GAMBLING WITH MURDER

BOOK FOUR OF THE WILBARGER COUNTY SERIES

DIANNE SMITHWICK-BRADEN

DSB
Mysteries

First printing

This is a work of fiction. Names, characters, businesses, places, events, and incidents are either the products of the author's imagination or used in a fictitious manner. Any resemblance to actual persons, living or dead, or actual events is purely coincidental.

Paperback ISBN: 978-1-7324735-3-9
ebook ISBN: 978-1-7324735-4-6

Published By DSB Mysteries
www.diannesmithwick-braden.com

Cover design by Dave King   kingsizecreations.com

Printed in the United States of America
Suggested retail price $15.95

For my "little" brother

GAMBLING WITH MURDER

CHAPTER ONE

GRACE STEWART WAS STOPPED at a red light. She cranked the air conditioning to high when beads of sweat began to form on her forehead. August in Nevada was too much for her old car. It was a struggle to stay cool even at that time of the evening. The Las Vegas traffic didn't help.

The light turned green, and she pressed the accelerator. A movement to the right caught her eye. She stomped on the brakes and swore under her breath. The driver of the SUV waved, mouthed the word sorry, and continued through the intersection.

Damn tourists, she thought.

Tourist traffic was the main reason she preferred to avoid the Las Vegas Strip. She was running late, and it was the most direct route to her destination. She didn't want to keep Todd Anthony waiting.

They'd met four years earlier when her car wouldn't start after a charity function. Todd was kind enough to stay and help. He captivated her with his warm personality, his twinkling blue eyes, and his boyish grin.

Grace moaned in frustration when she caught another red light. Her thoughts drifted back to Todd while she waited.

Todd was an undercover federal agent and was often kept away for long periods. He got in touch with her when he could. They'd have dinner and spend the night together when they had the chance. A different out-of-the-way diner and hotel were chosen each time.

She remembered a conversation they'd had in the early days of their relationship.

"My work can be dangerous," Todd told her. "Not just for me. Everyone around me could be in danger. I don't want to put you at risk. If we continue seeing each other, we can't tell anyone who doesn't need to know. We can't tell our families, friends, or coworkers.

Grace understood the desire for secrecy. She had secrets of her own.

She knew she could trust Todd with anything. Still, she hadn't told him about her past. It never seemed to be the right time.

At last, Grace drove into the parking lot of a little diner and parked near the entrance. She requested a table beside the front window in order to see Todd when he arrived.

A waitress approached Grace's table. "Hi, my name is Dana. What would you like?"

"Hi, Dana," Grace answered. "May I wait to order? I'm expecting a friend."

"That's no problem. Would you like something to drink while you wait?"

"Diet Coke, please."

"I'll have that right out," Dana promised with a smile and walked away.

Grace looked out the window and scanned the lot for Todd. She toyed with the ring she wore on her right hand while she waited. She had no idea what he'd be driving. He wasn't often in the same vehicle twice. She thought about their relationship while she waited.

Most women wouldn't be happy with their arrangement, but it suited Grace. She was able to focus on her career without the constant demands of a normal romantic relationship. It made the times they were able to meet all the more exciting.

She was startled back to the present when a tall man walked past the window and stopped beside her car. He took a small black object from his pocket and knelt beside the front tire. He reached into the wheel well for a moment, then pretended to tie his shoe. She could see that his hands were empty when he stood and strolled away.

Questions tumbled past each other in Grace's mind like slot machine reels. *Who was that? What did he do to my car? Didn't he see me sitting here?*

"Are you okay?" Dana asked and placed a drink on the table. "You look like you've seen a ghost."

Grace almost jumped from her chair. "I...I'm, yes," she answered with a weak smile.

"I didn't mean to scare you," the waitress apologized.

Grace laughed and said, "That's all right. I let my mind wander a little too far."

Dana patted her on the shoulder. "Give me a wave when you're ready to order."

"I will, thanks."

Grace looked out the window again. *Get a grip on yourself and think.* She twisted the ring on her finger and tried to organize her thoughts. *I'd better call the police and warn Todd. He won't want to risk being seen with the police.*

She stood and made her way to the Ladies' room. Once inside, she checked to make sure she was alone and locked the door. She dug her cell phone out of her purse and took a few deep breaths trying to ease the trembling in her hands and knees.

She tapped Todd's name in her contact list and prayed he would pick up. She needed to talk to him.

She swore in frustration when his recorded message began. At the tone, she left a brief explanation of what had happened.

Grace ended the call and tapped the number for the police. She explained what she'd seen to the dispatcher and was assured officers were on their way.

Her knees quaked during the short walk back to her table. She sat down and sipped her drink while she watched for the police. She hoped Todd would get her message and stay away.

Grace had regained most of her composure by the time a Las Vegas PD squad car pulled into the parking lot. She went outside to meet the officers.

She hoped she appeared braver than she felt when she extended her hand and said, "Hello, I'm Grace Stewart. I called about someone tampering with my car."

"I'm Officer Danny Burnett, and this is Officer Greg Hines. Tell us what happened."

Grace explained what she'd seen and described the man. "He was around six feet tall and weighed between one hundred eighty and two hundred pounds. He was wearing jeans and a dark gray T-shirt. His shoes were black or navy Nikes. His hair was brown and short, like a military cut. I didn't see his face."

"Did he have any distinguishing marks or tattoos?" inquired Burnett.

"There was a dime-sized spot on his right wrist. It might have been a mole or a birthmark."

"We'll check your car and meet you inside," said Hines.

"Thank you. I'm sure it's nothing. I thought it best to have someone check," Grace said, more for her benefit than theirs.

She walked back toward the entrance and glanced at the window where her table was located. The parking lot was reflected in the glass. *The man couldn't see inside. He didn't know anyone was watching.*

Grace went back to her table and watched the officers inspect her car. They took photos of the right front wheel well with a cell phone and made calls on their radios.

Officer Burnett entered the diner and saw Grace. She invited him to sit down.

"It doesn't appear to be dangerous. It looks like a tracking device," Burnett informed her. "We're calling in our tech guys to make sure. Do you know of any reason why someone would want to keep tabs on you?"

"I'm a reporter, but I work the anchor desk," Grace said with apprehension.

"Yes, Ma'am. I recognized you right away. Are you working on a story that might threaten someone?"

"Not at the moment."

"Are you meeting someone for dinner?"

"I was meeting a friend. I got a text saying that she can't make it after all," Grace told him, amazed at her own bluff. "I don't know of a reason anyone would be following her either."

Another police vehicle entered the parking lot. Officer Burnett excused himself and went outside.

Dana had been watching the police activity and looked at Grace. Grace waved her over.

"My friend can't make it after all. Could I order something to go?"

"You bet. Is everything okay?" Dana inquired.

"Someone tampered with my car. The police don't think it's anything to worry about."

"That's good news," Dana said, relieved. "What can I get for you?"

Grace scanned the menu. Her appetite had vanished, but she'd been there so long that she felt it would be rude to leave without ordering.

"I'll have a club sandwich with a bag of chips and another Diet Coke to go."

"Okay, I'll turn it in. It shouldn't take long."

"Thank you," Grace said and turned to watch the officers from the window.

The device was removed and on its way to the police station for analysis when Officers Burnett and Hines approached Grace's table.

"There's no doubt that it was a tracker," Hines told her. "The man you saw may try again when he realizes it isn't working."

"Did the man look at all familiar?" Burnett asked.

Grace pictured the man before answering and shook her head. "Silver Honda Civics are pretty common. Couldn't it have been a mistake?"

"It's possible," Hines said with a doubtful expression. "It would still be a good idea to stay on your toes."

"It could have been an overzealous fan," added Burnett. "We'll be in touch if we learn anything more."

Grace couldn't control the quiver in her voice when she said, "Goodbye, and thank you."

The words overzealous fan triggered a wave of anxiety. She did her best to calm her quaking body while she waited for her food.

Dana brought Grace's meal and the check to the table. Grace thanked her with a smile. She included a generous tip and left cash on the table before going outside.

She couldn't see anyone that seemed interested in her when she got into her car. She left the parking lot and drove home, watching the rearview mirror for any sign that she was being followed.

Why would anyone need to track me? Why follow me to a place I've never been to attach a tracker? I'm at the station and the gym almost every day. It had to have been a mistake.

Grace used the garage door opener and parked in her garage. She waited until the door closed to get out of the car. She opened the connecting door to the kitchen and waited, listening for any unusual sound.

She crept inside, leaving her purse and her food on the counter.

She tiptoed through the house, checking every room. She didn't relax until she was satisfied that she was alone.

Grace went to her desk and used her laptop to check her messages. There were no emails of importance and no messages on her answering machine.

She retrieved her purse from the kitchen counter and found her cell phone. No messages there, either.

Grace put her food in the refrigerator before going to the living room and flopping onto the couch.

She was disappointed with the outcome of the evening. She knew that seeing Todd was out of the question now, but was a phone call too much to ask?

She turned on the television and tried to find a movie to watch. She settled on a rerun of an old sitcom. This wasn't how she'd planned to spend her Sunday night.

Grace had spent the previous day preparing for their date. She looked at her fingers. She kicked off her shoes and looked at her toes. The mani-pedi wouldn't be a total waste, but she'd endured a bikini wax for nothing. *Next time, I won't bother with any of it. We'll see how he likes that!*

Anger and frustration had restored her appetite. She paused the TV and stomped into the kitchen. She took the club sandwich from the fridge and a hunk of cheesecake from the freezer. She eyed the to-go cup but reached for a bottle of wine instead.

* * *

Monday morning brought regret and a mild hangover. She'd have to spend extra time on the treadmill to pay for last night's choices.

Grace rolled over, looked at the clock, and groaned when she realized she'd overslept. She would have preferred to relax and nurse her hangover. Instead, she put on her workout clothes, laced up her shoes, and drove to the gym.

She thought about her life while she worked out. She'd chosen a career that preferred youth and good looks. At fifty-five years old, she knew her days as a female anchor were numbered. She'd spent a lot of time and money trying to conceal her age. She seldom took time off for fear that she'd have no job when she returned.

She found herself at a crossroads. She was too young to retire and too old to change careers. The thought of doing something else appealed to her, but what could she do?

She shortened her workout, left the gym, and drove to the post office. She went inside to collect her mail and stuffed it into her purse. She hurried back to her car and drove home.

Grace didn't see anything or anyone suspicious. *It was a case of mistaken identity or mistaken car. There's nothing to worry about.*

She showered and got ready for work. She was checking her appearance in the mirror when she felt that she was being watched. She looked at the bedroom window and the door. No one was there. A shiver danced through her body.

"Come on, Grace. You're letting your imagination get away from you," she said to her reflection in the mirror. "It was a mistake. No one is following you. It isn't like before."

The mirror image didn't look convinced.

Grace walked from room to room and checked to make sure all the windows and doors were locked. She went into the garage, set the security alarm, and got into her car. She opened the garage door, backed into the driveway, and waited for the garage door to close before backing into the street.

She drove to work and saw no evidence that anyone followed. She parked in her designated space and went into the station.

She said hello to the receptionist, poured herself some coffee, and went to her office. She took the mail and a bottle of aspirin from her purse before locking it in the bottom drawer of her desk.

She swallowed two aspirin with a sip of coffee. The workout hadn't helped her hangover.

Thumbing through the mail, Grace saw familiar handwriting. She smiled and opened it with the letter opener on her desk.

"Knock, knock," said the station manager.

Oliver Baldwin was an impeccably groomed man of stocky build with a wide toothy grin and shrewd brown eyes.

"Hi, Oliver."

Oliver stepped inside and closed her office door. "Are you working on a story that you've forgotten to mention?"

The suspicion in Baldwin's voice surprised her. "No, why do you ask?"

"I had an unusual phone call about you this morning."

"About me?" asked Grace. "Who was it?"

"He said he was with the FBI. Said his name was Melborn...or Welborn. Something like that."

"Why would the FBI be calling about me?"

"That's what I wondered. He wanted to know who you associated with and if there was anyone who was a special friend. He wanted to know if you were involved with anyone. I told him that if you were, it was news to me."

"That's strange," Grace replied and tried to ignore the feeling in the pit of her stomach.

"I thought so too." Baldwin paused before asking, "You have any idea what it might have been about?"

"I don't have a clue," Grace said. "Unless..."

"What?"

"Someone planted a tracking device on my car last night. I saw him and called the police. Do you think the two incidences are connected?"

"I'd wager they are," Baldwin said. "You're sure that you aren't working on a story?"

Grace looked him in the eye and said, "I swear I'm not."

"I don't like this," Baldwin said, shaking his head. "I could understand the harassment and stalking if you were working on something. It could be intended to discourage you."

The color drained from Grace's face. She gripped the back of her chair, trying to maintain her self-control. Those were the last words she wanted to hear.

"I'm sorry, Grace. I shouldn't have said that," Baldwin said and patted her on the back. "I didn't mean to bring up old memories. Why don't you sit down?"

Oliver was one of the few people who knew about her past.

Grace stood stock-still. She heard herself say, "I'd almost convinced myself that the tracking device was a mistake. Now, I'm not so sure."

"Did you know the man?"

Grace shook her head.

Their conversation was interrupted when the makeup artist opened the door. "It's time to get you ready."

"I'm sorry, Rhonda. It's my fault she's late."

"I'll be right there," Grace said with a nod and a forced smile.

Rhonda tapped on an imaginary wristwatch on her arm and left.

"Oliver, does anyone else know about that phone call?"

"No, I wanted to talk to you about it first."

"I'd appreciate it if you wouldn't mention either incident to anyone else. I don't think I'm up to whispers about it around the station."

"No one will hear it from me," Baldwin promised. "You'd better go before Rhonda invents something to add to the daily gossip."

Grace smiled, rushed to makeup, and braced herself for questioning.

Rhonda took pride in being the ultimate authority when it came to everyone else's business. She would have made an excellent reporter.

"I'm sorry I'm late," Grace began. "How was your weekend?"

"I heard some interesting news," Rhonda answered. "There are about to be some big changes made around here."

"You don't say," Grace said and relaxed.

Imaginary shakeups at the station were Rhonda's favorite topic of discussion.

Grace listened to Rhonda and nodded on cue. She'd heard this line of gossip so many times that she could quote it without a teleprompter.

"They're talking about replacing reporters. I heard it could even be one of the anchors," Rhonda said and waited for Grace's reaction.

Grace knew that Rhonda would use any response to support her speculations. She did her best to appear unconcerned and show no emotion. No surprise, no fear, no anger.

Disappointed, Rhonda tried another approach.

"You and Mr. Baldwin seemed to be in a serious discussion."

"We were talking about a story idea," Grace told her.

"I see," Rhonda said, unconvinced.

They both knew that news anchors at this station seldom investigated a story. Those jobs went to the younger reporters trying to work their way up. Grace hadn't done an investigative report in years.

She left makeup minutes before the first evening newscast. She settled herself at the anchor desk, pushed everything else to the back of her mind, and smiled at the camera.

"Welcome to the news at five," Grace began. "In today's headlines..."

"I suppose you've heard the latest from Rhonda," Barry said when the newscast ended. "Do you think there's anything to it?"

Barry Townson was Grace's co-anchor, and they made a good team. There were times when she wondered how much longer he'd have an anchor spot. He was a month older than Grace and was already an anchor at the station when she arrived.

"I doubt it. It's the same rumor we've heard from time to time. I wouldn't worry about it until you hear something from Oliver," she reassured him.

"That's true," Barry said with doubt in his voice. "There's no need to get worked up over a rumor."

"How was your vacation?" Grace inquired, changing the subject.

The pair spent the time between newscasts discussing Barry's recent trip to the Bahamas. Rhonda came by to do a few touch-ups, and the news anchors were smiling at the camera when the six o'clock news began.

Grace went to her office when the news ended. She'd have a few hours to relax and have dinner before the last newscast of the night.

She sat at her desk and looked at the letter she'd opened earlier. She took it from the envelope and smiled while she read. *August 20, 2016. That's this coming weekend. I wish I could be there.* She was lost in the handwritten pages when her cell phone rang.

Maybe that's Todd. She unlocked her desk, opened the desk drawer, and took her phone from her purse. She rejected the spam call and stared at the screen.

Why haven't I heard from Todd? Is something wrong? Is he angry with me?

Her thoughts were interrupted by a tap on her door. It was her dinner. She put her phone back in her purse, found her wallet, paid for the food, and tipped the delivery boy.

She picked at her salad and replayed the recent events like a movie in her mind trying to make sense of it all.

Barry tapped on Grace's door. "It's about that time."

Grace pushed her chair back and stood. The letter she'd been reading and the envelope fell to the floor. She picked up the letter and put it in her purse. She relocked the desk drawer before joining Barry in the hall.

"Was that a love letter? Barry teased.

"No, it was a letter from home," she replied with a wistful smile.

CHAPTER TWO

GRACE LEFT the TV station immediately after Tuesday evening's ten o'clock newscast ended. The past few days had been trying. She looked forward to a hot bath, hoping it would ease the tension from her muscles.

She drove home and pulled into her driveway. She pressed the button on the garage door opener. Nothing happened. She pressed it again. Nothing.

"What now?" she asked aloud and put the car in park.

She was about to get out when she realized that something wasn't right. The porch lights and recessed lighting around the house were set to turn on at nine. There was no glow of a lamp in the living room window. The house was in total darkness. *Is the power out?*

She got out of the car and looked around. Her neighbors' homes were well-lit on both sides of the street. It was then that she noticed her front door illuminated by the glow of her headlights. It was standing wide open.

Grace felt like she'd been zapped with a Taser. Her mind was blank, her body numb, her voice silenced. She stood frozen on the spot until she regained her senses. She fell into the driver's seat of her car and locked the doors. The engine continued to run while she tried to squash the panic that threatened her sanity.

She turned the air conditioning on high and pointed the vents at her face. She breathed in the cool air until her mind began to function again.

I know that I checked the windows and locked the doors before I left. I set the security alarm, too. What happened? Who did this? What am I going to do?

She couldn't stay in her car forever. Sooner or later, she'd run out of gas, and there'd be no more air conditioning. The thought of someone waiting for her in the dark house was horrifying.

She fumbled in her purse and found her cell phone. Her hands were shaking so hard that it was difficult to tap in 9-1-1.

Grace stayed in her car and tried to control herself until a police officer tapped on her car window. She was relieved to see Officer Burnett. She pushed the power button to lower the window, then turned off the engine.

"It's nice to see you again," she said, trying to keep her voice steady.

"I thought you might like to see a familiar face," Burnett replied with a kind smile.

"I can't tell you how happy I am," Grace answered with tears in her eyes.

"Would you like for me to wait here while these officers check the house?"

"If you don't mind. I'm kind of shaken up. Do you think this has anything to do with what happened at the diner?"

"I don't know, Ma'am. We don't have any leads. There was nothing on the tracker to give us a clue."

Grace answered Burnett's routine questions while they waited.

Their conversation halted when an officer walked from the house to the car, and the outdoor lights flickered on.

"There's no one inside," said the officer. "The power was shut off at the main breaker. Your security system is damaged, and so is the lock on your front door. We'd like for you to walk through the house and tell us if anything's missing."

"I'll go with you if you'd like," offered Burnett.

Grace nodded, got out of the car, and followed the officers into the house. She expected her home to be wrecked. To her amazement, it was just as she had left it. Nothing was missing, and nothing else had been damaged.

She went into her bedroom and saw nothing out of the ordinary until she turned toward her full-length mirror. She gasped and covered her face with her hands.

The words *We know who you are! You can't hide forever!* had been scrawled across the mirror with one of Grace's lipsticks.

"Is there somewhere else you can stay tonight?" Burnett asked, eyeing the mirror. "I don't think it would be safe to stay here, considering the circumstances."

"I…I can go to a hotel," she said, fighting back tears. "I need to book a room and pack a bag."

"I'll talk to the other officers to see if they've found anything else."

Grace nodded and thanked the young policeman. She went to her closet and pulled out the first bag she found. She stuffed random clothes and toiletries inside. She couldn't get out of the house fast enough.

She finished packing and went to her desk. She used her laptop to book a room at a busy hotel and casino. She knew she'd be safer in a large crowd.

She checked her messages and then turned off the answering machine. She unplugged her laptop and packed it in the duffel bag with her other belongings.

"I'm ready," she said when she joined the police officers in the living room.

"These officers will be investigating most of the night. I'll follow you to your hotel to make sure you get there without a problem," Burnett suggested.

"I appreciate that. Don't you need to get home to your family?"

"My wife would kill me if I let anything happen to her favorite news person," he said with a grin.

Grace smiled and followed the young man outside. She got into her car and backed into the street.

They reached the hotel, and Burnett escorted her inside. The young officer waited while she checked in, and he went with her to her room.

"Would you mind coming in for a minute?" asked Grace. "I want to write a note to your wife."

"That isn't necessary."

"I feel bad that I've kept you so long. I'd want to tell her how wonderful you've been to me. Please?"

Officer Burnett went inside and waited while Grace located a hotel notepad.

"What's your wife's name?"

"It's Kara."

"Kara Burnett. That has a nice ring to it," Grace told him.

She took her time to make sure she worded her thank you in the best possible terms. She signed it with a flourish and handed it to the officer.

Burnett read the note and blushed.

"Thank you. This will mean a lot to her," he said.

"It's my pleasure. I'd like to take you both to dinner sometime if that's allowed."

"It isn't against regulations. We should wait until this case is over to be on the safe side. Kara will be so excited!" he exclaimed.

"All right, we'll have dinner together when this is over," Grace promised.

"I'd better be going. It was good to meet you," he said. "I wish it had been under better circumstances."

"So do I. Thank you again!"

"Goodnight, Ma'am."

"Goodnight," Grace said and locked the door behind him.

She sat on the bed and cried until her eyes were almost swollen shut, and her face tingled. She went to the bathroom to splash water on her face and blew her nose. She grimaced at her reflection in the mirror.

She went back to the bedroom and picked up the hotel phone. She dialed a number and listened while it rang several times.

"Oliver, this is Grace," she said when he answered the phone.

"Grace? You sound upset. What's happening?"

"Someone broke into my house."

"What? Are you okay? Did you call the police? Where are you?"

"I'm rattled, but I'm okay. I'm in a safe place." She told him what the police had found.

"What are you going to do?" inquired Oliver.

"I need to disappear for a while," she answered and told him about the message written on her mirror.

"Damn!" he exclaimed. "Where will you go?"

"I don't know," Grace confessed.

"Is there anything that I can do to help?" The concern in his voice touched her.

"Will you cover for me?"

"Of course I will. You're on assignment as of now."

"That's perfect. I told Rhonda that we were discussing a story idea when she interrupted us."

"Is there anything else I can do?"

"I'd rather no one else knows anything, at least until the police have more information."

"You can count on me. How long will you be gone?" Oliver asked.

"I don't know. It depends on where I decide to go."

"When are you planning to leave?"

"There are a few things that I have to take care of first. I hope to leave before noon," Grace told him. "Oliver, I'm sorry about this and the short notice."

"Don't worry about that. I'll get Donna to fill in while you're away."

"That'll be great," she said, trying to sound pleased. "Thank you, Oliver. I'll be in touch."

"Be careful, and Godspeed."

The call ended, and Grace slammed the receiver down in frustration. Donna Triana would have been her last choice. She'd had an eye on the anchor position since the day she walked into the station. It was a good bet that she'd be the permanent female anchor by the time Grace got back.

It was getting late. Time to put aside her job worries and concentrate on plans for the immediate future.

She dumped the contents of her duffel bag on the bed. She changed into her nightgown and booted up her laptop. She needed a good plan if she was going to pull this off.

She searched the internet and made notes on a hotel notepad. She jotted down locations, addresses, and estimated travel times.

* * *

It was one in the morning before Grace closed her laptop and crawled under the covers. *I can do this. I'll take one step at a time and make changes if I need to.*

She was jolted out of sleep by a noise at her door. *What's that? Where am I?* She lay motionless, listening. She remembered where she was and why she was there. *Is someone trying to get in?* Her heart felt like a sledgehammer pummeling her ribcage.

"That's the wrong room, Dear," said a woman in the hallway. "Ours is further down."

She heard a man mumbling something before they moved away. She hadn't realized she was holding her breath until she let it out.

The clock on the nightstand read four a.m. She set the alarm and tried to go back to sleep.

Grace tossed and turned. She dreamed that she was tied down and couldn't move. She woke up, terrified, until she realized that her nightgown was wound around her.

She was still awake when the alarm sounded. She turned it off, got up, and showered. She ran through her plan for the day. Leaving the hotel without being noticed was the first hurdle she had to face.

Grace used the hotel phone and ordered room service. Then, she arranged to have her security system and her front door repaired. Her phone calls were interrupted when her breakfast was delivered.

She decided to leave her ten-year-old car in the hotel parking lot. She didn't want to take the chance that someone was watching or had put another tracker on it. She also didn't want anyone to know when she left. Her best option was to rent a car.

She finished eating and thought about calling an Uber to take her to the rental agency. That would require providing more personal information than she felt comfortable sharing. There were always cabs near the hotels.

Grace wanted to look like a tourist instead of a local TV personality. The fact that her eyes were still puffy would help. She decided to forgo makeup and pulled her long brown hair into a bun. She dressed in jeans and an old T-shirt.

She counted the cash in her wallet before repacking her bag. She eyed her cell phone on the bedside table. She picked it up and checked once for more a message from Todd. There were no messages from anyone.

She turned the phone off and packed it in her duffel. She wouldn't need it and didn't want to be tempted.

She walked through the room, making sure she didn't leave anything behind. She left the room key on the desk, put the notepad in her purse, and picked up her belongings.

Grace was ready. There'd be no need to stop by the front desk to check out. Her hotel expenses were to be paid with her credit card. Mustering her courage, she walked into the hall, closing the door behind her.

She made her way from the elevator through the casino and the front entrance. No one seemed to notice her exit.

She'd been standing in front of the hotel for fifteen minutes and began to second-guess her decision about calling an Uber. She knew that the longer she stood there, the higher the risk that she'd be discovered.

She was relieved when a cab arrived and was soon on her way to Budget Car Rental. She paid the driver and went inside.

Grace rented the cheapest car available, stored her duffel bag in the trunk, and drove to the Bank of America.

She parked in the lot and scanned her surroundings before going inside. She followed the signs to the safe deposit vault and requested access to her box. She took her key and identification from her purse, showed them to the clerk, and signed the paperwork.

She followed the clerk into the vault. The young woman unlocked the box and carried it to a nearby table. Grace waited until she was alone to open it and examine the contents.

The tools that she needed for a successful escape were inside. She'd left them there for safekeeping when she first moved to Las Vegas. She had hoped she'd never need them again. Yet, here she was.

Grace removed a large envelope from the box and shoved it into her purse. She put the safe deposit box back where it belonged and locked it before leaving the area.

She walked toward the tellers and waited in the shortest line.

"I need a prepaid Visa, please," she told the young woman.

The transaction was completed, and Grace left the bank.

A man was standing beside her car when she returned to the

parking lot. She fought the urge to scream and run. She was about to go back inside when she noticed a little girl.

The tiny blonde was straggling and staring at her feet. Exasperated, the man picked her up and carried her toward the bank.

"Daddy, I want to watch my new shoes walk," the child cried.

Grace smiled with relief and nodded at the pair. She saw no one else in the parking lot and rushed to the car. She locked the door once she was inside.

She drove out of the parking lot and out of Las Vegas checking her rearview mirror to be sure that she wasn't followed.

She drove until she reached Flagstaff, Arizona, and stopped at a convenience store for gas. She went inside for a bag of chips and paid for her purchases.

She drove to the rental agency, took the duffel from the trunk, and went inside. She handed the keys to the man behind the counter.

"May I use your phone to call a cab?"

"I'll call one for you if you'd like," answered the clerk.

"Yes, thank you."

A cab arrived fifteen minutes later, and Grace climbed in.

"Where to?" the driver asked.

"To a restaurant called Ahipoki. It's a seafood place close to the bus station."

"I'll have you there in a few minutes."

She arrived at the restaurant and paid the cab driver in cash. She went inside to the Ladies' room and locked the door behind her.

Grace altered her appearance as much as she could by changing her clothes and her hairstyle from a bun to a ponytail.

She removed all of the cards except the new Visa from her wallet and put them into the envelope from the bank. She transferred cash and a different driver's license from the envelope to her wallet.

She'd be using cash and false identification for the foreseeable future. The Visa card had no name on it and would be used for hotel and rental car deposits.

She left the restaurant and walked to the nearby bus station. She purchased a one-way ticket to Amarillo, Texas, and sat down to wait.

Grace twisted her ring around her finger and watched people come and go. She wondered what their stories were and if they, too, might be running from some unknown danger.

She was nibbling on the chips she'd bought when she heard the announcement to board her bus. She found a seat near the front and tried to make herself comfortable.

It was a long ride across Arizona and New Mexico. She got off the bus to stretch when it stopped, and each time she feared that someone might catch up to her before the bus was back on the road.

* * *

It was two in the morning when Grace got off the bus in Amarillo. She picked up her bag and trudged into the bus station, finding it almost deserted. The two passengers who got off the bus with her had a ride waiting for them. She watched them drive away before she used the phone on the counter to call a cab. She walked around, stretching her legs while she waited.

The taxi picked up her and deposited her at the front entrance of an Amarillo hotel. When she was secure in her room, she thought about the next leg of her journey.

She knew from her research that she could rent a car near the airport. The desk clerk told her that an airport shuttle ran hourly from the hotel. She'd take the shuttle to the airport and rent a car using another fake id.

It had been years since she'd been in Texas and even longer since she'd been home. She thought of the letter she'd gotten and dug it out of her purse. She read it again.

I'm so close. Should I risk stopping for a visit? It might be a good place to lay low for a while.

She pondered the idea while she got ready for bed. She set the alarm on the hotel clock and snuggled under the covers.

The alarm sounded at seven a.m., startling Grace from a sound sleep. She hit the snooze button and slept through the second alarm. She bolted out of bed when housekeeping knocked on her door.

Damn! She'd missed the eight o'clock shuttle. She'd have to hurry to catch the next one.

Grace showered, dressed, and packed her belongings. She thought again about going home. She didn't know when she'd have another chance. She checked out of the hotel and went outside to wait for the shuttle.

The day was not off to a good start. The shuttle was half an hour late because an accident on the way to the airport kept them at a standstill for almost two hours. It was eleven-thirty before she walked through the doors of Avis Car Rental.

The clerk was a new hire. He was slow and needed help from his counterpart for every task.

Grace tried to be patient. No one was expecting her, and she had plenty of time. Now that she'd decided to go home, she couldn't wait to get there. The delays were almost more than she could bear.

At last, she turned the rental car onto highway 287. She cranked up the radio and sang along. She looked forward to seeing her loved ones.

She felt confident that she'd managed to make it this far without being followed, but she still kept an eye on the rearview mirror to be sure.

Her stomach grumbled. She hadn't had a good meal since she left the hotel in Vegas. She knew there would be plenty of food where she was going. She didn't want any more delays and ignored her hunger pangs.

Between towns, her stomach made a fierce growl. Stopping for a quick snack didn't seem to be much of a delay after all. She remembered there once were some fast-food restaurants with drive-thru windows in the next town. She hoped they were still there.

Grace looked for a place to grab a bite when she entered the Childress city limits. She saw a local drive-in on the right side of the highway. She turned into the parking lot and the drive-thru. She ordered a small meal and was back on the highway in ten minutes.

Next stop, home. She laughed out loud at the thought.

CHAPTER THREE

JAMES FLETCHER STOOD on the front lawn of the Paradise Creek Inn and inspected his handiwork. He frowned, walked toward the porch, and repositioned his ladder under a bright-colored banner that read *Grand Reopening*. He adjusted the sign and let his mind wander to the past.

The Inn was located on the Fletcher family farm in Wilbarger County, Texas. It was his mother who had suggested that they turn the old house into an inn.

It was a family business. His daughter Lizzie had the education and experience needed to make the inn a success. She was the managing partner and lived at the inn.

James, his wife, Ellen, and his mom, Lois, lived a short distance from the inn. They helped with events and routine maintenance.

The inn opened in April of 2011, and business was slow in the beginning. Word soon spread, and within four years, they couldn't accommodate all of the events.

They found themselves turning away customers much too often. They needed more guest rooms and more space for indoor events.

In the spring of last year, they decided to build an addition to the south side of the house. They drew up plans and borrowed the money from the bank, with construction starting at the beginning of June.

Things took a turn for the worst when an arsonist came to the area. Crops had been burned in the fields, people were seriously injured, and others had been killed.

The memory of smoke pouring from the inn and the worry that Lizzie might be injured, or worse, was too painful to think about. He shook his head and forced his mind back to the present.

James climbed down the ladder and checked the banner again. Satisfied, he took the ladder to the storage shed and went back to the front lawn. He went up the porch steps and sat down in a rocking chair, letting his mind wander to the recent past.

All of the new construction had been destroyed by the fire. Part of the original house was burned, but the rest had smoke and water damage.

The fire resulted in the loss of their main source of income. Their customers found other places to stay and other venues for their weddings, parties, and meetings.

Lizzie and Ellen had to take jobs in town to make ends meet. He continued to work the farm while his mother took care of the household chores and kept them fed.

James was more thankful than he'd ever been for his hired hand, Dan Hayes. He recalled a conversation they had days after the inn burned.

"James, I think of y'all as family," Dan told him. "This has been a hard blow, and some hard decisions will have to be made. I want you to know that I'm not going to leave when you need my help the most. I know things will get better when the inn reopens. I want to be here working toward that day right along with you."

Since then, Dan had split his time between the Fletcher farm and other jobs. He never complained and was there every time James called.

Construction on the inn was finished six weeks ago. The new space was equipped with moveable walls so that it could be used for a variety of events. A hallway surrounded the large room to provide privacy for the six new guest rooms. The original house had been restored with four upstairs guestrooms and space for smaller indoor events.

There had been a whirlwind of activity since then. The décor had been updated, and finishing touches were made so that the inn could open again.

Flyers announcing the reopening were printed and distributed at businesses in Vernon and other nearby towns. An announcement was published in the local newspaper. Invitations were sent to previous and potential visitors to the inn.

The celebration was scheduled for Saturday, the day after tomorrow. The women had spent days getting the inside of the inn ready. He and Dan were in charge of the outside.

All that was left to do was wait. Wait for the reopening. Wait for the word to spread. Wait for the phone to ring.

James hated waiting.

He looked at his watch. *Three-thirty, Dan will be here soon.* He leaned back and closed his eyes. He prayed in silence for the inn's success and thanked God again for Dan Hayes.

The quiet afternoon was interrupted by the sound of a motor and wheels on the gravel drive. He heard the vehicle door open and shut. Footsteps crunched the gravel to the bottom of the steps and stopped.

James knew that Dan would understand if he finished his prayer before saying hello.

"Are you asleep, Little Brother, or playin' possum?"

His eyes snapped open. There was only one person who called him Little Brother. His head whipped toward the porch steps. He stared at the woman standing there.

"Grace!" he cried in disbelief and rose from the rocker.

Grace laughed and ran up the steps to meet him. They hugged, laughed, and cried tears of joy together.

"Why didn't you let us know you were coming?" James asked.

"And miss the surprise on your face? Not a chance!"

"I can't believe you're here," James beamed and hugged his sister again.

"Looks like everything's about ready for the party," Grace observed.

"Yep, there isn't much left to do. I'll give you a tour later. Right now, you'd better go in and surprise Mom."

"I can't wait!" Grace said with a wide grin.

James opened the front door and peeked inside. He motioned for Grace to follow, and they tiptoed into the lobby.

Lois was in the office on the telephone. Lizzie and Ellen were in the kitchen making refreshments for the reopening.

James indicated that Grace should stand by the front desk and stepped into the office. He tried to be patient while he waited for the phone call to end.

At last, he said with a straight face, "Mom, would you mind taking care of a guest?"

"A guest? We aren't booking guest rooms until next week."

"I know, but there's one in the lobby now."

"There must be some mistake," Lois said, perplexed. She stood and followed James to the next room.

James hurried ahead and stood behind Grace. He didn't want to miss his mother's reaction.

Lois glanced at James and frowned at his behavior. Then she looked at Grace and said, "Hello, do you have a room boo…"

Her jaw dropped in mid-sentence. She looked at Grace, then at James, and back at Grace.

"No, I haven't booked a room," Grace replied with a mischievous twinkle in her hazel eyes. "I was hoping that it would be okay to drop in."

"AAAHHH!" Lois screamed and wrapped her daughter in a tremendous bear hug.

Lizzie and Ellen ran from the kitchen, fearing that something terrible had happened. They saw three people laughing, hugging, and talking over each other. Two of them they knew well. The other was…

"Aunt Grace!" cried Lizzie.

"Hello, you beautiful girls," Grace cried. She disentangled herself from her mother's grasp to hug them both.

"It's so good to see you!" Ellen exclaimed.

"I can't tell you how good it is to see y'all."

"Am I interrupting something?" Dan asked and closed the front door.

"Not at all! Come in. You're just in time to meet my sister. Grace, this is my right-hand man, Dan Hayes," James said and clapped a hand on Dan's shoulder.

"It's nice to meet you," Dan said, extending his hand.

Grace shook his hand and said, "It's nice to meet you, too."

"Why don't we find a more comfortable place to visit?" Lois suggested.

"Wait a minute!" James said with mock exasperation. "I don't want to miss anything. Dan and I need to move the cattle before dinner. Can't we wait until dinner to catch up?"

"Wade will be here by then. He and Aunt Grace can get acquainted at the same time," Lizzie suggested.

"That's not until six o'clock," cried Lois.

Grace looked at the clock on the wall. "That's two hours from now. It's been a long trip, and I'd like to rest and freshen up. I'll go into town, get a hotel room, and be back by six."

She covered her ears. Their response was almost deafening.

"You'll do no such thing!" shouted Lois.

"We have ten empty guest rooms right here," Lizzie cried.

"No, you won't! James and Ellen shouted in unison.

"I'll wait outside," Dan said and slipped out the door.

"Okay, okay!" Grace shouted over the din. "I don't want to be in your way while you're getting ready for Saturday. I know you weren't expecting me."

"You won't be in the way," Ellen said with a smile. "You can stay right here. We'll let you rest, and we'll see you in the dining room at six."

"We insist," James said with a stern expression.

Grace was reminded of the stubborn red-headed boy she'd grown up with. "All right. I'll stay tonight. Only if you're sure, I won't be in the way."

"Since that's settled, Dan and I will get to work," James said and hugged his sister again.

"Would you like to stay in your old room, Aunt Grace?"

Grace beamed at Lizzie. "I'd like that very much."

"I'll get the key," Lizzie said and went to the office.

"I'd better get my things," Grace said and started to the door.

"I'll help you," James offered.

"I can do it. I just have one bag."

"This I've got to see," James teased and followed her outside.

Lizzie was waiting in the lobby when Grace returned. She led the way upstairs to one of the original rooms on the west side of the house.

"I hope you like it. I know it doesn't look the same," Lizzie said and opened the door.

Grace stepped inside and gazed at her old room. "This is beautiful, Lizzie."

Lizzie smiled and handed Grace the key. "I'll go and let you relax," she said and started toward the door.

"Lizzie," Grace began. "I'd prefer that no one else knows that I'm here.

"Is something wrong?"

"No, there's nothing to worry about. I'll explain at dinner."

Lizzie nodded and left the room. She went to the office and sat at the desk. She opened the reservations file on the computer.

I wonder how long Aunt Grace is planning to be here. It would be silly for her to stay in town. She looked at the blinking cursor. *Why doesn't she want anyone to know she's here?*

Her pondering was interrupted by an incoming call. She picked up the phone and said, "Paradise Creek Inn. This is Lizzie. How may I help you?"

"I'd like to book a room for the weekend," said the caller.

"Our rooms aren't available this weekend. I'd be happy to book one for a later date."

"None? I was hoping to stay there during your reopening?"

"We're leaving the guest rooms open for tours during the celebration. We felt that tours of occupied rooms would be inappropriate."

"Well, yes, I suppose it would," admitted the caller. "Your web page says that the event is come and go. May we come when it starts and stay until the end?"

"Yes, we'll be happy to have you."

"Wonderful! We'll see you Saturday afternoon."

"We look forward to it."

Lizzie hung up the phone and looked at the computer screen. *I'll take care of this when I know more details.* She deleted the entry, closed the file, and left the office.

Lizzie joined her mother in the kitchen.

"What time will Wade be here?"

"He said he'd be here before six." Lizzie paused, "Do you think Aunt Grace is okay?"

Lois stopped what she was doing and looked at her granddaughter. "What do you mean?"

"I don't know. She said she didn't want anyone to know that she's here. She said she'd explain at dinner."

"It's odd that she didn't tell us she was coming," Ellen began. "But that would have ruined the wonderful surprise."

"Yes, it would have," Lois answered with worry in her voice.

Her mother-in-law's knitted brows bothered Ellen. She knew that Grace's past was a constant source of concern.

"I hope James remembers to invite Dan for dinner," she said to change the subject.

Grace lay on the bed with her eyes closed. She tried to relax without much success. She tossed and turned. She counted sheep. She tried deep breathing exercises.

A nap wasn't going to happen. Tired as she was, her brain wouldn't take a break and let her rest. She sat up cross-legged on the bed and fidgeted with her ring.

Driven by fear and adrenaline, she hadn't taken the time to focus on anything other than getting away.

Thoughts passed through her mind, jumbled together like a jigsaw puzzle dumped out of the box. She knew she wouldn't be able to rest or focus until she sorted them out.

She was happy to be home with her family. She smiled at the memory of their surprised faces, but the smile faded when she realized that even this short visit could put them in danger.

I shouldn't have come, and I can't stay. I'll leave in the morning, but what excuse can I give them? I could tell the truth, or at least some of it. How much should I tell them? I could come up with a plausible lie. No, Mom always knew when I lied.

An idea flashed across Grace's mind. *Oliver said he'd tell everyone that I'm on assignment. There's no reason why I can't build on that. I'll be vague about it and create details if they ask questions. I'll have to be convincing, or Mom won't buy it. What sort of story should it be?*

Grace got up and paced around the room for several minutes. She stopped and smiled. *I'll tell them I'm researching a story about casinos. It makes sense. Gambling in Vegas compared to gambling in other states.*

Yes, that could work. I'll tell them that I'm supposed to be at a casino tomorrow and will have to leave in the morning to get there on time. I'll write a real story. Oliver may even run it.

The thought of Oliver Baldwin reminded her of her true situation. *Was I followed out of Las Vegas?* She reviewed her movements. *Was I careful enough? Did I make a mistake somewhere?*

I'm sure it's obvious by now that I've left. How long will it take whoever it is to find me?

I need to pull myself together and find out what's happening and who's behind it. I have to stop running, and I need answers.

Grace took a deep breath and squared her shoulders. She felt the tension easing from her body and looked at the clock.

"No time for a nap now," she said aloud.

She showered and dressed before appraising her reflection in the mirror. She applied fresh makeup to camouflage the dark circles under her eyes and the signs of exhaustion on her face. She brushed her hair so that it fell over her shoulders.

The aroma of home cooking wafted into her room, and her stomach growled. She left her room and started down the stairs.

Grace planned to give her family the highlights of her story before turning the conversation to their own lives. The art of distraction had served her well during her journalism career. Then again, these people were part of her family.

Lizzie appeared at the bottom of the stairs. "I was on my way up to get you," she said. "Everyone is here, and dinner is ready."

"Great, I'm starved," Grace said and joined her niece on the ground floor. "This part of the house looks fantastic. I can't wait to see the rest."

The pair went into the dining room to join the others. Grace's mouth watered, and her stomach rumbled when she saw the food on the table.

"Aunt Grace, I'd like you to meet my fiancé, Wade Adams. Wade, this is my Aunt Grace."

"It's nice to meet you," Wade said. His smile was warm and friendly.

"It's good to meet you," Grace replied. "Let me look at the two of you."

Grace assessed the young couple. Wade was at least six feet of lean muscle, with dark blonde hair curling a little around his ears and shirt collar. His green eyes twinkled when he smiled at Lizzie.

Lizzie's vivid blue eyes were bright with happiness. Her appearance hadn't changed since Grace last saw her. She was still petite with straight shoulder-length red hair and a few freckles across her nose.

"You have to be the most handsome couple I've ever seen," Grace told them.

The pair smiled at each other and back at Grace.

"Let's eat before it gets cold." Lois directed.

The group took their seats at the dining table and filled their plates. Few words were spoken other than pass the gravy or here's the salad.

Wade had been around the Fletchers long enough to know that this wasn't normal. He felt like he was in a poker game where no one could open. The silence made him uneasy.

"Grace, are you going to be here for a while?" Wade asked to break the tension.

"I'm passing through," Grace began. "Mom's last letter arrived before I left, and it made me homesick. I couldn't stand the thought of being so close and not stopping."

"Where are you from?" Wade inquired.

"Grace is a reporter in Las Vegas," Lois answered with pride. "She's the evening news anchor at one of the television stations there."

"I'm one of the evening anchors," Grace corrected and smiled at her mother.

"How long have you been in Vegas?" asked Dan.

"Going on ten years. I worked on the east coast for a long time. I couldn't pass up this opportunity when it was offered."

"You said you're passing through," James began. "Where are you going?"

"I'll be going several places. I'm researching gambling and

casinos for a story. My boss and I thought it would be better if I included casinos outside Nevada."

"That sounds interesting," Wade said.

"I've already been in Arizona and New Mexico. I'll visit casinos in Oklahoma, Missouri, and Kansas, then work my way back to Vegas."

"I didn't know you did story research," said James.

"I don't often," Grace answered and began to toy with her ring. "The station manager knows that I'm discreet and that I have investigative experience. He doesn't want to bring attention to the story until we're ready for the news to break. If we're right, there may be people who wouldn't want the information made public."

"Is that why you don't want anyone to know you're here?" Lizzie questioned.

"Yes, it's best if no one can track me and spread the word. I'll be moving around a lot. It's all over if anyone finds out what I'm doing."

Grace took a sip of tea to delay what she had to tell them. "I have an appointment with an informant tomorrow. I'll have to leave in the morning to get there on time."

"What?" Lois cried, surprised and disappointed.

"You just got here," James replied. "Can't you stay the weekend?"

"No, I wish I could," Grace apologized and twisted her ring around her finger. "I'm supposed to be in Oklahoma City by one o'clock tomorrow."

Lois watched her daughter and frowned. Grace avoided her mother's eye and changed the subject.

"Lizzie, tell me about your wedding plans."

Lizzie blushed when the attention shifted to her. "It's going to be September 10th. We wanted to wait until the inn was finished so that we could be married here. We've decided to keep it small, family and close friends."

"I understand you're the Wilbarger County Sheriff, Wade. Will your work interfere with wedding plans?" Grace queried.

"It's possible. Both our jobs have the potential to interfere with our plans," Wade said and winked at Lizzie.

"Yes, they do, and they have," Lizzie agreed with a laugh.

"So, you both have busy careers," Grace observed.

"There are times that we can't keep up and times that we look for things to do. It's a steady routine most of the time. That's how it is at my office, at least," Wade said.

"It's the same here," Lizzie added. "We've missed this year's wedding season, but the holidays are coming up. We were busy with parties for most of the holiday season before the fire. We hope that will be the case this year."

To Grace's relief, the conversation turned to inn business and small talk.

After the table had been cleared and the dishes were done, Grace said, "James, you promised me a tour of the inn."

"We'll start in here and work our way outside," he said, offering her his arm.

Grace took his arm and laughed. "Lead the way."

Lois watched her children leave the room. Wade felt something was wrong. He'd had watched the family during dinner, and they weren't themselves.

He was sure Grace was hiding something. *Why is Grace really here?*

CHAPTER FOUR

WADE'S THOUGHTS evaporated when his cell phone rang. He answered and listened with a frown.

"I'm on my way," he said and ended the call. "I'm sorry, Lizzie. I'm needed in town. It sounds like it's going to be a long night."

"What happened?"

"Reed said there's a bad accident on a farm-to-market road south of town. A bunch of kids were drag racing."

"Was anyone hurt?"

"I don't know," Wade replied. "I'll stay at my place tonight."

"Will you be here for breakfast?"

"I'll let you know. Tell everyone goodnight for me," he said.

Lizzie walked him to the door and kissed him goodbye.

"I need to go, too," Dan said. "I've got to be in Rayland by sunup. I'll be here Saturday morning."

"We'll see you then," Lizzie said and closed the door behind him.

She went back to the kitchen to help with what remained of the cleanup. Lois was standing by the back door, looking outside.

"What are you doing, Granny?"

Lois jumped and put her hand over her heart. "You scared me half to death!"

"I'm sorry," Lizzie said and laughed.

"I'm looking for James and Grace. Oh, there they are," Lois said and went outside.

She waited to join them until they'd finished their conversation.

The siblings sat down at a patio table.

"It's such a nice evening," Grace declared. "It's still too hot in Vegas to sit outside."

"This is my favorite time for sittin' on the porch," James agreed and paused. He looked at his sister and said, "What's going on, Grace?"

"I told you at dinner," Grace said without looking at him.

"Sis, that little duffel you brought wouldn't hold all of your clothes for an overnight stay when you were ten. Tell me the truth."

"I can't," Grace whispered.

"Can't or won't?" James demanded.

"That's what I'd like to know," Lois said and joined them.

Grace sighed and faced them. "I can't because I don't know. The truth is that some weird and scary things happened. I panicked and ran."

"What happened?" asked James with worry on his face.

Grace told them about everything except Todd. She didn't want to break her promise.

"Is anything you told us at dinner true?" Lois demanded with a scowl.

Grace nodded. "I did feel homesick when I read your letter, and I couldn't stand the thought of driving past when I was so close. I didn't plan to come here when I left."

"You don't have an appointment tomorrow, do you?" James accused.

"No, I realized after I got here that I could be putting y'all in danger. The best way to keep you safe is to leave."

James and Lois looked at each other and back at Grace.

"Lizzie doesn't know what happened to you in New York," James said.

"Why didn't you tell her?" challenged Grace astonished.

"She'd just gone through that nasty breakup with Drake and started a new job in Chicago. We thought she had enough on her plate," James explained. "We thought she was safe there."

"She needs to know," Grace said.

"Yes, she does. Let's talk about it inside," James said. "I'll get Ellen and Lizzie."

"It'll be all right," Lois told her daughter when they entered the kitchen. "We'll tell her together."

Lois filled five glasses with ice and set them on the table with a two-liter bottle of Coke. They each filled their glass.

"I'm going to need something a little stronger to get through this," Grace said.

James went to the liquor cabinet and came back with a bottle of bourbon. "We may all need something stronger," he said and sat down.

"What's wrong?" Lizzie asked, bewildered.

"Grace has something to tell you," Lois said and patted her granddaughter's hand.

"It sounds serious."

"It is," said James. "It involves all of us, but Grace is the most at risk."

Ellen looked at James with surprise. He nodded, and she said, "Yes, it's time."

"Time for what? What are you talking about?"

"Did you ever wonder why I never came home?" Grace began. "Why I never called? Why we've only kept in touch with hand-written letters?"

"Yes," Lizzie answered. "I've asked about it a few times."

"You're about to learn the reason for it all," said Grace. "You'll have to promise me that you won't tell anyone, not even Wade. At least not yet."

"I can't tell Wade? I don't understand."

"You will after Grace tells her story," Ellen said.

Lois nodded at Grace and said, "Go ahead. The longer you wait, the harder it will be."

Grace poured a healthy dose of bourbon into her Coke and almost emptied her glass. James refilled it for her.

"I always dreamed of being a news anchor with one of the national networks," Grace began. "I got my first job as a reporter in Virginia. My whole world revolved around my career and reaching my goal. That began to change when I met Bryan Meads.

Bryan was handsome, charming, and intelligent." Grace smiled at the memory. "We'd been dating for several months when I heard of a job opening in New York. I applied without hesitation.

It was also about that time that I began receiving love notes and gifts. I thought they were from Bryan at first. I realized they weren't when it began to get creepy. Fan mail is a normal part of being in the public eye. This was different.

As time went on, creepy began to get scary. I started getting photos of myself. There were pictures of me in my car, in front of my house, and on the job. There were even pictures of me and Bryan with his head cut out or scribbled over.

I had no idea who was responsible. I didn't have a name or a description of the man until Bryan hired a private detective. The detective followed me at a distance hoping to catch the person responsible.

It wasn't long until we had a name, address, and description. We took the information to the police and filed a restraining order against a man named Burl Sharp.

The notes, gifts, and photos stopped. I thought that would be the end of it.

Sharp somehow managed to hack into my home security system, my emails, and my phone. He monitored everything and knew where I was going the moment that I did. He was always watching from a distance, but he never violated the restraining order.

I bought a new laptop and a new phone. I changed my email address, phone number, and internet service provider. I put in a new state-of-the-art security system. He hacked into those in a matter of days.

Things went on like that for weeks, and I was a nervous wreck. I was terrified of what Sharp might do next.

I had a reprieve when I went for a job interview in New York. I invited Bryan to go with me, and we planned a nice weekend getaway.

I was offered the job on the spot. We spent the weekend looking for my new apartment. I was so happy and excited that I forgot about Sharp for a little while.

We went back to Virginia and started making all the arrangements. Bryan applied for a transfer to New York, and we decided to move in together.

Sharp began sending horrible emails to everyone in my address book while I was away. He made it appear that they were coming from me. He made phone calls to people using recordings of my voice. He'd managed to destroy most of my friendships and professional connections in Virginia by the time I left."

"I got one of those calls, too. It was terrible." Lois added and shivered. "I knew it couldn't have been Grace."

"Bryan and I moved to New York as soon as we could. We stayed in and ordered delivery until we both had to report to work the following week. I set up new accounts again and hoped that we were done with Sharp.

For weeks, there was no sign of him. Then, we went to dinner one night with one of Bryan's coworkers. Sharp was leaning on a car a few feet from us when we left the restaurant. He sneered at me and walked away.

He started sending things to me at work again. His letters were filled with anger and hate. The gifts were dismembered stuffed animals or broken objects smeared with red.

We filed a restraining order in New York. Sharp was always there but far enough away to stay out of trouble.

After a while, he stopped sending things, and we didn't see him following us. He seemed to have disappeared.

We were suspicious. We couldn't find any evidence that he'd hacked into my new accounts. It didn't occur to us that he'd hacked into Bryan's.

I'd been working at my new job for almost a year when Bryan proposed. We kept our engagement quiet and decided to elope. We didn't want to give Sharp an excuse to increase his activity again."

Grace stopped and gulped her drink. Lizzie sat wide-eyed with her hand over her mouth.

"The night before we were to be married, Bryan and I decided to stay in and had a pizza delivered. We went to bed early because we had an eight o'clock flight the next morning.

I woke up thinking I'd heard a noise. I listened for a few minutes. I didn't hear anything else, so I rolled over and went back to sleep.

It seemed like a second later that I woke up with excruciating pain in my left shoulder. I tried to sit up and saw a man standing over me with a knife in his hand.

I screamed, and he stabbed me again. Bryan woke up and dove at the man. He did his best to shield me. I didn't have the strength to help. I must have fainted because I don't remember anything else."

Tears streamed down Grace's face. She took another drink before she continued.

"I woke up in a hospital room the following afternoon. My nurse told me that I'd had surgery. She said that I would have died if the paramedics hadn't gotten there when they did. Bryan was already dead when they arrived.

The police came to the hospital a few days later. It turns out that one of our neighbors found us and called 9-1-1.

The officers said that the building superintendent had made a replacement key for a man who claimed to be Bryan. The super identified Sharp as that man.

There were no prints in our apartment other than ours. The police found traces of blood in our bedroom that didn't match either of us. There was blood and skin tissue on Bryan's knuckles that didn't belong to him. It all matched Burl Sharp. They believed that Sharp intended to kill us both while we slept.

The police didn't find the weapon. There was no other evidence or witnesses. It was my testimony that put Sharp away. When they led him from the courtroom, he looked at me and said, 'This isn't over.'

That was all I needed to hear. I quit my job and sold my apartment. I dropped the stage name I'd been using and changed my last name from Fletcher to Stewart.

I'd heard about a job in Las Vegas, so I took a chance. I've been there ever since."

"That's why we seldom talk on the phone or send emails," Lois said. "A handwritten letter can't be hacked. Using the post office and a post office box is more secure than a home address."

"I didn't want to take the chance that Sharp would use one of you to get to me," Grace added. "I've been trying to keep y'all safe by distancing myself from you."

"Why didn't you tell me sooner?" demanded Lizzie, anger flashing in her eyes.

"We thought the less you knew, the safer you'd be," said James. "You were in Chicago at that time and hadn't had any communication with Grace."

"I've been home for years, and you're just now telling me?"

"We thought it was over, and it wasn't our story to tell," said Ellen. "Sharp was sentenced to life in prison for killing Bryan and an additional twenty-five years for attacking Grace."

"I thought it was over, too, until this week," said Grace. She told Lizzie and Ellen what had prompted her unexpected visit.

"Do you think it's Sharp?" asked Lizzie with fear in her eyes.

"I have to find out," said Grace. "I'm still going to leave in the morning. I don't want to make calls or send emails from here. It's too risky."

"Where are you going to go?" Ellen inquired.

"I don't want y'all to lie for me," Grace answered. "I told everyone at dinner that I'm going to Oklahoma City. That's where I'll go."

"What will you do then?" queried Lois.

"I'll get a hotel room and make my calls from there. I'll decide my next move when I have more information."

"I have a suggestion," offered James. "You have to hear me out before you stop me."

Grace sighed and nodded.

"You shouldn't be here for the celebration," James began. "There's too much chance you'd be seen, and we won't know everyone who attends. Go to Oklahoma as planned. After you have the information you need, come back here."

"But...," Grace interrupted.

"You said you'd hear me out."

"Okay." Grace sighed and crossed her arms.

"You'll stay at our house," offered James. "No one else would know you're here. Wade and Dan won't even know. We congregate here at the inn most of the time. You'll be safer with people around. Someone is always here."

"You know the place as well as any of us," added Lois. "I'm sure you could find a place to hide if you should need one."

"We're all licensed to carry handguns," Lizzie said.

"You are?" Grace answered with surprise.

Ellen nodded and said, "Wade insisted after the fire."

"And you know that we've always had rifles," said James.

Grace looked at her family and realized that she didn't want to face this alone anymore. Tears rolled down her cheeks. "Are you sure that you want to take the risk?"

"We're sure," said Lois.

Lizzie, James, and Ellen nodded their agreement.

"I'm tired of running," Grace told them. "The worst part is being separated from y'all."

"Shouldn't we tell Wade and Dan?" Lizzie pressed. "Won't they be in danger too?"

"The fewer people who know Grace is here, the smaller the chance that she'll be discovered," said Lois.

"We know we can trust them both. The less they know, the safer they'll be," added James.

"Sharp can hack into anything. Any hint that I'm here could endanger all of you," said Grace. "You can tell them if you feel it's necessary. I don't want anyone to lie for me, and I don't want to cause problems."

"Now that that's settled, we need to make a plan to get you back unnoticed," said James to Grace.

Lizzie locked up after Grace went upstairs, and the others had gone home. She went to the office to turn on the security system. The insurance company had insisted they install one after the fire.

She went to her room and thought about everything she'd been told. It was a lot to take in.

Wade would be upset if he learned she might be in danger and didn't tell him. She'd given her word and understood that Grace was trying to protect everyone.

Lizzie had a solution before she went to bed. She'd ask her family not to tell her when Grace returned. There'd be no need to lie to Wade. She couldn't tell him what she didn't know.

She wondered if she should tell Wade about Grace's past. She had seen his doubts about her aunt's story on his face. She decided not to mention it unless he brought it up.

The next morning, Lizzie was startled by her alarm at six a.m.

She yawned and stretched before she remembered why she wanted to get up at that hour.

Breakfast was almost ready when everyone arrived in the kitchen. They ate and talked about old times. It wasn't until they cleared away the dishes that they discussed their plan again.

"I'll drive to Oklahoma City and find a hotel," Grace said. "I'll use their WIFI and set up a new email account. Then, I'll send word that I'm there. It may be a few days before you hear from me again."

"We know," said Lois. "Please, don't take off on your own without letting us know something."

"I won't, Mom," Grace promised. "I'll let you know whatever I decide is best. I'd better go upstairs and get my things together."

The Fletchers watched her go upstairs before anyone commented.

Ellen was the first to break the silence. "Do you think she'll come back?"

"I won't be surprised if she doesn't," replied James.

"It'll depend on what she can find out," said Lois. "She won't be back if the news is bad."

They waited until Grace rejoined them with her bag in hand. James looked at the duffel and shook his head.

Grace laughed and said, "I should have known this little thing would give me away. James always complained about my over-packing."

"That's not all that gave you away," said her mother with a grin. "You still play with your ring when you're nervous."

"I didn't realize I was doing that," Grace said with surprise.

"Be careful, and don't forget to let us know when you get there," Lois said and hugged her daughter.

James, Ellen, and Lizzie hugged her each in turn.

"See you soon," James told her.

Grace fought back tears and hurried to the car. She started the engine, backed out of the drive, and waved goodbye. Her family watched until they could no longer see the car before going inside.

She reached the hotel and casino on the outskirts of Oklahoma City. She went inside and booked a room for the night.

She went to her room and put her few belongings away. She went back downstairs to the business center. She created a new email account and sent the requested email.

Grace went back to her room and turned on the television for background noise. She picked up the phone, tapped in a number, and waited.

"Jackson and Willingham Attorneys at Law," answered the receptionist. "How may I direct your call?"

"I'd like to speak with Mr. Jackson, please."

"May I ask who's calling?"

"This is Grace. I'm calling about the Sharp case."

Grace waited on hold for a few minutes. She hoped Rick Jackson would have the answers she needed.

"This is Rick Jackson," said a deep masculine voice.

"Mr. Jackson, this is Grace Stewart."

"Grace! It's good to hear from you. How can I help you?"

"Some scary things have been happening," she answered and explained her situation. "Is it possible that Sharp could have been responsible?"

"Sharp is still incarcerated. He couldn't have done those things himself. However, he may have hired someone," Jackson suggested.

"Is there any way to find out? I'm afraid that my phones and emails have been hacked again."

"He was quite good at that, as I recall. Give me a couple of hours, and I'll find out as much as I can. How can I get in touch with you?"

"I'll call you," Grace said.

"Let me give you my private number just in case you should need it," said Jackson.

Grace jotted down the number. "Thank you, Mr. Jackson."

"I'll talk with you soon."

Her next call was to Oliver Baldwin's direct line.

"This is Baldwin," he answered.

"Oliver, this is Grace. Is it safe to talk?"

"How are you? Where are you?"

"I'm safe. Has anything happened there that I should know about?"

"I had a visit from a couple of men claiming to be FBI agents today. They were asking about a missing man and thought you might know his whereabouts. I told them that you were on assignment."

"Were they FBI?"

"Their badges looked real enough, and they had a warrant to search your office. I got the impression that they've searched your house. Do you have any idea who that missing man might be?"

"Did they give you a name?"

"Peter Crisp. They showed me a photo, too. It was hard to tell much. He looked to be in his mid-forties, with dark hair and blue eyes."

"Doesn't ring a bell," Grace said, wondering if it could be Todd.

"Do you have any idea who's behind your troubles?"

"No, I've been running scared," she admitted. "I'm ready for answers now."

"Don't take too many chances," Oliver advised.

"Should anyone ask, I'm doing a story about casinos in Nevada and other states," Grace informed him. "We're keeping it quiet until I get back."

"Got it," said Oliver and paused. "Yes, I'll get back to you on that next week, Mr. Scott."

Grace understood and ended the call.

Why would they search my office and house? Who is Peter Crisp?

She looked at the clock and walked around the room. She decided to play the slot machines downstairs until it was time to call her attorney again. Two hours later, Rick Jackson answered her call.

"Were you able to find out anything about Burl Sharp?"

"He's filed an appeal."

"What does that mean for me?" Grace asked, dreading the answer.

"First, the judge would have to determine if there are grounds for an appeal. If so, we'd have to prepare our case again."

Grace moaned. "What's the worst-case scenario?"

"The worst thing that could happen is that the appeal is granted, and he is released until the new trial. It could be up to a year before we return to court. You'd have to come back here to testify again."

"Do you think the appeal will be approved?"

"I don't know at this point," Jackson admitted. "It depends on what he claims to be the reason."

"How long will it take the judge to make a decision?"

"I'll try to find out," Jackson said. "Call again on Monday."

"Thank you, Mr. Jackson."

She stood and walked around her room. She couldn't imagine a judge granting the appeal. There was too much evidence against him. She stopped and put her hands over her mouth.

There was no doubt in her mind that her attacker had been Burl Sharp. She didn't see his face that night because it was too dark. Was his attorney basing the appeal on that fact?

The thought of Sharp being free to torment her again was terrifying. She knew he wanted her dead. Would he wait until she was in New York for a new trial or come after her the moment he was released?

Grace sat on the edge of her bed. She stared unseeing at the faces on the television screen. Her mind was blank, and her body numb.

Sometime later, she stood and went to the window. She stared at the sky and steeled herself. The terror she'd felt for the past week began to melt. Knowing what she could be facing made it easier to deal with. The fear was…changing… burgeoning into…determination…and anger.

Sharp was going to try to kill her, but she didn't have to make it easy for him.

CHAPTER FIVE

Saturday morning dawned with high hopes at the Paradise Creek Inn. The Fletchers had been looking forward to this day for more than a year. They hoped that the many phone calls asking for details indicated a good turnout for the reopening.

Dan arrived in time for breakfast. He and James were soon at work outside the inn while the ladies worked in the kitchen. They wanted to have everything ready by noon. That would give them time to have lunch and freshen up before their guests began to arrive.

Wade was there at noon with burgers and fries for everyone. He chose not to wear his uniform for the occasion. Today was about the inn, and he didn't want to be a distraction.

Dan and Wade were in charge of directing traffic and parking. James and Lizzie were to greet their guests and lead tours of the inn. Ellen would be tending to the refreshments. Granny would man the information and booking desk.

The entire inn was decorated with bright colors, greenery, and twinkle lights. Silk flower arrangements with red roses, yellow daisies, and bluebonnets adorned every guest room. Silk greenery and twinkle lights lined the doorways and stairway banisters.

Balloons and streamers of red, yellow, and blue decorated the hallways and the event rooms. The dining room and patio décor continued the colorful theme.

Guests could help themselves to refreshments at the serving bar. There were fresh savory appetizers, sweet treats, and trays of fruits, vegetables, and cheeses. Four varieties of punch were available to top it all off.

Everything was ready. All they needed were guests to end the opening day jitters.

The men sat on the front porch near a misting fan and waited. They took turns pacing the porch and looking toward the bridge.

"Looks like somebody's coming," Dan announced at last.

James opened the front door and shouted, "Our first guests are here!"

Wade stood back and waited for instructions. Dan was already directing the car to the parking area. He knew that his future father-in-law wanted to be the one to greet their first guests.

Dan escorted a middle-aged couple from the parking area to the front lawn. James met them at the bottom of the steps.

"Welcome to the Paradise Creek Inn," James began. "We're glad you could come."

"I know we're here a little early," said the woman. "I called a day or two ago hoping to book a room for the weekend."

"I'm Earl Ketchersid," said the man. "This is my wife, Beverly. We plan to stay until you kick us out."

"That's perfect," James assured him. "There are refreshments inside if you'd like to get out of the heat."

The couple followed James inside, where he introduced them. Lizzie led them away for a tour, and James returned to the front porch.

Deputy Maddie Clifton and her husband, Drew, were the next guests to arrive. Wade directed them to a parking space that would be easy to exit. He knew that Maddie was scheduled to work the night shift.

"Hey, Brody," Wade said to their toddler. "Give me five."

Brody grinned and slapped Wade's hand before hiding his face on his mother's knee.

"Howdy, Wade," Drew said. "How's it going?"

"Pretty good. How are you?"

The men exchanged pleasantries while Maddie struggled to keep Brody in check. They made their way to the porch, where James waited to greet them.

"Drew, Maddie," James said and nodded. "Thank y'all for coming."

"We wouldn't miss it," Drew said. "I can't wait to see how the inn turned out."

Maddie was about to agree when Brody started running across the porch. She caught him and picked him up.

"We won't be able to stay long," she told James. "The terrible twos are an issue today."

James laughed and said, "We're glad to have you, terrible twos and all."

"Will they go away when he turns three in a couple of months?" Drew asked with hope in his eyes.

Nope, they just morph into the next phase," James teased.

Drew moaned. They went inside, and James led them on a tour of the inn.

"Are you bored?" Lizzie asked when she joined Wade and Dan on the front porch.

"It'll pick up," Wade said and put his arm around her.

Dan stood up and said, "They must have heard you."

A line of cars made their way across the bridge toward the inn. Wade and Dan directed them to the parking area. Lizzie waited on the porch to greet the newcomers.

"Welcome to the Paradise Creek Inn," she said when the group had assembled on the lawn. "We're so glad you could come. If you follow me inside, I'll be happy to lead you on a tour of the inn and to the refreshments."

The Fletcher group was kept busy the rest of the afternoon. They had little time to talk or relax. They were ready for a break when the crowd thinned, and fewer guests arrived.

Dan and James went inside to cool off while Wade and Lizzie watched for guests.

"You've had a good turnout so far," Wade observed.

"Yes, we have. There are a lot of people who told me they'd come that haven't yet."

"My folks said they'd be here."

"We should enjoy this lull while it lasts," Lizzie suggested.

"Oops, looks like the lull is over," Wade said, nodding toward the bridge.

"I'll get Dan and Daddy," Lizzie told him and went inside.

Wade directed two cars toward the parking area. He grinned when he recognized the occupants. He hugged them all when they got out of their cars.

"I'm glad y'all could make it," he said to his family.

"Uncle Wade, is this your house?" questioned Bailee, his six-year-old niece.

"No, this is the inn where Lizzie lives and works.

"This is where you're going to live when you get married, isn't it?" asked his nine-year-old nephew, Gavin.

Wade didn't answer right away. The question surprised him. He hadn't thought about where he and Lizzie would live.

"We haven't decided," Wade answered.

"Don't you think it's time you did?" observed his dad, Sean.

"You don't have long to decide," added his mother, Gloria.

He led his relatives to the front lawn. Dan and James exited the house and greeted the group.

"This is Dan Hayes and Lizzie's dad, James Fletcher," Wade began. "Dan and James, this is my brother, Wyatt, and his wife, Becky. These two rug rats are Bailee and Gavin."

"Hey, we aren't rug rats," protested Bailee.

"We're little monsters," Gavin corrected.

The group laughed, and Wade continued the introductions. These are my grandparents, Gene and Peggy. You already know my mom and dad."

"It's good to see all of you," James said. "Thank you so much for coming. Wade, why don't you take your folks inside? Dan and I will handle things out here."

Wade grinned and led them inside. He and Lizzie showed them around the inn and made introductions.

The next guests to arrive were members of Lizzie's clan. Ellen's sister and brother-in-law, Barbara and Jimmy Pearson, drove up with their daughter, Jan, and her family.

James greeted them with hugs and tickled Jan and Eli's two-year-old daughter, Darcie. He led them inside and introduced them to Wade's family. Lizzie showed them around the inn.

Eli pulled her aside after the tour. "Lizzie, do you mind if Drake brings Mom and Dad? They'd like to see y'all and what you've done with the inn."

"Of course not. We'd love to see your folks."

"What about Drake?"

"Eli, we're practically family. Drake is your brother, and you're married to my cousin," Lizzie said. "Faith is my closest friend. We're going to see each other from time to time. There's no reason we can't get along."

Eli smiled at her and said, "I'll give them a call."

Lizzie excused herself to greet a new group of guests. Among the group was a man she didn't know.

There was something about him that bothered her. He didn't speak with any of the other guests and gave the impression that he was there alone.

He seemed to be interested in the people rather than the inn. Women of a certain age drew his attention. He stared at Ellen while he waited his turn in the refreshment line.

Lizzie excused herself and went outside to find Wade. He was talking with his deputies, Gordon Reed, Brandon Lodge, and Calvin Baker.

"Hi, Fletcher," Baker said with a mischievous grin.

Lizzie smiled and said, "Hi guys, thank you for coming."

"You know we never miss a chance for free food," said Lodge with a wink.

Lizzie laughed and said, "Y'all enjoy yourselves, but save some for the rest of the guests."

She turned to Wade and whispered, "Could I have a minute?"

"Refreshments are inside," he told his men, then turned to Lizzie. "You can have all my minutes, Darlin'."

"Mmmm, I'll remind you of that one of these days," she said and gave him a quick kiss.

"What's up?" Wade inquired with a grin.

Lizzie paused, then said, "There's a man here that seems out of place. I can't help feeling that he's up to something." She told Wade what she'd observed.

"Which man is it?"

"I don't see him right now."

"Describe him to me, and I'll keep an eye on him."

"He's about your height and build. His hair is brown and cut short. He's wearing jeans and a navy-blue T-shirt. It looks like he hasn't shaved in a couple of days.

Wade listened while she described the stranger. More cars were headed toward the inn. He couldn't be in two places at the same time.

"I don't want to leave Dan out here on his own," Wade said. "Tell Reed what you told me. He'll know what to do."

Lizzie went inside to find Wade's deputies while he helped Dan direct traffic. Reed joined him on the front lawn a few minutes later.

"Did Lizzie tell you about a stranger?"

Reed nodded. "She pointed him out to us. Lodge and Baker are keeping an eye on him."

"What do you think?"

"It's hard to tell," Reed replied. "I noticed him before Lizzie pointed him out. He doesn't seem to fit in with the rest of the crowd. I haven't noticed anything suspicious."

"Let me know if anything changes," Wade said. "Go back inside where it's cool. Uh oh!"

"What's wrong?" asked Reed.

"It's Tiffany!"

A mischievous smile spread across Reed's face. "Are you going to show her around the inn?"

Wade frowned at his deputy and ducked inside. James appeared on the front porch with a wide grin of his own.

Reed went inside and helped himself to some punch. He didn't want to miss a thing.

Wade went back outside after James led Tiffany and her young son away. His mood didn't improve when he realized he was directing Drake Wagner and his parents, Ben and Carol, to the parking area.

Lizzie was waiting on the porch to greet the next group of guests. He hoped that the Wagners wouldn't get there in time for Lizzie to lead them inside. Those hopes faded when he realized that the elder Wagner was now able to walk with minimal assistance.

It was Ben's stroke that prompted Drake to move back from Colorado last year. Wade didn't like the fact that Lizzie's ex was back in the area. He hated the fact that Drake tried to rekindle their romance.

Wade's attention was drawn by the arrival of more cars. He glanced toward the porch to see Lizzie guide the Wagners into the house. He gritted his teeth and continued to direct traffic.

Lizzie led Drake and his parents through the inn and to the refreshments. She was about to go back outside when she noticed a tall willowy brunette talking with Reed.

Lodge and Baker were sitting on the patio enjoying heaping

plates of appetizers. Lizzie walked outside and sat down at their table.

"Hi, Fletcher," Lodge said. "Did you make all this good food?"

"Mama and Granny helped," she replied.

"You should bring the leftovers to the office?" Baker suggested.

"I might do that if you two leave anything behind," she joked. "When did Tiffany get here?"

"You mean Wade's ex?" teased Lodge. "She got here a couple of minutes before your ex."

"Yeah, we're waiting for the fireworks to start," added Baker and leaned back in his chair with an evil grin.

"What fireworks?"

"You know the fireworks between you, Wade, and the two exes," Lodge teased.

Lizzie looked at the pair with a smile. "You know what they say about paybacks, don't you?" she said and stood.

Lizzie walked away with laughter ringing in her ears. She shook her head. *One of these days, I'm going to get even with those two.*

She went back to the front porch to find Wade chatting with a woman. She had long blonde hair and wore a short skirt with a halter top that showed off her hourglass figure. It was Megan Ford.

Lizzie resisted the urge to step between them. Megan had been a thorn in her side for years. She had caused the breakup with Drake. She also had her sights on Wade at one time.

That was supposed to be all in the past. Megan had had a rude awakening last year. She'd apologized to everyone she'd wronged. That was a big undertaking since she'd wronged almost everyone she'd ever met.

Lizzie and Megan were no longer enemies. They weren't friends either. Lizzie still didn't trust her enough to call her a friend. She had a wait-and-see attitude where Megan was concerned.

"Hi, Lizzie," Megan said when she reached the porch. "You know my friend, Terry Meaker, don't you?"

"Yes, how are you, Terry?"

"I'm good," Terry answered with an air of boredom.

Dr. Gerard Hughes joined them and said, "Lizzie, it's good to see you, my dear."

"Hello, Dr. Hughes. It's good to see you, too. Follow me for a tour of the inn and refreshments."

Lizzie led the way inside and looked over her shoulder at Wade. He was on his way to direct traffic.

Guests arrived all afternoon and into the evening. They enjoyed the tour, the food, and visiting with old friends.

Some of the day's guests were married at the inn, some wanted to be, and some wanted to book rooms. Granny was kept busy handing out information, answering questions, and making appointments.

The event was winding down, and many of the guests had gone when a young woman arrived. She had short blonde hair and wore dark sunglasses. She was tall, slender, and dressed in a form-fitting sundress. Her perfume entered the room before she did and lingered long after she'd gone.

She toured the inn and sampled some refreshments. She took a brochure, set up an appointment, and left.

"Who was that?" Lodge pointed out.

"I don't think she's from around here," replied Baker. "I'd remember her."

"Guys," said Lizzie. "You might want to wipe the drool off your chins."

Lodge and Baker looked at her as if they had no idea anyone else was on the planet. Their faces turned crimson with embarrassment and laughter when her words registered.

Wade sat on the front porch. More guests were leaving than arriving now. There was little more than an hour left in the celebration when the Ketchersids joined him.

"This has been such fun," Beverly told him. "We've booked a room so that we can experience everything."

"I'm glad you enjoyed it," Wade said and escorted them to

their car.

Wade and Dan went inside when the last guests left the parking area. They joined the Fletchers at the dining table. It was the first time the group had a moment to compare notes.

"Did you see the guy with the military haircut?" asked James.

"I did," answered Lizzie. "I told Wade about him. He gave me the creeps."

"Me too!" said Ellen. "He kept staring at me."

"Staring at you? Did he say or do anything?" James demanded with anger in his eyes.

"Nope," said Ellen. "Just stared. Then he went outside and sat on the patio for a while."

"I tried to make conversation with him when he left," said Dan. "He was a one-word answer kind of man."

Wade listened and made mental notes. He hadn't seen the man. He knew that his deputies would share their thoughts.

"What about that blonde woman?" Granny queried.

"She didn't talk to anybody either," said James.

"She asked for a brochure and made an appointment. She'll be back Wednesday to meet with Lizzie."

"What does she want to talk about?" Lizzie asked.

"She didn't say."

"There were some characters here today," Ellen observed.

"Speaking of characters," James began. "I was surprised to see Megan."

"I was, too," replied Dan. "I was expecting trouble and was surprised that she was on her best behavior."

"Was it hard to see her here?" inquired Granny.

"We've been divorced long enough that seeing her doesn't bother me," Dan said and paused, looking at the group. "Especially since I've been seeing a nice woman."

"Ooooo, is it serious?" Lizzie teased.

"I'll just say it's looking good," Dan answered and winked at her.

"When do we get to meet her?" asked Ellen.

"Soon."

Try as they might, he would give them no more information.

"Speaking of trouble," Lizzie began and looked at Wade. "Lodge and Baker were expecting to see fireworks between us."

"Fireworks? Between us?" Wade teased. "Why would there be fireworks between us?"

James roared with laughter.

Ellen frowned at her husband. "James, what on earth is so funny?"

James held up his hand to indicate that he needed a minute. When he stopped laughing, he said, "I was expecting fireworks, too. Wade ran into the office and shut the door like a demon from hell was chasing him. I went to find out what was wrong, and he told me his ex-fiancé was outside. He didn't want her to see him."

Wade groaned and covered his face with his hand. He was hoping the incident would stay between the two of them.

James roared again before he continued his tale. "I went out to meet her, and she introduced herself. I recognized the name. It was nice to have a face to go with it."

"You didn't tell her that did you?" Ellen was appalled.

"No, I enjoyed my private joke," James said and continued. "The next thing I know, here comes Lizzie with Drake and his parents. I thought there'd be a battle for sure."

Everyone enjoyed the story and the joke at Wade and Lizzie's expense. The young couple looked at each other and joined in.

"We'd better go home and get some rest," Granny suggested. "We'll need to get this place cleaned up for next week."

"You'll join us for dinner tomorrow, won't you, Dan?" invited James.

"I've already got plans, but thanks," Dan answered.

"Well, bring her along," Granny said. "The more, the merrier."

"I'm supposed to meet her family tomorrow," Dan said with a blush.

Everyone said goodnight leaving Wade and Lizzie alone. Wade locked up while Lizzie put away the leftover food.

She was rinsing dishes in the sink when he walked up behind her and wrapped her in his arms. She smiled and snuggled closer.

"Lodge and Baker were right. There are going to be fireworks tonight," he said and kissed her neck. "Not the kind I'd want them to watch."

"Why, Sheriff Adams, what do you have in mind?" she teased.

Without another word, he picked her up and carried her to the bedroom.

CHAPTER SIX

THE GRAND REOPENING WAS A SUCCESS. The Fletchers had been working hard and felt they deserved to rest on Sunday.

Wade and Lizzie slept late for the first time in weeks. They snuggled together until their stomachs began to rumble.

Brunch sounded good to them both. They each chose what they wanted from the pantry and worked together to make their meal.

They were eating at the dining table when Wade asked, "Have you thought about where we're going to live once we're married?"

"No, I haven't," Lizzie answered in surprise. "What do you have in mind?"

"I hadn't thought about either until Gavin and Bailee wanted to know where we're going to live."

"You're almost living at the inn now," Lizzie pointed out.

"I know, and our arrangement has been working well. But do we want to continue to have separate homes after we're married?"

"Oh! I hadn't thought about that either."

"That's something we'd better decide sooner rather than later," Wade suggested.

They ate in silence until they finished their meal. Both were lost in their own thoughts.

Wade broke the silence when he'd cleaned his plate. "Let's both think about it this afternoon," he suggested. "We can discuss it with your folks at dinner."

"That's a good idea," Lizzie answered with relief. "I'm a little stunned that we hadn't already thought about this."

"I know what you mean. I felt the same way after the rug rats, excuse me, little monsters, pointed it out."

Lizzie looked at him in confusion. He related the conversation he'd had with his niece and nephew.

She laughed and said, "I wonder how many times Wyatt and Becky have called them that?"

"I'd say quite a few," Wade said and laughed.

They cleared the table, and Lizzie asked, "Are you ready for your meeting with the County Commissioners this week?"

"I know what I want to say. I haven't had the time to write it up."

"Let me do these," she said, taking a plate from his hand. "Use the computer in my office and start writing."

"Are you sure? I don't mind helping with the dishes."

"I need something to do while you work," she said. "Besides, I want to think about our future living arrangements."

Wade went to Lizzie's office and sat in front of her computer. He thought about what he wanted to say to the County Commission.

He was shorthanded again and needed to hire more deputies. He'd been able to hire two new deputies last year. He'd needed a third deputy, but the Commission didn't approve the extra funds.

Clint Odom and Marina Gonzales were assets to the department. He hoped he could find two more who would fit as well with the rest of his staff.

The loss of Craig Dodson was hard on the entire department. They were all impacted by his death. Wade, most of all.

They had worked together and been good friends for years.

Craig was the one person he knew he could always depend on. Wade still struggled with the fact that he'd survived the explosion that had killed his friend.

He had been faced with a difficult task when he went back to work. He'd recovered from his physical injuries. Deciding who would take Dodson's place as second in command added to his emotional pain.

Gordon Reed and Maddie Clifton were equal in seniority and qualifications. Wade knew they were both dependable and capable of filling the position. He liked and worked well with both of them.

It would have made his life much easier if one of them had chosen not to apply. It had been a tough decision that he'd agonized over for weeks.

In the end, he'd chosen Reed. He still needed Maddie to oversee female prisoners.

Maddie was disappointed. Wade knew she could use the extra money. He also knew it wasn't about the money.

That was almost a year ago, and he'd waited long enough. His goal was to hire two more deputies and create another position that would put Maddie on an equal footing with Reed. It would be a good move for the department and give them all more freedom.

In the past, either Wade or Craig had to be available at all times. The new position would add another person to the rotation.

Wade hadn't told anyone in the department about his plan. He didn't want to see the disappointment in Maddie's eyes if the Commissioners didn't approve the funds.

He sighed in frustration. His plans for the department were in someone else's hands. The Commission could decide either way.

He expected them to approve at least one new deputy. He'd then have to take applications. It took a long time to find Odom and Gonzalez. He hoped the process would be faster this time.

Wade finished writing the proposal and printed it for Lizzie to proofread. He sat back and thought about their brunch conversation.

Where are we going to live? What we've been doing has worked out well. Will it still work after we're married? Why should I continue to pay rent on a house that I'll seldom use?"

Lizzie finished the dishes and cleaned the kitchen. She swept the entire inn while she thought.

Where are we going to live? I'll be here during the day. Someone will have to be here at night when the guest rooms are occupied.

She put the broom away and sat down at the table. *He stays here most of the time and drives into town for work. I don't see how moving in here will be much different than it is now. There are times when he needs to stay at his place.*

Wade startled her when he joined her at the table.

"I'm sorry," he said. "You were deep in thought. I should have cleared my throat or something."

Lizzie smiled and said, "I'm no closer to a solution to our problem than I was earlier."

"Neither am I," he admitted. "Want to take a break and proofread this for me?"

Lizzie took the pages and looked at the clock. "It'll be time to start dinner when I've finished."

"Tell me what you have planned, and I'll gather the ingredients," Wade offered.

Lizzie told him what she needed and went to her office to read his work. There were a few minor corrections that he needed to make. She marked them and made suggestions on sticky notes. She left the papers on the desk and went back to the kitchen.

Dinner and Wade's proposal were ready by the time the family arrived.

"Do you have enough for two more?" James asked. "Dan called. He's had a change in plans and wants us to meet his friend."

A smile spread slowly across Lizzie's face. "We have more than enough. Did he tell you anything about her?"

"No, he just asked if it was okay to bring her," James said with a smirk.

"I can't wait to meet her!"

"Now, don't go on about it too much," James scolded. "You know how secretive Dan is about his love life. He won't bring her back if we embarrass him."

"Daddy! I would never embarrass him in front of her," Lizzie said. "At least not until I get to know her."

"Wade, help me," James said with exasperation.

Wade laughed and said, "I'll do my best. I can't make any promises."

Dan knocked on the back door before he opened it. "May we come in?"

"Of course," Ellen said. "You know you don't have to ask."

"Everybody, this is Deanna Garnett. Deanna, this is everybody," Dan said, blushing.

The Fletcher family and Wade introduced themselves to the newcomer. Deanna had a bright smile, and her brown eyes sparkled.

"I've heard so much about y'all that I feel like I already know you," she said.

"We're so glad you could come," Lizzie said. "Why don't we sit down and get acquainted over dinner?"

Everyone sat down and filled their plates. Lizzie watched Dan while he watched Deanna. It was obvious that he was smitten.

"How did y'all meet?" James asked.

"We met at a party," Deanna said. "Dan was there with a friend of mine. By the end of the night, my date had left with Dan's date."

"I guess you could say we traded places," Dan added.

"We're still together, but they aren't," said Deanna.

"Are you still friends with the other girl?" Lois asked.

"No," Deanna began. "She says that I stole Dan from her."

"Not hardly," Dan said and shook his head.

The group laughed and chatted through dessert. The dishes were cleared, and everyone returned to the table.

"Lizzie and I want to discuss something with y'all," Wade

began. "We've realized that we need to decide where we're going to live once we're married."

"You haven't decided that yet?" Lois cried.

"We've both been so busy that we hadn't thought about it," admitted Lizzie.

"Where do you want to live?" James asked.

"Wade has been staying here since the inn repairs were finished. I stayed with him while I worked in town."

"Both arrangements have worked well. I think that's one reason why we hadn't thought about this sooner," Wade added.

"Our workplaces won't change. He'll still need to be in town every day, and I'll still need to be here. The issue is where we'll be the rest of the time."

"It's important that someone is here at all times when we have overnight guests," Ellen said. "It doesn't have to be Lizzie. We could share that responsibility."

"There will still be times that she'll need to be here late at night and back early the next day," Wade said. "It doesn't make sense for her to drive back to town."

"Wade needs to be in town when he has late nights and early mornings," Lizzie added.

"Are you renting or buying your place?" Deanna inquired.

"It's a rental," Wade said. "The lease is up in December."

"Could you sublet your house?" James inquired.

"I hadn't thought of that," Wade admitted. "Why do you ask?"

"I was going to suggest that you live at one place or the other to see how it works out. There's no need to pay rent if you choose to live out here."

"You might consider buying or building a house between here and town," Lois suggested.

"That would have to wait until the inn business recovers,' Lizzie pointed out. "It could be a long wait."

"I like the idea of subletting," Wade said. "Lodge said something about looking for a new place. He might consider taking over my lease."

"What about those late nights?" Lizzie asked.

"It has two bedrooms. I'll stipulate that one of them is mine when needed. I'll have to check with the landlord first."

"You'd better find out soon," Ellen pointed out. "The wedding is less than three weeks away."

"Speaking of which," Lois began, "I've marked that week as booked so that you'll have time to get everything ready."

"Thank you, Granny. I've been so busy that I hadn't thought of that either."

"Have you thought about your honeymoon?" asked Dan.

"That," Wade began with a mischievous grin. "I have thought about it. I've taken care of everything."

"You have?" Lizzie said with surprise.

"Yes, and I'm not going to tell you," he teased. "It's a secret."

Lizzie looked at her fiancé and smirked. "I'll bet I can find out."

"Uh oh," James said. "It sounds like you're going to have a hard time keeping it a secret."

"You may be right," Wade admitted. " But she'll have to drag it out of me."

Lizzie raised one eyebrow and said, "Challenge accepted, Sheriff Adams."

They laughed and joked a while longer before saying good-night. Wade and Lizzie locked up and talked while snuggled under the covers.

Wade looked into Lizzie's eyes. "What do you think? Where do you want to live?"

"It doesn't matter as long as we're together most of the time."

Wade smiled and kissed her. "I think it would be best for you to be here at least until business picks up. I'll talk to my landlord tomorrow."

"I do like the idea of having our own house someday," Lizzie admitted.

"We will, Darlin', we will."

"What do I need to pack for our honeymoon?" Lizzie teased.

Wade roared with laughter and turned out the light.

* * *

Grace's visit to Oklahoma was short. She knew it was a bad idea to stay in one place too long.

She'd used different modes of transportation over the weekend and made her way to St. Louis, Missouri. She stared out the window of her hotel room, planning her next move.

She needed to make a more drastic change in her appearance. She didn't want to be recognized by Sharp's people.

Changing her appearance meant going shopping. She needed different clothes and a bigger bag.

A trip to a hair salon would be a good idea. A new cut and color might do the trick.

I may need a new id or two as well. I've used all that I have at least twice. I can't risk using them too often.

Grace turned from the window and picked up her purse. She opened the envelope and took out what was left of her cash. It wouldn't last much longer.

She had money in the bank. She knew if she made a withdrawal, anyone monitoring her would know about it.

She knew that her credit card could be monitored too. She wondered if going to the bank or using her card would take longer to give away her location.

A familiar voice on the TV caught her attention. She looked at the anchor man's face on the screen. *I know him. I worked with him in Virginia.*

Grace watched the newscast and remembered some of the stories they'd worked on together. She wondered if he had the same types of connections that he'd had back then.

She waited until the six o'clock news ended. She picked up the phone and asked the hotel operator for the number to the local station, dialed the number, and waited.

"May I speak to Trent Cobb?"

"May I have your name, please?"

"I'd rather surprise him. Tell him it's a colleague from his Virginia days."

"Please, hold."

Grace waited for several minutes before her friend answered.

"Hi Trent, this is Grace."

"Grace? I can't believe it. Are you in town?"

"For a day or two," she said.

"Why don't we meet for lunch or dinner?"

"I can't. I may be in trouble."

"What kind of trouble? I hope it's not the kind you had in New York."

"It might be."

"What can I do to help?" he offered.

"I need local transportation for a couple of days and a new id. Do you happen to know where I could find those things?"

"I can help you with that, but I'll have to go with you. My guy doesn't like strangers." Trent told her.

"Are you sure you want to take the chance?" Grace asked. "It might be dangerous."

"How many times did you bail me out of scrapes? Now, I have a chance to return the favor."

"I can't risk my location being leaked. This has to be kept under wraps."

"Let me get in touch with my guy. Give me a call on my direct line in an hour," he said and gave her the number.

Grace watched TV for an hour and waited five minutes longer before dialing Trent's number.

"It's all set. He'll meet us tonight. If he agrees to help, it'll cost twenty-five dollars for the id and a hundred dollars for risk-free transportation."

"Would you mind picking me up?" Grace asked and gave him directions.

"I'll meet you at eleven-thirty," Cobb said. "We'll go to meet my friend from there."

"Thanks, Trent. I'll be waiting."

The call ended, and Grace returned her attention to the TV. There wasn't anything else she could do at the moment.

At eleven fifteen, she left her room and rode the elevator to the ground floor. She went outside, walked across the street, and a block north. She waited in the shadows until she saw a white Ford Mustang coming toward her.

There was no doubt that it was Trent. Grace stepped into the light, and he stopped the car. She got in, and they drove away.

"Thanks for doing this, Trent," Grace began. "I'm sorry it's been so long since we've talked."

"Hey, what are friends for? You look good. How have you been?"

"I was doing great until a week ago," Grace replied. "You seem to be doing all right. Nice suit, nice car, and you don't look like you've aged a day."

Trent smiled at her and said, "Neither do you."

"What's your friend like?" Grace queried.

"He's good, and he's careful. He's a fair man. That's the main reason I like him. He doesn't have a lot to say, but he'll be straight with you."

"That's what I need right now," said Grace.

"He'll ask questions about why you need his services and if the law will be involved." Trent looked at Grace with a raised eyebrow.

"I'm not hiding from the law," Grace reassured him. "I'm not sure who I'm hiding from at this point, but you could say that I'm acting with an abundance of caution."

"He'll want more information than that," Trent warned her.

"I'll tell him what he wants to know. I'll also tell him the less he knows, the safer he'll be."

They drove into the parking lot of a truck stop and parked in front. Trent escorted Grace inside the attached restaurant. There were few people there, and the waitress told them to sit where they liked.

Trent directed Grace to a secluded booth. They sat down and ordered coffee.

"Are you hungry? I'm starved, and the food here is good."

"I've already had dinner," Grace replied. "Order something for yourself."

The waitress brought their coffee, and Trent ordered his meal.

"Is Jolly around?" Trent inquired. "I haven't seen him in ages."

"Yea, he's in the back," said the waitress. "I'll let him know you're here."

A man stopped beside their table a few minutes later.

"Trent, it's good to see you in person instead of on the TV set," the man said and laughed.

Jolly Smith was not what Grace expected. She had imagined a shady-looking movie character. Instead, he was clean-cut, handsome, and dignified.

Trent invited the man to join them. They made polite conversation for a moment.

"Jolly, this is my friend, Grace. She needs your help," Trent told him.

"Why do you need my expertise?" Jolly demanded. He watched her while she gave him the highlights of her story.

Trent gasped. "Sharp?"

Grace nodded.

Jolly looked at Trent. "You know about this?"

"I wasn't involved. Grace and I worked together when Sharp started stalking her. I learned about the rest through other sources," Trent admitted.

Jolly stared at Grace for a moment. "What are you looking for?"

"I need transportation for a day or two at most," she began. "I'll need to make some changes to my appearance, and I'll need new identification."

"Do you want drastic changes or something subtle?"

"Something subtle," Grace said. "I have a lot riding on blending in."

Jolly nodded and clasped his manicured hands in front of him on the table.

"I'm going to help you, Grace," he said. "No one should have to go through what you went through, certainly not twice."

"Thank you, Mr. Smith," Grace beamed at him.

"My friends call me Jolly. I have a friend who can help you achieve a new look," he said and pulled a business card from his pocket. "I'll give her a call and tell her you'll be there at two o'clock tomorrow afternoon. When you've finished, come back here, and we'll make your new id."

He handed her a set of keys and said, "The blue Chrysler 300 parked behind the building is yours. I assume Trent gave you my terms."

"Yes," Grace said and reached for her purse.

Jolly held up his hand, and she paused.

"We'll balance the account tomorrow," he said and stood. "Trent, it's good to see you. Enjoy your dinner."

The waitress arrived, and Jolly walked away.

Trent finished eating and followed Grace to the back parking lot. They located the Chrysler 300 and opened the door. Grace sat behind the wheel and started the engine. She drove Trent around the truck stop to his car.

"Thanks for your help, Trent."

"You're welcome," he said and looked into her eyes. "Are you sure you know what you're doing?"

"No," she admitted. " But I have a plan now. That's more than I had when I came here."

"Take care of yourself," he said and hugged her. "Let me know if you need anything."

"I will," Grace said and smiled. "I'll let you know how it all turns out."

They said goodnight, and Grace drove back to the hotel. She went to her room and thought about what she needed to do the following day. It was almost two a.m. before she crawled under the covers and drifted off to sleep.

CHAPTER SEVEN

GRACE SLEPT in Monday morning for the first time since she'd left Las Vegas. She was exhausted, and she might not have another chance for several days.

She enjoyed a nice breakfast and a long hot shower before she started her day. After she dressed, she used the hotel phone and punched in her attorney's number.

"Mr. Jackson, this is Grace. Do you have any news about Sharp?"

"His appeal is still pending," Jackson told her.

"Do you have any idea what the judge will do?" she asked.

"I spoke with him and told him of the threat that Sharp made after the trial. I hope he'll take that into account."

"What about Sharp?"

"I asked a friend of mine to investigate his activities. His attorney has been his only visitor in the past six months. Sharp hasn't had computer access since he was incarcerated, and he rarely utilizes the postal service. He's corresponded with no one other than his attorney in the past year."

"Could he have hired someone through his attorney?"

"It's possible but unlikely," said Jackson. "I asked my friend to look into that as well. There's a chance that Sharp has had access to contraband communication devices. There's also a chance that he's been communicating through another inmate."

"I see," Grace said. "We don't know anything more than we did earlier."

"I'm sorry that I can't give you a definite answer," Jackson apologized. "However, Sharp has been a model prisoner for the past several months, according to my friend. Getting caught with contraband or sending online communication would put an end to his appeal."

"So, in your opinion, Sharp isn't responsible for the break-in at my house or the tracker on my car."

"I didn't say that," Jackson emphasized. "It would be difficult and foolish for him to hire a third party, but not impossible."

"When will the judge rule on the appeal?"

"He said he would announce his decision on Friday."

"I'll call you Friday evening then," Grace said and hung up.

She flopped face-first onto the bed and screamed into a pillow. Frustration gave way to despair.

She rolled over and stared at the ceiling. She was afraid to go back to Vegas, and afraid to go to the inn. She was tired of being afraid.

It had to be Sharp. Why would anyone else put a tracker on her car or break into her house?

Grace wiped the tears from her face and sat up. Nothing was missing or destroyed in her home. Sharp would have made sure that she knew he was responsible. Who could it have been if it wasn't Sharp?

The message on the mirror still rattled her. Oliver Baldwin was the only person in Vegas who knew she was hiding from her past. Could he be part of this? Could he be Sharp's outside contact?

Stop it, Grace! You're letting your imagination run wild again. You need to look at this situation as a reporter instead of a victim. Look at the facts and ignore the emotions.

Grace took out her laptop and plugged it in. She disabled the automatic WIFI connection and opened a blank document.

She typed every fact she could remember from the time she arrived at the diner until she left Las Vegas. She read through the file when she'd finished.

I wonder where the man from the diner is now? Could he have written the message on my mirror?

Grace looked at the clock on the nightstand. It was time to put her plan in motion. She got dressed and left the hotel.

She spent the rest of the morning shopping for new clothes. She bought enough to last her two weeks, along with a nice new piece of luggage to keep them in.

Grace needed to lead Sharp's people away from her family. The best way to do that was to resurface.

She went back to the hotel and organized her belongings. She still had time before she needed to be at the hair salon. She styled her hair and put on her makeup. She wanted to look like Grace Stewart, anchorwoman for the time being.

She spent some time in the business center looking for transportation out of St. Louis and for a branch of the bank that she used.

Grace checked out of the hotel and loaded her belongings into the trunk of the borrowed car. She drove to a Bank of America branch on the opposite side of town from her hotel.

She knew there would be cameras outside the bank as well as inside. She parked two blocks south of the building and walked to the entrance. She went through the main door and walked toward the first teller who met her eyes.

"May I help you?" the young woman asked.

"I need to make a withdrawal, please."

The woman handed her a blank withdrawal form. Grace completed it and handed it back to her with her real identification.

The teller looked at the amount and back at Grace.

"I'm traveling for work and am almost out of funds," Grace told her. "You'd think they'd give us an expense account. Instead, they reimburse us after the fact."

"That doesn't seem fair," said the woman.

"I know. I have to keep all of my receipts and do a mountain of paperwork before I get my money back."

The young teller shook her head in sympathy and asked, "How would you like that?"

"Big bills, please. They take up less room in my wallet."

Grace took the money and stuffed it into the bottom of her purse. She left the bank and walked two blocks west before turning south. She located the car and drove toward a casino before turning toward her true destination.

At two o'clock, she walked into the salon, told the receptionist that she had an appointment with Denise, and sat down to wait.

Grace surveyed her surroundings, and like Jolly, it wasn't what she expected. It appeared that the salon catered to clients with expensive tastes.

"Grace?" asked a plump woman with platinum hair.

Grace nodded and stood.

"I'm Denise. What can I do for you today?"

"I'm ready for a new look," Grace told her.

The two women discussed options before Denise began. Neither of them mentioned Jolly Smith.

Denise showed her some makeup techniques to give her face a different look. She colored, cut, and styled Grace's hair. Grace hardly recognized herself when she looked in the mirror.

"Thank you, Denise. I love it," Grace said.

"I'm glad you like it. Come see us again the next time you're in town."

Grace was pleased with her new look. She now had a chin-length auburn bob. Anyone who had seen her before wouldn't have known her right away.

She left the salon and drove across town to the truck stop. She parked the Chrysler in the back where she'd found it, took her belongings from the trunk, and walked toward an open back door.

Jolly was waiting for her with a look of approval on his face. "I didn't recognize you from a distance. I hope that's what you were expecting."

"It's perfect," she said.

He led her into a backroom that was set up with camera equipment.

"How many new ids would you like to have?"

"Three, please."

"Do you want new information or updated versions of the ones you have?"

Grace thought for a moment, then said, "I think new ones would be best. I've used these too much already."

"Let me see one of them to get the general information," Jolly said. "I assume you want different outfits for each one."

"Yes, I do."

Jolly pointed toward a screen in the corner of the room. "You can change over there while I put this information in the computer."

Grace took her luggage, went behind the screen, and chose her outfits for the photos. She changed into the first one and stepped from behind the screen.

"Stand in front of the blue screen, and we'll get started," he told her.

Jolly took multiple photos of Grace in each outfit. Each photo had a different facial expression. She looked at the pictures and chose the ones she wanted on her new identification.

She changed into jeans and a comfortable shirt while Jolly finished his work. She repacked her belongings and joined him at the computer.

"I've finished with the car," she told him. "I plan to leave here another way. How much do I owe you?"

She settled her account and said, "Thank you, Jolly. I'll be happy to return the favor if we should cross paths again.

"I'm glad I could help," he said. "I'll delete my files as soon as we're finished. I've never heard of Grace or any of these other women."

Grace laughed and thanked him again.

"I have a friend here who's leaving the state. He might be willing to give you a ride, provided you want to go the same direction," Jolly suggested.

"I had planned to take a bus. I like your suggestion better."

"I'll have him join us," Jolly said. "The two of you can talk it over."

He handed her the new ids for inspection. He deleted his files and left the room.

He returned a few minutes later with a tall man who appeared to be in his mid-thirties.

"It's up to the two of you to introduce yourselves if you wish," Jolly began. "This young man is a truck driver and hauls freight all over the country. This fine lady needs a ride. I'll leave you to work out the details."

Jolly left the room, and the truck driver said, "I'll be taking I-70 through Kansas, Colorado, and Utah. I wouldn't mind having some company if you're going that way."

Grace made a split-second decision and said, "May I ride with you to Salina, Kansas?"

"You've got a deal if you'll buy dinner," said the young man.

"It's a deal," said Grace.

"My rig is parked out back," he said. "Are those yours?" he said, pointing at Grace's bags.

"Yes," she said and picked up the duffel while the truck driver picked up the suitcase. "What should I call you?"

"No need to exchange names," he said with a grin.

"That's okay with me," she said and followed him to his truck.

"We ought to be in Salina by ten o'clock," he said. "I'll be ready to eat around six."

"So will I," said Grace, and they were on their way.

* * *

Wade was in his office working at his desk. The alarm on his cell phone sounded. He turned it off and found his landlord's number in his contacts. He tapped the icon and listened for an answer.

"Mr. Norton, this is Wade Adams. Do you have a few minutes to talk?"

"Hello, Sheriff," Norton asked. "What would you like to talk about?"

"I'm getting married in a few weeks," Wade began.

"Congratulations! I hope you'll have many happy years together."

"Thank you, Sir. We plan to live at her place. My lease isn't up until December."

"I see," said Norton. "Do you want to end your lease early?"

"No, I don't want to break the lease," Wade replied. "I've rented from you for years. I don't want to end on bad terms."

"Neither do I," Norton said with relief.

"How do you feel about subletting?" Wade asked. "One of my deputies may be interested."

"I'll need to think about that," Norton told him. "This has never come up before."

"I understand," Wade assured him. "I'll give you some time to consider it. I'll check to see if my deputy is interested in the meantime."

"All right, I'll get back to you when I've made my decision."

"Thank you, Mr. Norton."

Wade looked at the clock, stood, and stretched. He was supposed to meet Lizzie for lunch at the steak house. They planned to get their marriage license afterward.

He smiled, put on his hat, and walked out of his office.

"Lodge, I'm going to be a little late getting back from lunch. Call me if something comes up that can't wait."

"Yes, Sir," Lodge said.

Wade opened the door to find Megan Ford coming toward the station. He wondered what she was up to this time. Megan seldom came to the office without an ulterior motive.

"Hello, Megan," he said and held the door for her.

"Hi, Wade. I've lost a bracelet. Do you happen to know if Lizzie found one after the party?"

"I don't know, but I'll ask. I'm on my way to meet her for lunch."

"Thank you. I thought I'd file a report with your office. I might have lost it somewhere else."

"One of my deputies can help you with that. I'll see you later," Wade said and went to his truck once she was inside.

Megan smiled at Lodge. "Is Clint here?"

"He's out on patrol," Lodge told her.

"In that case, could I talk with Deputy Reed, please?"

Lodge turned toward Reed's desk and back to Megan. "He's on the phone at the moment. Have a seat. I'll let him know you're here."

Megan thanked him and sat down to wait. Reed appeared in the lobby a few minutes later.

"Hi Megan," Read greeted her. "How may I help you?"

"I lost a bracelet either at the inn or between there and home," she began. "I wanted to ask you if I should file a report in case someone turns it in."

"It can't hurt. Come on back, and I'll get the information from you."

Megan gave him her best smile and followed him to his desk. She sat down, crossed her legs, and pulled her skirt up above her knee.

Reed pretended not to notice and rummaged in his desk for the correct form. He handed her the form and a pen.

"Complete this form with a good description of the bracelet. We'll keep it on file," Reed told her.

"I hope an honest person finds it," Megan said. "I've had it for years. It belonged to my grandma. She gave it to me before she passed away."

Megan dabbed at an imaginary tear before she completed the form. "Is there anything else you need?"

"Do you remember where you last saw the bracelet?"

"I know I had it at the refreshment table. I had to hold it to keep it out of the food. It must have fallen off my wrist after that. The clasp sometimes comes unhooked."

"You think it was lost rather than stolen," Reed replied.

"Oh, I hadn't thought about it being stolen," Megan answered. "It isn't valuable other than for sentimental reasons."

"I'll go and make a copy of this for your records," Reed said and stood. "It won't take long."

"Thank you. I appreciate your help," Megan beamed.

Reed looked at her for a moment, puzzled. He went to the copier and made two copies of the form. He returned and gave her one for her records.

"I'll put a copy on the bulletin board and let you know if anyone turns in the bracelet."

"Do you have my phone number?"

"Yes, it's here on the form," Reed said.

"Oh, that's right. Thanks again." Megan said and stood.

She sashayed toward the office door with Reed and Lodge watching her every move.

Lodge looked at Reed when she'd gone. "What was that about?"

"She said she lost a bracelet and wanted to file a report," Reed answered. "Why didn't she ask Odom to take care of it? He's her brother."

"She asked for him first. She didn't seem to mind that he was out. I wonder what she's up to?" Lodge observed and refocused on his work.

"I don't know," Reed said and looked back at the office door. "Odds are that she's up to something."

Wade parked at the steakhouse and started toward the entrance. He stepped inside and saw Lizzie waiting for him at a nearby table.

"Hi, handsome," she said when he joined her. "How has your morning been?"

"It's been pretty quiet. How about yours?"

"It's been quiet at the inn, too. All we've had to do is wait for the phone to ring. I won't have to rush back today. I don't have an appointment until tomorrow morning."

"That sounds interesting," Wade said with a mischievous grin. "I told Lodge I'd be late getting back. I didn't tell him how late."

Lizzie was about to reply when the waitress approached their table. They placed their orders and resumed their conversation.

"Don't you think people will talk if you're late?" Lizzie teased.

"They might," Wade acknowledged and winked. "There's nothing they can do about it. I am the boss, you know."

They laughed at his joke, both knowing that he held himself to the same standards that he expected from his deputies.

"Before I forget," Wade began. "Was there a bracelet found at the inn or on the grounds?"

"I don't think so," Lizzie answered.

"I didn't either, but I told Megan I'd find out."

"When did you talk to Megan?" Lizzie asked with a hint of suspicion.

"I met her on the way out of the office. She wanted to file a report in case someone turned it in. I told her one of the deputies would help her."

"Did she lose a bracelet?"

"I don't know," Wade replied. "I wondered the same thing."

"I suppose we should give her the benefit of the doubt," Lizzie said. "I know she's trying to change, but…"

"I don't trust her either," added Wade.

Their waitress served their meal and ended the conversation about Megan. They'd almost finished eating when Tiffany Pruitt entered the restaurant with Drake Wagner.

"Look who's here," Tiffany said and walked toward Wade. "I missed you at the inn Saturday."

"Hi, Tiffany," Wade said. "Drake, how are you?"

"Doing fine," replied Drake. "Lizzie, it's nice to see you again."

"Hi, it's nice to see you, too," Lizzie answered. "Hi, Tiffany."

"We'd like to stay and chat," Wade lied. "We have an appointment in a few minutes."

He picked up the check and stood. Lizzie followed his lead. They waved goodbye, paid the bill, and left the restaurant.

Wade and Lizzie got into their vehicles and drove to the Wilbarger County Courthouse. They parked side by side and walked to the County Clerk's office together in silence.

Neither wanted to discuss it. Neither knew how to respond. Neither wanted to argue. They were there to get a marriage license.

They walked back to the parking lot with their marriage license in hand. They stopped and looked at each other. Both had worried expressions on their faces.

"Do you want to talk about it now or later?" Lizzie asked. "I know you need to get back to the office."

Wade shook his head and said, "Is there anything to talk about? I don't care that they were together."

"I don't either," Lizzie said. "The only man I want in my life is you."

Wade smiled and said, "You're the only woman I want."

"I guess that means we don't need to discuss it," Lizzie teased.

"You're right," Wade said and frowned. "But there is something we should talk about now."

Lizzie looked at him with surprise and concern. "What's wrong?"

"Why haven't you kissed me?" Wade said with a grin.

Lizzie beamed and wrapped her arms around his neck. Her kiss left him weak-kneed.

"We'll continue this discussion after dinner," she said with a sly smile. She got in her jeep and drove away.

Wade stared after her, wearing a goofy grin until the jeep was out of sight. He got into his truck and drove back to the office.

The rest of his Monday afternoon involved office matters. This was one of the times when he and his staff looked for things to do. He wasn't sure if he should relax and enjoy the quiet or prepare for an upcoming storm.

Lizzie returned to the inn and went to the office. She looked over her schedule for the next day.

She had a meeting at ten in the morning. Two meetings in the afternoon, and a couple booked a room for the remainder of the week.

The rest of the week consisted of a meeting or two each day. She had menus to plan and a shopping list to make. It felt good to focus on inn business again.

Lizzie knew it would take time to build the business back up. She hoped it wouldn't take long to reach the level of activity they'd had before the fire. They all depended on it.

She finished her menus and went to the pantry. She made her shopping list and pondered when she should go back into town.

She wouldn't be back in time for dinner if she went now. She'd risk being late for her first appointment if she went in the morning.

There wouldn't be time between meetings or before their guests arrived. Lizzie decided to ask her mother to do the shopping.

The office phone rang and brought her mind back to the present. She was occupied with business until her mother and grandmother came to help with dinner.

"The next couple of weeks are going to be busy," Lizzie said with a smile.

"That's good news," Granny said. "I hope it won't be too busy. You still have a wedding to think about."

"Did you get your marriage license today?" asked Ellen.

"We did," Lizzie replied with a frown.

"What's wrong?"

"I was so excited about getting our license, but it turned out to be anticlimactic."

"Why? What happened?"

"It's kind of silly," Lizzie answered. "We were finishing lunch at the steak house when Drake and Tiffany walked in together. We were both so concerned with how the other felt about it that we didn't talk again until we left the courthouse."

"Is everything okay?" asked Granny.

"We're fine. I think we were both expecting a fight. Neither of us wanted one," Lizzie said and shrugged her shoulders.

"That's good news," Ellen said. "You may both have prewedding jitters."

The office phone rang, and Ellen hurried to answer it. Lizzie and her grandmother began preparing dinner.

Ellen came back to the kitchen and said, "Next week is almost booked. I hope this is a good sign."

The women talked about the inn and their hopes for the future while they made dinner. James and Dan entered through the kitchen and sat at the dining table to cool off. Wade came in through the front door and joined them.

The family sat down and filled their plates. They talked about the activities of the day while they ate.

"Wade, what did your deputies think of the blonde woman and the man with the military haircut?" James queried.

"We all agreed that they didn't fit with the rest of the crowd," Wade answered. "They were different and a little rude. Those aren't reasons to begin inquiries. We also agreed that the man, in particular, could cross our paths again."

"I'll bet Lodge and Baker are hoping to cross paths with the blonde again," Lizzie joked.

"I wouldn't be surprised," Wade agreed.

"Mama, I've made a shopping list," Lizzie said. "I'm not going to have time to go into town. Would you mind going tomorrow?"

"I'm supposed to have lunch with Barbara, but I'll do it before I come home."

"That should be plenty of time," Lizzie said. "The Ketchersids will be here for dinner."

CHAPTER EIGHT

GRACE STAYED one night in Salina, Kansas. She lingered until check-out time, then rented a car and drove to Dodge City.

She planned to let her location be known before she moved again. She wanted anyone who might be looking for her to think she was working her way back to Vegas.

She looked at the clock. She still had some time before she had to check out, and she decided to make some calls.

She found her cell phone and pressed the power button. It was dead. She found the charger and plugged it in. She waited until it had enough charge to make a call.

She punched in Oliver Baldwin's direct number. The phone rang several times before he answered.

"This is Grace. Can you talk?"

"Hold on a minute," he said, and she heard the sound of a door closing.

"How are you?" Oliver asked.

"I'm fine," she told him. "How are things there?"

"Everything here at the station is under control."

"Would you look up the direct number to the police station for me, please?" asked Grace.

"Is something wrong?" Oliver asked with concern.

"I haven't checked with the police since I left. I don't know if they've made an arrest or have any suspects."

Oliver found the number and read it to her. "Where are you?"

"I'm in Dodge City," she said. "The story isn't panning out as we'd hoped. I still don't have the information I need."

"How long do you think it will take?"

"A few more days," she said.

"I see," Oliver said. "Take all the time you need."

"Thanks, Oliver. I'll talk to you in a few days."

Grace hung up and dialed the number for the Las Vegas Police. She asked to speak with Officer Danny Burnett. She didn't have to hold long before the young officer answered.

"This is Burnett."

"Officer Burnett, this is Grace Stewart."

"Hello, Ms. Stewart. What can I do for you?"

"I've been out of town on assignment since I last saw you. I wanted to check to see if you have any information about the tracker on my car or the break-in at my house."

"I'll get that information for you. I'll have to put you on hold."

"I'll wait," Grace said.

Anyone keeping tabs on her phone would have had plenty of time to find her location while she was on hold.

"Ms. Stewart, are you still there?"

"Yes."

"There were no prints on the tracker and none on your car. The security cameras around the diner showed a man matching the description you gave us. It didn't capture an image of his face. The type of tracker he used can be purchased online from several retailers. There were no prints found at your home other than your own."

"Do you happen to know if any of my neighbors have reported break-ins?"

"There haven't been any other reports of home invasions in that area in the past two months."

"There isn't much chance of catching either of them then," Grace replied.

"No, Ma'am," Burnett admitted.

"Thank you for the information and your time, Officer Burnett."

"You're welcome, Ma'am. I'm sorry I didn't have better news."

Grace ended the call and turned her cell phone off. She opened her laptop and added the information she'd been given to her document. She read through it again.

Based on the facts alone, there was no reason for leaving Las Vegas. There was no factual reason why she should stay away. She decided to wait until the judge ruled on Sharp's appeal before she considered going back.

Grace packed her belongings and checked out of the hotel. She planned to drive to Tulsa, Oklahoma, and turn in the rental car. She'd stay in Tulsa until she'd talked to her attorney again. Her next move would depend on the judge's decision.

* * *

Wade went home for lunch and made himself a sandwich, grabbed a bottle of water, and went to the living room. He sat on the couch and mentally patted himself on the back.

The meeting with the Wilbarger County Commission couldn't have been better. They approved the funds to hire two new deputies and the extra funds to create the new position. He could finally set his plan in motion.

He thought about the best way to share the news while he ate. Maddie should be the first person he talked with. He finished his lunch and went back to the office.

"Is Maddie back from lunch?" he asked Baker.

"Not yet," Baker replied. "She left a few minutes late."

"Tell her that I need to see her when she comes in," Wade requested. "I need to see Lodge when he finishes his phone call."

"I'll tell them," Baker said.

Lodge tapped on Wade's door ten minutes later. "Did you want to see me?"

"Yes, come in," Wade said.

Lodge stepped inside and sat in the chair in front of Wade's desk. He had no idea why Wade wanted to see him. He couldn't help feeling apprehensive.

"I overheard you and Baker talking the other day," Wade began. "Are you looking for a different place to live?"

Lodge sighed with relief. "Yes, Sir. My apartment is about to be remodeled. I need a place to stay until it's finished."

"I may have a solution for you," Wade said with a smile. "I'm going to be moving into Lizzie's place when we're married. The lease isn't up until the end of the year. Would you be interested in subletting my house?"

"That would be great!" Lodge exclaimed.

"I have to clear it with my landlord first. There will be times that I need to crash in the spare bedroom rather than drive back to the inn."

"That won't be a problem," Lodge said. "How would we handle the rent?"

"I'll have to discuss that with Mr. Norton if he okays our plan. I'll let you know when I've heard from him."

Lodge stood and said, "Thank you. I wasn't looking forward to living in my mom's basement."

Lodge left the office with a big grin on his face. Wade smiled and returned to his work.

Maddie Clifton tapped on his door a few minutes later.

"Come in, Maddie," he said. "Close the door, if you don't mind."

Maddie closed the door and sat down in the chair that Lodge

had vacated.

"Is something wrong," she asked.

"No, nothing's wrong," Wade said and smiled at her. "There's something that I need you to do."

"Okay," she said, curious.

"The meeting with the County Commission went well. Very well, in fact. I'll need you to draft and post an ad for two new sheriff's deputies."

"That's wonderful!" Maddie cried.

"One of those should specify that we need a deputy to help supervise female inmates."

Maddie stared at him for a minute before saying, "Marina isn't leaving, is she?"

"No, Marina isn't leaving," Wade said. "You see, the Commission also approved funds for another position."

"Oh? What position?" Maddie asked.

"I've wanted to create another position within the department for a long time. The position will be equal in pay and rank to Reed's current position. It will add another person to our on-call rotation. It will also give us another person to lead investigations."

"That sounds awesome," Maddie said. "Do you want me to draft an ad for that position, too?"

"No, the position is already filled," Wade said with a smile. "Assuming that you want it."

Maddie stared at him. His words began to sink in, and a broad smile spread across her face. "Yes, I want it!"

Wade laughed and said, "I thought you might."

"When do I start?"

"Right away, if you don't mind doing double duty until we can hire a new deputy."

"I don't mind at all!" Maddie beamed.

"I'll try to set your schedule so that you're working both positions at the same time. That way, you won't have to be away from Drew and Brody so much."

"Wade…I…thank you!"

"It's my pleasure. I'd have done this last year if I could have."

"I know," Maddie assured him. "You did what you felt was best for the department."

"I'd like to keep this between us until I have a chance to tell everyone in the staff meeting," Wade said.

"I'll do my best," she said and tried to wipe the smile from her face.

"Send Reed in, please. I should let him know what's happening."

Maddie left the office, and Reed was soon seated in front of Wade's desk. Wade shared the information about the new position and the new hires.

"That's awesome news!" Reed said.

"Will you send an email that we're going to have a staff meeting in an hour? I need to talk with Marina."

"Consider it done," Reed said. "Do you want me to send Marina to see you?"

"Yes, please."

Marina Gonzalez tapped on Wade's door. "Did you want to see me?"

"Yes, sit down, please."

Wade waited until Marina was comfortable. "Marina, I'm going to make some announcements in a staff meeting in a little while. There's something that I want to discuss with you first."

He gave her the highlights of his meeting with the County Commission.

"How would you feel about being the supervisor in charge of female inmates?"

Marina beamed. "I'd like that very much."

"The position includes a small pay raise," Wade told her. "That will be in addition to the merit raise that you have coming."

"Thank you, Sheriff."

Marina left the office happier than she'd been when she entered.

Wade liked sharing good news. He wished he could do so more often.

The phone on his desk buzzed. "Adams," he answered.

"You have a call from Gary Norton on line two," said Baker.

Wade pressed the button for line two and said, "Mr. Norton, I didn't expect to hear from you so soon."

"Well, I've thought about it and decided that your idea of subletting is a good one. However, I do have some stipulations."

Wade listened and assured his landlord that he would meet his conditions. All that remained was to tell Lodge and complete the paperwork.

He went into the staff meeting feeling better than he'd felt in a long time. He had good news to share. He hoped it would be a morale boost for the entire department.

"Lodge, I need to see you after the meeting, please," Wade said when he entered the conference room.

"Yes, Sir."

"I've got a lot of news for you," Wade began. "It's all good news for a change."

Wade shared information with the entire staff. The most well-received item was that they'd all be receiving a raise in their next paycheck. Lodge joined Wade in his office after the meeting.

"Mr. Norton had some conditions that we need to discuss," Wade told Lodge. "He wants to meet you before he makes his final decision."

"That's not a problem," replied Lodge.

"He wants the lease to remain in my name. That means that any damage or property issues that occur during the sublease will be my responsibility."

"I won't let you down."

"The last one is a little odd. He says that it will make his book-keeping easier. He wants me to pay the rent. That means you'll have to pay me, and I'll pass it on."

"That seems unnecessary," Lodge answered.

"I know," Wade agreed. "He said he knows my checks won't bounce, and he's never met you. We can deal with it for a few months, can't we?"

"Yeah, it isn't a big deal."

"Are we agreed that I'll have use of the spare bedroom when needed?"

"That's fine with me," Lodge said.

"I'll let Mr. Norton know that we agree to his terms and set up a meeting for tomorrow."

The two men shook hands and went back to their work.

* * *

It had been a busy day at the inn. Lizzie met with clients and answered phone calls. She'd booked four events and scheduled more meetings.

She looked at the clock. Her last client of the day had gone. She had a few minutes to relax before their guests arrived.

Lizzie left the office in search of a cold drink. She took a Coke from the refrigerator and went back toward the office. A middle-aged couple walked through the front door.

"Hello," Lizzie greeted them. "You must be the Ketchersids."

"That we are, Little Lady," said Earl.

"Welcome to the Paradise Creek Inn," said Lizzie. "I have some paperwork for you to sign, and then I'll show you to your room."

"We can't wait to try out your pool," said Beverly. "Our air conditioning has been out for days."

"It's supposed to be fixed by the time we get back," added Earl.

The paperwork was completed, and Lizzie showed the couple to a room on the west side of the house.

"We hope you enjoy your stay. Dinner will be available at six, and a breakfast buffet is available from seven until ten."

Lizzie went back downstairs and joined her grandmother in the kitchen.

"I wonder what's keeping Mama. I thought she would have been back by now."

"She may have lost track of the time," Granny said. "She doesn't get to visit with her sister often."

"I'd better make a backup dinner plan," Lizzie said and went to the pantry.

* * *

Ellen had enjoyed her lunch with Barbara. They'd spent far too much time talking, and she'd had to rush to get the shopping done.

She looked at the clock on the dashboard of her car. She'd still be back in time to start dinner for their guests.

These were the first guests since the reopening of the inn. She wanted everything to be perfect.

She turned west onto US highway 70 and thought about their plans. Everything depended on the customer service they provided. It had to be top-notch.

Ellen was halfway to the inn when she saw something large coming toward her on the highway. It appeared to span across both lanes. She slowed down and stared at the object.

It was a spray rig with a one-hundred-thirty-two-foot boom. The end sections of the boom were raised, making the machine look like a huge football goal.

Trees on the right side of the highway prevented the driver from moving over far enough for Ellen to pass. There was no place to pull over and wait.

Ellen's only choice was to swerve off the road into the tall grass. The driver of the spray rig waved his thanks while she waited for him to go by.

She pressed the accelerator and began to maneuver back onto the highway. The front passenger side of the car sank into the grass, and she couldn't move any further.

She put the car in park and got out. *It hasn't rained. What could I be stuck in?* She walked around the front of the car and looked at the tire.

"What have I done!"

"Sheriff, you have a call on line one," Baker told Wade.

"Adams," Wade said when he picked up the phone.

"Wade, I don't know what happened. I don't know what to do."

"Ellen? Where are you? What's wrong?" he asked, trying to stay calm despite his rapid pulse.

"I…I…think I've…killed…someone," Ellen sobbed.

"Where are you?"

"I…was…go…going home."

"Stay where you are," Wade told her. "I'm on my way."

Wade rushed out of his office. "Lodge, gather the team. There's been an accident. Call an ambulance and Dr. Hughes."

"Where are we going?" Lodge asked and picked up the phone.

"Somewhere on 70 between here and the inn. I'll meet you there," Wade said and ran out the door.

He started his truck and turned on his emergency lights. He tore out of the parking lot and sped toward the highway. He raced west through Lockett and didn't slow down until he saw Ellen's car on the side of the road. He stopped behind her sedan and radioed the location to his team.

Wade got out of his truck and rushed toward Ellen. She was leaning on the hood of her car, rocking and crying.

"Wade? What have I done?" she wailed.

He took her in his arms and hugged her. "It's going to be all right," he said and led her to his truck.

He helped her into the back seat and asked, "Have you called anyone else?"

"No, I…I…was stuck. Everyone's busy…we have guests… and…meetings…"

"My team is on the way," he said. "I'll call James, and then I'll look at your car."

Ellen nodded. Wade found some tissues and a paper bag in his glove compartment.

"Ellen, I need you to breathe into this bag for me. Can you do that?"

She nodded and began to breathe into the bag. He handed her the tissues and stood beside her while he called James.

"James, this is Wade. Ellen's been involved in an accident."

"Is she hurt?"

"She's fine physically. She's scared and hyperventilating," Wade told him. "I thought you'd want to be here with her."

"I'll be there in a few minutes."

James hung up, and Wade returned his attention to Lizzie's mother.

"Tell me what happened," Wade coaxed.

Ellen was coherent while she explained what had happened. She broke down again when she thought about what she'd seen. Wade encouraged her to breathe into the bag and relax.

He heard a car stop nearby and turned to see emergency lights flashing. Reed joined him beside his truck.

"What happened?" Reed asked.

Wade gave him the highlights of Ellen's story. "I don't know what she ran over. I haven't had the chance to look. She says she's killed someone."

"We'll block off the area and get started," Reed said.

"Reed, you'll have to take the lead on this," Wade told him. "I need to stay with her."

"I understand."

Wade didn't leave Ellen's side until James arrived. She was crying in her husband's arms when Wade joined his team.

The front left tire was on the shoulder of the highway. The front passenger side was in the ditch. The car was at an odd angle.

The right front tire had fallen into a culvert hidden by the tall grass. *No wonder she was stuck.*

Wade moved closer for a better look. A human leg was pinned

under the tire. It appeared that the rest of the body was wedged beneath the car.

Members of the Vernon fire department used a jack to raise the passenger side of the sedan. An EMT crawled under and examined the body. There were no signs of life.

The Sheriff's department took over. They gathered evidence and took photos.

It was difficult for Wade to stand by and watch. He longed to be a part of it. He went back to his truck and waited with his future-in-laws.

Dr. Hughes approached the trio after the body had been loaded into his van. He was a short, stout man with a full head of brown hair. He was one of six doctors in the city of Vernon and was chosen to serve as county medical examiner primarily because he had the convenience of a large basement beneath his office.

"How are you doing, Ellen?" he asked.

"I'm...I'm..." she began to sob and couldn't finish her sentence.

"She's not doing very well," James admitted.

"I thought not," said Hughes. "I'd be surprised otherwise."

He reached into his shirt pocket and handed James a medicine sample.

"She should take one of these right away and another at bedtime. Bring her to my office tomorrow if she isn't better."

Dr. Hughes was walking toward his van when Wade stopped him.

"Wade, I know you'd like to give Mrs. Fletcher some comfort," he said. "I won't know anything for certain until I've completed my examination. I'll let you know what I find."

"Thank you," Wade said. "We'd better do this by the book. Contact Reed first."

Dr. Hughes nodded and went on his way.

Wade walked toward his truck and saw Reed talking with James and Ellen.

"You can go home now, Mrs. Fletcher," Reed told her. "We'll

have to keep your car for a while. Is there anything inside that you need?"

"There are groceries in the trunk. Lizzie needs them for dinner tonight. What time is it?"

"Don't worry about that," James said. "Lizzie has everything under control."

"My purse is in the front seat...and my phone...where's my phone?"

"Your phone is in your hand," James told her.

"I'll get the rest of your things and take them to the inn," Wade told her. "You should go home and try to relax."

Ellen nodded, and James led her away. Wade transferred the groceries to his truck and retrieved her purse from the front seat.

He waved at his team and drove away. He hated being out of the loop. He knew only what Ellen had told him and what he'd seen with his own eyes.

Had Ellen killed someone? She should have seen anyone standing or walking nearby. Was the victim a man or a woman? All I saw was a leg.

Wade was so preoccupied that he missed the turn to the inn and had to turn around. It wasn't long until he was unloading the groceries and carrying them inside.

Lizzie met him at the back door.

"Where's Mama?" she asked with fear and worry in her voice.

"She's with your dad," he answered and pulled her close. "He said he was going to take her home."

"Is she okay? What happened?"

"She's not hurt, but she's had a terrible experience," Wade said and shared what he knew.

"Do you think she killed that person?"

"I thought about it on the way here. She should have seen anyone in her path unless she was distracted."

James opened the back door and joined them in the kitchen.

"Daddy? I thought you were taking care of Mama."

"Your granny is with her. She sent me to check with you. She won't rest until she knows that you have everything you need to tend to our guests. She's worried about being late with the supplies."

"The Ketchersids have been enjoying the pool, and dinner is almost ready," Lizzie told him. "Tell her there's nothing to worry about."

"That's what I told her. She feels bad about not getting it here on time."

"Everything's fine," Lizzie said and hugged her dad.

"Wade, is there anything you can tell us?" James asked with a hopeful expression.

"I don't know anything new at this point. Reed is running the investigation," Wade explained. "I'll share any information he gives me."

"I understand," James said.

James left with three plates of food. He was hungry and knew that his mother would be too. He hoped that Ellen would eat something.

The Ketchersids came down for dinner. Lizzie and Wade joined them and chatted with the couple.

"I never expected to be having dinner with the local sheriff," said Earl.

"And such a handsome one at that," added Beverly.

"Settle down, Beverly. I believe he's spoken for," teased her husband. "So are you."

"I know that," Beverly retorted. "I can still appreciate a nice view, can't I?"

"When are you two getting married?" Earl asked, changing the subject.

Lizzie shared the information, and the group talked about wedding plans. The Ketchersids excused themselves after dinner and ambled over the grounds.

Wade went to bed that night thinking about Ellen's accident. Something didn't feel right about it.

CHAPTER NINE

WADE GOT up the next morning, dressed, and went to the kitchen for a cup of coffee. He didn't plan to take the time for breakfast. Lizzie had a breakfast burrito and a travel mug filled with coffee ready for him.

"I know you want to get to the office," she said. "I thought you could eat on the way into town."

"Thank you," Wade said and kissed her.

Lois came in the back door and said, "Good morning."

"How's Mama?" asked Lizzie

"She was still asleep when I left. I could hear her crying during the night. She's having a hard time."

Lois looked at Wade and asked, "Have you heard anything?"

Wade shook his head. "I'll let you know when I do. I'm a bystander this time too."

"A bystander with a ringside seat," Lizzie pointed out.

"That's true. I need to go. I'll call you when I can," he said and rushed out the door.

"Do you think Mama will be okay?" Lizzie asked with worry.

"It'll take time. What's on the schedule for today?"

"I have six meetings," Lizzie said. "Would you mind tending to our guests?"

"I'll take care of the guests," Lois said with a wink. "You take care of the business."

"Thanks, Granny. Do you think Mama and Daddy will be here for lunch?"

Lois sighed and said, "I don't know. James may take Ellen to see Dr. Hughes. We'll have to wait and see how she's doing this morning."

Lizzie went to her office and looked at her appointment calendar. She'd already scheduled a Halloween party and two Christmas parties. There was also a reservation for a June wedding. She hoped the trend continued.

* * *

Wade walked into his office and looked around. His team was already there working on the case.

"Morning, Wade," Reed said. "How's Mrs. Fletcher doing?"

"Not good. Do you know anything?"

"We're trying to identify our Jane Doe. There was nothing on the body to give us a clue. We're still waiting to hear from Dr. Hughes about the time and cause of death."

"I was hoping I could give the Fletchers some good news,' Wade said.

"I know it isn't easy for you," Reed said and patted his boss on the back. "I've got everybody working on this."

"Thanks, Reed. Is there anything I can do to help?"

"You know how it goes. We have to wait until the lab results are in and Dr. Hughes finishes his autopsy. We're doing what we can until we have more information."

Wade nodded and went to his office. The meeting with Lodge and Mr. Norton was scheduled for ten. He needed to find something to do until then.

He checked his email. He cleaned his desk. He paced his office. He focused on what he knew about the case. *The victim was a woman. Why was she there? Was she out for a walk? I didn't see any cars near the road. Why didn't Ellen see her?*

"Sheriff?"

Wade was startled back to the present. "Good morning, Lodge."

"Isn't it about time to meet with Mr. Norton?"

Wade glanced at the clock and said, "I lost track of the time. We can take my truck."

Half an hour later, everything was settled. Wade would move some of his belongings into the guest room and put the remainder of his furniture into storage. Lodge would move in on Labor Day weekend.

They returned to the sheriff's department and met Dr. Hughes in the parking lot.

"Good morning, gentlemen," said Dr. Hughes.

Wade resisted the urge to ask what the doctor had to share. He knew he'd find out soon enough. Instead, he asked, "Have you heard from James or Ellen Fletcher this morning?"

"James called earlier and made an appointment. Ellen is having a difficult time."

Nothing more was said about the matter until they assembled in the conference room. Reed called the meeting to order.

"Today is Wednesday, August 24, 2016. We're here concerning the matter of Jane Doe, whose body was found yesterday at approximately four-thirty p.m. by Mrs. Ellen Fletcher. Mrs. Fletcher ran over Jane Doe while traveling west on US Highway 70. Deputy Brandon Lodge and Deputy Calvin Baker, what did you find?"

Wade leaned forward in his chair. He didn't want to miss anything.

"We found skin and fibers on the tire. There also skin, fibers, and hair on the undercarriage of Mrs. Fletcher's car," reported Baker. "All were a match to Jane Doe. There was blood at the scene that belonged to the victim. There was no blood found on the car."

"There was no damage to Mrs. Fletcher's car," added Lodge. "No dents, no broken headlights, not a scratch."

"Deputy Maddie Clifton, have you made progress with the victim's prints or DNA?" Reed inquired.

"There's nothing to report at this time," Maddie informed him.

"Deputies Marina Gonzalez and Clint Odom, do you have any news?"

"Gonzalez and I have been to several businesses. No one has recognized her," Odom reported.

"Thank y'all," Reed said. "Dr. Hughes, we're ready to hear your results."

Dr. Hughes stood and said, "Jane Doe appeared to be in good health before her demise. I'd venture to say that she ate a healthy diet and worked out regularly.

I can say without a doubt that Jane Doe was dead before Mrs. Fletcher ran over the body. I believe she died between midnight and two a.m. yesterday morning."

Wade sighed and said, "Thank God!"

"That should put Ellen's mind at ease," said Dr. Hughes.

"What was the cause of death?" asked Reed.

"She was shot in the back. The bullet nicked an artery causing her to bleed to death, but she didn't die right away.

The poor woman had several cuts, bruises, and contusions. The swelling and discoloration of her face were likely the results of being punched. Scrapes and cuts on her extremities indicate that she'd been crawling."

"Is there anything else you can tell us?" Reed queried.

"I've brought along the bullet and a dental impression," he said and handed a bag to Reed. "You may be able to identify her through dental records. I noticed that she had no shoes. Were they taken for evidence?"

"We didn't find shoes at the scene," Reed said.

"I see. That explains the bruising and cuts on the soles of her feet. She may have been running barefoot before she was shot."

"Thank you, Dr. Hughes," said Reed.

"If there's nothing else, I have patients to see," he said and left the room.

"I'd like to give the Fletchers the news," Wade told Reed.

"I don't see any reason why you shouldn't," Reed said with a smile. "Let's get to work and meet back here at two o'clock."

Wade went to his office and picked up the phone.

"Paradise Creek Inn, this is Lizzie."

"Hi, Sweetheart. I know you're busy, and I won't keep you. Is your mom there?"

"No, she's at home. Have you heard anything? Is it bad?"

"Your mom didn't kill anyone. The woman was already dead."

"Oh, thank God!"

"I have to go. I'll talk to you later. I love you."

"I love you, too."

Tears of relief filled Lizzie's eyes. She wiped them dry and went to the kitchen. Lois was clearing away the lunch dishes.

"Granny, Wade just called."

Lois stopped and stared at Lizzie. "And?"

"Mama didn't kill anyone," Lizzie said. "The poor woman was already dead."

Lois sat down in the nearest chair and wept. Lizzie went to her and wrapped her arms around her grandmother.

"I knew it had to be a mistake!" Lois exclaimed. "Do you know any details?"

"He said that the woman was already dead. He didn't have time to say more."

"We have to tell Ellen," Lois said and went to make the call.

The bell on the front door jingled. Lizzie's next appointment had arrived. The women returned to their work with lighter hearts.

Wade was waiting in the conference room at two. He could take part in the investigation now that Ellen had been cleared.

Reed joined him and sat down beside his boss.

"Do you want to take the lead now?"

"No, it's your case," Wade said. "Give me an assignment. I need something to do."

Reed smiled and said, "I've been wondering how Jane Doe ended up in that culvert."

"I've been wondering the same thing. Dr. Hughes thinks she was running. Who was chasing her? Why were they chasing her? Which direction? Where did the chase start?"

"Do you want to see what you can find at the scene?"

"I thought you'd never ask," Wade teased. "I'll get started after the meeting."

The rest of the team assembled, and Reed began the meeting. "Sheriff, how is Mrs. Fletcher?"

Wade smiled and said, "She's much better. James insisted that she see Dr. Hughes. The doc said that she may still have nightmares and anxiety for a while. He gave her some medication to help her sleep. Knowing that she wasn't responsible for the death lifted a huge weight from her shoulders."

The group applauded and patted Wade on the back.

"It's time to get back to business," Reed said. "We need to find out Jane Doe's true identity. That could be our best clue to her death."

"There are still no results from the fingerprint and DNA searches. I've started a dental search. That will take time, too," Maddie told him.

"Is it possible to get a better photo of our victim?" Marina asked. "It's difficult to see her features in this one. It was taken at the scene."

"Dr. Hughes may have one, or he may allow you to take a better photo," Reed suggested.

"People barely look at the one we have," Odom said. "It's kind of gruesome."

"We'll continue trying to identify the victim. Sheriff Adams is going to inspect the scene. His task will be to discover what led to her death."

"We've finished with Mrs. Fletcher's car," said Baker. "I'd like to assist Sheriff Adams."

"We could take the car to the Fletcher's and revisit the crime scene on the way back," Wade suggested.

"Lodge, I guess that leaves the two of us to run the office," said Reed. "We'll meet again tomorrow morning unless someone finds important information."

The team went to work. Wade drove Ellen's car, and Baker followed him in his patrol car. They stopped at the inn to find everyone there.

"We brought your car," Wade said to Ellen.

"Thank you so much," she said and hugged both men.

"Have the Ketchersids gone?" Wade asked.

"They went into town," Lois said. "I think they're getting bored out here."

"They said they wanted to do some shopping," Lizzie added.

"Have you finished meeting with clients?" Wade asked and kissed her.

"The last one is due any minute," Lizzie answered.

"We'll get out of your way," Wade said and turned toward the door. He turned back and added, "I'll stay in town tonight."

"In that case," Lizzie began and joined him by the door. She kissed him and said, "That will have to hold us until you get back."

Wade grinned and went outside, followed by his deputy. Baker got behind the wheel and looked at Wade with a smirk.

"What?" asked Wade.

"Does Fletcher have any single female relatives?"

"Her Granny is single," Wade teased.

Baker laughed, and they drove toward the crime scene.

The two men parked near the culvert and got out of the patrol car. They looked at the scene with a new focus. Wade took out his cell phone and started the video. He wanted to record everything they saw.

They searched the place where the body was found and the surrounding area. They talked while they searched.

"Cuts and bruises on her feet," Wade mused. "She may have been running. Which direction?"

"She may have run across the road and fallen into the culvert," Baker suggested.

"Why was she barefoot?" Wade pondered.

"She might have kicked her shoes off or lost them while running," Baker pointed out.

"It's going to be hard to find them in this grass," Wade added. "We should start across the road and see if we find anything.

They searched the opposite side of the highway, checking the pavement and vegetation for signs of blood. No blood or shoes were found. They went back to the culvert.

"Doc said she crawled," Wade began. "The grass ought to be flattened."

Baker walked a few feet away and stooped down for a better look. "Sheriff, look at this."

Wade joined him and saw a distinct path. They followed the path to the point where the victim had fallen. A faint trail led to it. They followed the trail until Baker stopped.

"Looks like a vehicle pulled over right here," he said and pointed at the flattened grass.

"She was in a vehicle of some kind," Wade began. "It stopped. Why did it stop?"

Baker walked ahead for several yards. He pointed at the pavement on the highway. "Are those skid marks?"

Wade joined him and examined the marks on the road. "Looks like skid marks to me. An animal might have been in the road."

"It looks like the victim's trail starts here," said Baker.

They searched the area and located one wedge sandal.

"Keep looking," Wade ordered. "The other has to be here somewhere. She'd have had a hard time running with one shoe."

Baker walked toward the fence line of the property beside the road. "Here's the other one."

They bagged the shoes. Baker took photos of the grassy area and the skid marks. They walked back toward the culvert, discussing what might have happened.

"The victim was forced into a car or vehicle of some kind," Wade began. "I'm guessing she was alone in the back seat."

"The car must have stopped or slowed down enough that she could jump out, "added Baker.

"She either kicked her shoes off or threw them so that she could run," Wade said. "He pulled over to try and catch her."

"A shot was fired, and she fell," Baker said, imitating the action with his hand. "Why didn't the shooter go after her?"

They walked along the trail to the point where she fell. They could see blood on the blades of grass. Wade photographed it, and Baker sealed it in an evidence bag.

"Why didn't we see this the first time we walked by?" Baker queried.

"We were looking for the trail and missed it, I guess," Wade said. "It's a wonder we saw it this time. This grass is tall, and it moves in the wind. I could get lost in this mess if I wanted."

"The shooter came after her. She hid," Baker said. "He couldn't find her."

"That's it," Wade agreed. "It was dark. She all but disappeared when she fell. The grass could have been blowing in the wind."

"She crawled to escape. Why did she crawl into the culvert?"

"She may have thought it was a safe place to hide, or she may have used all the strength she had to get to that point," said Wade.

"Did she know it was here or just happened to find it?" Baker wondered aloud.

"We may never know the answer to that," said Wade. "Why didn't whoever was in the car keep looking for her?"

"He could have been interrupted by oncoming traffic," suggested Baker. "He may have assumed she was dead."

"He may have found her here and left her for dead," Wade added. "Any evidence of that would have been destroyed when Ellen's car ran through here."

The two officers found no more evidence. They walked back to Baker's patrol car.

"I'll do the write-up if you'll take the evidence to the lab," Wade offered.

"It's a deal," Baker answered.

They drove back to the department. Wade went to his office to write the report. It was finished when Baker joined him. He printed a copy for his deputy to read.

"Feel free to make corrections and add anything I've forgotten," Wade suggested.

Baker read the report and handed it back to Wade.

"I've been thinking about the car," Baker said. "Why would you kidnap someone without making sure they couldn't get out? You'd think they have been at least watching her. Could she have been unconscious or pretending to be?"

"That's a good point," Wade agreed. "Dr. Hughes said she'd been punched. It could have knocked her out."

Reed tapped on Wade's door and walked in without waiting. "We've had a development," he said and handed Wade a photo. "Does she look familiar?"

Wade looked at the picture and handed it to Baker.

Baker gaped at the picture and looked at Reed. "Has Lodge seen this?"

Reed nodded. "Is this who I think it is?"

"She looks like the hot blonde that was at the inn," Baker said.

"Lodge, and I think so too," Reed said.

Wade picked up the phone and dialed the number to the inn. Lizzie answered.

"Lizzie, don't you have an appointment with the blonde from the party?"

"I did. She was supposed to be here at two, but she never showed up."

"Did she call or leave a message?"

"No, I tried to call yesterday to confirm her appointment. I got her voice mail."

"What's her name?"

"Let me go to the office and look to be sure," Lizzie said.

Wade waited for Lizzie to find the information.

"Her name is Jody Ratliff."

"Do you have any other information there?"

"All I have is a phone number," Lizzie said and gave him the number.

"Thanks, Babe. I'll talk to you later," he said and ended the call. "Gentlemen, we have a name and a phone number."

The investigation into the death of Jody Ratliff would be their top priority. They'd have to verify her identity and find out why she was in the area. That might give them a clue as to why she was murdered.

Wade went home and looked around his house. He wasn't sure where he needed to start. He walked to the guest bedroom.

He opened the door and sighed. It had become the junk room. It was going to take some time to clean out.

He took out his cell phone and ordered pizza. He went to the kitchen and took a beer from his refrigerator. He sat on the couch and waited for his dinner. He'd start cleaning after he ate.

* * *

Brandon Lodge sat at a table at the local Italian restaurant. His date should be arriving soon. They'd met online and chatted on the phone. This would be the first time they would meet face to face, and he was nervous.

He ordered a beer and looked around the dining room. *I wonder if she's already here waiting for me.* No one else was sitting alone.

He recognized the couple sitting at the table beside his. *Drake Wagner and Tiffany Pruitt are having dinner together? This could be interesting.*

Lodge's attention was drawn to a pretty brunette scanning the dining room. She smiled when he waved at her and joined him at the table.

"I'm sorry for being late," said Susan Ingle. "I was busy with a patient. A little boy swallowed a piece of one of his toys."

"Is he okay?" Lodge asked.

"He'll have a sore throat for a while, but he'll be fine."

"Sounds like an exciting day in the emergency room," Lodge joked. "Would you like a drink?"

"Yes, a glass of red wine would be wonderful," said Susan with a smile.

Lodge signaled their waitress and ordered the wine. They perused the menu in silence. They couldn't help overhearing the conversation at the next table.

"We're running out of time," Tiffany said to Drake. "I heard they're getting married next month. We've got to break them up now!"

Lodge missed Drake's response when the waitress returned with Susan's wine. They placed their order and grinned at each other.

"Would you excuse me?" Susan said.

Lodge nodded and watched her weave through the tables toward the Ladies' room. He overheard more of the next table's conversation while he waited.

"We could go to the inn and make a show of planning an event together. It could be something for work… or an engagement party," Tiffany said.

"Engagement party!" Drake exclaimed. "We hardly know each other, and you're talking about an engagement party!"

"Not a real one," Tiffany said with a dismissive tone. "No one has to know we've just met. We could say we've been dating for months."

Drake stared at Tiffany as if she'd lost her mind. He seemed to be speechless.

"We'll have to make sure Wade is there when we go. We need to make them both jealous enough to start fighting. Or we could say something that would make them angry with each other."

Drake requested that the waitress bring the check and said to Tiffany, "Your plan is too complicated and involves too many factors that you have no control over. What makes you think you can break them up?"

"I can't do it alone," Tiffany retorted. "That's why I need your help."

"Are you ready to go?" Drake demanded with a scowl.

Drake stood and walked toward the counter. Tiffany stared at him, gulped down her drink, and followed.

Lodge was concerned about what he'd overheard. He knew he needed to warn Wade and Lizzie. *How should I handle this?*

Susan came back to the table, and they talked about their jobs. She was fascinated by his work, and he was curious about the life of an emergency room nurse.

Their food arrived, and the pair enjoyed their meal with polite conversation. The waitress brought their check, and they prepared to leave.

"I've enjoyed having dinner with you. May I call you again?" Lodge asked.

"Yes," Susan said. "I've enjoyed this, too."

Lodge beamed and paid the check. They said goodnight in the parking lot and went their separate ways.

Megan Ford accosted Lodge before he could get into his truck. Her friend Terry stood back and rolled her eyes.

"Hi, Brandon. I'm so sorry to bother you," Megan said. "I was wondering if anyone might have found my bracelet. I forgot to mention losing it to Clint."

"Not that I'm aware," Lodge said with an artificial smile.

"I don't think I've ever seen you out of uniform. I almost didn't recognize you," Megan said. "You look quite handsome."

"Uh…thanks."

"Are you here with a date?" Megan pried.

"Yes, and I'm supposed to follow her to her place," Lodge lied.

"She's a lucky girl," Megan said. "I might be a little jealous."

"Megan, we're going to have to wait if we don't get inside," Terry said with irritation.

"Goodnight, Brandon," Megan said and followed Terry into the restaurant.

"What are you doing?" Terry challenged. "Is he the reason you dragged me to the inn Saturday?"

"I just wanted to say hello," Megan snapped. "They were all so good to me last year. I didn't want to be rude."

"He didn't even see you before you practically tackled him," Terry pointed out.

"It never hurts to be nice to people. Besides, I wanted to know if anyone had found my bracelet."

"What bracelet?" Terry quizzed with a raised brow.

"The one I lost Saturday," Megan retorted.

"You weren't wearing a bracelet that day."

The discussion ended when the women were shown to their table.

CHAPTER TEN

LODGE WAS SITTING at his desk when Wade arrived the next morning.

"Sheriff, can I have a minute?"

"I'll meet you in my office after I get some coffee," Wade told him. "Would you like some?"

"I've got mine, thanks."

"Brandon is everything all right," Wade inquired when he entered his office.

"Yeah, I'm good," Lodge began. "I want to give you a heads up."

"Me?" Wade asked with surprise.

"I started to call you last night. Then I decided it could wait until this morning. Now, I feel silly and wish I hadn't said anything."

Wade grinned at him. "You haven't said anything yet. What's the problem?"

"I had a date last night," Lodge began. "We were seated next to a couple that we couldn't help overhearing."

"You'll feel better if you get it over with," Wade prodded.

Lodge nodded and sighed. "Drake Wagner and Tiffany Pruitt were talking about causing a break up between you and Fletcher."

Wade sat back and stared at his deputy. "What are they planning?"

Lodge repeated the conversation he'd overheard.

"When are they planning to do this?" Wade replied with a scowl.

"They didn't say. Wagner told her it wouldn't work. I got the impression that he wasn't in favor of the idea. I didn't hear any more."

"Thanks for telling me," Wade said. "I'll let Lizzie know what they're up to."

Lodge nodded, and the two men joined the rest of the team in the conference room for updates and assignments.

"We caught a break in this case after most of you had gone home last night," Reed informed them. "Thanks to Gonzalez for suggesting that we needed a better photo."

He posted the picture on the wall. "This is our victim. She was at the inn Saturday and made an appointment for yesterday afternoon. She gave her name and phone number to Mrs. Fletcher."

Reed shared the woman's name and number with the team. "We need to verify her identity and find out everything we can about her. That may give us a clue as to why she was killed and who killed her."

"Was she staying at the inn," Odom queried.

"No," answered Wade.

"Adams and Baker examined the scene yesterday," Reed said. "I'd like you to hear what they found and their thoughts about what happened."

Wade shared the information with the team and added, "Baker uploaded the video for you to see when you have the time."

"Our victim had to have been staying nearby if she's been here since Saturday," Gonzalez pointed out. "She may have been taken from her hotel room."

"How did she get here," Maddie mused. "Did she drive?"

"She had to drive to the inn," Baker added. "Unless she rode with someone."

"I didn't see her arrive or leave. I don't think she was with anyone else," Wade countered. "The family said she didn't talk to anyone other than Lizzie's grandmother."

"We'll assume she had a vehicle. We need to find out if it belonged to her or someone else," Reed said. "Gonzalez and Odom will continue trying to find someone who recognizes Ms. Ratliff. The rest of us will verify her identity and dig into her history."

The meeting ended, and everyone went to work. Wade's task was to find a vehicle registered in the name of Jody Ratliff. He was searching the Texas DMV database when the intercom buzzed.

"You have a call on line one," Baker said.

"This is Adams."

"Sheriff, this is Drake Wagner."

Wade was stunned and took a moment to reply, "What can I do for you, Mr. Wagner?"

"This is a personal matter," Drake began. "Can you talk now, or should I call back later?"

"What's on your mind?"

"I've been seeing Tiffany Pruitt. I think you should know that she is dead set on causing the end of your relationship with Lizzie," Drake said.

"I see."

"I'm not sure what she's planning to do. I wanted you to know that I have nothing to do with it. I know that I don't have a chance with Lizzie because she's in love with you."

"I'm glad to hear that," Wade admitted. "Why are you telling me instead of Lizzie?"

"I didn't want to be misunderstood," said Drake. "I thought if I called Lizzie, you'd both think it was part of an attempt to get her back."

"You're probably right about that."

"Tiffany and I met for the first time Saturday at the inn. We went out a few times. I told her last night that I didn't want to see her anymore and wouldn't take part in her plan. I wanted you to hear the truth from me."

"I appreciate the information and your candor, Mr. Wagner,"

"I hope that we can put all of this behind us."

"I see no reason why we can't," Wade said.

The call ended, and Wade stared at the phone. He never dreamed that Drake would call him for any reason.

He picked up the phone and dialed the number to the inn.

"Paradise Creek Inn, this is Lois."

"Hi, Lois. Is Lizzie around?"

"She's with a client. I can have her call...wait, here she comes."

"This is Lizzie."

"Are you sitting down?" Wade began. "I have some news that might shock you."

"Bad news?"

"Yes and no," Wade teased.

He told her about his conversations with Lodge and Drake Wagner.

"I'm glad Drake isn't going to be a problem anymore," Lizzie said. "What are we going to do about Tiffany?"

"There isn't much we can do," Wade told her. "She isn't doing anything illegal."

"It's a good thing that we're aware of her intentions," Lizzie said. "My appointment schedule is going to be booked until after the wedding if she asks."

Wade laughed and said, "That should help until she comes up with another plan."

"This is another good reason for a small wedding," Lizzie joked.

The call ended, and Wade drummed his fingers on his desk. He knew the lack of an invitation wouldn't stop Tiffany if she decided to crash their wedding.

He'd tried to be nice. He'd tried being brutally honest. He'd tried being cold and distant.

He'd even hidden from her. He smiled at the memory of James' laughter.

He had no alternative. He'd have to be hard-nosed, even cruel, for the message to get through.

Wade focused on his task and continued his search. He found nothing registered to Jody Ratliff in the Texas DMV records. He began searching the Oklahoma DMV.

His vehicle search proved to be useless. He could find nothing registered in the name of Jody Ratliff in any of the databases he searched. It occurred to him that she might have rented a car. He began calling rental agencies in the surrounding area.

Reed tapped on Wade's door and said, "Gonzalez and Odom found something."

Wade looked up from his work and waited for Reed to continue.

"She was staying alone at one of the hotels along 287. Security video shows her driving away from the hotel Monday morning. She listed her car as a 2014 Black Nissan Sentra with a Texas license plate." Reed read the license plate number.

"That should help," Wade said and turned to his computer. He typed the information into the Texas DMV database and found what he needed. "The car belongs to a rental agency in Dallas," he told Reed.

"I'll send out a BOLO for the car," Reed said and left the office.

Wade called the rental agency and asked for the manager. He was on hold for half an hour. He hung up and tried again.

This time the manager answered his call. He explained the situation and asked for any information the agency might have gathered. Ratliff gave them a Las Vegas, Nevada address. Wade's phone rang immediately after he'd ended the call with the rental agency.

"Adams."

"This is Trooper Owen Holder. I understand you have a BOLO out for a Black Nissan Sentra."

"Yes, we do."

"It's parked on the northbound side of Highway 287 a few miles south of Vernon. Looks like it was abandoned. I was about to have it towed."

"We're on our way," Wade said and ended the call.

"Reed, the car's been found!" Wade shouted.

The two men left the office and raced to examine the car. They hoped it would provide the information they needed to find whoever was responsible for Jody Ratcliff's death.

* * *

Lizzie was sitting at her desk, making notes and waiting for her last appointment of the afternoon. She looked up when she heard someone tap on the office door.

Earl Ketchersid was standing in the doorway with a towel draped across his shoulders. His large belly hung over the waistband of his neon green and pink flamingo swimsuit.

"Hello, Mr. Ketchersid. Is everything all right?"

"There's an emergency at work that our boss says no one else can handle," Ketchersid informed her. "We'll be checking out after one more swim."

"I'm sorry to hear that," Lizzie said.

"We hate to cut our visit short. We've enjoyed our stay here. I'm gonna miss your homecooked meals," he told her.

"Would you like to stay for dinner tonight?" Lizzie offered.

"Don't tempt me," Ketchersid joked. "We'll have to go home and repack. We have to drive to Dallas this afternoon to catch our flight."

"What do you do for a living, Mr. Ketchersid?" Lizzie asked.

"We're company troubleshooters," he said. "We travel a lot."

"It's nice that you can work together," Lizzie said. "I hope you'll stay with us again."

"You can count on it," he said with a smile and left.

Lizzie could hear the characteristic sound of flip-flops as he made his way through the inn to the swimming pool. She went to the kitchen and found her grandmother making dinner plans.

"Granny, the Ketchersids won't be here for dinner. They're checking out this afternoon."

"Will Wade be here?" Lois asked.

"I'll call him and find out."

Lizzie went back to the office and called Wade's cell phone. It rang twice and went to voicemail. She left a message asking him to call her and hung up. She went back to the kitchen.

"Wade didn't answer," she told her grandmother.

"All right, I'll make dinner for us and make sure there's enough for him if he does come," Lois told her.

The bells on the front door jingled, and Lizzie went to meet her next client.

* * *

Wade and Reed met Officer Holder and examined the Black Nissan Sentra. The back tire on the driver's side was flat.

"It looks like the driver had a flat and walked away," said Holder.

"It does," agreed Reed. "The trouble is that the person who rented this car was found dead yesterday west of Lockett."

Wade took a rubber glove from his pocket and opened the driver's side door. He inspected the contents of the car while Reed spoke with the trooper.

The keys were still in the ignition. A purse and cell phone were in the passenger seat.

He opened the purse to look for identification. A wallet containing the victim's driver's license, cash, and credit cards was the first item he found. He dug deeper and found two things he hadn't expected. He bagged the items and got out of the car.

"I don't think our victim walked away. Most women wouldn't

leave their purse and cell phone behind, and a law officer wouldn't leave their gun and badge," Wade said, holding the bag for the others to see.

"I'll have a tow truck drag it to the office," Reed said and took out his cell phone.

Wade looked around the car.

"There's no sign of struggle. It looks like someone parked behind her," he pointed out. "I'd say that she got out of the car to see what happened. Someone stopped. She thought they were going to help."

"Instead, she's found dead several miles away," added Holder.

Wade searched the area around the car again. He got on his hands and knees to look underneath. He found nothing that would lead him to change his theory.

The tow truck arrived, and the car was taken to the sheriff's department for analysis. Wade didn't expect them to find anything useful. He was almost certain that the victim had been caught by surprise.

The sheriff and his deputy returned to the office. The driver's license and badge confirmed her identity. They examined the rest of the contents of Jody Ratliff's purse. They found a hotel key, a cell phone charger, and some miscellaneous items.

"Her phone is dead," said Wade. "I'll put it on the charger. There could be a lead on it."

"Why would an agent from Las Vegas be here?" Reed wondered aloud. "Was she here for business or pleasure?"

"Being from out of town would explain why she didn't talk to anyone at the inn. She didn't know anyone," Wade said. "It doesn't explain why she made an appointment with Lizzie."

"Could she have been investigating someone at the party?" Reed mused.

The Vegas FBI could tell us," Wade said. "I wish we had more to tell them."

Wade picked up the phone and dialed the number to the inn.

Lizzie answered, and he said, "Hi, Babe. "Is your Granny there?"

"Yes, I'll get her."

Wade waited less than a minute before Lois picked up the phone.

"I need to ask you about the blonde woman at the reopening. Tell me about your conversation with her again."

"She asked for a brochure and said she'd like to make an appointment," answered Lois.

"Did she say anything else?"

"She wanted the first available appointment. I told her that Lizzie was booked until Wednesday afternoon at two."

"Did it look like she was there with anyone or watching anyone?" Wade asked.

"She looked over her shoulder a time or two. That's all I remember," Lois told him.

"Thanks, Lois," he said. "May I speak with Lizzie?"

"She's checking our guests out. Can you hold for a minute?"

"If it won't be too long," he said.

He heard Lizzie's voice on the line sooner than he expected.

"Are you going to be here for dinner?" she asked.

"It doesn't look like I'll make it," he told her. "I'm sorry. We may have gotten a break on this case, so we'll be here late tonight. I'll stay at my place again."

"I was hoping to see you tonight," she told him. "Our wedding invitations are here, and I wanted you to see them."

"Do they look nice?" Wade asked with a grin.

"They do. We need to get them addressed and mailed this weekend."

"I may not be able to help you with that. Reed's a tyrant," he joked.

Reed's head popped up, and he stared at Wade. He pointed at himself and mouthed, "Me?"

"I'll do my best to be there for dinner tomorrow," Wade promised and ended the call.

Wade repeated what Lizzie's grandmother had told him.

"It's the team leader's responsibility to call the Las Vegas FBI to inform them that one of their agents is deceased," Wade told his deputy.

"I think that responsibility falls to the sheriff, who has more experience in such matters," Reed replied with a smirk.

"The best way to gain experience in an area is to do all the tasks," Wade said, grinning at his deputy.

"I've made calls like this before," Reed said, leaned back, and crossed his arms. He was still smirking.

"Flip for it?" Wade asked.

"If it's heads, I'll make the call," Reed said and leaned forward.

Wade took a quarter from his pocket and flipped it in the air. He caught it and slapped it on the desk so that both could see the results. It was tails.

"I'll just go to my desk so that you won't be interrupted," Reed gloated. "Do you want me to close your door?"

"Ha, ha, ha," Wade said and shook his head.

Reed laughed and left the room.

Wade looked up the phone number for the Las Vegas FBI. Calls about the death of a fellow officer were as difficult to make as those of family members.

He dialed the number and waited. He explained the reason for his call. He was transferred three times and put on hold for forty-five minutes.

"This is Agent Larry Collier."

"This is Sheriff Wade Adams in Wilbarger County, Texas. I'd like to discuss one of your agents, Jody Ratliff."

"I'm her supervisor," said Collier. "Is there a problem?"

"Yes, Sir," Wade began. "I'm sorry to have to tell you this. Miss Ratliff has been killed. The evidence points to abduction and murder."

"What?" Collier asked in disbelief.

Wade gave him the highlights of the investigation.

"Do you have any suspects?"

"Not at the moment," Wade admitted. "Was Agent Ratliff here on a case?"

"No, she was on vacation," Collier told him.

"Did she have any friends or family in this area?" Wade inquired.

"I can't answer that," Collier said. "I'll have to check her file. Was she there alone?"

"We haven't found any evidence pointing toward another person. It's still early in the investigation."

"We'll get in touch with her next of kin," Collier said.

"We'll need someone to identify the body," Wade told him.

"I'll take care of that, and I'll send you a copy of her file. It might help your investigation. May I have your contact information?"

Wade gave Agent Collier the department address, phone number, and fax number. The call ended, and he sat back, relieved that it was over.

The team met in the conference room to discuss the new evidence. It was agreed, based on the evidence, that Agent Ratliff was abducted from highway 287 after having a flat. There were no prints on the car other than those of the victim. The tire provided more evidence.

"Someone shot her tire," said Baker. "We found a bullet in the back driver's side tire that matches the nine-millimeter bullet found in the victim's body. They were fired from the same weapon."

"Wouldn't she have heard the shot and been suspicious?" Gonzalez asked.

"It might have sounded like a backfire," suggested Odom. "The radio was turned up loud when we processed the car. She may not have heard it at all."

"Did anyone hear the shot when she was killed?" asked Gonzalez.

"There aren't any homes near the place she was found," Reed said. "The closest one is at least a mile away. Those folks said they were asleep by ten that night and didn't hear anything."

"We have some news about her death," Lodge said. "Baker and I went back to the scene, and we parked the car in the same place that the shooter parked. Baker stood where our victim fell. We used a laser pointer to track the trajectory.

"The trajectory from the driver's side didn't match the wound," Baker added. "The bullet that killed her had to have been fired from the passenger side of the car."

"The shooter may have gotten out of the car," Wade said, picturing the possible scenario. "He might have fired and missed, then ran to the passenger side to fire again."

"Could there have been two people in the car?" Maddie posed.

"There could have been ten for all we know at this point," Wade said.

"I doubt there were ten people in the vehicle," Baker said. "The tires that made the skid marks on Highway 70 are common on passenger cars. We have a tread pattern that we could check against a suspected vehicle. The odds of finding the car using the skid marks alone are one in a million.

"I can't help wondering if this was a random abduction or it had something to do with her being an agent," Maddie said.

"Those are good points," Reed said. "We need to find the evidence to answer those questions. The victim's cell phone is locked. The tech lab is working to open it now. It might provide some information for us. What did the Vegas FBI have to say, Wade?"

"I spoke with her supervisor, Agent Collier. He said she was on vacation. He's sending us a copy of her file."

"We know how, when, and where she died. The who and why still need to be discovered," Reed said. "The information her supervisor is sending may provide a clue. Let's call it a night and start again in the morning."

Wade stopped for a burger on his way home. He sat on the couch and ate. The television was on, but he wasn't watching. His mind was on the case.

Ratliff lived in Las Vegas. Why vacation here? There has to be someone she knows in this area. Why the inn?

Could she have been engaged and looking for a venue? Again, why the inn? There are bigger, fancier venues in Las Vegas.

How did she know about the inn? Did she see a flyer at one of the local businesses, or did someone tell her about it?

He shook his head and stood. He stretched and went to the refrigerator for a beer. He popped the top and stared into space.

Lizzie's aunt showed up at the inn. The family didn't know she was coming. She's a news anchor in Vegas. Is that a coincidence?

Grace was nervous. She was hiding something, and she was lying. I'm sure of it. Could she be running from the FBI?

Could Ratliff have been in the area and at the inn because of Grace? Was Ratliff investigating Grace, or was she the source of Grace's story?

Wade walked back to the living room and plopped on the couch. There was no evidence to suggest that the two women knew each other. He couldn't help feeling that there was a connection. Ratliff couldn't tell him anything. He needed to talk to Grace.

CHAPTER ELEVEN

THE PERSONAL INFORMATION for Agent Jody Ratliff was on Wade's desk when he got to the office the next morning. He was reading through the file when Reed entered his office.

"Has the lab been able to unlock Ratliff's phone?" Wade asked.

"No, they've tried fingerprint and facial recognition. They're working on passcodes now. That's going to take a while."

"This might help," Wade said, pointing at the file. "Ratliff graduated from Midwestern State University in Wichita Falls. She had a volleyball scholarship."

"When did she graduate?" asked Reed.

"Two years ago," Wade said. "What are the chances some of her old teammates are still in Wichita Falls?"

"I'll call Midwestern and see what I can find out," Reed said.

Wade was still reading through the file when Reed knocked on his door.

"Agent Ratliff came to Texas for a bridal shower. One of her former teammates is getting married next weekend. How do you feel about a road trip to Wichita Falls?" Reed asked.

"Your truck or mine?" Wade said and stood.

"Your air conditioning works better," Reed said.

"Where are we going first?" Wade asked when they left the parking lot.

Reed consulted his notes. "The bride's name is Patricia Catlin. She works at a bank. We should be there soon after it opens."

Wade hoped Miss Catlin already knew about her friend's demise. He dreaded the thought of breaking the news to a loved one.

They drove to Wichita Falls, located the bank, and parked in the adjoining lot. They went inside and looked around. A young woman at a nearby desk greeted them.

"May I help you?"

"We'd like to see Patricia Catlin," Reed said.

"Do you have an appointment?"

"No, it's important that we speak with her."

"I'll see if she's available," said the woman. "Would either of you like some coffee?"

"No, thank you," the men replied.

"Won't you have a seat? I'll let her know you're here."

They sat down in nearby chairs to wait while the woman made a call. They waited ten minutes before a petite brunette approached them.

"I'm Patricia Catlin," she introduced herself. "I understand that you want to see me."

"Yes, Ma'am," Reed said, and both men stood.

"My office is this way," she said and looked at them with concern.

They followed her to her office and sat down in front of her desk. She settled herself in her chair.

"Is something wrong? Is this about Jody?"

"Yes, Ma'am," Reed began. "Miss Ratliff was killed early Tuesday morning."

"What! No!" cried Patricia.

The officers sat quietly while she wept.

"Are you sure it was Jody?" she asked when she'd composed herself.

"Yes, Ma'am," Wade said.

"I can't believe it," the woman said between sobs. "I knew something was wrong. I haven't been able to get in touch with her. What happened?"

Wade and Reed looked at each other neither wanted to be the one to tell her.

"She was murdered," Wade told her.

"Murdered? How? Why?"

"We believe she was abducted. It appears that she was shot while trying to escape," Reed told her. "We need to ask some questions about your friend."

"I'll tell you anything you want to know," said Patricia.

"We know that she was on vacation," said Wade. "We assume it was to attend your bridal shower."

Patricia nodded and wiped the tears from her face. "Yes, she's my maid of honor."

"When did Miss Ratliff arrive?"

"She got here Friday night."

"Did you know that she visited the Paradise Creek Inn Saturday afternoon?" asked Reed.

"I asked her to look into it for my bachelorette party. I wanted to get married there. They were closed when I was looking for a venue. She said that we might have to find a different place because the inn appointments were filling up fast."

"What did she do while she was here?" Wade inquired. "When did you last see her?"

"Jody stayed with me Friday night, and she was at my shower on Sunday. We had the final gown fittings on Monday, and then we had dinner."

"What time did she leave," asked Reed.

"It was around ten-thirty. I tried to get her to stay. She said all of her things were at the hotel."

"Why did she stay at a hotel in Vernon," Wade asked.

"I got the impression she was meeting a man in Vernon," said Patricia.

"Did she mention a name?" Wade asked.

"No, she said she'd run into a friend while she was there. She said he wasn't anyone that I would know."

"A few more questions," Wade said with a sympathetic smile. "Did she mention seeing anyone following her or anyone who turned up in more than a few places she'd been?"

"No."

"Did she seem to be afraid of anything or anyone?"

"Not that I noticed."

"Is it possible that she confided in someone else to avoid worrying you?" Reed asked.

"The only person that comes to mind is Janice Compton."

"Where can we find Miss Compton?" Reed asked.

Patricia gave them the address where Janice worked.

The men stood to leave. Reed handed her a card and said, "Please, call us if you remember anything that might be useful."

Wade and Reed left the bank and drove to the law firm where Janice Compton worked.

Miss Compton had nothing more to tell them. They left her with a card and instructions to call if she remembered anything.

The two officers crossed the Wilbarger County line when Reed asked, "Can we afford pizza and a working lunch today?"

"You're the team leader," Wade teased. "It's your decision."

"I'll call the meeting if you'll call in the pizza."

"Yes, Sir," Wade said with a grin.

They stopped to pick up the pizza before going back to the office. They were standing at the counter when the man with the military haircut walked past them and out the door.

Reed's arms were loaded with pizza when he saw the man and alerted Wade. Wade hurried to the door but didn't see anyone in the parking lot.

"He's already gone," Wade said when he went back inside.

"Is he a ghost?" Reed exclaimed. "How did he get away so fast?"

Wade shrugged and opened the door for Reed. They went back to the office and carried the pizza to the conference room. Everyone helped themselves and settled at the table. Wade and Reed filled them in while they ate.

"We need to find out if Ratliff was meeting a man while she was in town. He might have the information we need," said Reed.

"He could also be the shooter," added Wade. "I'd like to check out the stranger from the inn."

"I want a couple of teams to canvas the area again with our updated photograph. Find out if she was seen with a man, and find out the man's name if possible. I'll work with Wade."

"I need to talk with Wade for a few minutes," said Maddie.

Wade and Maddie went to his office and sat down. She handed him three applications for deputy sheriff.

"We need to set up interviews with these people," Maddie told him. "I know we're in the middle of an investigation. We need the help, and they may take other jobs if we wait. I've already checked their qualifications."

Wade read the first two applications. Both appeared to be good candidates.

He looked at the third application. He looked at Maddie and back at the name. He looked at Maddie again and asked, "Is this a joke?"

Maddie grinned and said, "It's no joke. He applied, and he's qualified. The only things against him are his lack of experience and the fact that he's Lizzie's ex."

Wade stared at his deputy. He looked at the application again and tossed it at her. "How am I supposed to work with him?"

"Look at it this way," Maddie began. "You'd be able to keep an eye on him."

Wade shook his head. "I don't see how this is going to work."

"We can't discriminate," Maddie pointed out. "We have to interview him."

"All right, schedule the interviews. Make sure it's a group interview like it was with Gonzalez and Odom. I don't want to be the only one making this decision."

"I think that's a good plan," Maddie told him. "I was as surprised as you when I read this. I never dreamed Drake Wagner would want to join our department."

Maddie's amusement ended when the intercom on Wade's desk buzzed.

"Keep this to yourself as long as you can," Wade said. "The harassment from the rest of the team is gonna be terrible."

Maddie stood and smiled. "They already know," she said and hurried out of the room.

"Yeah, what is it?" Wade asked with a surly attitude.

"There's an Agent Welborn from the FBI here to see you," Baker said.

"FBI? I'll be right out."

Wade walked into the outer office and offered his hand. Welborn ignored it and showed the sheriff his badge.

"Brock Welborn, FBI," he said and handed Wade a business card. "I believe you found one of our people."

"I wasn't expecting to see anyone so soon," Wade said. "Come to my office, and I'll give you an update."

Brock Welborn was a large man with dark hair and eyes. He squinted at Wade and followed him. He sat in the chair in front of Wade's desk.

"Can I get you anything?" Wade offered.

"No, let's just get on with it," Welborn said.

Wade settled in his chair and took stock of Welborn. The man hadn't made a good impression.

"We used the information you sent us and learned a bit more about Agent Ratliff."

Wade shared the information that he and Reed had gathered.

"Do you have any leads on the man she might have been meeting or the murderer?"

"We have two teams working on that now," Wade told him.

"What are you doing about it, Sheriff?" Welborn sneered.

"I was about to look into a person of interest," Wade retorted.

"Who is the person of interest?"

"All we have is a vague description, no name," Wade said. He didn't intend to share any more information until he had to.

"I see," said Welborn. "We haven't been able to get in touch with Agent Ratliff's next of kin. I've come to identify her and take the body back with me. I have the paperwork giving me the necessary authority." He opened his briefcase, extracted the forms, and handed them to Wade.

Wade took his time reading the paperwork. "I'll show you to the morgue," he said and stood.

Welborn followed him. He said nothing until he'd seen the body. "Yes, that's Jody Ratliff. My flight leaves from Dallas tomorrow afternoon. I'd like to take possession in the morning."

Wade looked at the attendant in charge of the morgue.

"She'll be ready before I leave tonight," said Dennis Balser.

"You can pick her up after eight in the morning," Wade told the agent.

The two men returned to Wade's office.

"May I have a copy of your reports?" Welborn asked.

"Certainly," Wade said. "Baker, get Agent Welborn a copy of all the reports regarding Agent Ratliff."

"Yes, Sir," Baker replied and began to print the files.

"I'd like to talk with you about another matter," Welborn said. "In your office if possible."

Wade led the way, and the men took their seats. Welborn took a photo from his briefcase and passed it to Wade.

"Does this man look familiar?"

Wade looked at the picture. "No, I don't recognize him."

"Does he match the description of your person of interest?"

"No, he doesn't."

"Does the name Peter Crisp mean anything to you?"

"Not at all. Do you think this man is connected with Agent Ratliff?"

"I don't know," Welborn said and looked at the photo when Wade gave it back to him. "He's one of our agents. He's been missing for weeks. I thought I'd take a shot."

"We could make a copy and post it here," Wade offered. "We can keep an eye out for him."

"I don't suppose it would hurt," Welborn said.

Baker tapped on the door. "I have the files you wanted."

"Thank you, Baker. Would you make copies of that photograph and post it around the station?" Wade requested.

Welborn handed the picture to Baker and said nothing while waiting. Baker returned the photo, and Welborn stood.

"Thank you for your help, Sheriff. I'll be here in the morning for Agent Ratliff."

"He's a nasty character," Baker said when Welborn left the office.

"Yes, he is," Wade agreed. "I hope tomorrow is the last we see of him."

Their conversation was interrupted when Tiffany and her son walked into the outer office.

"Hi, Sheriff," said Ross.

"Hi, Deputy Pruitt," Wade said and smiled.

"I hope you don't mind," Tiffany said. "We were passing by, and Ross wanted to stop to see you."

"It's always nice to see a fellow law officer," Wade said and patted the boy's shoulder. "We're pretty busy right now. I can't give you a tour today."

"That's okay, Sheriff," said the boy. "It can wait until I get back."

Wade smiled. "Where are you going?"

"I'm going to my dad's house for the weekend."

"I hope you have a safe trip and a great time."

"Thanks, Wade," Tiffany said and steered Ross toward the door.

Wade went to the conference room and sat down. *I wondered if Ross wanted to stop or if it was Tiffany's idea. It could be part of her plan to come between Lizzie and me.*

The team didn't find anyone who had seen Agent Ratliff with a man. Reed and Wade weren't able to locate the man with the military haircut.

"We'll start fresh in the morning," Reed said during their meeting. "We've worked late every night this week, and we all deserve a rest."

Wade left the office and drove straight to the inn. He was greeted with an enthusiastic hug and kiss from Lizzie.

"I've missed you," she said and held him close.

"I've missed you too," he said and kissed her again.

"I hope you're hungry," Lois said.

"I've been eating take-out all week," Wade said. "I'm ready to taste your good cookin'."

James and Ellen walked in the back door with Dan close behind.

"How are you feeling, Ellen?" Wade asked. He'd been so busy that he hadn't thought to check.

"Better," she answered. "I've been able to sleep, and I didn't have a nightmare last night."

"That's good news."

"She's almost back to normal," James said with a grin.

"Dinner's ready," Lois called.

The men stood out of the way while the ladies put the food on the table. Everyone settled into their chairs and filled their plates.

"How's your investigation going?" James asked Wade.

"We've learned a lot about our victim. We still don't have a lead to her killer."

"That poor girl," Ellen said, and tears glistened in her eyes.

"Do you have any idea why she wanted to meet with me?" Lizzie asked.

Wade swallowed a mouth full of mashed potatoes before he

answered. "It turns out she wanted to have a bachelorette party here. The wedding is next Saturday."

"That was cutting things close," said Lois.

"Was she the maid of honor?" Lizzie asked, horrified.

Wade nodded and took a drink from his glass.

"Can you imagine losing your maid of honor just days before your wedding?" Ellen exclaimed.

"No, I can't," Lizzie said wide-eyed.

The conversation turned to their own wedding plans. Lizzie brought the box of wedding invitations to the table when they'd cleared away the dishes.

"These did turn out nice," said Wade.

"Do you happen to have your guest list finished?" Lizzie chided.

"I'll finish it tonight. I need to look up a few more addresses."

They were still discussing the guest list when the bells on the front door jingled.

"Who could that be?" Ellen asked.

"I'll get it," said James.

He went toward the lobby and saw two men standing near the check-in desk.

"May I help you?" he asked.

"My name is Brock Welborn. This is my partner, Charles Brittain. We're with the FBI." The men showed James their credentials.

"I'm James Fletcher. Would you like to book a room?"

"We'd like to ask you some questions," said Welborn.

"May I ask what this is about?"

"Are there others here? We'll need to speak with them as well."

"Everyone's in the dining room," answered James and indicated that they should follow him.

James introduced the FBI agents to the family and asked them to sit down.

"I didn't expect to see you here, Sheriff Adams," said Welborn with a nasty smirk.

"I can say the same about you," Wade retorted.

"I'm sure you're wondering why we're here," said Brittain trying to ease the tension.

"Yes, we are," answered Lois.

"We're investigating a disappearance," Brittain said. "We hope that you can help us find him."

Welborn opened his briefcase. "This is one of our undercover agents," he said and handed a photo to James. "He hasn't made contact with us in three weeks."

James looked at the picture and passed it to Ellen. Welborn watched their faces as they looked at it in turn.

"Do any of you know the man?" asked Brittain. "Does he look familiar?"

They all shook their heads.

"Does the name Peter Crisp mean anything to you?" Brittain continued.

Again, they shook their heads.

"Why do you think he'd be here?" Wade queried.

"Because of this woman," Welborn said and handed another photo to James.

James looked at the second picture and passed it on. Wade looked at the photo but said nothing. Dan followed Wade's lead.

"What does this woman have to do with us?" Lois asked with a straight face.

"You tell me. We found this in her office," Welborn said with a sneer. He passed an envelope to Lois. It was the envelope that had held her last letter to Grace.

"How do you know this woman?" Brittain asked with a kind expression.

Wade felt as though he was watching a good cop, bad cop exhibition. He was tempted to intervene, but he wanted to know what this was about.

"She's my daughter," Lois answered. "What does she have to do with this man?"

"We aren't sure," Brittain admitted. "They were seen together a few days before our agent's last contact. Has she ever mentioned him?"

"No, she hasn't," Lois replied.

"When did you last speak with your daughter?" asked Welborn.

"Is she in some sort of trouble?"

"Not that we're aware."

"Why do you need to know?"

Welborn's grin was anything but pleasant. "I asked you first."

Lois glanced at James and said, "She was here Thursday evening, and we had dinner together. She left Friday morning."

"She was here?" Welborn asked with excitement.

"Why don't you tell the Fletchers why you're here before they answer more questions?" Wade suggested with an edge to his voice.

Welborn leaned back and glared at Wade. "Miss Stewart may be a particular friend of our missing agent. We think she might know where he is or how to contact him."

"Why don't you get in touch with her?" Wade asked.

"We haven't been able to find her," Welborn admitted.

"Correct me if I'm wrong," Wade began. "You aren't certain that Miss Stewart even knows your agent. Yet, you come here and worry her family on the off chance that she might have mentioned him."

"Sheriff Adams, we understand that this is upsetting," Brittain said. "I'm sure you'd go to any lengths to find one of your men no matter how unlikely the lead."

Wade nodded and said no more.

"Was there anything that your daughter said that might give us a clue?" Brittain asked.

Lois told them about Grace's assignment and that she would be traveling to different places to research the story.

"The rest of our conversations were family-related and none of your business," Lois said with defiance.

Wade looked at her with surprise.

Welborn sighed and leaned back in his chair. "That matches the story we were given by her station manager."

"Then why did you come here looking for her?" James demanded, his temper flaring.

"She left under unusual circumstances," Welborn. "We thought she might be attempting to make contact with our agent."

"What unusual circumstances?" asked Wade.

"Miss Stewart filed two police reports before she left. One involved a tracking device on her car, and the other a home invasion. The next day she was gone. Off the grid."

Wade looked at the family. Dan was the only person who looked truly surprised.

"What do you mean off the grid?" Lois asked.

"We tracked her to Flagstaff, Arizona. She hasn't used her cell phone or her computer since then. There are no records of her credit cards or identification being used."

"Why would she do that?" Ellen asked.

"That's what we want to know," Brittain said.

"We've told you all that we can," James said. "She didn't mention anyone other than her boss while she was here."

"Do you know where she planned to go from here?" asked Brittain.

"I believe she had a meeting in Oklahoma," Ellen said.

"Did she say where she was staying or who she was meeting?" Welborn asked.

"No, she didn't," replied Lois.

"Thank you for your time," Brittain said. "We'll be on our way."

Welborn reluctantly stood and said," Please, have her contact us if you hear from her again."

The Fletchers gave a noncommittal answer and saw the agents to the door.

CHAPTER TWELVE

BROCK WELBORN and Charles Brittain ambled to their car. They didn't speak to each other until they were driving away from the inn.

"I thought I was supposed to play the bad cop," Brittain challenged.

"That's the sheriff I spoke with today," answered Welborn. "He wouldn't have bought me as the good cop after our previous meeting."

"I don't think he bought the whole act. He seems to be pretty sharp," observed Brittain.

"Yes, and he plays his cards close to the vest," Welborn said. "I had the feeling he wasn't telling me everything this afternoon."

"Your intimidation act didn't work with him, did it?"

"Nope, he clammed up. We may have to lay our cards on the table before this is over."

"I had a feeling the Fletchers weren't telling all they know either," said Brittain. "We should check their backgrounds."

"I thought so too," admitted Welborn. "I wanted to find out what they knew."

"I believe they were truthful about not knowing Stewart's whereabouts. The rest, I'm not sure about. The mother seemed to be worried."

"She did, didn't she," said Welborn with an evil grin. "What else did you notice?"

"I was curious about the reason the Sheriff was there," Brittain began. "The redhead was wearing an engagement ring. There was a box of wedding invitations on the table. Either Adams or the other man is her fiancé."

"I'll bet it's Adams. He was being protective of the whole group," Welborn agreed.

"Why didn't you tell them what we know about Stewart?" asked Brittain.

"Suppose the Fletchers tell the Stewart woman about our interview. Suppose she talks to our man and mentions Peter Crisp."

"That's a lot to leave to chance," said Brittain. "How long do you think it will take the sheriff to make the connection between Ratliff and our man?"

"It won't take long. They'll start digging elsewhere if they run out of leads."

"What about Ratliff? Was she here on vacation?"

"It seems so. I read through the reports the Sheriff's department gave me. They were thorough."

"Her presence here was either a coincidence, or she kept some information to herself," said Brittain. "What are the chances that the man she met here was our man?"

"Anything is possible," said Welborn.

"In that case, our man could be with the Stewart woman," suggested Brittain.

"Her movements are more in line with being on assignment," said Welborn. "We know she was in Flagstaff and that she visited her family. They believe she went to Oklahoma. She turned up in St. Louis and went from there to Dodge City."

"She could be meeting him somewhere," Brittain pointed out.

"Then why all the travel?" Welborn queried. "She may not be connected with our man at all. The trouble is that she's our last lead. It's weak, but it's all we have at this point."

Wade watched the agents until he was certain they had gone. He was uneasy. Welborn and Brittain seemed to know more about Grace than they wanted to share.

Why were they so sure that Grace was involved? Did they come to the inn because they were already in the area? Did they use Agent Ratliff's demise as an excuse for coming to the inn?

Dan watched Wade and asked, "What's going on?"

"I'm about to find out," Wade said with determination. "Will you make sure all of the exterior doors on the west side are locked? I don't want those two to walk in while we're talking. I'll take care of this side of the house."

Dan nodded and left the room. Wade locked the front and side doors. He checked to make sure that the security system was on. He joined the family and listened while they talked.

Dan walked into the kitchen and locked the back door. He sat down at the table with the Fletchers.

"I despise that Welborn character," Lois said and scowled.

"He acted like Aunt Grace is a criminal."

"Ms. Stewart might know him and might have some idea how to contact him," Ellen said, making quotation marks in the air when she said the word might.

"Who is Ms. Stewart?" asked Dan.

"Oh, we didn't tell you, did we? Aunt Grace's last name is Stewart instead of Fletcher," Lizzie replied.

"Stewart was my husband's first name. Grace wanted to use a family name when she…" Lois paused. "When she became a journalist. She needed a stage name to protect her privacy."

Wade looked at Lizzie's grandmother. She wouldn't meet his gaze.

It was obvious to him that they were hiding something. Something that had to do with Grace.

"There's no doubt that Welborn is a nasty character," Wade said.

"He certainly is," said Ellen.

"He acted as if Grace was on the most wanted list," added James.

"Is there anything that Dan and I should know that you didn't want to share with those agents?" Wade queried.

They all shook their heads.

Wade clasped his hands on the table in front of him, looked down, and sighed. He lifted his head and looked at the group.

"You are good people, honest people," Wade said. "That's probably why you're so unconvincing when you lie."

"We told him the truth," James said.

"Not all of it," Wade challenged. "I know all of you pretty well now."

"I should hope so," Lois said with a smile.

"Do you remember when we first met?" Wade asked. "I knew that you were holding something back from the beginning. It wasn't until you decided to share that information with me that I could exclude you from the suspect list."

Wade saw them exchange guilty looks. "Welborn's nasty, not stupid. I'm sure that he and his partner think you're hiding something."

The family made no reply.

"He had to have had a warrant to get this address from the post office. He'll be back, and he'll be nastier. Next time, he'll have a warrant and tear this place apart."

The family remained silent.

"I know y'all are hiding something. Dan and I don't want to be implicated in whatever Grace has done."

Dan looked at Wade with a raised eyebrow.

"I don't want the sheriff's department to be implicated either," Wade continued. "I can't protect you from Welborn or the FBI."

"Grace hasn't done anything," said Lois at last.

"That we know about," James added.

He looked at his mother and squeezed her hand. Lois looked at her son and sighed.

"They need to know," she said.

"I'll go and let y'all sort things out," Dan said and stood.

"No, please," James said. "You should hear this too."

Dan sat back down, still as bewildered and uncomfortable as he'd been since the FBI agents arrived. Lois looked at Wade and Dan with tears in her eyes.

"I want you to understand that we never intended to hurt either of you," she began. "We've been trying to protect you."

"Go on," Wade encouraged.

"Grace has been on the run for a long time. We've kept it a secret for her protection and ours."

Lois and James took turns telling Grace's story. The tale ended, and James said, "Any hint that we've had contact with Grace could endanger us all. We thought you'd be safer if you didn't know about it."

"I understand why Grace ran in the beginning," said Wade. "Why is she running now?"

"She told us about her car and her house," Lois said and gave Wade the details. "That would have scared anyone. It was a message written on a mirror in her bedroom that sent her into a panic. 'We know who you really are! You can't hide forever!'"

Dan whistled and said, "I'd have taken off, too."

James nodded and said, "She thinks it might be connected to Sharp. She plans to keep hiding until she can find out."

"Her boss has known all along about her past," Ellen said. "He decided to tell everyone she was on assignment. She built on his story to make hers plausible."

"Did she mention anyone else?" Wade pressed.

"No, she didn't," said Lois.

"Do you know where she is?"

"No," James answered. "We haven't spoken to her since she left."

"You've heard from her, haven't you," Wade surmised.

"Yes," Ellen said. "She sent word to let us know that she had reached a hotel in Oklahoma on Friday. We haven't heard from her since."

Wade knew they were telling the truth. He also felt they were still keeping something from him.

"What does she plan to do when she has the answers she needs?"

"We don't know," Lois said. "We told her she could come back here. She won't if she feels we're still at risk."

"When are you supposed to hear from her again?" Wade queried.

"She said she'd let us know what she finds out," James said. "She didn't give us a timeline because she didn't know how long it would take to get answers."

Lizzie had been listening to the conversation and watching Wade's reactions. He was angry and hurt.

"Is that everything?" he asked.

"That's all we know," James said.

Wade stood and paced around the room. He ran one hand through his hair and looked at his future in-laws. He sat down again and shook his head.

"I can't believe after all we've been through that you didn't trust me enough to tell me about this," Wade said with pain in his voice. "What about Dan? He's known you longer than I have!"

"We're sorry," James said. "We thought we were doing what was best. We never meant to hurt either of you. We didn't want you to be in danger."

"You didn't want us to be in danger!" Wade exclaimed. "What about all of you? Don't you realize this is the first place Sharp would look for Grace? She moved away and took precautions. You didn't do any of that! You've been in danger all along!"

"We thought it was over," Lois said with tears running down her face. "Sharp has been in prison for years."

"I'm sorry," Wade said, trying to control himself. "I shouldn't be yelling at you. I love y'all and don't want to lose any of you."

"I have a question," said Dan. "Why is Grace still hiding if it's over?"

The older Fletchers stared at Dan. It was obvious that they hadn't considered that question.

"I can't answer that," said Lois. "I guess it made sense to me because she was Sharp's target."

"You're both a part of this family, too," James said. "I can see now that we were wrong to keep it a secret. We should have told you long ago. I'm sorry."

Ellen and Lizzie apologized to the two men.

"It's my fault," said Lois. "I insisted that we all kept Grace's secret all these years. I was trying to protect everyone. I'm sorry."

Dan sat in silence, looking at each of them in turn.

"Dan, say something," James coaxed. "Yell at me, call me an SOB, anything.

"Wade covered it pretty well," Dan told him. "I don't know what else there is to say except that when you hired me, part of the job was to look after Lizzie. I was ready for whatever might come. I don't understand why you didn't tell me about this."

He looked at Wade and asked, "What should I do if those agents question me?"

Wade sighed and ran his hand through his hair again. "My official advice is to tell them the truth. My instincts tell me that we shouldn't mention Sharp or Grace's past unless they bring it up. Do what you think is best. That goes for all of us."

Dan nodded and stood up. "I'm going home," he said. "I need to sort this out."

"Will you be here tomorrow?" James asked.

"I don't know," Dan said and walked out the door.

James nodded and hung his head in sorrow.

Wade looked at Lizzie. "I can't believe you didn't tell me."

"Wade," Lois began. "Lizzie didn't know anything about it until last week. We kept it from her, too."

"I think we should go," Ellen suggested. "Wade and Lizzie need to talk."

Lizzie was sitting at the table with her hands over her face. Tears pooled on the table at her elbows. She got up and hugged her family goodnight.

She turned and faced Wade when they'd gone.

"You've been in danger all this time. Why didn't you tell me?"

"I didn't know until last Friday. I was just as angry as you are."

"Why didn't you tell me when you found out?" Wade demanded. "Don't you think that's something your fiancé should know?"

"I meant to tell you. I haven't had the chance with everything that's been happening," she answered.

"There haven't been a few moments in the past week to let me know that your life could be at risk," he said with a healthy dose of sarcasm.

Lizzie's temper flared. "We've been busy doing other things," she said. "The reopening, wedding plans, inn business, and your cases! You've stayed in town more than you've been here this week!"

They glared at each other until Wade stood.

Lizzie moved toward him and said, "Granny and Daddy confronted Aunt Grace after you and Dan left Friday night. That's when they decided to tell me. They wanted me to be aware of the situation."

"What aren't you telling me?" Wade asked.

Lizzie reached for his hand and held it tight. "I could see in your face that you had doubts about Aunt Grace's story. I thought it was your law enforcement instinct in overdrive until I heard the truth."

"And?

"I've been waiting for the right time to tell you or for you to bring it up," Lizzie admitted. "I'm sorry, and I promise I'll never keep anything from you again."

Wade looked at her, dropped her hand, and took a step back. She could see the doubt in his eyes.

"I'm going back to town. I need some time."

Lizzie began to cry again. "Please, stay. We can work this out."

"I need to leave before I say something that I can't take back," Wade told her and walked to the door.

"Will you be here for breakfast?"

"No!"

Wade opened the door and left Lizzie standing there. She heard his truck start and the sound of his tires on the drive. She locked the door, turned out the lights, and went to her room, where she cried herself to sleep.

* * *

Grace picked up the phone in her Tulsa hotel room. She dialed her attorney's number and prayed that he'd have news, any news this time.

"Mr. Jackson, this is Grace."

"Hello, Grace. How are you holding up?"

"I'll be better if you can give me some answers," she said and held her breath.

"I have good news," he said. "Sharp's appeal was denied. He'll stay in prison, and you won't have to testify again."

"Is there any chance that he could get out of prison early?"

"There were no grounds for the appeal. His sentence of life without parole plus twenty-five years stands. He'll die in prison."

"Do you know if Sharp had anything to do with my car and house?"

"Sharp was thoroughly questioned on the subject," Jackson told her. "He swore he had nothing to do with it and volunteered to take a polygraph. His statements during the test showed him to be truthful. There's no evidence that he had hired anyone."

"It's finally over?"

"Yes, indeed," said Jackson with glee.

"Thank God!" she said. "Thank you for your help, Mr. Jackson."

"My pleasure, Grace," Jackson exclaimed. "I hope that any future communications we have are purely social in nature."

Grace laughed and said, "I hope so too, Mr. Jackson."

The call ended, and Grace dialed Oliver Baldwin's number.

"Oliver, this is Grace."

"Hello, Mr. Scott," he said. "May I call you back? I'm in a meeting at the moment."

"I'll call back later," she told him and hung up.

Grace contemplated calling her family. She decided to wait and talk with Oliver first. He was in a hurry to get her off the line. She hoped his meeting had nothing to do with her.

She had time to kill. She was hungry, and she wanted to celebrate. She went downstairs and ate dinner in one of the casino's restaurants.

Celebrating with strangers and drawing attention to herself didn't appeal to her. She celebrated alone by choosing the most expensive meal on the menu and a carafe of wine.

It was almost two hours before she got back to her room and dialed Oliver's number again.

"Can you talk?" asked Grace when he answered the phone.

"Yes, I'm sorry about earlier. Rhonda has Barry Townson stirred up. He was in here asking if you'd been fired. One thing led to another, and he was in here for over an hour."

"That's terrible," she sympathized. "Is Barry all right now?"

"I don't know. I hope I convinced him that I didn't fire you and have no plans to replace him."

"Until Rhonda gets him worked up again," Grace said and laughed.

"Rhonda may be the only one getting fired," Oliver told her. "I had a long talk with her after Barry left. I told her that if she didn't play her cards right, she'd be looking for another job."

"I'll bet she didn't take that well."

"No, she didn't," Oliver confessed. "We may have a new makeup artist when you get back. How are you?"

"I'm great!" she said and told him about the conversation with her attorney.

"That's wonderful news!" Baldwin exclaimed. "Are the authorities certain that Sharp wasn't responsible for the two incidents here?"

"They seem to be," Grace said.

"Have you considered the implications?" Oliver asked.

"What do you mean?"

"If it wasn't Sharp, who was it?" asked Oliver. "You saw a man tamper with your car, and you saw the words on the mirror."

"I've been so relieved about Sharp that I hadn't thought of that," Grace admitted.

"You need to think about it. I've thought about it a lot since you've been away," said Oliver. "The incident with your car may have been a mistake. It's not likely, but possible. The message on your mirror is another matter. It had to have been someone who knew about your past."

"I haven't told anyone else. How could someone have found out?" Grace asked with alarm.

"Do you have any enemies? Is there someone vindictive enough to dig into your background and use it against you?"

Grace was stunned.

"Are you still there," Oliver asked after a long pause.

"Yes, I'm here. I was trying to process your questions."

"Did anyone come to mind?"

"No," Grace replied. "I'll have to think about it."

"It's a good sign that you didn't think of someone right away., but it doesn't get us any closer to an answer."

"Could it be someone who wants my job?" Grace suggested.

"Hmmm, I look into that," said Oliver. "There's more news for you to think about."

"More?" Grace asked, concerned.

Those two FBI agents were here again Wednesday afternoon," Oliver informed her.

"Were they asking about me?"

"They wanted to know if I'd heard from you and so on. I told them that you were in Dodge City the last time I spoke with you."

"Are they still looking for their missing agent?"

"Yes, they are," said Oliver. "The search seemed to be more urgent than the last time they were here. I told them that you didn't recognize the name or the description of the missing man. I also told them that I had never heard you mention anyone by that name or seen you with the man in the photo. Yet, they keep coming back here asking where you are and if I've heard from you."

"Do you think the FBI has done more than ask questions?"

"I can't say for sure, but I think it's a good possibility. They knew you were in St. Louis, and I'm sure they knew you were in Kansas before I told them."

"The FBI is tracking me?"

"I didn't know you'd been in St. Louis, but they did," Oliver told her.

"That's my fault. I let my location be known, hoping to lead Sharp's people on a wild goose chase. I never dreamed the FBI would be watching."

"My gambler's instinct tells me they're running a shell game. It doesn't feel right," Oliver said. "I think you're being set up."

"I don't understand," said Grace.

"One of the agents, Agent Welborn, gives me the impression that you're a suspect in their agent's disappearance," Oliver told her.

"Why would I be a suspect?"

"They didn't say you were. I think you should take a little more time and investigate who might be behind this," Oliver suggested. "Otherwise, you could still be at risk."

"Thanks, Oliver. You've given me a lot to think about."

"Take care of yourself," said Oliver.

"I will, and I'll keep in touch," she said and ended the call.

Why would someone set me up? What are they planning? Who in Vegas knows about my past? How did they find out?

Oliver's right. I can't go back to Vegas until I've figured this out.

CHAPTER THIRTEEN

JAMES FLETCHER KNOCKED on the back door of the inn. No lights were burning inside, and no aroma was coming from the kitchen.

James knocked again.

"They must have overslept," said Lois.

"I have my key here somewhere," Ellen said, digging in her purse.

"Wade's truck isn't here," observed James.

"Lizzie would have let us know if she was going to stay in town," Ellen replied.

"This doesn't look good," Lois added.

Ellen found her key and unlocked the door. They went inside and divided the morning chores.

James started the coffee while Lois gathered ingredients for a quick breakfast. Ellen went in search of Lizzie.

Lizzie was lying in bed, staring at the ceiling. Streaks of mascara ran from her red, swollen eyes to her splotchy cheeks. Her hair was splayed over a tear-stained pillow.

Ellen sat on the edge of the bed and brushed a strand of hair from Lizzie's forehead.

"Honey, what happened?"

Lizzie turned to her mother and said, "Wade went back to town last night. I don't know if he's ever coming back."

Ellen held her daughter in her arms and stroked her hair while she sobbed. "Honey, things may not be as bad as they seem. Wade loves you. I'm sure he'll come around."

"Mama, I don't know what to do," Lizzie said between sobs. "He was so angry. I don't know if he'll ever forgive me."

"I know. We're here for you, and we'll help you get through whatever happens," Ellen promised. "The first thing you should do is get out of this bed and get into the shower. You don't need to wallow in misery all day."

"I don't feel like it, Mama," Lizzie whined through her tears.

"You get out of that bed right now, young lady," Ellen ordered. "You have client meetings today. I know that you don't want them to see you looking the way you do right now."

Lizzie sniffed and stared at Ellen. Her mother hadn't used that tone of voice with her since she was in high school.

"Fine!" Lizzie said and stomped toward the bathroom.

Ellen followed her daughter, turned on the shower, hugged Lizzie, and left the room.

"How is she?" asked James.

"She's miserable," Ellen answered. "Wade left and hasn't called. She doesn't know what's going to happen?"

"Is the wedding off?" asked Lois.

"I didn't have the heart to ask."

Lizzie looked in the mirror. *Mama was right. I can't see clients looking like this. I'd scare them away.*

She blew her nose and squared her shoulders. She had a long hot shower before returning to her room to get dressed. She did what she could with makeup to improve her appearance.

She joined her family in the kitchen and poured herself a cup of coffee.

"I'm sorry, Honey," James said and hugged his daughter.

"Have you heard from Dan?" Lizzie asked.

James shook his head. "I don't know that I will."

"We've sure made a mess of things," Lois pointed out.

The family sat at the table and picked at their breakfast in misery. There was nothing more they could do to remedy the situation.

"Do you think they'll ever forgive us?" Lois asked.

"I don't know that I would be forgiving in their shoes," said James.

"I have to believe they will," said Ellen. "I don't want to think about the alternative."

"If they do forgive us, we have to tell them when Aunt Grace comes back here," Lizzie demanded. "Promise me that we'll tell them."

"Lizzie's right," Ellen said. "A second betrayal would end everything. We'd have only ourselves to blame."

"Yes, Wade and Dan should be told everything from now on," said Lois.

James nodded his agreement and said, "Telling them won't be an issue if we can't get past this. I'll see you at lunch. I need to start plowing."

The Fletcher women needed to stay busy. Lois answered phone calls and made appointments. Lizzie and Ellen cleaned the inn until it shined.

The family hadn't heard from Wade or Dan by lunchtime. They sat down to their midday meal in somber spirits. They had little to say as they filled their plates.

They were startled by a knock on the back door. Dan Hayes stepped inside.

"I'm sorry to bother you at lunch," said Dan. "May I come in?"

"Yes, of course," James beamed.

"It's no bother at all," said Ellen. "We just sat down."

"Sit down and join us," Lois said and went to the kitchen for another place setting.

"James, if you don't mind, I'd like to talk with you outside," Dan said.

The smile faded from James' face. He nodded and followed Dan to the patio.

"Dan, I want to apologize again. We were wrong. I was wrong. I should have told you that you might be in danger. Can you ever forgive me?"

Dan grinned and said, "You're forgiven. I hope you'll forgive me."

"You haven't done anything wrong," James said.

"I'm sorry for leaving the way I did last night," Dan said. "I should have stayed and talked it out. That's what families do."

They shook hands, and James said, "I'll let you know if Grace comes back. I won't keep anything else from you."

"I'd appreciate that," answered Dan.

Lois had been watching through the window.

"They're shaking hands," she said. "James is patting Dan on the back. Here they come."

She rushed back to her chair. The men went back into the kitchen and sat down. Ellen passed a plate of fried chicken to Dan.

"We're sorry, Dan," said Lizzie.

"Apology accepted," Dan said and smiled. "I'm sorry for running out of here last night."

"I would have done the same thing and added a few choice words on the way out," Lois said with a wink. "We won't keep you in the dark again."

They ate and discussed their plan for the remainder of the day. For Lizzie's sake, no one mentioned Wade.

Lizzie met with her scheduled client at two. The man wanted to surprise his wife for her birthday. He wanted the entire family to stay the weekend at the inn. He reserved every guest room and the large party room for the occasion.

She looked at their event calendar after the meeting ended. There were two Halloween parties and a large event scheduled for

October. There were holiday parties booked every weekend between Thanksgiving and Christmas. Four more were booked on weeknights.

Business looked good for the near future. She wished she could say the same about her personal life.

She looked at the box of wedding invitations. She picked up an invitation and ran her fingers over the embossed flowers in the corner. She read the text and smiled.

Lizzie's smile disappeared, and tears filled her eyes. *Should I address these? Wade never gave me his list. Should I call him?*

She reached for the phone and began dialing. She stopped and hung up. *I'll wait until tonight. He needs space, and I don't want to pressure him. I may not want to hear his answer anyway.*

She wiped the tears from her face and picked up a pen. *I can't send these back. I may as well get started.*

She addressed half the envelopes using her guest list. She put invitations inside and sealed them. She was about to attach the postage when she decided to put everything away. *No point in wasting stamps.*

* * *

Wade slept little that night. He woke up with a horrible headache and a bad attitude.

He scrounged through his kitchen, trying to find something suitable for breakfast. *Lizzie would have a good breakfast, ready and waiting.*

He stopped and ran his hand through his hair. *I can't think about Lizzie right now.*

He picked up his keys and got in his truck. He drove to the donut shop, where he bought two donuts and a large coffee.

Wade drove to the office and went inside. He was an hour early, but he'd be able to enjoy his donuts without being disturbed.

He settled at his desk and took a bottle of aspirin from the drawer. He swallowed two with his coffee and took a big bite from a donut.

This time alone will be good. I can focus on what I need to do today. I'll sort out the personal stuff when I get back to my place.

He sighed. It wouldn't be his place much longer. Lodge would be moving in next week. He needed to rent a storage building for his furniture or find a new place to live.

Wade glanced at his calendar and saw the eight o'clock appointment with Welborn written there. He picked up the phone and called Reed.

"Reed, will you do me a favor?" Wade asked.

"That depends on what it is," Reed joked.

"That FBI agent Brock Welborn is supposed to be here at eight. Will you help him when he gets here?" asked Wade. "I'm in no mood to deal with him right now."

"Anything I can do?" Reed offered.

"There's nothing anyone can do," Wade said.

Reed was curious. He sensed that it wasn't the right time to ask questions. "I'm less than a mile away. I'll be there soon."

"I'm going to be out of the office for a while. I have an idea that might help us find our mystery man."

"Yes, Sir," Reed said.

Wade left the office moments before Reed arrived. The office was alive with activity by the time Agents Welborn and Brittain arrived.

"We'd like to see Sheriff Adams," Welborn said to Lodge.

Reed stepped up and said, "Sheriff Adams is out of the office. I'll be glad to help you."

"We're here to collect the body of Jody Ratliff," Brittain informed him.

"Let me call the morgue and make sure she's ready," Reed said and picked up his phone.

"I was told that she'd be ready before the attendant went home last night," Welborn said with a sneer.

"I'm sure she is. It never hurts to double-check," Reed answered. "I also want to make sure Balser is there. I don't have the key."

Reed made his call and led the agents to the morgue.

"Is Balser often late to work?" asked Welborn with an air of superiority.

"No, Sir," Reed replied. "It's Saturday morning, and he has small children. Sometimes his work schedule overlaps with his wife's. She's a nurse who works the night shift. There are times that she doesn't get off when she's supposed to."

Balser was waiting when Reed and the FBI agents entered the morgue. Ratliff's body was wheeled to an open bay door.

"I'll get the van," Brittain volunteered and hurried across the parking lot.

"Sheriff Adams didn't want to see us today, did he?" Welborn asked with a sneer.

"I wouldn't know. He's looking for a person of interest in this case."

"Uh huh," Welborn grunted. "When is he getting married?"

"Next month," Reed said.

They said nothing more and watched Brittain back the van toward them. Welborn opened the van door, and the two agents loaded Ratliff's body while Reed signed the release papers.

"Tell the sheriff that we'll be in touch," Welborn said and climbed into the van.

Reed watched them drive away and closed the bay door. *How did he know Wade was getting married?"*

Wade knew that the establishment he wanted to visit wouldn't be open before nine o'clock. He used the time to drive past storage facilities around town. He jotted down the phone numbers so that he could call them when he got back to the office.

He still had time to kill, so he drove around looking at homes that were for rent or sale. He abandoned that endeavor when he realized it made him think of Lizzie.

He drove downtown and parked in front of a small shop. He got out of his truck and walked to the door. A chime sounded when he opened it.

An old man with glasses, a smock, and a beret sat painting in front of an easel. Arthritis made it necessary for him to turn his whole body to greet his customer.

"Hello, Sheriff," Duke Shultz replied. "It's nice to see you."

"Are you working on your next masterpiece, Mr. Shultz? How are you doing?"

"I'm doing okay. We agreed you should call me Duke."

"We also agreed you'd call me Wade."

"So, we did, so we did," the man cackled.

"That's a nice outfit," Wade teased.

"It looks good for my customers, and it serves a purpose. The smock keeps paint off my clothes, and the beret hides my bald head," Duke said and laughed at his own joke. "What can I do for you today?"

"Would you be able to sketch a person's face from a description? We don't have a sketch artist in the department since Dodson passed away."

"I'll give it a try," Duke said. "Is it a man or a woman?"

"It's a man," Wade answered.

"Let me get my sketch pad and a charcoal pencil," Duke said. "I'll be right back."

Wade looked at the completed artwork hanging in the store while he waited. *Lizzie would like...* He shook his head, trying to chase the thought of Lizzie from his mind. He didn't want to think about her right now.

Duke Shultz climbed onto a stool at the front counter with a pad and pencil in hand. "Describe him to me while I sketch. We can make changes afterward."

Wade described the man with the military haircut and watched Duke sketch. It wasn't quite right at first. A few changes to the nose and eyes were made. Soon, the face of the mysterious man stared at him from the artist's sketch pad.

"That's him," Wade said. "How much do I owe you?"

Duke quoted him a price, and Wade reached into his pocket. It was empty.

"I'm sorry, Duke. I managed to leave the office without the checkbook. Would you write up an invoice? I'll bring you a check before you close today," Wade told him.

"That's no problem," Duke said.

Wade left the shop with an invoice and sketch in hand. He called Reed from his truck to make sure the FBI agents had gone.

"They're gone, and I know why you didn't want to talk to them," Reed said.

"I'll be back in a few minutes," Wade told his deputy and ended the call.

Megan Ford was getting out of her car when Wade parked in his space. She waited to walk to the entrance with him.

"Hi, Wade," she said with a sweet smile.

"Good morning, Megan. What brings you here?"

"I came to see Clint and tell y'all that I found my bracelet. It was wedged between the front seat and the console of my car."

"I'm glad you found it," Wade said and opened the door for her.

She gave him her best smile and said, "Thank you."

They went inside, and Wade looked around the outer office. He knew Baker and Lodge picked up their phone the minute they saw Megan. Reed wasn't so lucky. He walked in with a cup of coffee.

"Reed, Miss Ford has some information concerning her lost bracelet. Would you help her while I take care of this invoice?"

Reed pasted a smile on his face and indicated that Megan should sit beside his desk. Wade tried not to laugh and walked away.

He went to the copier and made one copy of the invoice. He made multiple copies of the sketch. He went back to his office and wrote a check for Duke Shultz.

Wade buzzed Baker's desk on the intercom.

"Yes, Sir," Baker answered.

"Is Miss Ford still out there?"

"Yes, Sir," Baker said with a chuckle.

"I'm going to slip out the side door. I'll be back soon."

Wade went out the back door and took the check to Duke Shultz as promised. Shultz marked the invoice paid, and Wade drove back to the office.

Megan's car was gone when he parked his truck in the lot. He felt it was safe to go back inside and explain his plan to Reed.

"Did you have a nice visit with Miss Ford?" Wade teased when he stopped at Reed's desk.

"Thanks a lot," Reed said.

"Did she get to see Clint?" Wade asked.

"She didn't ask for Clint," Lodge said with a wicked grin.

"She only had eyes for Reed," Baker added and laughed.

Wade joined in the laughter at Reed's expense. He remembered a time when he was the target of Megan's attention. His deputies never missed a chance to tease him about it.

"I noticed that you disappeared soon after she got here," Reed accused.

"I was working on our case," Wade said and smirked. He went to his office and came back with a folder in his hand.

"I went to see our local artist," he said and took the sketch from the folder. "Does this look enough like our mystery man to show people?"

"It does," Reed said. "We should be able to identify him in no time."

"Unless he left the area," Baker pointed out.

"We won't know until we try," said Reed. "I'll get this photo out to the rest of the team."

Wade spent his lunch hour calling storage facilities. He needed to move most of his belonging out of the house before Lodge moved into it. He arranged to view a storage unit when he left work. He'd decide where he was going to live when he'd dealt with his feelings toward Lizzie and her family.

He pushed thoughts of Lizzie from his mind again. He didn't want to think about her or the plans they'd made. Not until he was alone and had the time.

He went to the conference room at one o'clock. The team was meeting to discuss the progress in the Ratliff case.

Reed called the meeting to order. "Has anyone discovered the name of our mystery man?"

"We've been to all the hotels, motels, and camping areas. He isn't staying at any of them," said Clint Odom.

"He's been seen at most of the restaurants in town," added Gonzalez. "No one knows his name or what sort of vehicle he drives."

"No one we spoke with saw him with our victim," Odom said.

"Could he be staying with a friend or relative?" Wade queried.

"That's possible," Maddie said. "It's also possible that he isn't visiting or passing through. He may live or work in this area."

"That's a good point," Reed replied. "We need to change our approach. We assumed he was visiting because we didn't know him and because our victim was visiting.

"There's a good chance that he doesn't know anything about our victim," Wade said. "We need to keep looking for other leads."

"That's true," said Reed. "Half of us will continue the search for this man. The rest of us will focus on finding more information about the victim."

The meeting ended, and Wade went back to his office. He sat down at his desk, and his cell phone rang. He looked at the caller id before he answered.

"Hello, Wyatt."

"I'm sorry to call you while you're at work. I need an answer right away, or I would have waited until later," said Wade's brother.

"What about?"

"I have an idea for your bachelor party," Wyatt told him. "Will you be off work next weekend? I thought we could take a long fishing trip."

Wade had forgotten about his bachelor party. He didn't know what to tell Wyatt, given his current situation with Lizzie.

"That sounds like a good idea, but I don't know," he said. "We're in the middle of a murder investigation. Can I call you back?"

"Oh, I should have realized," apologized Wyatt. "Call me when you have a chance. I'll work out the details."

The call ended, and Wade ran his hands through his hair. His thoughts were on the bachelor party, the wedding, and Lizzie.

He walked around the office looking for something to do that would take his mind off of it all, especially Lizzie.

Ratliff's personal information lay on his desk. He opened the folder and read through it again. *I wonder if her next of kin would have any answers.*

He dialed the number listed in the file. It went directly to voice-mail. He left a message and a call back number. There was nothing else he could do today.

Wade told Reed about the message he'd left for Ratliff's next of kin and left the office. He drove to the storage facility and rented a unit. He drove to a local grocery store to collect empty boxes and went home to pack.

He stopped long enough to have a sandwich and a beer. He thought about Lizzie while he ate. He knew he should call her, but he wasn't ready.

He resumed his packing and was interrupted by someone knocking. He braced himself for another argument with Lizzie and answered the door. Tiffany stood on his front steps.

"Hi," she said and smiled. "I drove by and saw your truck. I thought I'd stop to visit. May I come in?"

"I'm kind of busy right now," he told her. "I'm packing, and there's nowhere to sit."

"I don't mind sitting on the floor," she said. "I wanted to talk to you about Ross."

"Let's talk out here," he told her and stepped outside, closing the door behind him.

"Oh...well...okay," she said, disappointed.

"What's wrong with Ross?"

"He's growing up so fast. He'll soon be at the age when he'll need someone to look up to," she said.

"What does that have to do with me?" Wade asked with suspicion.

"His father lives hours away, and he doesn't see him often enough," she explained. "Ross needs a good strong man in his life."

She moved closer and put her hand on Wade's arm. She looked into his eyes and said, "So do I."

Wade stared at her a moment before he said anything. He pushed her hand away and took a step back.

"Tiffany, I've told you more than once that I don't love you. I haven't for a long time. I don't want anything to do with you. I love Lizzie. I'm going to marry her, and there's nothing you or anyone else can do about it."

Anger flashed in Tiffany's eyes. "What about Ross?" she spat.

"Ross is a good kid, and I like him," Wade began. "He's not my responsibility. He's yours. Think about what your son needs for a change, and stop using him to get what you want."

He went inside and slammed the door leaving Tiffany standing in a rage on the front porch. He waited until he heard her drive away before picking up his cell phone.

"Lizzie, can we talk?"

CHAPTER FOURTEEN

WADE WOKE UP BEFORE LIZZIE. They'd talked into the early hours of the morning. He wanted to let her sleep.

He got up and went to her office to finish his guest list. He put the list on top of the box of invitations and went to the kitchen. *I'll make breakfast for Lizzie for a change.*

He started a pot of coffee and found a frying pan. Omelets were his specialty. He was gathering the ingredients when he heard a knock on the back door. The smiling faces of Lizzie's family greeted him when he opened it.

"Good morning," he whispered. "Lizzie's still sleeping."

"I hope this means the two of you have made up," Lois whispered.

Wade nodded.

"Let's go outside so we can talk without waking Lizzie," James said.

Wade followed them to the patio.

"Wade, we're sorry about keeping secrets from you," Lois said.

"We'll never do that again," said James.

"We hope you'll forgive us," added Ellen.

"I'm sorry that I lost my temper," Wade said.

"Are we good?" James asked with concern.

Wade grinned and said, "We're good."

The four hugged and went back into the kitchen to find Lizzie sitting at the table drinking coffee.

"I was going to let you sleep," Wade said.

"I smelled the coffee and decided to get up," Lizzie said with a yawn.

"I'll make breakfast," Ellen said. "James has something to tell you both."

"What is it, Daddy?"

"We heard from Grace," he said. "She sent an email and wants me to pick her up in Wichita Falls this afternoon."

"Is she going to stay here for a while?" asked Lizzie.

"I don't know. She didn't say anything else."

"I hope it means this business with Sharp is over," Lois said.

"We'll have to wait until she gets here to find out," Ellen said.

"How is your case going, Wade?" asked Lois.

"We know her name and why she was here," Wade replied. "We aren't any closer to finding out who killed her."

"I'm sure it doesn't help that you're short-handed again," James observed.

"Speaking of that," Wade began. "I have something to tell y'all before you hear it from someone else," Wade said. "Drake Wagner applied for one of the deputy positions."

"You're kidding!" Ellen exclaimed.

"I wish I were. I thought it was a joke, too, at first. He interviews tomorrow afternoon."

"I'll bet that's going to be awkward," James said with a grin.

"It will be," Wade told them. "I wanted to pitch his application in the trash."

"What are you going to do?" Ellen asked.

"Ethically, we have to give him an opportunity. We can't afford to pass up qualified candidates," he said. "We have two open positions and three applicants. We could have more applications before we have to make a decision."

"What happens if you have to hire him?" Lois asked.

Wade shook his head and shrugged. "I'll guess I'll have to make the best of it."

"I'd like to be a fly on the wall for that discussion," Lizzie joked.

"There's another discussion that you should know about," he said. "You should thank Tiffany the next time you see her. She came to my house last night."

"Oh, really," Lizzie said with a raised brow.

Wade told her about their conversation.

"I was thinking about postponing or even canceling the wedding," he said. "I found myself telling Tiffany that I was going to marry you whether she liked it or not. That's when I realized that I could never be happy without you and that calling off the wedding would be a huge mistake. I called you after Tiffany left."

"Thank you, Tiffany!" Lizzie shouted.

They were laughing when Dan arrived. They let him in on the joke and told him about Grace's pending return.

"What should we do about Grace?" Lois asked.

"I think you should wait to hear what she has to say," Wade suggested.

"We told her that she'd be safe here," said James. "I don't know if she's coming back for a short visit or if she's still in trouble."

"I think she's still hiding," said Lois. "She'd have called or driven here herself otherwise."

"I could arrange for her to stay at the jail in protective custody," Wade offered.

"Like Megan did last year," Lizzie said with a nod.

"Speaking of Megan, you don't have to worry about her," Wade said with a wide smile.

"Why not?"

"She's after one of my deputies," Wade said.

"Poor, man," said Dan with a grin.

"Which one?" Ellen asked.

"I'm guessing all of them, except Odom," he said and grinned. "I think she's hedging her bets in the hopes that one of them turns out to be a winner."

They talked during breakfast until James and Dan had to start their project for the day.

"I won't be around much for a few days," Wade said when they were ready to leave. "Lodge is going to sublet my place. I'm trying to get moved out so that he can move in next weekend."

"Let me know if you need help moving anything," James offered.

"I will, thank you. I need to go too, Lizzie. I need to finish packing."

"Do you want me to help?"

"You have wedding invitations to finish and mail," Wade teased. "I'll let you know if there's anything you can do."

"Will you be here for dinner?" Lizzie asked.

"I'll be here unless something comes up at the office," he said and kissed her goodbye.

"Lizzie, go get dressed," Ellen suggested. "I'll clean this up."

"I can help," Lizzie said and yawned again.

"Go finish those invitations," Lois said. "They need to go in the mail today. I'll help your mother."

"Why do I have to get dressed to address envelopes?" Lizzie queried.

"It'll make you feel better," Ellen told her. You'll be tempted to go back to bed if you stay in your pajamas."

"Fine, I'll get dressed," Lizzie said and shuffled toward her room.

Ellen and Lois grinned at each other and cleaned up the breakfast dishes.

"What time are the girls supposed to be here?" Lois asked.

"At eleven-thirty," Ellen told her. "They plan to take her to lunch. Jan wouldn't tell me the rest of their plans."

"Wade said he'd be here for dinner," Lois reminded her daughter-in-law. "Will she be back in time?"

"I don't know," Ellen said. "I'll talk to Jan."

"Here she comes," whispered Lois.

"I'm dressed and ready to finish the invitations," Lizzie announced. "I'll save one for Aunt Grace instead of mailing it."

She went to the office and found Wade's guest list. She sat down and opened the box of invitations.

She addressed the remaining envelopes and stuffed them. She was putting the postage on the last few when the bells on the front door jingled.

Lizzie got up and went into the foyer.

"Are you ready?" Jan asked.

"Ready for what?"

"Lunch," Faith said.

"I didn't know we were going to lunch," Lizzie answered, confused.

"Well, we are," Jan told her.

Lizzie smiled and said, "Let me finish these invitations first."

"Do you need help?" Faith offered.

"I have just a few left."

"I'll tell Aunt Ellen that we're taking you with us," Jan told her.

Ellen was waiting near the stairs. "Wade will be here for dinner tonight. Will she be back in time? I'll need to let him know if you'll be late getting back."

"She should be back before six," Jan told her. "Six-thirty at the latest."

"You girls have a good time," Ellen said and hugged her niece.

Jan went to the office to find Lizzie and Faith waiting for her.

"Where are we going?" inquired Lizzie.

"It's a surprise," said Jan.

"I need to send these out," Lizzie said, pointing at the box of invitations. "Do you mind if we stop by the post office first?"

"We can do that," said Faith.

The women got into Faith's car and drove into town. They stopped by the post office as promised. The wedding invitations were on their way.

"Put this on," Jan said and handed Lizzie a sparkly pink blindfold.

"Why do I need a blindfold? What are you up to?"

"It's all part of the fun," Faith said.

Lizzie reluctantly complied. "How long do I have to wear this thing?"

"Sit back and enjoy the ride," Jan chided.

"We could have had lunch at the inn," Lizzie said.

"No, we couldn't," Faith said. "You would have been cooking and cleaning."

"We want you to relax and enjoy," Jan added.

"I have so much to do," Lizzie began.

"Lizzie," Jan scolded. "You deserve a break."

"You work at the inn," said Faith. "You eat at the inn."

"You sleep at the inn," added Jan. "You're getting married at the inn."

"You need a break from the inn!" the pair said in unison.

Lizzie laughed, "Okay, you win. So, where are we going?"

"We're here," said Faith.

Lizzie felt the car slow down and make a right-hand turn. She reached for the blindfold.

"Leave it on," Jan ordered. "I'll let you know when you can take it off."

"Yes, Ma'am," Lizzie teased.

Faith parked the car and helped Lizzie get out. The gravel under her feet didn't give Lizzie a clue to her whereabouts.

Jan and Faith led her across the parking lot and through a door. Lizzie could smell the aroma of hot pizza when they entered.

"You can take off the blindfold now," said Jan.

Lizzie uncovered her eyes and blinked. The room was pitch black.

"Where are we?"

All at once, bright lights blinded her, and the cry of "surprise" deafened her.

Lizzie was amazed. The large room was decorated with greenery and twinkle lights. There were arrangements of yellow roses placed on tables set for six.

A buffet table held large pizzas and an assortment of wine on one side of the room. A table laden with gift bags and boxes stood on the other side. Photos of Lizzie and Wade adorned the walls.

Lizzie beamed. "I can't believe you did this."

"Do you like it?" Jan asked.

"I love it!" Lizzie answered.

She hugged Jan and Faith. They led her to a rocking chair draped with an emerald green bedsheet. A yellow bathrobe was wrapped around her shoulders, and a sparkling toy tiara was placed on her head.

"We crown you, Queen Lizzie," Faith said with an air of authority. "

Jan handed Lizzie a glass of wine and said, "A toast to Queen Lizzie."

Lizzie watched her friends raise their glasses and heard the distinctive clink. She took a drink and raised her glass to her friends.

"Thank y'all. This is so nice. I had no idea," she said.

"What is your first command, my queen," Jan said with a bow and a grin.

Lizzie sat up straight, squared her shoulders, and said, "I'm starved. Dig in."

She whispered to Jan, "What do I do now?"

Jan laughed and led the way to the buffet. Everyone filled their plates and found a seat at one of the tables.

Lizzie made a point to talk with and thank everyone while they ate.

Jan and Faith had set up several games for the occasion. The room was filled with laughter and good-natured competition.

Faith took Lizzie's hand and led her back to the rocking chair throne. "It is now time to bestow gifts on our Queen."

Everyone dragged a chair to form a semi-circle in front of Lizzie. Jan stood next to her and spoke loud enough for everyone to hear.

"Faith and I decided that a traditional bridal shower wouldn't do for you, Lizzie. You already have everything you'll ever need at the inn. We still wanted to show you how much we love you and how happy we are for you."

"This shower is as for much Wade as it is for you," Faith teased. "Bring on the lingerie!"

Lizzie opened the gifts one by one and held them for everyone to see. The lingerie ranged from elegant and pretty to naughty and "where's the rest of it." There were all sorts of colors and styles.

Faith stood when all the gifts had been opened. "It is with great sadness that I must announce the end of Queen Lizzie's rule."

"I want to thank you all for coming and for the lingerie. I'm sure Wade thanks you, too," Lizzie joked. "This has been so much fun. I especially want to thank Jan and Faith for putting this together. I love y'all."

"The wine's gone, but there's still some pizza left," Jan said. "Please, take some home with you."

The guests left, the venue was cleaned, and the gifts were loaded into Faith's car.

Lizzie had had a bit too much wine. She was dizzy and extra happy by the time they got into the car. She was sound asleep when they got back to the inn.

Jan and Faith left her snoring in the back seat while they each took an armload of gifts inside. Wade went back to the car with them. He lifted Lizzie out of the back seat and carried her to her room.

Lizzie woke up when he kissed her forehead. "Wade, wait 'til you see what I got."

"I'll see it later," he said and brushed a strand of hair from her face.

Wade left her on the bed and helped carry in the remaining gifts.

"How much did she have to drink?" he asked Jan.

"Not as much as you'd think. She didn't eat much. Some food should sober her up."

"Did she have fun?"

"We all did," said Faith. "The bachelorette party will be even better."

"I thought this was her bachelorette," Wade said with a raised brow.

"Nope, this was a lingerie shower," Faith informed him. "She got some things that I think you'll find interesting."

Wade looked at her with a mischievous smile. "Oh yeah?"

"Oh, yeah!" said Jan with a grin.

The two women said goodnight and drove away. Wade and Lois let Lizzie sleep while they made dinner together.

"When are James and Ellen going to be back?" Wade asked.

"They should be here any minute."

* * *

Grace drove from Tulsa to Wichita Falls. She turned in her rental car and took a cab to Sikes Center Mall. She waited in the coffee shop for her brother.

She saw him before he saw her, and she was pleased to see Ellen with him.

She waited while James and Ellen ordered coffee. They sat at a distant table, acknowledging each other with a wink and a slight nod.

She collected her belongings and left the shop. She strolled through the parking lot toward their car, dragging her luggage behind her. She stopped when she located their car.

James and Ellen finished their coffee and strolled outside. Grace was near their car when James remotely opened the trunk and unlocked the car doors.

Grace stored her luggage inside, closed the trunk, and got into the backseat. James and Ellen took their places in the front seat. No one spoke until they had driven out of the parking lot.

"It's so good to see you two," Grace said.

"I almost didn't recognize you," James said.

"I thought it would be smart to change my looks a bit."

"You look great," said Ellen.

"How are things at home?" Grace queried.

James and Ellen looked at each other before James said, "We had to tell Wade and Dan the truth."

"Why? What happened?"

"Two FBI agents came to the inn looking for you," Ellen said. "Wade and Dan were there."

"After the agents left, Wade wanted to know what we were hiding. We had to tell them. It ended in a big fight."

"Wade was on the brink of canceling the wedding," Ellen added.

"I'm so sorry," said Grace. "I didn't want to cause problems. Have you worked everything out?"

Ellen nodded, "We've all made up, but there have to be some changes."

"We promised we wouldn't keep anything from them again," James said. "They're part of our family now. They know we came to pick you up."

"I understand," Grace said and paused. "It's a good thing Wade knows about my predicament. I might need his help."

"Are you still in trouble?" Ellen asked.

"I'm not sure," Grace replied.

"What were you able to find out?" James asked.

Grace told them about her conversations with Rick Jackson and

Oliver Baldwin. They discussed possible implications and solutions for the remainder of the drive.

They arrived at the inn to find dinner ready, and Lizzie still tipsy.

Lois met them at the door and hugged Grace. "I'm so glad you're back here where you belong."

"Me too, Mom."

Grace approached Wade and said, "I'm so sorry about all the secrecy. I never meant to cause problems for you. I've been hiding and keeping secrets for so long that it's second nature."

"I understand," Wade said. "It's time to stop running now."

"You're right," Grace said. "I'll do my best."

"Where's Dan?" James asked.

"He called and said he was running a little late," Lois said. "He should be here soon."

"We need to lock up while Grace is here," said James.

"I'll take care of that," Wade said and left the room.

"How was your party," Ellen asked Lizzie.

Lizzie giggled and said, "It was so much fun. You should see what I got. Aunt Grace, I saved you an inv…inv…invitation."

Wade walked into the room and grinned. "She had more wine than food."

"We'd better feed her then," James smirked.

Dan opened the door and said, "Is there any left?"

"We haven't started," Lois said. "We were waiting for you."

James locked the back door behind Dan. They all sat at the table and began to eat. Wade made sure that Lizzie ate enough to dilute the wine still in her system.

"Did you get everything moved?" James asked Wade.

"I moved my things into the spare bedroom and packed up everything I won't need. I still have to move those boxes and my furniture to storage. I thought I'd do that a little at a time over the next few days."

They continued to make polite conversation until they'd

finished eating. The dishes were cleared away, and the family gathered around the dining table again.

"I understand the FBI has been here," Grace said. "What did they want to know?"

Lois told her about the encounter.

"I'm sorry for the trouble I caused. Wade, Dan, I'm sorry that you've been caught in the middle of it."

"Grace agreed that we shouldn't keep secrets from each other anymore," James told them.

Grace nodded.

"Is Sharp still a threat?" Lois asked.

"Not according to Mr. Jackson."

She shared the news about Sharp with the group.

"If Sharp or his people aren't looking for you, then who is?" asked Dan.

"That's why I'm still taking precautions," Grace told him. "I spoke with my boss last night. He seems to think that someone else is responsible for the tracker and the break-in. He said that the message on the mirror points to someone who knows about my past. He thinks that I'm being set up."

"Set up for what?" asked Ellen.

"I don't know," Grace said. "Oliver told me that the agents were more aggressive when they last questioned him. One of them more so than the other. They've been tracking my movements. I let my location be known twice, and they knew about those before they talked to Oliver."

"Why did you do that?" asked Lois.

"I wanted to lead Sharp's people away from here and make them think I was headed back toward Vegas."

"When did the agents visit your boss?" asked Wade

"Oliver said they were there on Wednesday."

Wade scowled and said, "Either the agents that were here didn't have that information, or they chose not to share it with us. Did Oliver mention either of the agents' names?"

"I believe one of them was Welborn. He didn't mention the other."

"He's the nasty man that was here asking questions," Lois said with a frown.

"Oliver said he gave him the impression that I was a suspect," said Grace.

"Grace, I know you've told the family everything," said Wade. "I have to ask. Is there even the slightest chance that you know Peter Crisp?"

"I've never heard of or met anyone by that name," Grace said. However, I am acquainted with an FBI agent."

Grace told them about Todd and explained their relationship.

"You know Todd Anthony?" asked Wade, amazed. "Have you ever met Jody Ratliff?"

"No, who is Ratliff?" Grace replied.

"She was a young woman who was murdered here last week. She was FBI from Las Vegas," Wade told her. "Todd Anthony is listed as her next of kin."

Grace stared at Wade. She shook her head and said, "I never met her. We didn't talk about our families. How were they related?"

"The file didn't specify their relationship," Wade told her. "When did you last see Todd?"

"We were together on the fourth of July," Grace told him. "I haven't seen him since then. I was waiting for him the night the tracker was put on my car."

"This is too weird to be a coincidence. I'm pretty sure the FBI knows more than they've told us," Wade said. "They'll be back looking for you if you're a suspect."

"What should we do if they come back?" asked Lois.

"Unless they have a warrant, we won't tell them that Grace is here," answered Wade. "We won't lie to them. We won't volunteer any information either. At least not until they've been upfront with us."

"Are you sure they'll be back?" asked Lizzie.

"They'll be back," Wade replied with a scowl.

Together they discussed what Grace's next move should be. It was decided that her presence shouldn't be common knowledge. She'd stay on the farm while trying to sort things out, and go into protective custody if needed.

They said goodnight when everyone was satisfied with the plan. Grace went home with James, Ellen, and her mother.

Grace went to sleep that night, happy to be with her family again.

CHAPTER FIFTEEN

WADE DROVE into the parking lot the next morning and saw Megan go into the office with a big box. His mind flashed back to a time when she brought goodies for him.

He laughed and hurried inside. He didn't want to miss his deputies' reactions.

Odom and Megan were alone in the outer office. Wade passed by them and overheard part of their conversation.

"I decided to bring you some donuts," Megan was saying.

'Thanks!" Clint said. "Why did you bring so many? I can't eat all of these."

"I thought you'd like to share with everyone else. I was going to bring coffee until I remembered there's a coffee machine here."

"I appreciate this, Megan," said her brother. "I'm sure the rest of the staff will too."

Megan lingered until Odom told her that he had to get to work. She smiled, said goodbye, and left the office.

Odom carried the box of donuts to the break room. Lodge had been standing out of sight until Megan had gone. He went to his desk with a donut in one hand and a cup of coffee in the other.

Baker walked in red-face and flustered. Megan had stopped him in the parking lot. He wore a splotch of lipstick on his cheek where she'd kissed him. He went to the Men's room and scrubbed his face before going to his desk.

"Want a donut?" Lodge asked with a wicked smile.

Baker glared at him and didn't answer.

Reed came into the office, and Lodge said, "Megan Ford brought donuts. Baker got extra frosting."

Reed watched Baker's face redden.

"Knock it off!" Baker shouted. "At least she didn't ambush me while I was on a date."

Lodge laughed and looked at Reed. "You could be next."

Reed smiled. "I think she's interested in one of you. You'd better be on your toes."

"Come on, guys," Odom said. "She was trying to do something nice."

"We don't mean to be disrespectful," said Reed. "This isn't the first time she's tried to get attention with baked goods."

"Hey, Sheriff!" shouted Lodge. "Tell Odom about the time Megan brought you sweet treats every day."

Wade stood in the doorway of his office and said, "Have a little consideration for Odom. He hasn't known Megan as long as we have."

"I've heard stories about her," Odom admitted. "I saw how she behaved last year. Why did she bring things to you?"

"Lizzie and I weren't dating at the time," Wade answered. "She was working with us as an interim deputy. It was unethical to date a subordinate."

"Megan saw an opportunity," Odom said, nodding in understanding.

"She was trying to hurt Lizzie," Wade told him. "They didn't get along."

The ringing of a telephone ended their conversation. The deputies returned to their work and Wade to his office.

He drummed his fingers on his desk. He picked up the intercom and buzzed Reed's desk.

"Yes, Sir," Reed replied.

"Would you and Maddie come to my office, please?"

"Maddie's in the lab. I'll call over there and let her know," Reed replied.

Wade was moving a second chair in front of his desk when Reed entered his office. Maddie appeared in the doorway a moment later. Wade indicated that they should sit down.

"I want to discuss how to handle the interviews, especially the one this afternoon," Wade told them.

"When are the other two interviews?" asked Reed.

"One is tomorrow morning, and the other tomorrow afternoon," Maddie said. "We need to handle them all in the same way. We don't want to risk a lawsuit."

"I agree," Wade replied.

"Do you expect a lawsuit?" Reed asked.

"We don't want to take the chance, given Wade's relationship with Mr. Wagner," Maddie pointed out.

"That's true," Reed agreed.

"We've already talked about using the same method used when hiring Gonzalez and Odom," Wade said. "Everyone will ask questions and rank the candidates. Do you both agree to that?"

"Agreed," Maddie said.

Reed nodded.

"I've given the matter a lot of thought since Maddie informed me that Wagner is a qualified applicant," Wade told them. "I've decided that I won't take part in the interviews."

"Why not?" Maddie asked, surprised.

"I think it would be best that I avoid Mr. Wagner's interview. There would be too much tension for a fair assessment. That means that I shouldn't attend the other interviews either."

"That makes sense," said Reed. "How will you make the final decision without interviewing?"

"The final decision won't be mine," Wade said and smiled. "It belongs to the two of you."

"Us!" the deputies cried in unison.

"Yes," Wade said. "You'll be working more closely with the new hires than I will. You both have good instincts, and I trust your judgment. I can't trust mine in this instance."

"You'll abide by our decision?" asked Maddie.

"Yes, I will, whether I like it or not. I want you to choose the best people for this department. Don't consider my personal feelings."

"Well, okay then," said Reed. "It's about time for our team meeting."

The trio left Wade's office and made their way to the conference room. Reed called the meeting to order. They discussed their lack of progress in solving the case and brainstormed their next moves.

"Everyone has an assignment," said Reed. "Half of us will continue the search for the mystery man, and the rest of us will focus on finding more information about the victim. Maddie, did you want to talk about our upcoming interviews?"

Maddie shared their plans. "Wade wants us to make our choices based on what's best for the department and disregard his personal feelings. Our first applicant will be here this afternoon.

Take some time to come up with questions that you'd like to have answered by all of the candidates. There may be others that you think of while we're interviewing. You'll have the opportunity to ask those questions before the interviews are over.

Keep in mind that the application window won't close until the end of September. We don't have to hire anyone right away."

Wade returned to his office and started a nationwide search of law enforcement. He suspected that Anthony had lied to Grace about being an undercover agent.

Lodge tapped on Wade's door and asked, "Do you have a minute?"

"Sure."

"I thought that I'd be able to move the refrigerator from my apartment since they're remodeling. It turns out that I can't. Would it be possible to rent yours?"

Wade beamed at his deputy. "I've been wondering what to do with mine. You just saved me the trouble of storing or selling it."

"How much would the rent be?"

"It's a loan," Wade said. "I'll decide what to do with it when you go back to your apartment."

Lodge smiled at his boss. "Thanks, Wade. Do you need help moving anything?"

"I'm waiting until the last minute to move the couch. I may need help with it."

"You've got it," Lodge said, grinning.

Wade worked in his office until lunchtime. He went home to have a quick meal and relax. He hoped taking his mind off the case for a while would help him focus when he started again.

He went back to work a few minutes early. He knew Wagner would soon be there for his interview.

His job during the interview was to answer phones and deal with anyone who came to the office. He had all calls routed to his phone. The outer office would be quiet enough that he'd be able to hear the door if anyone came in.

He kept himself busy until Drake Wagner arrived. He greeted Drake and shook his hand.

"I won't be participating in the interviews or making the final decision. I've left that in the hands of my lead deputies."

Drake seemed to be relieved and said, "I appreciate the information."

Wade led Drake to the conference room and introduced him. Reed waited until Wade had left the room to begin the interview.

Wade went back to his office and checked his computer. He heard the main door open, and he went to greet the visitor.

"I understand that you're looking for me," said the man.

Wade couldn't believe his eyes. "Yes, I'm Sheriff Adams."

"Layne Reece," the man said and shook Wade's hand.

"Please, come into my office. I need to ask you some questions."

The man followed Wade and sat down in front of his desk.

"Do you live around here, Mr. Reece?"

"Temporarily. I'm working with a construction crew. I've been living in a trailer at the site. What's this about?"

Wade took Jody Ratliff's photo from a file and handed it to Reece. He noticed a blemish on the man's right wrist.

"Do you know her, or have you seen her with anyone?"

Reece looked at the photo and clenched his jaw. "No, what does this have to do with me."

"Her body was found Tuesday afternoon. She'd been shot in the back. We located one of her friends who said she ran into a man that she knew here in town. Her friend didn't have a name or description."

"Why me?" Reece said and scowled.

"You and this woman were at the Paradise Creek Inn at the same time."

"There were a lot of people there that day." Reece challenged.

"Yes, there were. We've talked with everyone except you."

"Wait, was she the good-looking blonde in the tight dress?"

"Yes," Wade answered and tried not to smile.

"I do remember her, but I didn't talk to her."

"Did you see anyone talking with this woman or anyone who seemed to be interested in her?" Wade asked.

Reece grinned. "I think every man there was interested in her. I didn't see anyone do more than stare."

"Why were you at the inn?" Wade asked.

"I was bored. I saw a flyer about the reopening and went just to pass the afternoon."

"May I have your phone number and address? There may be other questions that come up in the investigation."

Reece gave him a phone number. "I don't have an address. I'm not in one place for more than a day or two."

"I don't anticipate more questions. The phone number should be enough," Wade told him. "Thank you for coming in."

"I'm sorry that I can't help you," said Reece and stood.

Wade walked him to the door and went back to his office. Their last lead was gone.

"Mr. Wagner," Reed began. "What makes you a good candidate for Wilbarger County Deputy?"

"I was a forest ranger in Colorado for many years. One of the responsibilities was to patrol the area and enforce the laws and regulations within the national park."

"Have you had other training?" Maddie inquired.

"I completed police academy training last month," Drake replied.

"Why the Sheriff's department rather than the police department?" queried Baker.

"I prefer country living to city life," Drake said. "Patrolling and answering calls across the entire county is more appealing to me than being stuck in town."

There were more questions about his experience and his reasons for leaving his job in Colorado.

"Do you have any questions for us?" offered Maddie.

Drake asked the standard questions about the pay, hours, and overtime.

"Does anyone have anything else to ask Mr. Wagner?" asked Maddie.

"I have a question. We need to get this out in the open and be done with it," said Lodge. "Mr. Wagner, we all know you have a history with Lizzie Fletcher. Do you think you can work alongside Sheriff Adams, considering the circumstances?"

"I'm glad you asked," Drake said. "I've thought this through and talked it over with my family. I wouldn't have applied if I didn't think I could work with the sheriff. My relationship with Miss Fletcher is in the past, and I'm moving on with my life. I need a job, and I need to stay near my family. I hope that I can be part of this family too."

"Thank you, Mr. Wagner," Maddie said. "We have two more interviews this week. The application window is open until the end of September. We'll make a decision then and contact you either way. Please, let us know if you take another position before then."

"I will," Drake said. "Thank you for your time."

Drake left the building, and the deputies discussed their thoughts.

"He interviewed well," Maddie said. "The only professional problem is his lack of experience."

"I agree that's the one professional issue," Reed said, stressing the word professional.

"All right, let's talk about the elephant in the room," suggested Maddie. "We shouldn't disqualify him because of his past relationship with Wade's fiancé. We should disqualify him if that could cause problems in this department."

"We have two more interviews scheduled," Reed added. "It's possible that we could have more applications before time runs out."

"Do the other two applicants have more experience?" asked Gonzalez.

"Yes," Maddie answered. "We shouldn't rule out any of the applicants before we've finished all the interviews. We need to choose someone who will be a good fit with our team."

Wade knocked on the conference room door before he opened it and said, "I'm sorry to interrupt your discussion. Our mystery man was just here."

Wade shared the contents of the conversation with the team.

"I guess that means that the investigation is stalled unless we catch a break or find new evidence," Reed said.

"I'm afraid so," Wade agreed.

"Does anyone have any suggestions?" Reed asked.

"We should question everyone again," Maddie said. "Ratliff's friends were upset when you spoke with them. They may have more to tell us now that the initial shock has passed."

"We need to ask more specific questions," Odom suggested.

"We'll start again," Reed said. "And we'll keep digging into Agent Ratliff's background. "She may have been on vacation, but her murder still could have been case-related."

"I'll let you finish your discussion," Wade said and started toward the door.

"I have a question for the sheriff," Lodge said. "It pertains to Wagner."

Wade turned and said, "All right."

"Do you think that you can work with Wagner considering his past relationship with Fletcher?"

Wade nodded and said, "I've been expecting that question. I've been thinking about this since I read his application. I want you to choose the best people for the job. Should you choose Drake Wagner for one of the positions, I'll put my personal feelings aside and make the best of it."

"Lodge asked Wagner the same question," Reed told him. "He said he wouldn't have applied if he thought he'd have an issue."

"That's good to know," Wade replied.

He went back to his office and left the deputies to their discussion. He prayed that the other two applicants, that anyone, would be a better fit than Drake Wagner.

He wondered if he and Wagner might have been friends if not for Lizzie. He wondered if they'd ever get past the rivalry.

Noise from his computer got his attention. The search was finished, and a photo of Todd Anthony filled the screen.

He picked up the phone and called the inn.

"Paradise Creek Inn, this is Ellen."

"Ellen, this is Wade. I need to talk with all of you, especially Grace."

"Is it bad news?" asked Ellen.

"I haven't made up my mind," Wade told her. "Will everyone be there for dinner?"

"I'll make sure they are," Ellen told him. "We'll see you at six."

Wade frowned at his computer screen. He printed the information and put it in a file folder. He went to the outer office and took down photos of the missing agent and Jody Ratliff.

He made copies of the photos and returned the originals to the bulletin board. He put the copies in the file folder with the computer information.

Wade looked up a Wichita Falls phone number. He dialed and asked to speak with Patricia Catlin.

"This is Patricia. How may I help you?"

"Miss Catlin, this is Sheriff Wade Adams. We spoke last week."

"Do you have any news about Jody's death?"

"No, I'm sorry. We're still investigating," Wade told her. "I have more questions if you have the time."

"I have a few minutes," the woman said. "What can I help you with?"

"Did Miss Ratliff ever mention a man named Todd Anthony?"

"He's her uncle."

"Do you happen to know how to reach him?"

"No, I'm sorry.

"Do you have any idea where he works?" asked Wade.

"No, why do you ask?"

"Mr. Anthony is listed as her next of kin," Wade told her. "I haven't been able to get in touch with him. Do you happen to know if there are other family members that I should contact?"

"Jody's dad passed away from cancer when she was little. Her mother died in a car accident when we were in college. Todd is her mother's brother."

"Do you happen to know her mother's name?" queried Wade.

"Her name was Valerie," Catlin replied.

"Did Miss Ratliff have any siblings?"

"No, she was a baby when her dad died. Her mother never remarried."

"Did she ever mention any coworkers or friends in Las Vegas?"

"Not that I recall. Jody was a shy and private person," Patricia told him. "It took her a long time to make friends."

"I have one more question," Wade told her. "You said that she told you she ran into a friend in Vernon. Was that before or after she visited the inn?"

"It might have been at the inn," Patricia suggested. "She would have driven through a fast-food place or ordered delivery rather than go into a restaurant. I doubt she would have socialized with anyone she didn't know."

"Thank you for your time, Miss Catlin. You've been a great help," Wade said and ended the call.

He dialed Lizzie's number.

"Hi, Sweetheart," she answered.

"Hi, Darlin'," Wade replied. "Were the inn's surveillance cameras on during the reopening?"

"I'm pretty sure they were," she told him.

"Have the videos been erased?"

"Hold on, and I'll check."

Wade waited for Lizzie to search for the video.

"It's still here," she said at last.

"Will you email it to me?"

"I can try. It's a big file," she told him. "It might be better to share it through the cloud."

"Save it to your computer first," he said. "I don't want to risk losing it. There might be a lead there."

"I'll let you know when I've uploaded it," Lizzie told him.

"Thanks, Babe," he said and hung up.

Wade went to Reed's desk. He told him what he'd learned from his conversation with Miss Catlin.

"I've decided to try to find her family," he told his deputy.

"They may know something that will point us in the right direction."

"We need something to go on," Reed agreed. "I'm getting tired of stumbling around and grasping at straws."

Wade went back to his office and started a general search for Valerie Ratliff. This time the information was easy to find. It listed Todd Anthony as her brother and both her parents as deceased. There were no other living relatives listed.

Wade's cell phone rang half an hour later.

"The file is too big," Lizzie told him. "I could download it to a flash drive, but I don't have one here with enough memory."

"I'll get one and bring it to you," Wade said. "I need to see that video."

"Get one with the highest memory you can find," Lizzie advised. "Mama said that you need to talk with us. Will you be able to stay for dinner?"

"Yes, but I may need to come back to town tonight," he told her. "It depends on what we can find on the surveillance video."

"I'll see you soon," Lizzie said, and the call ended.

It was four o'clock, and Wade didn't want to wait any longer to look at the surveillance video. He picked up the file folder and told Reed that he'd be back in the morning. He drove to the local super-center and bought two of the highest-capacity flash drives he could find.

CHAPTER SIXTEEN

WADE DROVE to the inn and went inside. Ellen was sitting at the dining room table, flipping through pages of a cookbook.

"Hello, Wade," she said. "I wasn't expecting you before dinner."

"I need to look at some of the surveillance videos," he told her. "Is Lizzie in her office?"

"She's with a client," Ellen told him. "It may be another thirty minutes before she's finished. Can I make you a snack or a glass of tea?"

"You don't have to wait on me," he told her. "I'll make us both a glass of tea."

Ellen smiled and said, "Thank you."

Wade went to the kitchen and took a pitcher of tea from the fridge. He filled two glasses with ice and poured the tea.

He went back to the dining room and sat down beside Ellen. She took a sip from her glass.

"I could get used to this," she said and winked at Wade.

He looked at the cookbook in front of Ellen. "What are you planning to make?"

"I'm browsing for something different," she told him. "I like to add some variety to our menu now and again."

They were chatting about food when Lizzie joined them.

"We have another event booked for November," she said.

"What kind of event?" Ellen asked.

"It's an early Thanksgiving banquet for a large family," Lizzie answered. "Wade, my office is free. We can download that video when you're ready."

"Do you have more clients today?"

"That was the last one for the day," she replied.

"We'd better lock up then," Wade told her.

"I'll go get Grace and Lois," Ellen said. "I'll be back in a few minutes."

Wade and Lizzie locked all of the exterior doors to the inn. They left the back door unlocked so that Lizzie's family could get in while they worked.

They went to Lizzie's office. Wade drug an extra chair behind the desk and watched her pull up the requested video.

"This could be a waste of time," he told her. "We'll wait to download it to the flash drives until I've watched it. Can you fast-forward it to the point that Jody Ratliff got here?"

Lizzie ran the footage to the point that Jody Ratliff entered the inn and backed it up a few seconds. She let it run at normal speed while Wade stared at the screen.

"What are you looking for?" she inquired.

"Ratliff's friend thinks she might have met someone she knew that day," Wade said. "She may have talked with someone that we didn't notice."

They watched the footage of Jody on the inn tour and at the refreshment tables. They didn't see anything of interest until she was talking with Lois at the information desk.

"Wait!" Wade exclaimed, "Right there! Did you see that?"

"I didn't see anything," Lizzie said and rewound the recording.

"Your Granny said the woman looked over her shoulder a few times. Get ready to pause it. Now!"

The young woman was looking at someone in a group of people. It was difficult to tell who had drawn her attention.

"Granny wasn't looking at her in this frame," Lizzie said.

"Can you zoom in on the crowd there?"

There was one person in the group who was looking toward Jody Ratliff. It was the man with the military haircut, Layne Reece.

"Can you move it forward in slow motion? I want to see if they talk to each other."

They watched Layne Reece approach Ratliff at the information desk. She was listening to Lois when he brushed her arm in passing. She looked over her shoulder and watched him go out the front door. She followed when she'd finished her conversation with Lois.

"It looks like they knew each other," Lizzie observed.

"Let's look at that again and zoom in," Wade suggested.

Lizzie backed up to the point that Reece approached Ratliff. She enlarged the image and advanced it frame by frame.

"Right there, it looks like he touched her to get her attention," Wade said with excitement.

The recording was advanced again. They paused it when Grace entered the office.

"What are you watching?" she queried and moved behind them. She gasped and put a hand over her mouth.

She saw a man with a military haircut wearing jeans and a T-shirt. He had his back to the camera.

"What's wrong?" Lizzie asked.

"That's him," Grace said and pointed at the screen.

"Who?" Wade asked and looked at her in confusion.

"That's the man that put the tracker on my car?"

"Are you sure?" Wade asked, stunned.

"Yes! His T-shirt is a different color, but that's him."

"What does he look like?" Wade asked, already knowing the answer.

"I only saw him from the back," Grace said. "I saw a mole or something similar on his right wrist. You can't see it in this photo."

"Does the name Layne Reece mean anything to you?" asked Wade.

"No," Grace answered.

"Lizzie, back it up so Grace can see the man's face."

The recording was rewound to the point that Reece was looking at Ratliff. Lizzie zoomed in so that Grace could see clearly.

"Does he look familiar from this angle?" Wade asked.

Grace stared at the image. Something niggled at the back of her mind.

"There's something familiar. I might have seen him somewhere," Grace said. "But I don't know him. Is this what you wanted to talk with me about?"

"No, this is brand new information," Wade said. "I want to talk with everyone about what I learned today. I need to finish with this video first."

"I'll go help with dinner," Grace said and left them alone.

"What else do you want to see?" Lizzie asked.

"I want to see what the outdoor cameras recorded. Pull up the videos from out front and the parking area."

Lizzie located the files from the front camera. They could see Layne Reece exit the inn and walk toward the parking area. Jody Ratliff soon followed. They had no contact.

"Try the parking area now," Wade said.

The parking area video showed no direct contact between the two. Reece dropped something near a tree, went to his car, and drove away. Ratliff followed a few minutes later, picked up the item, and went to her car.

Wade leaned back in his chair and scowled.

"What's wrong?" asked Lizzie. "Isn't this what you needed?"

"That man came to see me today. He told me that he didn't know Ratliff and hadn't seen her before that day."

"Why would he lie about knowing her?" Lizzie asked, then realized what that could mean. "Did we have a murderer at the inn that day?"

Wade looked at her and winked. "It wouldn't be the first time."

Lizzie stared at him. "I know, but I don't have to like it."

"Think about it, Darlin'," Wade said. "We might never have met if there weren't bodies found here. You could be married to Drake Wagner."

"Wade Adams!" Lizzie said with a smirk. "You should be ashamed of yourself!"

He took her in his arms and kissed her. "I'm sorry. I'm just grateful that you're in my life."

Lizzie kissed him and snuggled close. "I've missed you this past week. Do you think Layne Reece could be responsible for Ratliff's death?"

"He just moved to the top of the suspect list," Wade told her. "Especially since he's the only one we have."

"Do you want me to download all of these files?"

"Download those we've already seen," he said and handed her the flash drives. "Save the rest if there's room."

Dinner was almost ready by the time Lizzie finished downloading the video files.

"Ellen said you wanted to see us," said James.

"We need to talk," Wade told him. "I left a file in my truck. I'll get it, and then we'll get started."

Wade left and went to his truck. He returned with the file folder in hand and locked the back door behind him.

"I think we should all sit down. There have been some developments in the case," Wade said.

Wade waited while they sat down. He took a chair near Grace.

"Grace, I'd like for you to look at these photos."

He handed her a picture. "Do you recognize her?"

"No, who is she?"

"That is Jody Ratliff, our murder victim. It turns out that she's Todd Anthony's niece. I haven't been able to find any other living relatives."

He handed her another picture. "Do you know this man?"

Grace looked at the image and smiled. "That's Todd."

"I had a feeling," Wade said. "This is the photo the FBI showed us. He's their missing agent.

Grace stared at the photo for a moment, speechless. Tears filled her eyes. "That explains why I haven't heard from him," she said when she regained her voice. "How long has he been missing?"

"Welborn told me it had been three weeks," Wade said and patted her arm.

"If Todd is the missing agent, who is Peter Crisp?" Grace queried.

"I wish I had an answer," Wade said. "When did you last hear from Todd?"

"It was the end of July. He called to tell me Happy Birthday on the twenty-ninth," Grace said. "We arranged to meet for dinner on August fourteenth."

"That would put his disappearance on or around August fifth," Wade surmised.

"What do you think is going on, Wade?" Dan asked.

"It's always bothered me that Ratliff turned out to be Las Vegas FBI," Wade said. "At first, I thought Grace was being investigated and on the run."

"Thanks," Grace said with sarcasm.

"Sorry, it's the cop in me," he said to Grace. "I also thought that Ratliff could have been the source for your casino piece. Now that I know your story and the reason for Ratliff's visit, I could see it as a coincidence if it weren't for our mystery man with the military haircut."

"What about him?" Lois asked.

"Grace recognized him from the surveillance video as the man who put the tracker on her car. It's obvious from the video that he and Ratliff knew each other."

"What does this have to do with us?" asked Lizzie.

"I don't know," Wade admitted. "Grace, Todd Anthony, and Jody Ratliff all live in Las Vegas. I was able to verify that Todd is an undercover agent. Jody Ratliff worked in the forensics lab. Do you have any idea what Anthony was doing undercover?"

"He never told me," Grace answered in a whisper.

"I think you all need to be extremely careful until I can get to the bottom of this," Wade told the family. "I agree with Grace's boss. Something isn't right. Someone may be trying to set her up. Whoever is behind this won't care about taking the rest of us down with her."

Wade stayed for dinner, then drove back to town with his mind spinning. He went to the office and sat at his desk. He marveled at how much quieter it was in the evening. He opened a file and dialed the number that Reece had given him.

"Mr. Reece, this is Sheriff Adams. Would it be possible for you to come back to my office and answer a few more questions?"

"Sheriff?" answered Reece. "What are you talking about?"

"You came to my office this afternoon about the Jody Ratliff case. I have more questions," Wade said with apprehension.

"Who's Jody Ratliff?" Reece asked. "I've been in Louisiana for the past two weeks. I got back late last night."

Wade gritted his teeth and said, "Someone came to my office this afternoon claiming to be Layne Reece. Would it be possible for me to meet you at the construction site and show you a photograph of the man?"

"What construction site?"

"Aren't you working with a construction crew?" Wade asked, already knowing the answer.

"Nah, I'm a cook at the truck stop restaurant on 287."

Wade sighed and said, "Are you there now?"

"Yeah, come on by," he said.

"I'm on my way," Wade said and hung up.

He picked up a copy of Layne Reece's photo and strode out of the office. He got in his truck and slammed the door. He beat the steering wheel with his fist a few times before he started the engine and drove to the truck stop.

The real Layne Reece was a huge man who appeared to eat most of what he cooked. He wore a grease-stained apron across his middle and several days of stubble on his chin.

"Mr. Reece," Wade began. "I'm Sheriff Adams. I spoke with you on the phone a few moments ago."

"Come in, Sheriff," said Reece and wiped two greasy chairs. "Have a seat."

Wade eyed the grimy furniture and said, "Thanks, I won't be here long. Do you know this man?"

He handed a photo to Reece.

"Nope, I don't know him," replied Reece. "You say he was passing himself off as me?"

"Yes, Sir. Do you have any idea how he might have gotten your phone number?"

"No, I've always got my phone on me except while I'm workin'. I keep it over there so I don't drop it in the food or the sink," Reece said and pointed at a table near the back door of the kitchen.

Wade looked at the unattended phone and said, "Thank you for your time, Mr. Reece."

He left the man to his work and went back to the office. He took the flash drive with the inn videos to the technology lab. He loaded the videos on a machine and saved copies of the relevant segments.

He spent a lot of time trying to identify the make and model of the car driven by the bogus Mr. Reece. The license plate wasn't visible in the videos from the inn.

Wade printed the best image he had of the white Chevy Malibu and the man's face. He made multiple copies and returned them to his office.

He typed up the pertinent information and wrote *Prime Suspect* in red across the top of each photograph. He left copies on each deputy's desk.

He had an idea while he worked. He went back to the technology lab and searched for office surveillance videos from that afternoon. He viewed the video until he found the Malibu parked in front of the department.

The license plate was partially visible. It would be easier to run a search with the entire number. He tried his best to get a better view.

Wade went back to his office and began a license plate search with the little information he had. He knew it was a long shot, but he had to try.

He sent out an all-points bulletin with photos of the false Layne Reece and the white Malibu. He leaned back and rubbed his eyes. It was getting late.

He picked up the phone and called Reed.

"Reed, I'm sorry to bother you at home," he said. "I wanted to fill you in."

Wade told Reed what he'd discovered and about the APB. They agreed to meet with the team first thing in the morning to bring them up to date.

He drove home with his mind on the case. He went inside, took a beer from the fridge, sat on the couch, and turned on the television. He wanted to think about something else for a while.

He was watching a rerun of *Friends* when his cell phone rang. He grimaced when he saw the name on the caller id. He'd forgotten to return Wyatt's call.

"Hi, Wyatt," Wade said. "I'm sorry that I didn't call you back."

"You forgot, didn't you?" Wyatt said. "I knew you would. You always forget when you're working on a case."

Wade laughed and said, "You're right."

"Do you have time to talk?" asked his brother.

"Yeah, I'm home and need a distraction."

"You told me that you didn't want a wild bachelor party. I've got an idea that I think you'll like."

"I'm listening," Wade said.

"I was looking into a fishing trip to Lake Texoma."

"Yeah, you mentioned that," Wade said.

"I have a friend who has a cabin there," Wyatt said. "He'll rent it to us at a reasonable rate. We can get three days for the price of two since it's going to be Labor Day weekend."

"I don't think that I need to be away that long," Wade said.

"I had a feeling you'd say that. That's why I've checked into a shorter trip," Wyatt told him. "How would you feel about an overnight trip to Lake Kemp?"

"That sounds like a better plan," Wade told him.

"We'd have to camp out," Wyatt said. "We can fish off the bank or the boat dock."

"That's fine with me," Wade replied. "When are you planning to do this?"

"I thought we'd leave after lunch Saturday afternoon. We can set up camp and fish all night. We won't have to leave until five o'clock Sunday night."

"That sounds good to me, Wyatt. Who are you planning to invite?"

"Family members and your deputies are on the list. Is there anyone else you'd like to invite?"

"Did you include James Fletcher and Dan Hayes?"

"I did."

"I can't think of anyone else," Wade told him. "Can I ask you something?"

"Ask away," Wyatt replied.

"Did you have everything figured out before you married Becky?"

"We thought we did. It turned out we were wrong," Wyatt said and laughed.

"What happened?"

"We had an apartment all picked out and made plans to move in. Neither of us had ever lived on our own. We didn't know the first thing about renting apartments. We should have asked for advice, but we wanted to do it ourselves."

"I think I remember this story," Wade said. "It turned out to be a dump, didn't it?"

"Yep. The apartment we looked at was amazing. We thought they'd all look that way. We ended up in a trashed-out, rat-invested apartment with a leaky roof. The only good thing about it was that we were on the second floor. The first floor had sewage problems."

Wade roared with laughter. "I don't have to worry about that."

"I take it you've decided where you're going to live," said Wyatt.

"We're going to live at the inn and see how that goes. We may end up moving into town," Wade said.

"It's not going to be easy living under the nose of your in-laws," Wyatt advised.

"It hasn't been a problem so far."

"Wait until you have your first big fight," Wyatt warned. "You'll find out then if they're going to be meddlers."

"Are Becky's parents meddlers?" Wade asked.

"They were at first. I'm sure it's natural. We may be meddlers when our kids get married."

"How did you handle it?"

"Becky took care of it. I don't know exactly what she said, but the gist of it was that we're adults and have to make our own decisions."

"How did they take that?" asked Wade.

"Pretty well," Wyatt said. "We haven't had any issues since then."

"Lizzie and I had a pretty big fight the other night," Wade confessed. "Her family didn't get into it, so I don't anticipate them being meddlers."

"Every couple has fights," Wyatt said. "Becky and I had a doozy the week before our wedding."

The brothers lived in different parts of Texas and seldom saw each other. The distance between them shrank as they talked for more than an hour about married life and life in general.

The call ended, and Wade was grateful for the break from the case. He went to bed that night and slept better than he had in more than a week.

CHAPTER SEVENTEEN

WADE WAS at the office early the next day. He wanted to make sure the clips from the Inn video could be seen when his team arrived.

The team gathered in the conference room, and Wade shared what he'd learned. Their top priority was to find the bogus Layne Reece and his car.

"I want to know what he left for Ratliff to pick up," said Reed.

"Her personal effects are still here," Maddie said. "It could be with them."

"It would have been small," Wade said. "It could be almost anything, a scrap of paper, a pen, or a flash drive. They both held it in one hand."

They discussed the new information and their options. Having a suspect to focus on gave the investigation a new outlook.

"Before we adjourn," Maddie began, "Sherri Logsdon will be here soon for her interview."

"What time will she be here?" asked Reed.

Maddie looked at the clock on the wall and said, "In twenty minutes."

"Take a quick break and gather your interview notes," Reed told the team. "We'll meet back here in fifteen minutes."

Wade went to his office and had all incoming calls routed to his phone during the interview. The team was assembled in the conference room when he heard the outer door open. He went to greet the visitor.

He extended his hand and introduced himself. "I'm Sheriff Adams. Are you Miss Logsdon?"

"Yes. It's nice to meet you," she replied.

Sherri Logsdon was a tall woman with an athletic build. She wore little makeup, and her hair was pulled into a tight bun. Wade guessed her to be in her mid-thirties.

"The team is ready for you in the conference room," he said and led the way.

Introductions were made, and he left the conference room. His phone was ringing when he returned to his office.

"Sheriff's office, this is Adams," he answered.

"This is Brock Welborn. I want to know why you're investigating one of our agents."

"We've been researching everyone who might be able to give us a lead. Who are you concerned about?" Wade asked, intentionally antagonizing the man.

"Agent Todd Anthony," Welborn replied through gritted teeth.

"I'm sure you're aware that he's listed as the uncle and next of kin of our victim," Wade said.

"Was your search helpful?"

"Not in the way I expected. Why did you tell us your missing agent was Peter Crisp when in reality, it's Anthony?" Wade demanded.

"Peter Crisp is code," Welborn admitted. "Our undercover agents know to check in with their handlers when that name is used."

"You expected him to get the code through Grace Stewart," said Wade.

"We hoped he would," Welborn said. "We still need to speak with Ms. Stewart. Have you heard from her?"

Wade hesitated before answering. He didn't want to tip their hand. He knew the FBI was more aware of Grace's movements than they admitted in their previous meeting.

"I know that the family heard from her over the weekend," he said. "I know that she's safe. I don't know any other details of the conversation."

"Sheriff, I have a difficult time believing that you don't know exactly where Ms. Stewart is at the moment," Welborn accused.

"It doesn't matter what you believe," Wade retorted. "I've been busy trying to find the person responsible for your Agent Ratliff's death. Everything else has taken a backseat."

"Including your wedding?"

"I'm trying to solve this case before my wedding," Wade informed him. "I'd prefer to focus on my bride at that time."

"Searching for Agent Anthony won't help your case. His body was found yesterday."

"You have my condolences," Wade said. "Do you know what happened?"

"We're still waiting for the autopsy report." Welborn sighed. "I know that he'd been shot."

"Is it possible that our cases are connected?" Wade asked.

Welborn ignored Wade's question and said, "Ms. Stewart is a person of interest in this case. We need to speak with her soon, or we'll be forced to issue a warrant for her arrest."

"I'll let her family know," Wade said. "I'm sure they'll give her your message if they hear from her again."

Welborn hung up without another word. Wade dialed Lizzie's number and waited.

"Hi, Sweetheart."

"Lizzie, I have some bad news for your aunt," he told her and shared the news about Todd Anthony. "She needs to know. I thought it might be easier to hear coming from one of y'all."

"Do you know any details?"

"No," Wade told her. "There isn't much chance that I will unless our case is connected to his murder."

"I'll tell Granny," Lizzie said. "She'll know the best way to handle telling Aunt Grace."

"Tell her that she needs to stay away from the inn," Wade warned. "Welborn could show up at any time. Y'all need to devise a way to alert her when he does. She needs a good place to hide."

"I have an idea," Lizzie began.

"I don't want to know," Wade interrupted. "Welborn is liable to do anything to get the information. I can't tell him what I don't know."

The phone call ended, and Wade stared at the wall. His mind replayed the conversation with the FBI agent. *What if these two cases are connected? The FBI may take over the Ratliff case. We need to solve this one. On the other hand, handing it over to the FBI would free us up for deputy interviews and routine business.*

I should let Maddie and Reed know something in case Welborn shows up here. Too many closed-door meetings might arouse suspicion with the rest of the team. I'll have to make time to talk with them.

Reed tapped on Wade's door, interrupting his thoughts. He invited his deputy inside. Reed sat down in front of the desk.

"How did the interview go?" Wade asked.

"It went well," Reed told him. "Logsdon will be a good addition to our team."

"What time is the next interview?"

"It's going to be at four. She has to finish her shift at her current position and then drive a couple of hours to get here."

"I've forgotten where she's from," Wade said.

"She's coming from Anson, Texas," Reed informed him. "I think she's originally from somewhere around Houston."

"Has Maddie had any more applications?"

"Not that I'm aware," Reed said.

"It would be nice to have a bigger pool to choose from," Wade pointed out.

Reed smirked at his boss. "That would make it less likely for Drake Wagner to be hired."

Wade looked at him with surprise. "I wasn't thinking about that. I'd like to have the best people we can get to join the team."

"I don't suppose there have been any case developments since our meeting," Reed said.

"Welborn called and wanted to know why we were checking into one of his agents," Wade said and gave him the highlights of their conversation. "I didn't share our most recent information with him."

"He wasn't forthcoming with us," Reed observed. "I don't think we're obligated to share."

"I don't plan to share anything else until I have to," Wade told him.

Reed left the office, and Wade picked up his phone. He buzzed the intercom on Maddie's desk.

"Yes, Sir," Maddie answered.

"Do you have lunch plans?"

"No, Sir,"

"I'll buy," Wade said. "I'll meet you at my truck at noon."

"Yes, Sir."

Maddie was standing beside the passenger door of Wade's truck when he left the office. They climbed in, and Wade backed out of his parking space.

"Would you mind if we go to Sonic? I need to discuss something with you, and I don't want to be overheard."

"I had a feeling this wasn't a purely social engagement," Maddie teased.

They discussed the case and Sherri Logsdon's interview. The conversation ended when Wade parked in one of the drive-in stalls. They placed their order, and Wade rolled the window up.

"What I'm about to tell you can't leave this truck?" Wade said.

"I've been trying to keep the department out of it. I can't tell you everything, but I want you to be aware."

"What's wrong?" asked Maddie.

"The FBI is looking for Lizzie's aunt. Agent Welborn and his partner came to the inn and questioned the family while I was there Friday night. They believe that Grace knows something about their agent's disappearance."

"Do you think she does?"

"I can't tell you how I know this," Wade warned. "She knows the man. She says that she hasn't heard from him for some time. Welborn said the man had been missing for weeks."

"Why do you need to keep the department out of it?"

"I think Welborn will do whatever it takes to get what he wants," Wade said. "He may arrest the Fletchers or me. I don't want him coming after any of you."

Their food arrived before Maddie could respond.

"What are the chances you'll be arrested?" Maddie asked when the carhop walked away.

"I don't know," Wade admitted. "I'd say they're pretty high if Welborn can come up with a valid charge."

"Do you know where Lizzie's aunt is?"

"All I'll say is that I don't know where she is at this second," Wade said. "The less you know, the better."

"Are you going to tell Reed what's going on?" she asked.

"I'll find a reason to get him out of the office and tell him this afternoon," Wade said. "I don't want to arouse suspicion with the others by meeting in my office too often."

"What should we do if you are arrested?" asked Maddie.

"Be truthful," Wade said. "Run the department as usual."

"Yes, Sir."

They finished their lunch and returned to the office. Wade waited until Maddie was inside before getting out of his truck. Reed was waiting for him.

"We found the Chevy Malibu," he told Wade. "The owner called while you were out. It was reported stolen last week from her driveway. It's been returned and is parked in front of her house. Do you want to go check it out?"

Wade grinned and said, "Let's go!"

They climbed into Wade's truck. Wade took the opportunity to discuss his situation with Reed.

Reed sat back and stared at Wade with wide-eyed disbelief.

"Wow," he said at last. "Is that why you didn't want to see them when they came to pick up Ratliff's body?"

"That's one of the reasons," Wade said. "Welborn's visit led to a terrible argument with Lizzie and her family."

"Keeping this from the rest of the team won't be easy," Reed replied. "They'll want to know what's happening."

"I know," Wade agreed. "Tell them what you know if it's necessary. Otherwise, they shouldn't have any information to give the FBI."

The two men arrived at the home of Brenda Schur. Reed questioned her while Wade examined the car.

Mrs. Schur was an elderly woman who drove the car to run errands and visit friends. She parked the car in the driveway after a trip to the grocery store. The next morning it was gone.

She was shocked to see the car parked on the street when she checked her mailbox earlier that day. She walked out to make sure it was her car before reporting its return.

Wade dusted the car for prints and checked the car for other evidence. He found nothing useful.

The car appeared to have been detailed before it was returned. It was spotless. He joined Reed and Mrs. Schur on her porch.

"The car was hotwired and then repaired," he told them. "I can't find any other damage."

"Whoever took it didn't get far," said Mrs. Schur. "It was almost out of gas when I parked. I was going to fill up the next time I used it."

"It's got a full tank now," Wade told her. "The thief must have had it cleaned and filled it with gas before bringing it back to you."

"Well, how nice! I expected to find out it had been totaled in a high-speed chase," said Schur with a grin. "I've never heard of a stolen car being returned."

"Neither have we," Reed told her. "We need to tow it to the Sheriff's department to process any evidence that we can find. We'll get it back to you as soon as we can."

"I don't need to go anywhere," she told them. "Do what you need to do."

The men said goodbye and drove back to the office. Both were glad that Mrs. Schur's car had been returned. Neither expected it to give them any clues.

Maddie approached them when they entered the office. "We might have a lead," she said.

"I hope it turns out better than ours," Reed replied.

"There was a matchbook among Ratliff's belongings," she said and handed it to Reed. "Open the cover."

Reed opened the matches. The words *tomorrow night at seven* were written inside. He looked at the outside. It came from a restaurant in Quanah.

"Do you think we'll be able to get there and back by four?" Reed asked Wade.

Wade looked at the clock and said, "We have two hours. It'll be an hour round trip. The rest depends on how long it takes to question folks."

"I don't want to miss the last interview," Reed said. "You go ahead. I'll stay here."

"I'll try to be back in time," Wade said and hurried to his office.

He found the file folder that held the suspect's and victim's pictures and rushed to his truck. The half-hour drive to Quanah, Texas, gave him time to reflect on the case and his conversation with Welborn. He wanted to solve Ratliff's murder before Welborn could make his next move.

Wade moaned when he saw that the restaurant was attached to a truck stop. The chances were already slim that anyone would remember the pair a week later. This made them almost nonexistent.

He went inside and asked for the owner of the restaurant. The owner acknowledged that the matches came from his restaurant. He didn't recognize Ratliff or the mystery man. One of the waitresses said that she had seen them.

"I noticed them because she was so pretty, and he was so…not," said the waitress.

"Did you happen to overhear any of their conversation?" Wade asked, hopeful.

"A little. He asked her why she was here. She said something about a wedding."

"Did they leave together?" asked Wade.

"No, she left first. He asked for a coffee to go and paid the check before he left."

"Did she appear to be afraid of him?"

"Not that I could tell."

"Is there anything else you remember?"

"They both seemed to be upset when they left. She had tears in her eyes. That's all that I remember."

Wade gave her his card and asked her to call if the man returned. He went back to his truck and drove back toward Vernon.

The third interview had already begun when Wade got back to the office. He checked his email and wrote up his report while he waited for the interview to end.

He heard the conference room door open and Maddie's assurance that she'd be in touch. He joined her in the outer office.

"How was the interview with Christy Truly?" Wade asked.

"She seems eager to work here," Maddie answered. "She interviewed well. I think she's had lots of practice. She said she's been on several interviews.."

"I have a feeling there's something you aren't telling me," Wade prodded.

"She had a little attitude when she learned that you wouldn't be taking part in the interview or hiring process. She thought that it was irregular."

"I'm sure it is," Wade admitted. "What else?"

"She's flirty. That could make her a distraction. I should get back in there. I don't want to miss any of the discussion."

"Let me know when you've finished. I have news."

It was five fifteen when Baker told Wade they'd finished their discussion. He followed his deputy into the room and shared what he'd learned in Quanah and what they'd discovered with the Chevy Malibu.

Lodge asked, "Could they have had a second meeting?"

"We have no clues as to where or when they did," Reed said.

"There wouldn't have been much time to meet again," Wade pointed out. "She was busy with her friends in Wichita Falls before she was killed."

"I started a facial recognition program earlier today," said Maddie. "I'm searching for our suspect on the criminal databases. Should I expand it?"

"It can't hurt," Reed said. "We might get lucky and have a name by morning."

Wade went home and ordered pizza again. Lodge would be taking possession of the house in three days. He had to move his unneeded belongings into the storage building.

He loaded his truck with boxes while he waited for his food. He took a short break to eat and drove to the storage facility. He unloaded the boxes and called Lizzie on his way back to his house.

Hi, Darlin'," he said when she answered. "How did Grace take the news about her friend?"

"Granny said she's okay. She was upset. She expected bad news since he'd been missing for so long."

"Did Grace find a good place to hide?"

"We have it all worked out," Lizzie told him.

They chatted a bit longer and ended the call. Wade went to bed feeling uneasy. He was certain that Welborn was going to cause trouble.

* * *

The Fletchers spent the afternoon planning their alert system and an emergency hiding space for Grace. She needed to stay hidden until she found out who might be setting her up and why.

"I have an idea," James said. "Do you remember how we used to hide and seek?"

Grace laughed and said, "Yes, and there was one place where I could never find you. I always thought it was in the barn."

"No, it's too hot to hide in the barn," James said. "We need a cooler place, and it needs to have power. Otherwise, our alert system won't work."

"I think I know what you have in mind," said Lois. "The hidden room in the cellar."

James nodded. "We can set you up in there with everything you need. There's already an outlet on that wall. We can tap into it for power in that room."

"Wade seems to think that Welborn can show up any minute," Lizzie pointed out. "We'd better get started."

The small room had been there since before Lois was born. They didn't know what its original purpose had been. It was so well camouflaged that only those who knew of its existence could find it. The Fletchers used it for storage.

The family worked all afternoon cleaning the space and getting it ready for Grace. James rewired the outlet so that she would have electricity.

Lizzie found a lamp and table while Lois and Ellen set up a small dresser. One of the cellar sofas was moved into the room for

Grace to sleep on. It had all the comforts of home when they'd finished.

A small alarm was set up to alert Grace of danger. It had a red LED bulb that would light up if anyone in the house pressed a particular number and symbol on their cell phones. That was the signal to turn off her appliances and to wait in silence until the light glowed again.

James and Grace moved her belongings from the house into her new room while Lizzie and Ellen made dinner. Lois removed all evidence of Grace's presence in the house.

They ate dinner together and cleaned up the kitchen. Lizzie's parents and grandmother stayed longer than they normally did for Grace's sake.

Grace paced the floor and tried to watch T.V. She needed to take her mind off of Todd. She needed something to do. She eventually said goodnight to her family and went to her room, closing the hidden door behind her.

She took out her laptop and looked over the notes she had made while she was traveling from casino to casino. She'd spent her downtime observing each casino and asking questions. She'd tried a few games as well.

The information she'd gathered wasn't what she would call newsworthy. She supposed she could embellish here and exaggerate there.

That wasn't Grace's style. She was known for truth and accuracy. She didn't have enough information to make a good story.

Grace stood and paced the floor again. *I don't have anything to give Oliver. I wanted to have something written to justify being away for so long. I'll have to come up with something else.*

She stopped pacing and looked at the laptop. She sat down and read over her notes again. She'd written notes when she was bored and when she needed to focus.

I could write about being on the run. That might make a good news piece. It could even be background information for a short story or novel.

She let her imagination run wild while she typed. She cried when she wrote about Todd. She trembled when she wrote about how afraid she'd been.

Grace wrote until she could hardly keep her eyes open. She saved her work, turned off the laptop, and got ready for bed. She fell asleep when her head touched the pillow.

CHAPTER EIGHTEEN

"WHY ARE we going back to Texas?" Brittain asked Welborn while they waited for their flight at the Vegas airport.

"Call it a gut feeling," Welborn said.

"What do you expect to find? Stewart's family won't tell us anything even if they know where she's hiding."

"I think that sheriff knew more than he was willing to tell me," Welborn said. "It's time to show our hand."

"What hand?"

"We may have to come clean with the Fletchers if we want them to come clean with us," Welborn said.

"That's need-to-know information," Brittain said, staring at his partner.

"We have to find out what the Stewart woman knows," Welborn said.

"What if she doesn't know anything? We don't want to give out information without cause."

"We won't," Welborn said. "We'll tell them what we must to get that evidence."

"What do you have in mind?" Brittain asked.

"I've already arranged a meeting with the FBI in Dallas. We'll explain our situation," Welborn said. "With their help, we'll get a search warrant and search every inch of the Fletchers' property. If Grace Stewart is there, we'll find her."

"What about the sheriff?"

"I have an idea about how to keep him busy," Welborn said. "He wanted to know if Anthony's case was linked to the Ratliff case. You'll go to his office and show him the autopsy report. Keep him occupied comparing the two cases while I handle the Fletchers."

Their discussion ended when it was announced that their flight was boarding. They found their seats and made themselves comfortable. It was going to be a long day.

Welborn's plan to involve the Dallas FBI didn't go as well as he'd hoped. Their flight to Dallas was delayed due to weather conditions in the Dallas-Fort Worth area.

They arrived at the airport to find that the agents who were to meet them had been called away. They had to take a cab to the FBI headquarters.

They were late for their meeting because of their flight delay. They found themselves waiting in a conference room until the agent that Welborn had spoken with was free.

"I'm Agent Luis Paredes," said a tall young man when he entered the room. "Which of you is Agent Welborn?"

"I'm Welborn. This is my partner Agent Brittain."

Paredes looked at them both and nodded. He flipped through some pages on a legal pad before he spoke again.

"Let me make sure I understand," he began. "You're looking for a suspect in the disappearance of an agent. You believe she's in Texas with her family."

"Yes," said Welborn. "Our agent's body was found two days ago. It's imperative that we find and question the suspect."

"You believe the suspect will be located on some farmland outside of Vernon."

"Her family owns and operates the Paradise Creek Inn," Brittain said. "The Inn is located on their farm."

"I see," said Paredes. "What do you want from us?"

"I told you when we spoke on the phone. We'll need a search warrant and a team," Welborn said, his patience wearing thin.

"We have a team waiting for instructions," Paredes told him. "The search warrant is still pending. I expect to hear from the judge any moment."

"Is there any way to hurry this up?" Brittain asked, sensing trouble from his partner. "It's a long drive from here."

"It's approximately a two-and-a-half-hour drive to Vernon," Paredes answered. "How far is it to the search area from there?"

"Another half-hour at least," Welborn said through gritted teeth.

"I'll see what I can do about transportation," said Paredes and left the room.

Welborn stood and paced the room. "Sheriff Adams could well be at the Fletchers for dinner before we get there."

"Do you have an alternate plan for keeping him busy?" Brittain asked with a smirk.

Welborn glared at him. "I'll put him in cuffs in I have to."

Brittain relaxed in his seat. He amused himself watching Welborn pace until Paredes returned with a map of Texas.

"Show me where we're going," he said and unrolled the map.

Welborn and Brittain looked at the map. They pointed out the general area of the Fletcher farm.

"Are these open fields," Paredes asked, pointing.

"I know there's a pasture to the east of the inn," said Brittain. "I saw it when we were last there."

"You've already been there? Do you have the address or coordinates?"

"We used GPS to find it with the address," Welborn snarled. "I assume that you have GPS."

"We aren't from the stone age, contrary to your opinion of us,"

Paredes said and sneered. "I'm trying to determine the quickest route."

They were interrupted by a knock on the door. The search warrant had arrived.

"Gentlemen, we can go now," said Paredes.

Welborn and Brittain followed Paredes to the roof. A helicopter was loaded with men and equipment.

"Agent Welborn, if you give our pilot the address, we can be on our way," said Paredes.

Welborn shared the information with the pilot, found a seat near Paredes, and sat down.

"How long will it take to get there by air?" he asked.

"Forty-five minutes to an hour tops," Paredes answered.

Welborn looked at his watch. It was three-thirty. *That should put us there before the sheriff leaves his office.*

The Wilbarger County Sherriff's Department spent the day searching for their lone suspect. They had no other leads to pursue.

Maddie's facial recognition search was still running. They were no closer to finding the man than they'd been in the beginning.

The APB was still active. They'd had no reports about their suspect.

Wade ran the office while the rest of the team split up into pairs and canvassed the area. They were armed with photos of their suspect and the determination to find him.

They returned to the office by noon with nothing new to share. No one had seen the man since he'd visited Wade in his office. They met before going to lunch to discuss other options.

"I think we should visit nearby towns," suggested Odom. "We know he was in Quanah last week. He might be there."

"I'll need to visit with those county sheriffs before we do that,"

Wade informed him. "They may want to run the search themselves."

"They'd probably get a better response than we would," Maddie pointed out. "They're known by their constituents."

No one had a better idea. They broke for lunch and hoped that someone would come up with a solution by the time they returned to the office.

They met in the conference room when everyone returned from lunch. Reed opened the meeting and asked if anyone had a suggestion.

"I've contacted the sheriffs in all of the nearby counties," Wade told them. "I didn't request permission to search ourselves. I faxed the photograph to them instead. The more eyes we have looking for our suspect, the better our chances are of finding him."

"That frees all of us to search here at home," Reed said.

"The facial recognition program is still running," Maddie said. "I had an idea during lunch."

"We're all ears," said Reed.

"If our suspect is still in our area, he has to be staying somewhere," Maddie began. "He could be camping in an abandoned house or a vehicle somewhere outside of town. I think we should patrol those areas and investigate anything that looks suspicious."

"You're right," said Reed. "He could be camping across county lines out of our reach."

"I'll get in touch with those sheriffs and ask them to look for someone camping," Wade said.

"I'll get in touch with the Vernon Police Department," said Reed. "They can check abandoned houses within the city limits."

"What are the chances this guy is moving around?" asked Gonzalez.

"Or already gone," added Baker.

"Odds are that he has moved on and is no longer in our area," Reed admitted. "The patrols and searches might give us a clue to where he's been hiding. We don't have any other leads to follow right now."

Wade volunteered to patrol the rest of the afternoon. He wanted to get out of the office for a while. He contacted the neighboring sheriff departments and shared his team's suspicions before leaving.

"I'll see you in the morning, Reed," he said and went to his truck. He was to patrol the area between Lockett and the county line.

Wade patrolled Highway 70 to the Foard County line. He turned around and patrolled county roads looking for abandoned buildings and vehicles in odd places. He gradually made his way toward the inn. He didn't want to miss the opportunity to see Lizzie.

He parked at the inn and got out. He could hear something coming toward him, but he couldn't see anything. He went to the back door and knocked before opening it.

"Hello, Wade," said Lois. She went to greet him and gave him a big hug. "We've been missing you around here."

"I've missed y'all too," he said and stepped back outside. The noise was louder.

"What's wrong?" Lois asked.

Wade went back inside and closed the door. "There's a helicopter out there. It looks like it's about to land."

"I'll alert Grace," Lois said and took out her cell phone.

"What on earth is that noise?" Ellen called from upstairs.

Lizzie ran out of her office and shouted, "There's a helicopter landing out front!"

Grace was in her room writing with the door open. She saw the red LED light glow out of the corner of her eye. She jumped up and closed the door. She turned off her laptop and the lamp before she sat on the bed to wait.

The temperature in her hideaway was comfortable. She knew it was fear that caused beads of sweat to form on her brow. Her body trembled with it.

She tried to occupy her mind with memories of her childhood. She and James had climbed every tree that they could reach. They played in the barn and swung from the rafters onto the loose hay below.

Their grandmother would make them snacks when they got hungry. They'd take a homemade picnic basket and eat under the trees.

The picnic basket was an old shoebox. Its lid was bent in the middle so it would open from either end. A piece of yarn or twine was the handle.

Grace recalled the time they'd made a playhouse out of an old stock trailer. It was equipped with dishes and paintings on the wall. A discarded rug served as the carpet.

The trailer had two wheels and would lower when you got too close to one end or the other. They spent as much time seesawing in it as they did playing house.

A tear rolled down her cheek. She enjoyed being near her family and sharing their lives again. She wished it could last forever.

She shook her head and wiped her face. *Not like this. I want to be able to live a life of freedom. No more fear for me or my family. I can't think about moving home until this is over.*

Grace stretched out on the sofa and waited. She wondered how much longer she'd have to hide. She listened, hoping to hear something from upstairs.

James and Dan were working in the field and saw the helicopter hovering near the inn. They stopped what they were doing and jumped in the pickup. They arrived as the chopper touched down. The rest of the family watched from the front window.

"It's Welborn!" Wade said and cursed under his breath.

"You said it was just a matter of time," Lizzie said.

"Are you sure that Grace is safe?" he asked.

"Safer than we are," Lois observed. "Are they expecting to find terrorists in here?"

Armed men in protective gear disembarked from the helicopter and moved toward the inn. James and Dan met them on the lawn.

"What's going on here?" James asked, bewildered.

"We have a warrant to search your property," said Welborn with an evil grin. "These men are here to help in the search and make sure there's no threat to our lives."

"What threat?" James asked, his temper flashing. "We never threatened you. We answered all of your questions. What do you want from us now?"

Welborn handed the warrant to James and said, "Just stand aside and let us do our job."

Wade walked out and stood on the porch. "Welborn, what are you doing?"

"I didn't expect to see you at this time of the afternoon," Welborn said and sneered. "Shouldn't you be at your office?"

"I've been patrolling and stopped to say hello," Wade replied. "Turns out I was just in time."

"Stay out of our way, Sheriff," Welborn warned. "We're going to search every nook and cranny of this place."

"Mind if I ask why?" Wade said and leaned on the porch railing with his hands in his pockets.

"We're looking for Grace Stewart. If she's here, we'll find her."

"It would be best if you'd all wait inside," Brittain said. "It will be cooler and more comfortable."

The family went into the dining room, followed by Brittain. They sat at the table and waited.

"I need something to drink," James said. "Would anyone else like something?"

Everyone said yes except Brittain.

"I'll help you," Ellen said. "I'm sure we'd all like one. Agent Brittain, would you like something."

"No, thank you."

Ellen filled glasses with ice, and James found a two-liter bottle of Coke. They carried them to the table so that everyone could pour their own.

"Are you just going to sit there and stare at us?" Wade asked Brittain.

"I do have something I'd like to show you," Brittain said and took an envelope from his pocket. "This is the autopsy report for Agent Anthony. Welborn thought you might be interested."

Wade took the envelope and opened it. He read through the report and then read it again.

"May I make a copy of this?" he asked. "I'd like to compare it with our current case."

"That copy is yours," Brittain said.

"Are you certain about the date and time of death?" Wade asked.

"I'm sure you understand that, given the circumstances, it was difficult to determine the precise moment of death," answered Brittain. "Our medical examiner believes those dates are accurate."

"According to this report," Wade began. "Your agent was killed after Ms. Stewart left Las Vegas."

"That is my understanding."

"Then why are you here searching for her?" James demanded.

"Everything will be explained in due time," said Brittain.

"Wade, what does it say?" James asked.

Wade looked at Brittain before answering. "Todd Anthony was shot twice in the chest at close range. His body had been frozen. The medical examiner estimates his date of death to be August eighteenth."

"Grace was here that day!" Lois exclaimed and glared at Brittain. "Young man, you'd better start talking."

"I'm sorry, Mrs. Fletcher," Brittain stammered under her gaze. "Agent Welborn requested to be here for this discussion."

The FBI agents from Dallas searched every building on the Fletchers' property. They combed through the tall brush and the nearby shelterbelts. When they'd finished, they entered the inn with Welborn.

"Search every room and closet," Welborn told the men. "Don't forget the cellar. I'll be in the dining room with the family."

Grace heard a noise in the cellar and froze. She heard furniture being moved and cabinets opened. She prayed that her hideaway wouldn't be discovered.

Agent Paredes approached Welborn in the dining room. "There's no one else on the property. We did find some guns, mostly rifles.

"We're all licensed to carry weapons," James informed him.

"May I see your licenses?" Paredes asked.

The family presented their licenses to Paredes.

"There's nothing here, Welborn," he said.

"I still need to question these people," Welborn said.

"My men and I will wait outside," Paredes told him. "I suggest you hurry."

Welborn waited for the other agents to leave before turning his attention to the Fletcher family. "I'm sure you've been informed of the death of Agent Todd Anthony."

"I think that I can speak for the Fletchers," Wade said. "We want the truth. All of it."

Welborn sighed and sat down. He dropped his tough-guy demeanor before he spoke.

"Agent Anthony was working undercover. The last time he made contact with his handler was during the first week of August.

He was close to completing his assignment. He said he had evidence that would put the criminals away for a long time. He was supposed to meet his handler the next day. He never showed up."

"What does that have to do with my daughter?" Lois demanded.

"Anthony's handler had seen them together during one of their scheduled meetings. He didn't know the status of their relationship. He recognized her and thought they might have been more than acquaintances."

"Why are you still looking for her?" Wade asked. "You know Anthony was killed while she was here."

"We need to know if Anthony gave her anything for safekeeping," said Brittain. "We thought he might have given her a copy of his evidence."

"That would explain her sudden departure and staying off the grid while she traveled," added Welborn.

Lois looked at Wade, and he nodded.

"Grace left Las Vegas because she was scared," Lois told them. She explained about the tracking device and the message on her mirror.

"She didn't know who was responsible or why?" asked Brittain.

"No, she didn't," Lois said.

"I knew you were holding out," Welborn said, sighing. "I can't say that I blame you."

"This is concerning," said Brittain.

"What do you mean?" asked James.

"It confirms our suspicions," answered Welborn. "We believe there's an informant in our department."

"You mean those criminals are after my daughter," Lois said.

Welborn and Brittain looked at each other.

"Yes, Ma'am," answered Brittain.

"When did you last speak with her?" asked Welborn. "Do you know where she is?"

"She contacted us on Saturday," said James. "She's safe."

"We know you were tracking her movements," Wade began. "I'm pretty sure you knew more about her whereabouts than the Fletchers did."

Welborn nodded.

"Does that mean the men that killed Anthony know as well?"

"We don't know for certain," answered Welborn. "It's likely they do."

"They're either tracking her themselves or someone in our department is keeping them informed," said Brittain.

"Why this search for Grace?" asked Ellen. "Wouldn't your spy know if you found her here?"

"We wanted to find out about Anthony's evidence," answered Welborn. "We also wanted to move her to protective custody. She'd be in a safe house that only Brittain and I would know about."

"You're telling us that you're trying to protect her and recover your evidence," said Dan. "Why don't I believe that?"

"I don't blame you for doubting us," said Welborn. "We haven't been upfront with you."

"We want to protect Ms. Stewart," added Brittain. "Whether she has the evidence or not."

"Will you tell us more about the criminals who might be looking for her?" asked Lois.

"I can't go into details," said Welborn. "They're a group similar in organization to a cartel or the mafia. They take part in every crime imaginable."

"We believe they plan to take control of Las Vegas and branch out from there," added Brittain. "It's possible that they have representatives in every part of Vegas government."

"Gentlemen, would you give us a moment to discuss this privately," asked James.

"We'll go outside and make sure our ride doesn't leave without us," Brittain said

He stood and indicated that Welborn should follow. James waited until they were on the front porch before saying anything more.

"Wade, Grace is nearby. Should we let her talk with these men?" he whispered.

"I don't know," Wade replied in a low voice. "I don't trust them."

"Will they stop looking for her if she talks to them?" Ellen whispered.

"They might," Wade answered. "If they have a mole, the criminals will know where to find her."

"Don't you think Aunt Grace should be the one to make that decision?" Lizzie asked.

They all looked at her for a moment, then nodded.

"Are we agreed that we won't tell these two anything until we've talked with Grace?" asked Wade.

"I think that's best," said Dan. "We'd be in a pickle if we convinced her to meet with them, and she was arrested or killed."

"What are we going to tell them?" asked Lois.

"Leave that to me," said James.

He went to the door and invited the two agents to come back inside.

"We've talked it over, and we agree that we'll give Grace your message the next time we talk to her," James told them. "We don't know when that will be. She gets in touch with us when she can. We don't know where she is or how to get in touch with her."

Welborn nodded and extended his hand. "We appreciate your cooperation. Sheriff Adams has my contact information."

"We 're sorry for disrupting your evening," said Brittain.

The Fletcher family watched the men climb into the helicopter. They watched the craft take off and fly out of sight before going inside.

Lois pressed the alert so that Grace would know the coast was clear. They were sitting at the dining table when Grace entered through the back door.

"What's been happening?" she asked.

"The FBI agents were searching the property for you," Lois said.

"Lizzie, why don't we make some sandwiches while they tell Grace what happened."

Lizzie reluctantly followed her mother to the kitchen. They made sandwiches and listened to the conversation while they worked. Grace listened to them and sat in silence for a few minutes.

"They don't believe that I had anything to do with Todd's

disappearance or death," Grace repeated. "They think he gave me something with the evidence he'd gathered."

"Yes," said Wade. "That could explain the tracker on your car and the message in your house."

"He never gave me anything," Grace said. "He was never at my house, and I was never at his."

"We know," James said. "We're wondering if you should tell the FBI agents those facts."

"Keep in mind that if you do," Wade began. "The people that Todd was investigating will know where to find you if they have an informant."

"Who else would have done those things in Vegas?" asked Lois.

"It could have been the FBI," Wade pointed out.

"Or the mole in their department," added Grace.

The family ate and discussed their options for two hours.

"I need to think about this," Grace said. "I'll let you know what I decide in the morning."

Grace returned to the cellar and locked the cellar door behind her. She went back to the hidden room. James, Ellen, and Lois went home for the night.

Lizzie made sure all the alarms and security systems were on and working. Wade locked all of the doors. He decided to stay the night rather than go back to town. He didn't feel right about leaving them alone. He wasn't satisfied that the FBI had gone.

CHAPTER NINETEEN

GRACE GOT up the next morning with her mind made up. She'd been awake most of the night thinking it over. She had to leave the farm.

She left her hideaway and went into the kitchen. She knew her family wouldn't be happy with her decision. She waited until they were all enjoying their breakfast before she brought up the subject.

"We need to talk," she said.

"Here it comes," Lois said and sat back in her chair.

James looked at his sister and said, "Running away isn't the answer.

"I know," Grace replied. "I have something else in mind, and it involves Wade."

Surprised, Wade looked at Grace and said, "Me?"

"Well, not only you," Grace began. "I want to talk about protective custody at the jail. How would that work?"

"There are a couple of options," Wade said. "You could be in full lockdown. No one would be able to reach you without authorization. The other option would give you the freedom to move around the office during the day. You'd be in lockdown at night."

"I see," Grace said. "I'd be more restricted than I am here."

"Yes," Wade admitted. "You'd also have armed guards twenty-four seven."

"What are you thinking about, Grace?" asked her mother.

"We were lucky last night. We wouldn't have been prepared if the FBI had shown up a day earlier," Grace said. "I might have been caught in the open. The people who killed Todd won't be in a helicopter."

"That's true," Wade agreed.

"This can't go on forever," she said. "We all need to get on with our lives. The only way to end this is to talk with the FBI."

"What?" Lois exclaimed. "Their spy would know where to find you."

"That's the whole point, Mom," Grace said. "I want the people who killed Todd to show their hand."

"You want them to come after you?" Ellen asked, astonished.

"I don't want to look over my shoulder for the rest of my life. I want to know who and what I'm facing."

"Won't that be dangerous?" Ellen asked.

"That's why I was thinking of protective custody. They'd have no reason to show up here," Grace said.

"Wade, what do you think?" Lois asked.

"I think it's a good idea," Wade answered. "You have a good security system. However, it could take up to half an hour for help to arrive."

"We're all willing to do what it takes to protect each other," said James.

"I know," Wade said. "The problem is that you have other jobs to do. If Grace talks with the FBI, she'll need round-the-clock protection from trained professionals. I can't spare the manpower to protect her out here."

"What do y'all think?" asked Grace.

"I've always thought this was the safest place for you," said

Lois. "Last night, we had a little warning. We may not be that lucky again."

"The people responsible for Todd Anthony's death aren't amateurs. They'll send someone to tie up the loose ends," Wade said. "He or she could just walk in and start shooting. You may not have time to return fire."

"That won't happen if I'm not here," Grace said.

"You don't know that for sure," said James.

"Why would they come here if they know I'm at the jail?" said Grace.

"What's to keep them from storming the jail?" asked Ellen.

"It would be potential suicide for the shooter," said Wade. "Everyone in the department carries a sidearm at all times. They'll all be on alert if Grace chooses protective custody."

"Grace is right," said Lois. "We can't live this way forever. I'll support you if you're sure this is what you want to do."

"It is," Grace replied. "What do the rest of you think?"

James, Ellen, and Lizzie nodded their agreement.

"I'll make the arrangements when I get to the office," said Wade. "Grace, you'll need to stay undercover until I come back. I'll drive you into town."

"What should I bring with me?" she asked.

"You can bring whatever you need that will make you feel more comfortable," he said.

"Will we be able to visit?" asked Lois.

"Certainly," Wade said with a smile. "Let me know when you're planning to be there, and I'll authorize the visit."

"Wade, do you think I should be in full lockdown?" Grace asked.

"I'll leave that up to you," he said. "I would recommend it after you speak with the FBI. We won't know who could be walking into the office."

"I'll make sure that I have enough to keep me occupied," Grace said. "How do you want to handle the FBI?"

"I think it would be best to wait until you're at the jail," Wade replied. "Someone may already be in town looking for you."

"Are you serious?" asked Ellen.

Wade nodded and said, "We haven't caught the person who killed Agent Ratliff. I don't think it's a coincidence that she and her uncle were both murdered."

Grace packed her things and waited for Wade's return. She stayed near her hideaway as a precaution.

She prayed that she was making the right decision. The lives of the people she loved most depended on it.

She dreaded being locked down. She didn't like the idea of being so restricted. Finding out who killed Todd and ending the nightmare would be worth it.

Wade drove to work and thought about what Grace wanted to do. It would be dangerous. Even so, he felt it was the right move to make. *How am I going to explain this to my people?*

He thought about it during the drive. He parked his truck and went into the office.

"Good morning, Wade," Maddie greeted him when he walked in.

"Good morning. Would you and Reed join me in my office?"

The two deputies followed him. He closed his office door behind them and moved a second chair in front of his desk.

"Have a seat," he said. "I have some news, and I'd like your advice about the best way to handle it."

"What's wrong?" asked Reed.

"Do you remember what I told you about Lizzie's aunt?"

Both deputies nodded.

"She's at the inn and has requested to be in protective custody," he said and waited for his deputies' reactions.

"Why does she need protective custody," Maddie inquired.

"The FBI came to the inn last night searching for her. They believe that Grace has some important evidence. They also believe that they have a spy in their department."

"Does she have the evidence?" Reed queried.

"She says she doesn't," Wade said. "I believe her. She has a tell when she lies."

"Are you saying that she needs protection from the FBI and a criminal element?" asked Maddie.

"Yes, and no. She wants to talk with the FBI once she's in custody. I'm going out to the inn to get her in a little while. I'll need some deputies to go along as armed escorts."

"What do you want us to do?" asked Reed.

"I have a personal stake in this," Wade began. "How do you suggest I handle it with the rest of the staff?"

"I'll handle it," Maddie replied. "We have a meeting in a few minutes. I'll explain the situation, and we'll ask for volunteers for the escort."

Wade looked at her and smiled. "Thank you, Maddie. I didn't mean for you to take responsibility."

"I know," she said. "Where do we want to put her? We could give her an interrogation room or a holding cell."

"We need to be able to put her in full lockdown," Wade said. "I don't want Welborn to have access to her. We don't know who else we're dealing with."

"I want to make sure that I understand," said Reed. "She hasn't been accused of a crime. The FBI still insists on speaking with her."

"They are more than insistent," Wade said and told them about the FBI's arrival and search of the property.

Reed raised an eyebrow and said, "Could Welborn be the mole?"

"That thought crossed my mind, too," said Wade. "That's why I don't want him to have access to Grace."

"It's about time for our meeting," Maddie said. "Do you want to join us or wait here until I've explained the situation?"

"I'll wait here," Wade said. "I want them to speak freely. My presence might be an issue. Besides, someone has to run the office."

"We'll yell when we're ready for you," said Reed.

Maddie and Reed went to the conference room for their morning meeting. Maddie explained the situation without giving any names.

The entire team agreed that the person in question should be in protective custody, and all were willing to do their part. They were more supportive when they learned that Lizzie's aunt would be under their supervision.

Reed tapped on Wade's door and said, "We're ready."

Wade stood and followed him into the conference room.

"Sheriff Adams," Maddie began. "We all agree to protect Lizzie's aunt."

Wade beamed at his staff. "Thank y'all. Having her here will enable us to continue working on the Ratliff case and avoid a lot of long hours."

"You should know that everyone volunteered to be part of the escort," Maddie said. "We've decided to draw names out of a hat."

"We want to make sure Fletcher and her folks are safe," said Baker.

"We can't let anything happen to such good cooks," Lodge teased. "Does this lady cook too?"

Wade laughed and said, "You'll have to ask her."

The topic of the meeting turned to their case. There were no new leads in the death of Jody Ratliff.

The facial recognition search for their suspect continued to run. Patrols for someone camping in a vehicle or abandoned building would continue.

Wade called the inn after the meeting ended.

"Lizzie, I need to speak with Grace," he said when she answered his call.

"She's right here," Lizzie said and handed the phone to Grace.

"Hello?"

"Grace, this is Wade. Are you sure this is what you want to do?"

"I'm sure."

"I'll be there in less than an hour with my deputies to pick you up," he told her.

"I've packed everything I'll need," she said. "I'm ready."

"See you soon," he said and ended the call.

Maddie knocked on his door and said, "Her room is ready. It doesn't feel right to call it a cell in this case."

"I know what you mean," Wade replied. "I don't like putting her there."

"Does she realize what this means?" Maddie inquired.

"I don't think anyone can until they've experienced it," Wade told her.

"I'll be riding with you," she said. "Baker and Odom will be in the second truck."

"I'm glad to have all of you," Wade said and smiled.

Wade and Maddie went to his truck and climbed in. They drove to the inn, followed by Baker and Odom.

They arrived at the inn and parked near the back door. Baker and Odom stood guard while Wade and Maddie went inside.

"Grace Stewart, this is Maddie Clifton," Wade said. "I'm going to load your things into the truck. Maddie's going to explain how this is going to work."

Grace nodded and shook Maddie's hand. Wade gathered Grace's belongings and went outside.

"You're now in protective custody," Maddie said. "We need your word that you'll do what we tell you to do right away and without question."

"I will," said Grace.

"Wade will come back inside and give us the all-clear," Maddie continued. "You'll get into the back seat of his truck and lie down. We don't want you to be seen."

"I understand," Grace said and twisted her ring around her finger.

"We'll drive into a garage area when we get to the office. We'll take you from there to your cubicle," Maddie said. "Do you have any questions?"

Grace shook her head and swallowed hard. She hugged her family members and said goodbye.

Wade entered the room and said, "I'll let y'all know when she's safely tucked away. You can visit or call anytime."

"Thank you for doing this," said Lois to both Wade and Maddie.

"That's what families do," Maddie said and smiled.

Wade opened the door and nodded at the deputies outside. They moved to the back door of his Ford F-150 super crew and opened it. Wade led Grace outside to the truck, followed by Maddie.

Grace climbed inside and lay down on the back seat. Wade covered her with a tarp and closed the door. He waited until Maddie was in the passenger seat before he got in.

They drove away from the inn, followed by Baker and Odom. Their trip to the sheriff's department was uneventful.

They drove through an open bay door into the garage. Lodge closed the door behind them and secured it.

Maddie and Wade got out of the truck and helped Grace out of the back seat. Maddie led her to the cell that she'd be occupying while Wade collected her bags.

"I'm sorry this isn't a nicer space," said Maddie. "We tried to make it comfortable for you."

Grace looked around the small space and said, "It's bigger than the space where I've been hiding. I appreciate all you've done."

"Someone will be checking on you," Maddie told her. "Let us know if there's anything we can do for you."

Wade waited until Maddie left the room to take in Grace's luggage.

"I'll make sure you get better meals than we serve the prisoners," he told her. "I have a feeling I'll be bringing food from the inn if your mom doesn't bring it herself."

Grace laughed and said, "I wouldn't be surprised. She doesn't like this idea."

"I know she doesn't," Wade said. "I honestly believe you'll be safer here. When do you want me to make the call to Welborn?"

"The sooner, the better," she said. "I want to get this over with."

"Would you like to listen?" Wade asked, grinning.

"I think I would," said Grace.

"I have his number in my office," Wade said. "You'll have time to settle in here when we've finished."

Grace followed him to his office. He closed the door and picked up the phone. He put it on speaker so that Grace could hear.

"Welborn."

"Agent Welborn, this is Sheriff Adams."

"What do you want, Sheriff?" Welborn demanded.

"I have some news that I think you'll be interested in hearing," Wade said.

"What kind of news?"

"Grace Stewart came to see her family," he said.

"When? Is she still there?"

"She's in town, and she wants to talk with you," Wade told him.

"We're still in Dallas waiting for our flight," Welborn said. "We can be there this afternoon."

"There's something else you should know," Wade said. "She'll be at my office in protective custody."

"Your office?"

"Yes, my office," said Wade.

The sound of someone running echoed through the receiver. "We'll be there," said Welborn.

Grace and Wade could hear him say, "Hurry up, Brittain," before he hung up the phone.

"Is Welborn as nasty as Mom says?" Grace asked.

"He's not a pleasant person," Wade answered. "It could be an act. He'd be a great actor if that's the case."

"How should I handle him?"

"Don't let him rattle you," said Wade. "He thinks you have something he wants. He's going to try everything he can think of to get it. Tell him the truth."

"How long do you think it will take the informant to find out I'm here?"

"I'm not sure," Wade admitted. "It depends on where the spy is and when Welborn informs his office about meeting with you."

"Is it possible to be scared and happy at the same time," she asked. "I'm happy to be taking a stand, but I'm scared about how it might end."

"I think that's a perfectly normal response in this situation," Wade said. "Would you like a tour of the office?"

"Yes," said Grace with a smile. "I'd like to thank your staff too."

Wade showed Grace around the office and introduced her to his deputies. Grace thanked each of them for helping to keep her safe. Wade showed her an interrogation room and a small office.

"You may want a change of scenery after a while," Wade said. "You can hang out or work in one of these rooms when we feel it's safe. You can't be seen from the outer office."

"That's nice to know," Grace said.

Wade looked at his watch and said, "I'll take you back to you to your room. I don't know how long it will take Welborn to get here."

"Where will I be meeting with him?"

"I don't think you'll like what I have in mind," Wade said and smirked. "I know he won't."

Grace laughed and said, "That works for me."

Wade left Grace to settle into her space and went back to his office. Welborn stormed in an hour later with Brittain trailing in his wake.

"Where is she?" Welborn demanded when he saw Wade.

"You must have broken the sound barrier getting here," Wade observed with a smirk.

"I want to see her now!"

"She isn't going anywhere," Wade said. "Sit down, relax. Would you like some coffee or a soft drink?"

"I'd like a Coke," said Brittain.

Welborn looked at him and scowled.

"I need something to calm my nerves after that wild ride," Brittain said and sat in a nearby chair. "Deal with it."

Welborn gritted his teeth and balled his fists. "I would like to see Ms. Stewart right away," he said, attempting to be polite.

"Have a seat, and I'll have her moved to a room," Wade said.

Welborn sat down beside Baker's desk and put his hand over his face. He made a slight growling sound and said nothing more.

Wade somehow managed to avoid laughing out loud. He found Grace in her cell, typing on her laptop.

"Welborn and Brittain are here," he told her. "Are you ready?"

Grace saved the file she'd been working on and stood. "Let's get this over with."

The room that Wade led her to had two cubicles. Each cubicle had a chair and a telephone handset. A wall of plexiglass divided them from an identical cubical on the other side.

"This is just like the movies," she said.

"The ones in the movies are bigger," Wade said with a grin. "Maddie is going to stay in here with you. I'll be in the other room with the agents."

"How does this work?" she asked.

"You'll each pick up a handset so that you can hear and speak to each other," Wade explained. "You can tell Maddie that you're finished if you think he is getting out of line. You're in control of this situation, not him."

"Is the plexiglass to protect him or me?" Grace joked.

"It's intended to keep visitors from passing things to inmates and vice versa," he said. "In this case, it keeps the agents from touching you."

"He can't shoot me through that, can he?"

"It's bulletproof," Wade said. "I'll make sure he doesn't have a weapon before I bring him in here."

"That's good," said Grace. "I think I'm ready then."

"Your meeting will be recorded," Wade told her. "I think it's better to be safe than sorry."

"Me too," Grace said.

Wade left the room, and Maddie stepped inside. She waited near the door. She would be able to see everything from her vantage point.

Wade returned to the main office and approached the two agents.

"Ms. Stewart is ready," he told them. "Will you both be meeting with her?"

"I think it best that we both hear what she has to say," said Brittain.

"I'll have to ask you both to remove your weapons," Wade said. "Baker will secure them for you."

Wade knew that Welborn was offended and was surprised that he didn't argue. Both men handed their guns to Baker and watched him place them in a gun safe. Wade escorted them to the visitation room and held the door open for them.

Welborn looked inside and said, "What is this?"

"It's our visitation room," Wade said. "You'll talk with Ms. Stewart in here or not at all."

Welborn gritted his teeth and went inside. Brittain followed and sat down. Grace picked up the handset and waited. Brittain was the first to speak.

"Are you Grace Stewart?" he asked.

"I am," she replied. "I understand that you want to ask me some questions."

Welborn opened his briefcase and handed a photo to Brittain. Brittain held the photo so that Grace could see it.

"Do you know this man?"

"Yes, that's Todd Anthony."

"When did you last see Mr. Anthony?"

Grace answered his questions and wondered when they'd get to the point.

"You look different than I expected," said Brittain. "If you don't mind my saying so."

"I've made some changes since I left Las Vegas," she replied.

"Why did you leave Las Vegas?"

Grace explained her reasons for leaving. She didn't mention her history with Sharp.

Welborn lost his patience and snatched the handset from Brittain. He leaned on the countertop with his nose less than an inch from the glass.

"Did Anthony leave anything with you for safekeeping?" he demanded.

"No, he didn't."

"Did he ever tell you where to go or what to do if he went missing or was killed?"

"No, he didn't."

"Could he have hidden something in your house or office?"

"He was never at my house or my office," Grace said, annoyed. "If he hid anything, it was without my knowledge or permission."

"What sort of relationship did you have with Anthony?"

Grace had had enough. "I don't think that's any of your business," she said with an icy tone.

Welborn backed away from the glass and glared at her. "Do you know what evidence Anthony had or where he hid it?"

"I do not," Grace said with defiance. "We didn't talk about our work. We didn't talk about our families. We enjoyed being together when we could."

"Where were you on the night of August eighteenth?" Welborn asked.

"I was at the Paradise Creek Inn having dinner and visiting with my family," she replied.

"Was anyone else there to verify your story?"

"Sheriff Adams and Dan Hayes were there as well," she said with a smirk.

Welborn looked at Wade and gave the handset back to Brittain.

"Ms. Stewart, I want to make sure that I understand you," Brittain said. "You didn't hear from or see Agent Anthony in any way after July twenty-ninth."

"That's correct," Grace said.

"He never gave you anything to keep for him or tell you what to do in the event of his demise."

"That is also correct," Grace replied.

"I think we have all we need," Brittain said and looked at Welborn, who nodded. "Thank you for your time and cooperation, Ms. Stewart."

Wade escorted the men back to the main office. They collected their guns and went on their way.

"How'd I do," Grace asked when Wade came to say goodnight.

"You were great!" Wade exclaimed. "I'm going to watch the tape tomorrow so that I can hear both sides of the conversation."

Later that night, someone in Las Vegas received a text message. It read. *She's in Texas.*

CHAPTER TWENTY

GRACE COULDN'T SLEEP. The meeting with Welborn and Brittain had rattled her. She could tell that they doubted her story. She didn't know what they would do next.

She tossed and turned for a while before she gave up. She opened her laptop and began typing. She hadn't talked to Oliver in several days. She needed to let him know what was happening.

She decided to send him an email. This time she wanted to give away her location. It might speed things along.

Grace typed and retyped the message. She still wasn't satisfied. She wanted to give Oliver the information, but she didn't want anyone to suspect that she had set a trap. She decided that a phone call would be the best way to contact Oliver.

The time on her laptop read two fifteen a.m. She shut it down and tried again to sleep.

Wade met Lois in the parking lot of the Sheriff's department bright and early that morning. She had two grocery bags filled with food and snacks for Grace.

"Good morning, Lois," he said.

"Good morning. I hope it's all right that I brought this," she replied. "I couldn't sleep last night thinking about Grace in a cell."

"You can bring anything you want," Wade said and opened the office door for her. "I'll find out if Grace is awake and have someone take you to her."

"Thank you, Wade," said Lois.

"You can wait in my office," he told her. "Lodge and Baker will be here soon. If they smell that food, it may not get to Grace."

Lois laughed and said, "I'm quicker than I look. I brought extra just in case."

Wade winked at her and went to the technology lab. He looked at the live feed from the cells. Grace's light was on.

"It looks like she's awake," Wade told Lois when he returned. "I'll ask Maddie to take you when she gets here."

"I brought lots of homemade burritos," Lois said, grinning.

"Have I ever told you how much I love you?" Wade joked when she handed him his breakfast. "This is the next best thing to being at the inn with y'all."

Lois giggled. "There's plenty here for your deputies."

"Do I smell food?" Lodge said when he entered the building.

"You'd better take enough out for Grace before they track you down."

"I've got this," Lois replied.

She took two burritos out of one bag and put them in the other. She stood and went to Wade's door carrying the bag of burritos in her hand. She put the burritos on a nearby table and called, "Come and get it!"

Lois stepped back into Wade's office to watch the stampede. Wade stood beside her and laughed while his deputies rushed to the table.

"What on earth?" Maddie said when she saw the commotion.

"Lois is here to see Grace," Wade told her. "She brought food."

"Looks like I'd better bring more next time," Lois joked. "Do these boys get meal breaks?"

"They do," said Maddie with a laugh. "You'd never know it looking at them now."

"Would you mind taking Lois to see Grace?" Wade asked Maddie. "I don't think I should go over there at this hour of the morning."

"It will be my pleasure," Maddie said.

Lois went into Wade's office to get the food she'd brought for Grace and followed Maddie. She was uncomfortable being there and wasn't pleased to see where Grace was staying.

"Hi, Mom," said Grace. "Something smells wonderful."

"I brought you some breakfast burritos and a few snacks," Lois said and eyed her surroundings.

"It's okay, Mom," Grace assured her. "It's not that bad."

Lois sat in a chair while Grace ate. "When are you supposed to talk to the FBI?"

"I saw them last night," Grace said. "I answered their questions and told them what little I know about Todd."

"What happens next?"

"I don't know," Grace admitted. "I guess we'll have to wait and see."

"How long do you plan to stay here?"

"I'll have to go back to work sooner or later," Grace told her. "I can't afford to lose my job."

"Have you talked to your boss?" asked Lois.

"No. I need to talk to Wade about calling him," Grace answered after swallowing a mouthful of a burrito. "He needs to know what's happening. I don't know how long the story that I'm on assignment can last."

Mother and daughter discussed the situation and possible options. They were talking about the upcoming wedding when Wade joined them.

"I thought I'd see how you're doing this morning," he said.

"I'm all right," Grace answered.

"Does she have to stay in here all the time," Lois asked.

"She can roam around the office as long as she stays out of sight," Wade said. "We'll hurry her back in here if there's a problem."

"I need to call my boss," Grace said. "I haven't talked with him for days. He should know what's going on."

"You can use the phone in my office," Wade told her. "You can watch the video of last night's interview with me if you'd like."

"It could be interesting to see from a different point of view," Grace told him. "Mom, you were right about Welborn."

"Was he here?"

"In all his glory," said Wade. "You can watch too if you want."

Grace finished her meal and found a place to keep her snacks. The trio went to Wade's office. He and Lois waited outside while Grace made her call.

"Oliver, this is Grace. Can you talk?"

"I have a few minutes," he replied. "How are you?"

"I'm fine. I wanted to touch base with you. How are things there?"

"Rhonda decided to leave us," Baldwin told her. "The anchors are doing their own makeup. It's not a problem for Donna, but Barry hasn't got a clue."

Grace laughed and said, "That sounds about right."

"It's good to hear you laugh," Oliver said. "Does that mean that things are clearing up?"

"A lot has happened since we last talked," Grace told him.

She told him where she was and about the FBI. She told him that they might have an informant and what type of criminal element was involved.

"That doesn't sound good, Grace," he told her. "Are you sure you aren't making a mistake?"

"I'm not sure of anything," she told him. "How long can we use the excuse that I'm on assignment?"

"You have a point there," Oliver admitted. "The owner of the station is starting to ask questions."

"I have a lot of vacation time built up," Grace said. "Can I use some or all of it if I need to?"

"You can," he said. "It would be even better if you had a story when you come back. You are coming back, aren't you?"

"I have every intention of it," Grace assured him. "I don't have enough information for the casino story, but I have another idea."

Grace pitched the idea of running a story about her experiences while on the run. She offered to write one piece or a series of stories.

"I think that's an amazing idea," Oliver told her. "The possibility of exposing corruption in the Vegas FBI office could make national news."

"How long do I have to get the story?" Grace asked.

"That's a good question," Oliver said. "I may need to bring the owner in on this."

"I'd like to wait a little longer," Grace told him. "I don't want to tip my hand too soon.'

"I agree. This would all be for nothing if you don't find out who's out to get you," Oliver said.

"I may be able to speed things along," Grace said. "I almost sent you an email last night before I decided to call. If my communications are being monitored, it should get a quick reaction."

"Don't write or do anything foolish," Oliver warned.

"I don't plan to," she said. "I'm going to tell you where I am and that my story is coming along. I'll mention a few routine items."

"Do what you think is best, and be careful," he told her. "We need you back. It turns out that our viewers aren't fans of Donna."

"I'll talk to you soon," Grace said and hung up. She was wearing a bright smile when Wade and Lois joined her.

"What are you so happy about?" asked Lois.

She beamed and said, "My viewers don't like my replacement. I was worried she'd have my job before I could get back."

The rest of the day was uneventful. Grace sent the promised email to Oliver Baldwin. They heard nothing more from agents

Welborn and Brittain. Wade and his deputies met in the conference room that afternoon to discuss their tasks for the weekend.

"I'm sorry that this protective custody ordeal landed on Labor Day weekend," Wade told them. "Some of you have time off scheduled. I don't want you to give it up. All I ask is that you keep your cell phones charged and nearby in case we need you."

"You haven't canceled your bachelor party, have you?" asked Reed.

Wade stared at him and shook his head. "I'd forgotten all about it, to be honest. I'll call my brother and explain."

"Don't do that," Maddie told him. "I'll handle things here. You guys need a break."

"What about your time off?" Wade asked.

Maddie shrugged and said," Our trip was postponed. I'll take off when we've rescheduled."

"I don't know," Wade said with hesitation.

"The bachelor party is one night," Reed said. "You won't be out of town for twenty-four hours."

"You'll have the radio in your truck," Lodge pointed out. "We can call you if there's an emergency."

"Aren't y'all going too?" Maddie asked.

"We've talked about it," said Baker. "We're going to go in shifts."

"We'll all get to be there, and the office will be staffed," said Lodge.

"What do you say?" asked Reed.

"It sounds like I'm going to have a bachelor party," Wade said and smiled at his staff. "Thank y'all."

Wade and Lodge worked together that evening to move the rest of Wade's things into the storage unit. They moved Lodge's furniture into the house. Wade said goodnight and drove to the inn. He wanted to see Lizzie and reassure the family about Grace's safety.

He had a bad feeling about leaving them for any length of time.

He knew that Grace's plan to force her pursuer into the open could work at any moment.

Wade and Lizzie had dinner with her family and spent the rest of the evening alone.

"You're stuck with me now," Wade told her. "Lodge is moving into my house at this moment."

"Does it feel strange to know you won't be living there anymore?"

"It doesn't feel real," Wade replied.

"Are you excited about your bachelor party?"

"I was at first. Now, I'm not sure it's a good idea," he confessed.

"Because of Aunt Grace?"

He nodded and said, "I can't shake the feeling that something bad is about to happen."

"Are you sure it isn't prewedding jitters?" Lizzie joked.

Wade pulled her close and kissed her.

"I'm not nervous about the wedding," he said. "I worried that we'll have to postpone it."

"I've thought about that too," Lizzie said. "Would that mess up your honeymoon surprise?"

Wade looked at her with a raised eyebrow and a smirk. "I'm not going to tell you where we're going. I can postpone that too if needed."

"I'll need to start packing next week," Lizzie teased. "Can't you give me a little hint?"

"Nope," he said and kissed her again.

* * *

They woke up early the next morning. Wade wanted to check on Grace and get as much work done as he could. He needed to get a fishing license before his bachelor party.

"I'll be home tomorrow night," he told Lizzie. "What do the girls have planned for your bachelorette?"

"Jan promised it will be low-key," Lizzie told him. "She said something about dinner and live music."

"Promise me one thing," Wade said. "Don't drive home. Stay the night with one of the girls."

"I think that's the plan," Lizzie said and arched her brow. "Are you expecting me to have too much to drink?"

"No, not intentionally," Wade said and smirked. "Make sure you eat more than you drink this time."

They kissed each other goodbye, and Wade drove into town. He went into the office as Gonzalez was leaving.

"How was your shift?" he asked.

"It was quiet," she told him. "No calls, no arrests, and no visitors."

"That's good," Wade said. "Enjoy your time off."

"I will. Enjoy your party," she said and left the building.

Wade settled behind his desk, and his phone rang.

"Sheriff's office, this is Adams."

"This is Brock Welborn. I appreciate that you allowed us to speak with Ms. Stewart yesterday."

"It was her decision," Wade replied. "What can I do for you?"

"Brittain and I are waiting for our flight back to Vegas," he said. "We were wondering if Ms. Stewart would agree to protective custody in Las Vegas."

"Why should she do that?"

"We have more men and resources than you do," Welborn told him.

"What's in it for you?"

Welborn sighed and said, "Her presence could provoke the informer into revealing himself."

"Don't you think your visit with Ms. Stewart yesterday could have the same result?" Wade asked.

"I think he'll wait until she's back within reach," Welborn admitted.

"I'll talk with Ms. Stewart and let you know," Wade said. "Is this a good call-back number?"

"It's good until we board," replied Welborn. "We still have half an hour."

"I'll get back to you," Wade said and ended the call.

He pressed the intercom and buzzed Maddie's desk.

"Yes, Sir."

"Is Grace awake? I need to talk with her?"

"I was about to go and check on her," Maddie replied. "Do you want me to bring her to your office?"

"Yes, please."

Grace tapped on Wade's door a few minutes later and said, "Maddie said that we need to talk."

"Come in," Wade said. He waited for her to sit down before he said anything more. "Agent Welborn called. He wants to offer you the opportunity to go into protective custody with them in Vegas."

Grace stared at Wade. She shook her head and said, "He wants me to go back to Vegas. With him?"

"That's what he said. I have his number if you want to speak with him."

Grace cleared her throat and leaned back in her chair. She shook her head and rolled her eyes.

At last, she nodded and said, "I'll talk to him."

Wade dialed the number and handed the phone to Grace.

"I'll wait outside," Wade told her.

"No, please, stay," Grace said. "I want you to hear what I have to say."

"Agent Welborn, this is Grace Stewart. I understand you wanted to talk with me."

"Did Sheriff Adams tell you that we'd like for you to enter protective custody with us?" Welborn asked.

"Yes, he did," Grace replied. "I appreciate the offer, but I prefer to stay here."

"I understand that you'd like to be near your family, but we can offer more security. We have more men and more resources."

"I'm safe where I am. What guarantee do you have that I'd even make it to Vegas?"

Welborn was silent a moment before he replied, "I can't guarantee anything."

"If I'm going to be bait, it's going to be on my terms, not yours. I prefer to stay here with my family and attend my niece's wedding." Grace handed the phone to Wade, sat back, and crossed her arms.

"Welborn?" Wade said into the phone.

"Yes."

"I don't think she's interested," Wade said and hung up.

He grinned at Grace and said, "That was awesome."

"He had a lot of nerve thinking I'd go anywhere with him," Grace said. "I feel safer right here than I've felt since I left Vegas."

"We'll do our best to keep you safe," Wade said pleased.

"I know you will," Grace said. "There's a bonus to this too."

"What bonus?"

"I can spend time getting to know my new nephew," Grace said and smiled.

"Wade beamed at her and said, "I hadn't thought of that."

They chatted a little longer. Wade didn't want to tell her what he had planned for the weekend. He'd be leaving soon, and he had no choice.

"Grace, I hate to say this," he began. "We're going to be short-handed since it's a holiday weekend. I think you should stay in lockdown until Monday morning."

"I understand," she replied. "Have you told my family?"

Wade shook his head and said," I haven't had the heart. I will before I leave today."

"I'll tell them," Grace volunteered. "We can ask them to bring us lunch, and I'll explain it to them."

"I'm pretty sure they've already planned to bring lunch for

you," Wade told her. "I'll call to double-check. We could all eat in the conference room."

"That's a great idea," Grace said. "Would it be okay if I call my boss again? He was going to check into something for me. I need to know what he found out before lockdown."

"Be my guest," Wade said. "I'll give you some privacy."

Wade left the room, and Grace made her call. The Fletchers arrived at the office at eleven-thirty with enough food to feed an army. They invited everyone on duty to join them for lunch.

Grace told her family about the conversation she'd had with Welborn.

"What possessed him to believe you'd consent to go with him to Las Vegas?" asked Lois.

"I don't have any idea, Mom. He knows that won't happen now," Grace told her. "I've spoken with Oliver too."

"What did you find out?" asked James.

"He explained everything to the owner of the station," Grace said. "I'm officially on assignment until this is over. I have to have a story ready when I get back."

"That's wonderful," said Lois.

"I'm going to be spending a lot of time writing," Grace said. "Wade thinks it best that I stay in lockdown this weekend. I'll have a lot of uninterrupted time to work on my story."

"I'm sorry, y'all," Wade said. "It's a holiday weekend. Some of the deputies will have to be on patrol. Others put in for time off weeks ago. We'll all be available in case of emergency."

"We know you're doing what you think is best to keep Grace safe," said James. "We can't ask for more."

"I have my cell with me," Grace said. "I can check in with you if you'd like."

"I'd like to hear from you once or twice this weekend," Lois said.

"I'll call at nine o'clock every night," Grace assured her.

"Now that that's settled," James began. "Wade and I have a bachelor party to get to. Wyatt is going to meet us at the lake."

"I have two requests," Wade said. "I need to get a fishing license before we leave town, and we need to take my truck, so I'll have the radio if needed."

"That's fine with me," James said. "We'd better get moving."

"Have a good time," Lizzie said and kissed Wade goodbye. "Be safe."

"You do the same," Wade told her. "I'll see you tomorrow."

CHAPTER TWENTY-ONE

WADE AND JAMES drove back to town Sunday afternoon. The bachelor party had been a success. They'd had a good time and caught more fish than they'd expected.

They were both tired and in need of a shower. Wade wanted to stop by the office to check on Grace before going to the inn.

He led the way to Grace's cell and tapped on the glass window. She looked out and waved at them. Wade used his key to open the door.

"How was the party?" Grace asked.

"We had a great time," James told her. "How have you been?"

"It's been really quiet," she told her brother. "Maddie comes to see me when she can."

"That's good," Wade said. "Is there anything you need?"

"No, I'm fine," Grace told him.

"How is your story coming along?" James asked.

"It's taking shape," she said. "I don't know how it's going to end. The rest is looking good."

"None of us know that," said Wade. "Have you heard anything from your boss?"

"Not since yesterday."

James wrinkled his nose and sniffed the air. "I think we need to get home and shower."

"We are getting ripe," Wade agreed.

"I didn't want to say anything," Grace joked.

"I'll be here in the morning," Wade told her. "I'm going to lock you in again."

"Was it something I said?" Grace teased. "See you tomorrow."

Wade smirked and locked the door. The men went back to the office and the parking area.

"It looks like the girls took my truck home," James observed. "Mind if I ride the rest of the way with you?"

"Let's go," said Wade.

They climbed into the truck and drove home. Wade dropped James at his house and backtracked to the inn.

Lizzie was at the table making floral arrangements for their wedding. She smiled when she saw Wade. She wrinkled her nose when he got too close.

"Ewww, did you wrestle every fish in the lake?" she joked.

"Nah, I missed a few," he told her.

"Did you have a good time?"

"We did and caught quite a few fish," Wade told her. "How was your party?"

"It was great!" Lizzie told him. "We had dinner at a fancy restaurant in Wichita Falls and then went to a bar to hear a live band. We spent the night at a hotel and drove back to town this morning."

Wade reached for her and pulled her close. He kissed her and saw an odd look on her face.

"What's wrong?"

"Sweetheart, I love you," she told him. "Right now, I want you to shower."

Wade pretended offense. "You don't like my manly smell?"

"I love your manly smell," Lizzie said, covering her nose. "It's the fishy smell that I can live without."

"I remember a time not so long ago that you had an unpleasant aroma," Wade said.

"You said it wasn't that bad," Lizzie cried.

"I lied," Wade said, smirking. "You reeked."

Lizzie flung a bouquet at him. He dodged and laughed. She picked it up, ready to try again.

He ran toward the bathroom. The flowers hit him in the back before he reached the door.

Lizzie laughed. She waited until she heard the shower running to retrieve the bouquet from the floor. Wade was waiting inside the door. She screamed when he grabbed her and drug her into the shower with him, fully clothed.

"I missed you, Darlin," he said.

"I missed you too."

* * *

Wade went to the office after breakfast the next morning. He was anxious to find out how the search for their suspect was going.

"How was your trip?" Maddie asked when she arrived.

"It was great!" he told her. "Thanks again for taking care of things here."

"You're welcome," she said. "Grace is awake and dressed. She wants to know if she can come out and play."

Wade smiled and said, "I think it would be safe for her to have a short break from that room. I'm sure Lois will be here sometime today."

"I'll tell her," Maddie said.

Lodge and Baker came in together. They were arguing about who had caught the most fish.

"Wade, you can settle this," Lodge said. "Which of us caught the most fish."

"It's no contest," Wade told them. "I did."

"No way!" said Baker.

"Think about it, boys. I was there longer than either of you."

"That's true," said Lodge. "We'll break it down to make it fair. Who caught the most fish in two hours?"

"I did," Wade said with a wicked grin.

"I can see we aren't going to win this one," said Baker and pointed at Lodge and himself. "Which one of us caught the most fish."

"I don't know. I was too busy with my own," Wade said and laughed at the expressions on his deputies' faces.

"We were never going to win that argument, were we?" Lodge joked.

"Nope!"

The outer door opened, and the men turned to see Megan Ford coming inside with a big bakery box. Wade was close enough to his office that he was able to duck out of sight. Lodge and Baker weren't so lucky.

"Good morning," Megan sang when she saw the two men. "I thought you might like some breakfast. It's a shame you have to work on a holiday."

Baker was rescued by the ringing of his phone. Lodge had no choice. He took the box and talked with Megan.

"Clint is off today," he told her. "I'm sure you can catch him at his place."

"He isn't there," Megan replied. "He went to visit one of his friends."

"I'll put this in the fridge in the break room. He can have it tomorrow," said Lodge.

"I didn't bring it for him, silly," Megan said and patted his arm. "I brought it for all of you."

"Oh, well, thank you," Lodge stammered. "That's very nice. We appreciate it."

"I'll get out of your way," Megan said and turned to leave. "She waved at Baker with one finger and left the office.

Wade stood in his doorway and leaned on the frame. "What did she bring you?"

Lodge scowled at Wade and said, "She didn't bring it to me. She brought it for all of us."

"It smells good," said Baker. "It smells like those cinnamon rolls from the bakery."

Yeah, they do, don't they," said Lodge. He put the box on his desk and opened it. He took a hot gooey roll from the box.

"I'm taking one first because you made me talk to her," Lodge said and bit into it. "Mmmm."

He sat at his desk and enjoyed the cinnamon roll to the point that Baker and Wade could stand it no longer. They both helped themselves.

"Those look good," said Grace. "May I have one?"

"Help yourself," said Lodge. "They're amazing."

Grace went in search of paper towels. She brought one back for each of them before taking a cinnamon roll from the box.

"Are you trying to tell me something, Grace?" asked Wade.

"What do you mean?"

"Yesterday, I smelled bad. Today you give me a napkin," Wade joked.

"Well, you are a little messy," Grace said with a grin.

They were all laughing together when they heard the outer door open. Wade grabbed Grace, pushed her into his office, and shut the door. He relaxed when he saw James and Ellen.

He opened the door and said, "False alarm. I think y'all should visit somewhere out of sight."

"We'll go back to my room," Grace told him.

Grace led her brother and sister-in-law to her cell. They brought her two books and a movie to occupy her time. Lois sent another bag of snacks.

"I'm going to gain a hundred pounds if this keeps up," she told them. "Do they have a gym or workout equipment here?"

"You'll have to ask Wade," said Ellen with a smile.

"Have you heard anything? Has anything happened?" James asked.

"Not a thing," Grace told him. "I thought something would have happened by now."

"The day isn't over," Ellen told her. "It could take time to get here from Las Vegas."

"Flying is faster than driving," Grace said. "They'd still have to drive part of the way."

"What are you going to do if this doesn't work?" asked James.

"I've been thinking about that," she said. "I haven't made a decision. I'm staying put for now. I don't want to miss Lizzie's wedding."

"I wish you didn't have to stay in this cell," said Ellen.

"It could be worse," Grace said. "I'm making the best of it."

James and Ellen said goodbye and returned to the inn. Lizzie was looking at her flower arrangements and frowning.

"I need to go into town," she told them. "I didn't buy enough ribbon to finish these."

"I would have picked some up for you," Ellen said.

"I didn't realize I needed more until just before you came home."

"Can't it wait until tomorrow?" asked James. "We can get it for you when we go to see Grace."

"I'd rather finish these today," Lizzie said. "I'm supposed to meet Jan and Faith tomorrow."

"What do you girls have planned now?" asked Ellen.

"We're having lunch and then getting mani-pedis for the wedding."

"That sounds like fun," Ellen said. "What do you have in mind for dinner tonight?"

"Oh no! I forgot all about dinner," Lizzie admitted.

"Why don't I go into town with you?" Ellen suggested. "We can get what you need and pick up something for dinner."

"Wade should be home by the time we get back," Lizzie said.

"I'm going to see if Dan needs any help," James said. "You girls have fun."

Ellen made a shopping list while Lizzie determined how much ribbon she'd need. They got into Lizzie's jeep and started toward town.

Lizzie looked at the fuel gauge and said, "I'm going to need gas before we start home."

"We can get what you need from the craft store first," Ellen suggested. "Then we'll do the grocery shopping and get gas."

"That should put us back in time to get everything done before dinner," Lizzie said.

The two women finished their errands and stopped at a gas station. Lizzie got out of the jeep and started toward the pump.

"Hello, Lizzie," said a familiar voice.

Lizzie turned around and saw Ben Wagner at the next pump.

"Hello, how are you?" Lizzie asked.

"I'm doing fine?" he said. "Aren't you about to be married?"

"On Saturday," Lizzie said with a bright smile.

"Are you closing the inn for the occasion?" asked Ben.

"Yes, but it will reopen on Monday," Lizzie replied. "I won't be back at work until the beginning of next month."

"We have some friends coming to visit. I thought they'd enjoy a trip to the inn," said Ben.

"We'd love to have y'all," Lizzie said.

Ben Wagner waved, got into his car, and drove away. Lizzie filled the gas tank of her jeep and returned the nozzle to the pump.

They went back to the inn and unloaded the jeep. Lizzie finished the floral arrangements while Ellen put away the groceries and planned dinner.

The family gathered around the dinner table at six o'clock.

"How is Grace doing today?" Lois asked Wade.

"She's doing all right," he said. "I checked on her before I came home. She was burning up the keyboard on her laptop."

"What's she writing?" Dan asked between bites.

"She's writing a story about her experiences," James said. "They plan to air it on the news when she gets back to Vegas."

"That could be interesting," Dan said. "There might be some things that you don't know about."

James looked at Dan before replying. "I hadn't thought about that. I'm sure she hasn't told us everything that she's been through. She doesn't like to worry us."

"Do you think she could be keeping something important from you?" asked Wade.

"I don't think so," Lois said. "I can always tell when she lies."

"Maybe she isn't lying," suggested Dan. "Maybe she's leaving out details."

The Fletchers didn't respond. They knew Grace well enough to know that what Dan suggested was a real possibility.

"I could talk with her tomorrow," Wade offered. "She might tell me things that she wouldn't want to tell y'all."

"That's true," said Lois. "I don't think she's keeping anything from us. It would be nice to be sure."

"How are the wedding arrangements coming along?" James asked, changing the subject.

"The flowers are done," Lizzie told him. "I'll start decorating when I get back from town tomorrow."

"I can decorate while you're gone," Ellen offered. "I need something to do."

"I'll help," Lois offered. "We might have it finished before you get back."

"What about your tux, Wade?" asked Ellen.

"I'm supposed to pick it up tomorrow afternoon," he answered.

"Have you decided where you'll be on the day of the wedding?" Lois queried. "You know it's bad luck to see the bride before the wedding."

"I thought we were going to skip that tradition," Wade said, knowing that was out of the question.

"You can stay at our house," James said. "No point in staying in town when all of your stuff is here."

"Thanks. That should make it easier," Wade replied and took a big drink from his glass.

"Wade and his groomsmen can use one of the upstairs rooms," Ellen suggested. "Lizzie and the girls can use her room and the office."

"That leaves one more thing," said Lizzie.

"What's left?" Lois asked.

Lizzie looked at her grandmother and winked. "Where are we going for our honeymoon?"

Wade spewed tea through his nose. He gasped for air and laughed at the same time.

The rest of the family laughed with him. He mopped his face and looked at Lizzie. She batted her eyelashes at him and beamed.

"Darlin," he said. "That's for me to know and you to find out."

"I'm trying to find out," she replied. "You won't tell me."

"I haven't told anyone else either," he said and leaned toward her. "You'll find out this weekend."

"What am I supposed to pack?"

"I'll pack for you," he said with an evil grin.

"That'll be interesting," Dan said with a smirk.

The family talked and joked until it was time to say goodnight. Wade and Lizzie locked up when the others had gone and snuggled together under the covers.

"Are you serious about not telling me where we're going?" Lizzie asked.

"I'll give you one hint," he said. "Where would you go if you could go anywhere in the world?"

Lizzie sat up and looked at him with wide eyes. "Are we going to the Bahamas?"

"Nope," Wade said and laughed at the look on her face.

"Where are we going?"

"I said I'd give you one hint," he said, trying to keep a straight face. "That was it. We aren't going to the Bahamas."

"Wade Adams, you're a rat," she said and tried to cover his face with her pillow.

He blocked the pillow and wrapped his arms around her. "I don't want to spoil the surprise. You'll want to pack light clothes."

"Thank you," she said. "That helps more than you know. I don't care where we go. I just want to be with you."

"I feel the same way, Darlin."

* * *

The Fletcher women began decorating the inn the next morning after the men had gone and the dishes were done. Lizzie lined the banisters with yellow roses, greenery, and twinkle lights.

Ellen and Lois decorated the fireplace mantel and the lobby with the same theme. The flower arrangements that Lizzie had made were strategically placed around the inn. Yellow roses, white daisies, and silver satin ribbon adorned the registration desk and the side tables throughout the inn.

The wedding would take place in the original house. Chairs were placed facing an archway where the bride and groom would stand to make their vows.

"Lizzie, we'll work on this," Ellen told her daughter. "You need to get to town."

Lizzie looked at the time on her phone. "I hate to leave you to do all the work."

"We'll leave some for you to do," Lois said. "Now go on and have a good time."

"All right," Lizzie replied. "Promise you won't work too hard."

"We promise," Ellen said. "Get moving, or you'll be late."

Lizzie obeyed and rushed to her room. She showered and put

on fresh clothes before hurrying to her jeep. Jan and Faith were already at the restaurant when she arrived.

"I was just about to call you," said Faith.

"We were decorating, and I lost track of the time," Lizzie told her friend.

They were seated at a corner table and ordered their drinks. Jan almost burst with excitement.

"Are you excited? Are you nervous? How is Wade? Does he have the jitters?"

Lizzie waited until Jan paused for breath to answer. "Yes, I am excited and a little nervous. Wade seems to be fine."

"What are you nervous about?" Faith asked.

"I'm nervous about the wedding," Lizzie said. "I feel like I've forgotten something. Something important."

Jan and Faith took turns naming items and prewedding chores. They ordered their meal and continued trying to make Lizzie feel more at ease.

"Have you checked on the cake?" asked Faith.

"Yes," Lizzie answered. "It will be at the inn at one. The caterer will be there at four."

"I can't think of anything else," Jan said. "You picked up your dress."

Lizzie's eyes widened, and her mouth dropped open. "I forgot to pick up my dress!"

"When were you supposed to get it?" Faith asked with alarm.

"Friday afternoon. We've been so busy that I totally forgot."

"That's no problem," Jan said, trying to remain calm. "I'll call the dress shop and tell her you'll be there this afternoon."

"How could I have forgotten my dress?" Lizzie said, not hearing her cousin."

Jan took out her cell phone and dialed the number to the dress shop. Lizzie was too stunned to hear the conversation. Faith tried to console her and patted her shoulder.

"Lizzie, it's all set," Jan told her. "We'll pick it up before we go to the salon."

"Here, drink some of your tea," Faith said and handed Lizzie her glass.

Lizzie obeyed and took a big gulp. "We were talking about Wade's tux last night. It didn't register that I hadn't picked up my dress."

"It's going to be all right," Faith said. "It's better than standing in your undies on your wedding day and discovering you don't have a dress."

Lizzie looked at her friend with horror. Jan burst into laughter at her cousin's expression. Faith and Lizzie joined in. They were still laughing when Tiffany approached their table.

"Hello, Lizzie," she said.

"Hi, how are you?" Lizzie replied, wondering what Tiffany was up to.

"I want to congratulate you on your upcoming wedding. Wade's a great guy. You're a lucky woman."

"Thank you," Lizzie said.

"I hope you'll have a long and happy marriage," Tiffany said and walked away.

The three women looked at each other with raised brows. They finished lunch and drove to the dress shop. Lizzie didn't relax until the wedding gown was safely locked in her jeep.

They went to the salon and enjoyed an afternoon of pampering. Lizzie hated for it to end. The women said goodbye and got into their cars. Lizzie drove home and sang along with the radio.

Wade went to see Grace before he left the office. He picked up his tuxedo and drove toward the inn. He passed a vehicle parked on the side of the highway. *Was that Lizzie's jeep?*

He turned around and went back for a better look. A green Jeep Wrangler was parked on the shoulder with a flat tire.

The hair on his neck and arms stood on end. His heart felt as though he'd been hit with a defibrillator. He didn't remember getting out of his truck. He forgot to breathe.

He looked inside. Lizzie's purse and cell phone lay in the passenger seat. Something lay across the back seat in a plastic zippered bag.

"Lizzie!" he screamed. "Lizzie, where are you!"

He sank to his knees. His mind reeled, and he felt sick. He knelt beside the driver's door. He put his hands on the ground and hung his head.

"NO! This can't be happening! Lizzie can't be dead!"

CHAPTER TWENTY-TWO

WADE REMAINED on his hands and knees until the dizziness and nausea passed. He tried to stand. His knees were too weak to hold him.

He sat on the grass and wrapped his arms around his legs. He rested his head on his knees and prayed for Lizzie's safety.

His senses gradually returned. He took out his cell phone. His hand shook when he dialed his office.

"Sheriff's office, this is Clifton."

"Maddie, call out the team. Highway 70 near the Rayland exit."

"Wade, what's wrong?"

He struggled to explain. "I found…I…found…Lizzie's jeep…abandoned.

"We're on our way!"

It seemed an eternity before Wade saw flashing lights in the distance. He tried again to stand, but he didn't have the strength. Tears rolled down his face when his team rushed to him.

"Wade? Are you okay?" Maddie asked.

Wade nodded and said, "Lizzie, where's Lizzie?"

"We'll find her," Maddie said. "Let's get you into your truck."

Lodge and Baker lifted Wade to his feet. They led him to his truck, and Maddie opened the passenger door. He somehow managed to climb in and sit on the passenger seat. The deputies moved a few feet away from Wade to discuss their plan.

"I'll call Dr. Hughes," Maddie told Baker. "You and Lodge start processing the scene."

The men nodded and went to work. Maddie dialed Dr. Hughes and explained the situation.

"I'm on my way," said Dr. Hughes. "Has anyone notified Lizzie's family?"

"I don't know," Maddie answered. "Wade may have called them. If not, I'd rather wait until we've processed the scene."

"That's a good idea," said Dr. Hughes. "I'll be there soon."

Maddie approached Wade and asked, "Wade, have you called the Fletchers?"

He looked at her with confusion, then shook his head and said, "No, I haven't called anyone else."

"Dr. Hughes is on his way," Maddie told him. "Can you tell me what happened?"

"I was on my way home and passed the jeep. I wasn't sure it was Lizzie's until I turned around and came back."

"Then what happened?"

"I called for Lizzie. She didn't answer. I couldn't find her. I opened the door and saw…"

Wade's eyes were wide, and his face blank. Maddie knew he was picturing the scene.

"What did you see, Wade?"

"Maddie, it's the same as the Ratliff scene."

The abrupt change in Wade's demeanor surprised his deputy. "What?"

Wade was all business. "Lizzie's jeep looks the same way."

He slid out of the seat and paced near his truck. "Ratliff's keys were still in the ignition. Her personal items were on the passenger seat."

Maddie realized what Wade was trying to tell her. "You're saying it was the same perpetrator."

"Yes!" Wade said and sat down in his truck again. "We have to find her before…"

"We will," Maddie said. "What did you do after you looked in the jeep? We need to know what evidence you left."

Wade nodded and said, "It's kind of a blur. I don't remember doing anything else. I think I sat down and stayed there until you got here."

"Dr. Hughes is here," Maddie told him. "I'm going to help Lodge and Baker while you talk with him."

"Maddie, you have to take the lead," Wade said, his eyes pleading. "I don't know what I'll do if Lizzie's…"

"I know," she said and patted his shoulder.

Maddie met Dr. Hughes before she joined the other deputies.

"How is he?" the doctor asked.

"He's starting to come around," she told him. "He says the scene is like the one in the Ratliff case."

Dr. Hughes shook his head and said, "I'll stay with him while you do your work."

"Thanks, Doctor," she said. "He said he didn't call anyone else."

"I'd prefer to keep it that way for now," said Hughes.

Lodge was examining the flat tire when Maddie joined him.

"I don't see a nail or a cut in the tire," Lodge told her. "It could be underneath."

"We'll take it to town when we're done here," Maddie said. "Have you looked inside?"

"No, Baker and I have been working the outside."

Baker joined them and shared his findings.

"The grass is flattened behind the jeep. It looks like she pulled off the pavement back there," he said, pointing. "Someone else pulled over behind her. Someone may have stopped to help."

"I hope that's what happened," Maddie said. "Do you have any idea how long the jeep has been sitting here?"

Lodge went around the front of the jeep and touched the hood. He lifted it and held his hand over the engine. He closed the hood and walked toward Maddie and Baker.

He shook his head and said in a low voice, "It doesn't look good. The engine is cool."

Maddie nodded and took a pair of rubber gloves from her pocket.

"We need to process the jeep. The sooner we get Wade away from here, the better."

Maddie opened the door and looked inside. She examined and bagged Lizzie's belongings. She took them to her car and put them in the trunk. She used the raised trunk lid to keep Wade from seeing her. She dialed a number on the cell phone and waited.

"This is Maddie Clifton with the sheriff's department," she said. "I need a tow truck to move a vehicle to our garage."

She gave directions and ended the call. She dialed a second number.

"Mr. Wilkinson, this is Deputy Maddie Clifton. We have a missing person. Would it be possible for you to bring your search dogs right away?"

Maddie hung up the phone and closed the trunk. She spoke with Lodge and Baker before approaching Wade and Dr. Hughes.

"The tow truck is on its way," she told them. "Baker and Lodge are going to finish here. I think it's time we talked with Lizzie's family."

"I don't think Wade should be driving just now," Dr. Hughes told her.

Maddie nodded and looked at Wade. "Do you mind if I drive your truck?"

Wade looked at her and said, "I think you'd better."

"I'll follow you," said Dr. Hughes.

Wade put on his seatbelt and closed the door. Maddie climbed in and started the truck. They drove away, leaving Lodge and Baker at the scene.

"I don't envy Maddie right now," said Lodge.

"Neither do I," Baker replied. "How long do you think it'll take them to get here with the dogs?"

"Twenty minutes to half an hour," Lodge said.

"Do we have something of Fletcher's for them to get her scent?"

"Maddie found a jacket on the floorboard. She left it with the other evidence in the trunk. She didn't want Wade to figure out what she planned to do."

"It's going to be hard to keep Wade away from this case," Baker pointed out. "That's another job I don't envy doing."

"Yep, he's scared and worried now," said Lodge. "It's going to be ugly when he gets mad and determined."

The tow truck arrived, and the two deputies supervised the removal of the jeep from the scene. Mr. Wilkinson and his dogs reached the scene as the tow truck drove away.

Lodge explained the situation to Mr. Wilkinson while Baker took the jacket from the trunk of Maddie's car.

Wilkinson held the jacket for his dogs to smell. He gave them the command, and they began searching the area.

The dogs concentrated on the area around the jeep. They'd move away for a moment and return to the vehicle. The men watched the dogs for twenty minutes.

"They can smell her near the front of the jeep," Wilkinson said. "They lose her scent when they move away."

"Thank you, Mr. Wilkinson," Baker said. "I think that's all we can do for now."

Wilkinson called his dogs and loaded them in his pickup.

"I'm sorry, they didn't find her trail," said Wilkinson. "Someone may have given her a ride."

"That's what we're afraid of," Lodge said under his breath.

Baker got into Maddie's car, and Lodge got into his. They drove back to the sheriff's department. They wanted to begin processing the evidence right away.

* * *

Maddie parked Wade's truck near the front door of the inn. They got out and waited for Dr. Hughes to join them.

The trio walked up the steps and stood on the front porch. Wade swallowed hard and opened the front door.

Lois heard the tinkle of the front door bells and met them in the lobby. She smiled and started toward them, then stopped.

"Something's wrong," she said.

Wade nodded.

"Are James and Ellen here," asked Maddie.

"They're on the patio," Lois said and led the way.

James and Ellen were arranging the patio tables and chairs for the wedding reception. They didn't see their visitors at first. They turned and saw grim expressions on their faces.

Wade looked at them and said, "I'm sorry." A tear leaked from his eye.

"Sorry, for what?" asked Ellen.

"What's happened?" asked James.

"I think we'd all better sit down," said Dr. Hughes.

James and Ellen sank into the nearest chairs. Dr. Hughes led Lois to a seat while Maddie led Wade. They sat down with the family.

"Lizzie is missing," Maddie said. "Wade found her jeep on the side of the road."

"Missing!" Ellen exclaimed. "What do you mean?"

"Her jeep was parked. There was no sign of Lizzie," Maddie told them. "Have you spoken to her this afternoon?"

"I haven't talked with her since she went into town," said Ellen.

James and Lois said they hadn't heard from her.

"She's probably at a friend's house," James said, taking his phone from his pocket. "I'll call her."

"She doesn't have her phone," Wade said in a whisper. "It's in her jeep."

James stared at Wade and lowered his phone.

"I don't understand," said Lois. "How can she be missing?"

"I know this is difficult," said Dr. Hughes. "I'm sure Deputy Clifton and the others will find her soon."

"Wade?" Ellen said. "What happened?"

"I was on my way here," he began. "I passed the jeep and turned around to see if it was Lizzie's. She was gone. Her stuff was inside. She was gone."

Ellen put a hand over her mouth. Tears welled in her eyes. She grasped James' hand for comfort. Lois put her hand on her son's shoulder.

Maddie's phone rang, and she excused herself. Dr. Hughes spoke with the family.

"Wade has had quite a shock," he said. "I've given him a mild sedative. He may not be able to respond to your questions when it takes effect."

Maddie came back to the patio and explained what they'd found at the scene. The Fletchers listened in silence to Maddie's voice. She tried to comfort them as best she could.

"We didn't find anything at the scene that would indicate foul play," she told them. "The search dogs didn't find her scent. We know she didn't walk away. Chances are that someone picked her up. She may have left her things expecting to be right back."

"Then where is she?" James asked.

"It may have taken longer than she expected," Maddie told him.

"You don't believe that's what happened, do you?" asked Lois.

Maddie sighed and said, "I don't know what happened. I'll have a better idea when the evidence is processed."

Lois nodded, unsatisfied.

"Do you feel up to answering some questions?" asked Maddie.

They nodded and prepared themselves to answer.

"When did Lizzie leave to go into town?"

"It was eleven-thirty this morning," Ellen said. "She was going to have lunch with Jan and Faith."

"What time did you expect her back?"

"She didn't say," Ellen replied. "I assumed she'd be here in time for dinner."

"Did she have other plans while she was in town?"

"The girls were going to have mani-pedis after lunch. They wanted to look nice for the wedding."

Ellen's eyes widened, and she looked at Wade. "The wedding! We have to find her in time for the wedding!"

"Did she mention going anywhere or doing anything else?" Maddie asked, trying to keep their minds in the present.

Ellen shook her head and said nothing more.

"She planned to come back to help with the decorating," Lois said.

"Who are Jan and Faith?" asked Maddie. She thought she knew, but she wanted to keep their minds focused.

"Jan Wagner is our niece, Lizzie's cousin," James answered. "Faith Foreman is Lizzie's best friend."

"Do they live in town?"

James nodded.

"Do you happen to know their addresses or phone numbers?"

"I do," Wade said and handed her his cell phone. "They're in my contacts. I should have called them. Lizzie could be with one of them."

"I'm sure Deputy Clifton will take care of that," said Dr. Hughes. He sensed that Wade was recovering from the initial shock.

Maddie copied the numbers and addresses into her phone. She excused herself and called both women. She returned to the patio with a grim expression.

"They haven't spoken with her since they left the salon at four o'clock," Maddie told them. "Is there anything you can remember that could help us find her?"

The family shook their heads. Wade looked at Maddie. His eyes were glazed. The tranquilizer was beginning to work.

"I think Wade needs to go to bed," said Dr. Hughes. "He shouldn't be left alone."

"I'll stay with him," said James. "He's taking this hard."

"We'll all stay," said Ellen. "We need to be together."

"I think that's a good idea," said Dr. Hughes.

He stood and helped Wade to his feet. James led the way to Lizzie's room, and the two men made sure that Wade was comfortable. He was snoring by the time they left him alone.

Dr. Hughes chatted with the rest of the family to determine their state of mind. He left a few tranquilizers in case Wade should need them.

The family was dealing with the situation better than Wade. He hadn't given them any details about the Ratliff case. They didn't know that he believed Lizzie had been killed.

Maddie and Dr. Hughes said goodnight and drove back to town. Ellen and Lois went to their house to gather what they'd need for a few days.

The Fletchers had a light dinner and waited for the phone to ring. They expected Lizzie to call at any moment.

Dr. Hughes dropped Maddie off at the office. She found Lodge and Baker to discuss what they knew.

"No prints in the jeep other than Fletcher's. We found Wade's prints on the driver's door handle," Baker told her.

"I found the cause of the flat," Lodge said. "This was inside the tire."

He handed Maddie an evidence bag with a nine-millimeter bullet inside.

"Does it match the one from Ratliff's car?"

"It's going to be hard to tell," Lodge said. "It must have hit the rim. We can check with this one."

Maddie took the second bag and asked, "Where did you find this one?"

"In the wheel well," Lodge said. "The shooter must have missed and fired a second shot."

"Were there any prints on Lizzie's things other than hers?"

"The garment bag in the back seat had someone else's prints," Baker replied. "It was Fletcher's wedding dress. The prints could belong to someone at the store where she bought it."

"Have you had a chance to check her cell phone?" asked Maddie.

"The technology department has gone for the day," Baker said. "I thought I'd give it a try when I've finished here."

"Aren't y'all supposed to be gone too," Maddie asked.

"So are you," Lodge pointed out. "We don't want to leave until we've gone through the evidence."

"I know," Maddie said and frowned. "I don't either. I'll call Reed to let him know what's happened."

"Order some pizza while you're on the phone," suggested Baker. "It might be a long night."

"Got it," Maddie said. "I'll help you process this when I get back."

Maddie went to her desk and picked up the phone. She dialed Reed's number and waited.

"Reed, we have a problem," she said and explained.

"What's going on?" Reed asked. "Is it bad?"

"It's bad," Maddie said. "Lizzie Fletcher is missing."

"Do you think it's the same perpetrator?" he asked.

"It looks that way," she said. "How do we want to handle this?"

"We'll work together on both cases," he said. "You're the lead on Fletcher's, and I'll continue the lead on Ratliff's. How's Wade?"

"Not good," Maddie replied. "He processed Ratliff's car. He knows what this means. Her family is doing a little better."

"Have you told our guest?" asked Reed.

"I've been so busy that I forgot," admitted Maddie. "I'll tell her. I still need to talk to the women Lizzie met for lunch."

"I'll be there in a few minutes," Reed said.

"It's your night off," Maddie protested.

"You're going to need help," he said. "Odom and Gonzalez aren't expected back at work until tomorrow. Wade can't help."

"I wish we had our new hires in place," Maddie said and ended the call.

She went to the cell area and tapped on Grace's door.

"Come in," Grace called.

Maddie unlocked the door and stepped inside. "I have some news."

Grace listened while Maddie explained what had happened. She stood and paced when Maddie finished.

"This is all my fault," she said. "I never dreamed they'd go after my family."

"We don't know that this is connected to your case," Maddie told her.

Grace stopped pacing and faced Maddie. "You don't know that it isn't either."

"We don't know anything for sure right now," Maddie said.

"Have you told my family?"

"Yes, they're at the inn," Maddie replied. "Wade is with them. They're not doing well."

Grace sank onto her cot. "I'll never forgive myself if this is my fault."

"This isn't your fault," Maddie told her. "You did what you thought was best to keep everyone safe. We don't know that the people looking for you had anything to do with this."

Grace looked at the deputy with doubt in her eyes. "Would you tell me the truth if you did know?"

Maddie looked at Grace and then sat down beside her.

"I would," Maddie told her. "I believe that it's better to deal with the truth from the beginning rather than try to sort it out later."

"What do you think happened?" Grace asked her.

"Don't mention this to your family when you talk to them," Maddie said. "Everything we've found so far indicates that it's connected to a current case. Wade knows because he processed the other vehicle. I don't think he told the family any details about it."

Grace looked at Maddie and said, "Thank you for telling me. Do you think Lizzie is dead?"

"We didn't find any evidence at the scene that would lead us to believe that," Maddie said.

"That's not what I asked," Grace pressed.

Maddie didn't answer right away. She thought about it before answering.

"It's possible," Maddie admitted. "But I have to believe that she's still alive."

Grace's phone rang, and she looked at the caller id.

"It's my mom. I'd better answer."

"I'll get back to work," Maddie said. "I'll lock you in again."

Grace nodded and answered the phone. Maddie locked the door and went back toward the office. Her mind was reeling when she reached her desk.

Reed came in and said, "What do you want me to do?"

Maddie didn't answer. She was typing, changing the facial recognition search parameters.

"Maddie?"

Maddie looked up and stared at Reed. She shook her head and said, "I'm sorry. I didn't hear you."

"What do you want me to do?" he asked again.

"I was just talking with Grace," Maddie said. "She said something that struck a nerve."

"Tell me," Reed said and pulled up a chair.

"She believes that Lizzie's disappearance has to do with her. What if she's right?"

"Ratliff was killed before Grace got here," Reed pointed out.

"What if her death is connected to the Anthony case?" Maddie asked. "What if it's all connected?"

"Ratliff was Anthony's niece," Reed said, reflecting. "Grace was dating Anthony. You may be onto something."

"We need to interview Lizzie's friends," Grace said.

Their conversation was interrupted by the pizza delivery. They called Baker and Lodge to join them. They discussed their ideas and the evidence while they ate.

"I've expanded the facial recognition search to the Las Vegas area," Maddie told them. "Every available database, not just the criminals."

"Will that speed things up?" Baker asked and took a big bite from his pizza.

"I doubt it," Maddie said. "It would go a little faster if I could use multiple computers to search. We don't have enough available computers to do that."

"Where are you running the searches now?" asked Lodge.

"I have two running, one at each of the vacant deputy stations," she said.

"You can run one on mine," Baker offered. "I can use the one at the counter or pause the program if I need a machine."

"Mine too," said Lodge.

"We can talk with the technology lab," Reed said. "They may let us use one or two of their machines."

"That could speed up the process," Maddie said. "I don't want to stop these. One of them has been running for days. I'm afraid it'll start over."

"We won't touch those," Reed said. "Start new ones on Lodge's machine and Baker's machine. You boys can use my computer if you need one. We might be able to use Wade's when needed too."

"What are we going to do about Wade?" asked Baker. "You know he's going to want to be in the middle of this."

"I'll handle Wade," Reed said. "At least, I'll try."

CHAPTER TWENTY-THREE

DAN ARRIVED the next morning to find Wade and Fletchers in poor condition. The men needed a shave, and the women still wore their nightgowns and robes.

"Is something wrong?" he asked when he joined them at the table.

Wade looked at Dan, ran both hands through his hair, and nodded.

"Lizzie is missing," James said with tears in his eyes. "We don't know where she is or what has happened to her."

Ellen told him what little they knew. Dan sat back and tried to process the news.

"What are we going to do?" Dan asked. "Someone is out looking for her, right?"

"My deputies are doing everything they can to find her," Wade said. "There aren't any leads for them to follow."

Dan knew that the family needed him more than the field needed to be plowed. He got up and rummaged through the pantry and the refrigerator.

"What are you doing?" Lois asked.

"When was the last time any of you ate?" Dan asked.

"We had a sandwich last night," Ellen said.

"I'm going to make breakfast," he informed them. "Y'all need to eat."

The family didn't have the strength to argue. Ellen helped him find what he needed. James and Lois set the table. Wade took out his phone and called the office.

"Sheriff's office, this is Reed.

"Reed, do you have any news?"

"We're still processing everything," Reed lied.

"What do you know now?" Wade asked.

"Nothing for certain," Reed said.

"Then what do you think!" Wade shouted. "Tell me something!"

"Wade, stand down!" Reed replied with authority. "We'll find her."

"I'm sorry, I'm sorry," Wade said. "I'm going crazy with nothing to do and no news."

"Do you trust us?" asked Reed.

"Of course, I trust you," Wade replied. "Why would you ask?"

"Do you trust us to find Lizzie?" Reed asked.

Wade hesitated before answering. "I trust you. It's just…it's Lizzie."

"Yes, it's Lizzie," Reed said with compassion. "You need to remember that she's ours too. She's part of our law enforcement family, just as you are. We'll find her."

"Thank you, Gordon," Wade said. "I'm sorry that I blew up at you."

"I understand," Reed told him. "We're doing everything we can think of to find her."

"Do you want me to come in?" asked Wade.

"You need to be with Lizzie's family," Reed said. "Maddie and I will drive out in person to update you later today. There's nothing more to do until we've finished processing the evidence."

The call ended, and Wade looked at the family. They stared at him, waiting to hear what he'd learned.

"They're still processing the evidence," Wade said. "Reed and Maddie will come out and update us this afternoon."

"They don't know anything?" asked James.

"Nothing that they're ready to share with us," said Wade.

* * *

Reed met with the rest of the team in the conference room. Maddie led the meeting and shared the evidence they'd found the previous evening.

"Lodge, what did you find out about the bullets?" she asked.

"They're a match to the one found at the Ratliff scene," he said. Baker and I determined that the shots had to have come from the passenger side of the car. We believe they were traveling in the same direction as Fletcher."

"Did they shoot the tire, pass her, and then turn around?" Gonzalez queried. "Or were there two vehicles?"

"Either scenario means that we're looking for more than one person," said Baker.

"Are we sure those two FBI agents are agents?" Odom suggested.

"That's worth looking into," said Maddie. "I went through Lizzie's phone last night. There's nothing there that will give us a lead."

"What's our next move?" Odom asked.

"We have to interview the women that Lizzie met for lunch yesterday," Maddie replied. "Gonzalez and I will talk with them. I'd like to continue our patrols for the suspect and look into the two FBI agents. There've been no hits with the facial recognition searches. They're still running."

"We're open to any suggestions," Reed said. "Wade isn't doing well. We'd like to have some good news for him."

"Have you talked to Wade today?" Maddie asked.

"Yes, he called earlier," Reed informed her. "He's scared, worried, and mad."

"It's going to be hard to keep him out of the office," Lodge said.

"We need to find Lizzie as soon as possible," said Maddie.

The meeting adjourned, and the team went to work. Maddie and Gonzalez went to Faith's office. Faith told them everything that they'd done before Lizzie's disappearance.

"We did one thing that we hadn't planned," Faith told them. "We went to pick up Lizzie's wedding gown. She was panicked because that was the one detail she'd forgotten."

"Did you notice anyone following you or listening to your conversations?" asked Maddie.

"No, I didn't," Faith replied.

"Did Miss Fletcher mention any other plans that she might have had?"

Faith thought for a moment and shook her head. "I don't think so. I assumed she was going home."

"Thank you for your time, Mrs. Foreman," said Maddie. "Please, call us if you remember or hear anything."

"You have to find her," Faith said with worry. "She's my best friend. I don't know what I'd do if…"

"We understand," said Gonzalez. "We'll keep in touch."

The deputies left Faith's office and drove to meet with Jan at her office. Jan's recount of their afternoon matched Faith's except for one detail.

"Tiffany Pruitt spoke to Lizzie while we were eating lunch," Jan said and repeated the conversation.

"Was Mrs. Pruitt angry with Miss Fletcher?" asked Gonzalez.

"She wasn't yelling or anything like that," Jan said. "She wasn't what you'd call friendly either."

"Did Miss Fletcher mention any other plans that she might have had?" Maddie asked.

"No, she wanted to get home to finish decorating for the

wedding," said Jan. "She might have stopped to see Wade, but she didn't mention it."

"She didn't come to the office," Maddie told Jan. "Call us if you remember anything that could be useful."

"I will," Jan said. "She's the closest thing I have to a sister. I'll do anything to help you find her."

Maddie and Gonzalez said goodbye and went back to their car. Maddie called the office. Lodge answered.

"Lodge, I need to find Tiffany Pruitt," Maddie told him.

She heard the sound of typing and waited for Lodge to find the information.

"She's an insurance agent," he said and gave Maddie the address.

"Thanks," Maddie said and ended the call.

They drove to the insurance agency and went inside.

"We'd like to speak with Tiffany Pruitt," Maddie told the woman at the front desk.

The woman peered into the next office and said, "She's on the phone with a customer. I'll tell her you're here when she's finished."

Maddie nodded, and the two deputies sat down to wait. Ten minutes later, they were escorted to Tiffany's office.

"What can I do for you?" Tiffany asked with a fake smile.

"We'd like to talk with you about Lizzie Fletcher," said Maddie.

"What about her?"

"We understand you interrupted her and her friends at lunch yesterday," said Gonzalez.

"I congratulated her on her upcoming marriage," said Tiffany. "Is that a crime?"

"No, Ma'am. Where were you yesterday afternoon between three and six p.m.?" asked Maddie.

"I was here working," Tiffany answered. "What's this about? Has Lizzie accused me of something?"

"No, Ma'am," Gonzalez replied. "Can anyone verify your whereabouts?"

"My secretary was here all afternoon," Tiffany said with suspicion. "What's going on?"

"Lizzie Fletcher is missing," said Maddie and watched the woman's reaction.

"Missing? How horrible! Wade must be devastated," Tiffany said, covering a smirk with her hand.

"Did you see or hear anything that might help us find her?" Gonzalez asked.

"No, I left the restaurant after I spoke with her and came back here," Tiffany said. "I hope you find her in time for their wedding."

"Thank you, Ma'am," Maddie said and handed her a card. "Please, call us if you remember anything."

Tiffany dropped Maddie's card in the trash when the deputies left the room. Gonzalez verified Tiffany's alibi with her secretary. The pair drove to the office, pondering the case in silence. Reed was waiting for them when they returned.

"Agents Welborn and Brittain are the real deal," he told them. "I ran a search of Vegas FBI. There's no doubt they're the same men who were here."

"That doesn't mean that one of them isn't the mole," Maddie pointed out.

"You're right about that," said Reed with a smirk. "Look who else I found."

He handed her a photo of another FBI agent. She stared at it and looked back at Reed.

"Our prime suspect is an FBI agent?" Maddie asked in disbelief.

"Yep," said Reed beaming. "Agent Marty Henson has been on medical leave. I'm waiting for his office to return my call to find out the details."

Maddie smiled at Reed and said, "Now we have a name to go with the face. Did you update the APB?"

"I finished right before you came in," Reed told her.

"Have you shown this to Grace? She might know something about him."

"No, and it's time for someone to check on her."

"I'll go," Maddie told him and left the office.

She knocked on Grace's door and unlocked it when Grace replied.

"I'm glad to see you!" Grace exclaimed. "Do you have any news?"

"Nothing new about Lizzie," Maddie said and handed her the photo. "We have a name to go with this face."

Grace stared at the picture and the name. "This guy keeps turning up!"

"Do you know him?" asked Maddie, surprised at her reaction.

"You already knew that he put the tracker on my car," Grace said. "It's the name. I've heard Todd mention Marty. They were friends."

Grace stared at the picture, and the niggling feeling in the back of her mind returned. She had seen the man somewhere before.

"I saw him!" she cried. "It was the last time I was with Todd. It was the fourth of July, and we were at a park watching fireworks. He spoke to Todd, and they talked for a few minutes."

"Are you sure?" Maddie asked with excitement.

"Yes, I think he was Todd's contact, or whatever they call it."

"His handler?" Maddie suggested.

"Yes, that's it."

"Thanks for your help, Grace," Maddie said. "I'm sorry I haven't been checking on you as much as I should."

"I'd rather you look for my niece instead of babysitting me," Grace said.

"Is there anything you need?" asked Maddie.

"I hate to ask. Would you mind bringing a hamburger and fries?"

Maddie laughed and said," That does sound good. Tell me what you want, and I'll bring one back for you."

She wrote down what Grace wanted for lunch and went back to the office. She shared the new information with Reed and went to lunch. She came back and ate with Grace in her cell.

"Have you talked to your family today?" Maddie asked.

"I have. Mom said Wade is blaming himself. The rest are coping by taking care of him. Dan Hayes is there trying to keep them all together."

"This is hard for all of us," Maddie said. "I know it's worse for your family."

"Have you made any progress?"

"We know a lot more about our suspect," Maddie answered. "We aren't any closer to finding him."

"I'm sure you've already thought of this," Grace began. "I'll say it just to get it off my chest. Don't mention him to Welborn or Brittain. I don't trust them. I know that Todd trusted Marty Henson."

"What if he's the informant?" Maddie asked.

"What if he's not?"

"Were you ever in law enforcement?" Maddie teased.

"No," Grace said with a grin. "I've noticed that investigators tend to think alike no matter what their line of work. I've had a lot of time to think since I've been here."

"This is my cell number," Maddie said and gave Grace the information. "Text or call me if you need anything or if you have any other thoughts you want to share. I'll come back before I leave for the night."

"Thanks, Maddie. Go and find my niece."

"Yes, Ma'am."

Maddie closed and locked Grace's door. She went in search of Reed to share what she'd learned.

"Just because Todd Anthony trusted this man doesn't mean that he isn't the informer," Reed pointed out.

"I know, and I agree with you," said Maddie. "Think about the surveillance video from the inn. It was obvious that Ratliff knew him and wasn't afraid of him."

"That's true," said Reed. "Wade said the waitress in Quanah assumed they were a couple."

"I'm not saying we should remove him as a suspect," Maddie said. "I'm saying we should keep an open mind."

"Then why is he here, and why did he lie to Wade?" Reed asked.

"We'll have to ask him when we find him," said Maddie.

"You don't think he had anything to do with Lizzie's disappearance, do you?" asked Reed.

"I have my doubts," Maddie told him. "Remember what Lodge and Baker said about the shots being fired from the passenger side of a car."

"There had to be a driver and a passenger," said Reed.

"Did you happen to find out if Welborn and Brittain went back to Vegas?" asked Maddie.

"I'm still waiting for their office to return my call," Reed said. "I'll see if I can get an answer before we see Wade."

* * *

Lizzie woke up with a pounding headache. She opened her eyes. She was having trouble seeing. Her left eye seemed to be swollen. She touched her face with her fingertips and winced.

She looked around, trying to figure out where she was. She was in a small dark space. It was hot, dusty, and smelled of oil and rubber.

She could see light coming in from what appeared to be a door. She stood up, and the little room began to spin. She sat down again.

She'd been lying on a pile of dirty burlap bags. There was enough light coming in that she could see an old chainsaw and some other power tools on a bench.

I think I'm in a toolshed. How did I get here?

Lizzie stood again and waited for her head to stop spinning. She crept toward the door and pushed. It opened a little wider. She could see that it was chained and padlocked.

She heard footsteps outside. She started to call for help but went back to the pile of bags instead. She didn't know who was out there.

She waited and listened. She heard keys jingling and the lock being opened. The chain was dragged through the handle of the door. It opened, and bright light streamed into the shed.

Lizzie shielded her eyes. She could see only the shadow of someone in the doorway.

"Who are you? Why am I here?" she asked.

"Aw, good, you're awake," said a male voice. "I apologize for hitting you so hard. I didn't want you to wake up too soon and try to run."

"I asked you a question!" Lizzie said, her temper flaring.

"You asked two questions. I have no intention of answering either. I've brought you a blanket along with some food and water. Stay where you are, and I'll leave them inside the door."

Lizzie moved to stand. She stopped when the man spoke again.

"Don't make me use this gun, Miss Fletcher," the voice warned. "I don't want to hurt you more than I already have."

"What do you want?" Lizzie asked through gritted teeth and settled herself on the crate.

"That's a question that I will answer," said the voice. "I want you to read a little script for me. I'll record while you read."

He tossed a folded piece of paper toward her feet. She bent down and picked it up. She unfolded the paper and looked at it.

"I'm ready when you are," said the man.

Lizzie looked at the page and began to read. She'd almost finished when she stopped and stared toward the shadow.

"You want my Aunt Grace!" she shouted.

The man sighed and said, "Read it as it's written without stopping. Otherwise, I'll be forced to take other action."

Lizzie could hear the threat in his voice. She didn't want to read it.

She glared in his direction and shifted her weight on the crate. She tried to position herself so that the tool bench would show in the background of the video.

"Start again!"

Lizzie obeyed his command and read the note without faltering.

"Very good, Miss Fletcher," said the man. "Thank you."

"What now?" she asked.

"You'll be released as soon as my demands are met," he told her. "In the meantime, relax and enjoy your meal. I'll bring more tomorrow."

Lizzie sat still while he closed and chained the door. She waited until she was sure he'd gone before she got up.

She didn't look forward to facing the night locked in a tool shed. She had to find a way out.

She picked up the bag of food and the water bottle. She held the cool bottle to her swollen eye with one hand and dug into the bag with the other. It was a Big Mac and fries.

Lizzie tore into the burger and looked around the shed. There was light coming from the wall beside her. There was a stack of wood pallets in the corner.

She put the burger down and investigated the source of the light. It was a small window. She moved the boxes that blocked it and could see that it pushed out. She wasn't sure that she could squeeze through, but she had to try.

The light was waning, and she had to work fast. She moved some of the pallets and positioned them to form a ladder.

Lizzie climbed up so that she could reach the window. She pushed it open and started to climb through. The slat she was standing on splintered.

She tumbled off her makeshift ladder and landed hard on her right foot. She lay on the floor until the pain subsided.

She tried to get up and fell to the floor again in pain. She was pretty sure her ankle was broken.

She was lying on something hard. She wiggled around until she could get hold of it with her left hand. It was a flashlight. She tried the switch, and a weak beam of light shone across the room.

Lizzie examined her ankle and looked around the shed. She managed to crawl back to her burlap bed.

I won't be getting out that way. This flashlight won't last long. I'd better turn it off.

She picked up the rest of her burger and pushed the switch on the flashlight. She finished the burger in the dark. She drank some water and then tried to make herself comfortable. She folded the blanket as best she could and propped up her injured ankle.

The tool shed grew darker as night fell. She listened to the howl of coyotes in the distance and thought about her family. She prayed that they wouldn't be too worried and that they would find her soon.

She knew that her captor's demands wouldn't be met. They couldn't be. She drifted off to sleep thinking about Wade.

Lizzie woke up startled and confused. She lay still and listened. Her ankle throbbed.

She remembered what had happened. She remembered that she was in a tool shed.

She could hear a noise that sounded like it was coming from the corner of the shed. She found the flashlight and switched it on, and shined the beam toward the corner.

Lizzie shrieked when she saw them. Rats had found the remains of her dinner. They had chewed holes in the paper bag and were eating the French fries.

She shivered and moved as far away from them as she could. She knew there were more that she hadn't seen. She wanted to keep the flashlight shining on them, but the beam was already fading. She had to turn it off.

Lizzie lay on her bed listening to the rats rustling in the corner. She held on to the flashlight and planned to use it as a weapon if they decided to join her.

CHAPTER TWENTY-FOUR

MADDIE CHECKED in with Grace once more before driving to the inn with Reed. Neither of the deputies looked forward to talking with Wade. They knew he wasn't going to like the news.

They parked in front of the inn to find James sitting on the porch in a rocking chair. He stood when they arrived and greeted them.

"How are you, Mr. Fletcher?" Reed asked.

"I've been better," he replied. "I can tell that you don't have good news."

"It isn't bad news," Maddie said. "We don't know much more than we did last night."

James nodded and led them into the house. Ellen and Lois were making dinner. Wade and Dan sat at the dining table talking.

Wade jumped up when he saw Reed and Maddie. "Did you find her?"

"Not yet," Reed told him.

Maddie was appalled at his appearance. His hair stood out in all directions. He looked like he hadn't slept in days. He needed a shave, and he wore the same clothes he'd worn the day before.

"I promised we'd be here to give you an update," Reed told his boss. "There isn't much to tell that you don't already know."

"Sit down," James said.

The deputies complied and were joined by Lois and Ellen.

"This isn't going to be easy to hear," Reed said. "I'd rather have better news to share."

He explained what they'd found and what they'd discovered during the day. Wade ran his hands through his hair while he listened, making it stand out all the more.

"What about our suspect?" Wade asked, his eyes boring into Reed's.

"We caught a break," Reed said. "He's Las Vegas FBI."

"Another one?" James exclaimed.

Reed nodded and continued, "His name is Marty Henson, and he's on medical leave."

"Why is he here?" Wade demanded.

"We'll ask him when we find him," Reed replied. "Maddie has a little more information about him."

Maddie shared the highlights of her conversation with Grace and said, "He could have come here looking for Todd Anthony or the evidence that everyone seems to think he gave Grace."

"Anthony's dead," Wade pointed out.

"Henson may not be aware of that," said Reed. "He hasn't been in contact with his office since Anthony's body was found."

Their conversation halted when Maddie's phone rang. She left the room to take the call. She rushed back in and said, "Reed and I need to get back to the office. There's been a development."

"I'm coming with you," Wade said and stood to follow them.

"Wade," Reed said and put his hand out. "You're needed here. You can't do anything at the office. I'll keep you updated. I promise."

Wade glared at him and began to argue.

"Wade! You put me in charge of this case," Maddie shouted. "Do you think I can do the job or not?"

Wade stared at her, blinked a few times, then nodded. "You're right," he said, "You're both right. I'm sorry. I know you'll do everything you can."

"I know you need something to occupy your time and your mind," said Reed. "There's just nothing you can do right now."

Wade nodded and looked at Lizzie's family. "I'm sorry."

James looked at Reed and Maddie and said, "Get going. We've got this."

The deputies ran out the door to their car. Reed turned on the emergency lights and the siren. He pushed the car to its limits on the way back to the office.

They rushed inside and saw Baker and Odom standing in front of Lodge's computer. Lodge waved them over.

"It's a video message," he told them.

The deputies stared at the screen while Lizzie read from a sheet of paper.

"It's Tuesday evening, September 6th. My name is Lizzie Fletcher. I'm being held in a safe place. I'll be released unharmed under the following conditions.

The evidence that Grace Stewart is holding is to be placed in a large manilla envelope. She is to take the envelope to the deserted hotel on Highway 287, north of Vernon.

Ms. Stewart must drop the envelope in a barrel near the door and walk away. She is to come alone. I will suffer the consequences if anyone is seen following her. I'll be released when my kidnappers are satisfied with the evidence. You have until Friday at noon to comply."

The video ended, and the deputies looked at each other.

"What are we going to do?" Lodge asked.

"Make copies of this," Maddie said. "We need to show it to Wade and her family. Use the original to try and find out who sent it and from where."

"She doesn't look good," said Baker. "Are you sure you want Wade to see this?"

"It's proof that she's alive," Reed said. "They need to see that for themselves."

"We don't have a lot of time," Lodge observed. "How are we going to give them something we don't have?"

"We need to find her before the deadline," Reed said. "Analyze every detail of that video."

"I'm going to talk with Grace," Maddie told them. "What do you want to do about telling Wade and the rest of the family?"

"Wade said that Grace has a tell when she's lying," Reed said. "I don't know what it is, but Wade and her family do. They need to be together when they see this."

"I'll call them," Maddie said and picked up the phone.

"Make sure we can see this in the conference room," Reed told Lodge. "We'll meet with the Fletchers in there."

"They're on their way," Maddie said when she hung up the phone.

"They've had a difficult twenty-four hours. Their tempers are short, and they look exhausted," Reed warned.

"I'll bet Wade is ready to tear someone apart," Baker said.

Reed nodded and said, "Let's get to work. The sooner we find Fletcher, the better it will be for all of us."

Wade and the Fletchers were led to the conference room when they arrived.

Maddie brought Grace from her cell.

"What's happening," Wade asked.

"Lizzie's alive," Reed told them. "She's been abducted, and there's been a ransom demand."

"How much?" James asked. "We'll do whatever it takes to get her back."

"They don't want money," Maddie said. "We wanted you to hear this for yourselves."

Reed pressed the play button, and the video started. They watched in silence. Grace gasped when she heard the demand, and tears welled in her eyes.

The video ended. Grace looked at her family and said," I never dreamed anyone would hurt Lizzie."

"Grace, I have to ask again," Wade said. "Did Todd Anthony give you anything to hold for him?"

"No, I swear," she answered.

"Did Anthony ever give you anything?" Maddie asked. "A gift, a package, anything."

"He gave me a locket last year," she said.

"Do you have it with you?" Wade asked.

"It's in my suitcase," she said. "I don't think it's big enough to hold any evidence."

"May we see it?" asked Maddie.

"Yes, I'll get it," Grace said and hurried to her cell.

Reed waited until she'd gone and asked, "Is she telling the truth."

"I think so," said Wade. "Lois, what do you think?"

"She's a terrible liar," Lois said. "She always gives herself away. I'm sure she's telling us the truth."

"What if Anthony did give her something? What if it's still in Vegas?" asked Ellen.

Grace returned and handed the locket to Reed.

"We'll examine this in the lab," he told her. "It may not be in one piece when you get it back."

"Do what you have to do," she told him. "I'll do anything to save Lizzie."

"Is it possible that he gave you something that didn't mean much at the time?" Maddie asked. "Something that might still be in Vegas."

"He never brought gifts," she said. "He didn't want to attract attention. The only thing he ever gave me was that locket."

"Can you tell us anything about the case he was working on?" asked Reed.

"No, he never talked about his work," she said.

"Think back," Wade said. "Was there ever a slip of the tongue or an unintentional mention of a name or place?"

Grace stared at the ceiling, trying to recall their conversations.

"I can't think of anything," she said at last. "What are we going to do?"

"We could buy time by giving them something they'll believe is the evidence," suggested James.

"They said they wouldn't release her until they're satisfied with the evidence," said Maddie.

"You could arrest them at the hotel when they pick up the evidence," James suggested.

"They'd have no reason to tell us where they're keeping Lizzie," Reed pointed out.

"May we watch the video again?" Dan asked. "There's something I'd like to check."

The video was restarted, and Dan moved closer for a better look.

"What's wrong with her face?" asked Ellen.

"I'd say she was punched," said Reed without looking at Wade.

"You know Lizzie would have put up a fight," said Wade through clenched teeth. "That would have been a quick way to overpower her."

"That looks like a tool bench," Dan said. "She could be in a tool shed somewhere."

"She's mad," said James. "Look at the flash in her eyes when she looks up."

"I've seen that look a few times," said Wade. "She's ready to fight if she has to."

"I'll think she'll try to find a way out," Lois said with confidence.

"It doesn't look like she's tied up. Could they be watching her?" Ellen asked.

"That depends on how many there are," Maddie said. "One person can't be in two places at once."

"Unless she's near that hotel," said Reed.

"What are we waiting for?" Wade said and stood.

"Wade, we'll handle this," Reed said. "I don't want to have to arrest you on assault or murder charges."

"Chances are that they won't be there," said Maddie. "You can stay here. We'll report to you when we get back."

Wade started to argue. Ellen spoke up before he could.

"Wade, Lizzie wouldn't want you to be arrested or hurt. That's no way to start your lives together. It would destroy everything you've worked to achieve."

"You don't want to put your people in that position either," James pointed out.

Wade sank into his chair and ran his hands through his hair. He looked at Reed and said, "I'll stay out of your way, but I'm staying put until you get back."

"Fair enough," said Reed. "Baker, get started analyzing that video. We'll check the hotel and surrounding area before it gets too dark."

The deputies went to work, leaving Wade and the Fletchers in the conference room. The image of Lizzie on the screen gave them some comfort. She was alive. There was still hope.

"Wade, you should call your folks," James suggested. "They'll want to know what's happening."

Wade went to his office to make the call.

"I'm so sorry," Grace said to James and Ellen. "It never crossed my mind that these people would go after any of you."

Ellen stood and walked toward Grace. She hugged her and said, "We know. It didn't occur to us either."

Reed, Maddie, and the rest of the team rushed to the old hotel and searched the area. There was no one in or around the hotel. There were no outbuildings of any kind nearby. They returned to the office and gave Lizzie's loved ones the news.

* * *

Lizzie woke up to a bright light shining on her face. She shielded her eyes with her hand and looked for the light source.

Sunshine was streaming through a hole in the side of the shed. The morning sun better illuminated her prison.

She sat up and looked at her swollen ankle. She crawled on the dirt floor to the tool bench and tried to stand. She winced and leaned on the bench for support.

She looked around the space for something that she could use to make a splint. She could see a crowbar on the tool bench. She stood on her good leg and hopped toward the bench.

She picked up the crowbar and laid it near her bed. She searched the bench for anything else she could use. A pair of tin snips hung on the wall. *Those might be useful.*

Lizzie hopped back to the wooden pallets. She knelt on the floor and pushed one toward the burlap sacks. She picked up the crowbar and began to pry one of the boards up.

It was getting hot, and sweat began to drip into her eyes. She wiped her face with the hem of her T-shirt and eyed the water bottle. There wasn't much left.

She ignored her thirst and kept working until she had loosened two boards. She rested a few minutes and looked at the burlap sacks.

She picked one up and tried to tear it into strips. It was in better shape than she thought. She'd needed to find something sharp.

She looked at the pair of tin snips. She crawled to the bench and pulled herself up. She stretched as far as she could. They were too high.

Lizzie thought about climbing onto the bench. It didn't look very sturdy, and she didn't relish the idea of falling again.

She leaned toward her bed and picked up the crowbar. She used it to knock the snips from their hook. She grabbed both tools and sat down again.

She tried the snips on the bag and was able to cut several long strips. She heard a car and stopped what she was doing.

Lizzie hid her tools and the wooden slats under the burlap sacks. She heard the jingle of keys, and she lay down. She covered herself with the blanket. She wanted her captor to believe he'd woken her.

"Miss Fletcher," said the voice. "I have your lunch. Stay away from the door."

Lizzie didn't reply. She pushed herself up on one elbow and waited. She welcomed the fresh air when he opened the door.

"Did you sleep well?" asked the man.

"What do you think?" Lizzie said with an edge to her voice.

"Well, it won't be much longer," he said. "The video was delivered, and the sheriff's department is on the move."

Lizzie tried to see the man's face. The sun was again behind him. She could see only shadow. She wanted to keep him talking. She wanted him to move where she could see him.

"What do you mean?" she asked.

"Your friends have investigated the hotel and have searched the area around it looking for you. I anticipated that, of course," he said.

There was something familiar about the man. Lizzie tried to keep him talking so that she could figure it out.

"You won't get away with this," she said. "The sheriff is my fiancé. He'll hunt you down whatever it takes."

"I'm aware," the man said with a chuckle. "All he has to do is get us that evidence, and this will all be over."

"Us?"

The man chuckled again and said, "I brought some chicken for you today. Enjoy!

"Who are you?" Lizzie demanded.

He didn't answer. He put the food and a fresh bottle of water in the corner and chained the door. Lizzie waited until she was sure he'd gone before returning to her work.

The aroma of fried chicken filled the shed, and her stomach

grumbled. She ignored it and tied the pieces of wood to her leg with the strips of burlap.

She crawled to the tool bench and pulled herself up. She tested her ankle. It still hurt, but she could put a little weight on it.

The heat began to build again in the shed. She wiped the sweat from her face and drank some of the water. She had no intention of spending another night with the rats. She'd eat when she was free.

Lizzie picked up the tin snips and started to work on the hole in the wall. Her arms ached, and blisters formed on her hands.

She sat down to rest and sipped more water. She was tired, and her body ached. Her ankle throbbed. She stared at the opening she'd made.

I might be able to open it wide enough with the crowbar. I need to rest first.

She lay down and propped her ankle on the blanket. She thought about the chicken. She was too tired to eat. She drank more water and fell asleep.

Lizzie woke up confused. She didn't know how long she'd slept. Sunlight came in at a different angle.

She realized the water was drugged. She couldn't drink any more if she hoped to escape. Her stomach growled. She was hungry and weak. She feared that the food was also drugged.

She picked up the crowbar and put one end in the cut she'd made. She pushed and pulled, trying to pry it open. Her ankle began to throb, and she decided to try something else.

Lizzie put her good foot on the leg of the tool bench for leverage. She grabbed the metal with both hands and pulled with all her might.

"It's working," she said aloud. "Just a little more."

She pulled again. The metal gave a bit more, and she stopped to examine her work.

It'll be tight, but I should be able to squeeze through. I won't get far on this ankle. I need something to use for a crutch.

There wasn't much light left. She crawled on the floor until she found the flashlight. She switched it on and made a quick sweep of the shed. She knew it wouldn't last much longer.

Something lay under the tool bench. She crawled toward it and pulled it out. It was an old broom.

She struggled to her feet and tested the height. "I think it'll work," she said. "I just need to modify it a little."

She sat down and picked up the tin snips. She cut away the bristles and tested the crutch again. She cut more burlap strips and wrapped the hilt of the broom. She tied them around the handle to secure them.

Lizzie hobbled around the shed for a few minutes using the crutch. "It's not great. It'll have to do," she said aloud.

She sat down to rest and planned her next move. *There has to be a road nearby. I wonder if there's a house too. What am I going to do if he's in a house where he can see me? Maybe, I should wait until dark.*

The thought of meeting the rats or the coyotes face to face changed her mind. She'd take her chances and get out now.

She crawled toward the hole and laid the broom on the floor. She put her head through and inhaled the fresh air.

She squeezed one arm and shoulder through. She began to push with her healthy leg, and she inched a little farther. Both arms and shoulders were free.

Lizzie pulled and pushed until she felt a sharp pain in her side. She could feel wetness spreading across her ribs. She touched the place with her hand. She winced and brought her hand back toward her face. It was covered in blood.

She had to stop the bleeding before she went any further. She wriggled back inside and sat on the floor. She took off her T-shirt and picked up the flashlight.

She had a long gash between her ribs and her hip. She knew it was going to need stitches. She folded her shirt and pressed it onto the wound. She leaned against the wall and closed her eyes. The fresh air felt good.

Lizzie woke to the sound of paper being torn. The shed was

dark. She knew the rats were back. She was too hot and tired to care.

She put her tools on her bed and lay down beside them. She made herself comfortable and checked her wound with the flashlight.

Her shirt was soaked with blood. She could see that it was still bleeding, although not as much. She applied pressure again and tried to stay awake. The beam of the flashlight faded, leaving her in darkness.

CHAPTER TWENTY-FIVE

THE SHERIFF'S department worked through the night analyzing the ransom video, searching for Lizzie, and trying to devise a plan in the event they didn't find her in time.

They knew the shed where Lizzie was kept wasn't facing the sun. They surmised that they were looking for a building with a door facing southeast.

It was determined that the shed was made of barn metal. It appeared to me handmade instead of purchased. It had been standing for a long time, judging by the holes they could see in the video.

Four patrols had spent the day scouring the county. It would have been difficult with a full staff. It was near impossible, with only four deputies searching.

Baker continued to analyze the video. He knew it had been recorded with a cell phone. He'd been unable to find any other useful information.

Maddie and Reed ran the office. They devised and rejected plans to catch Lizzie's abductors at the hotel. Each one endangered Lizzie's life.

"We've got to try something," Reed said. "We're running out of time. The patrols haven't found anything, and Baker is stuck.

"Odds are that they are watching the drop zone at least part of the time," Maddie said. "We should put someone at the hotel across the highway with a telescope. We might get lucky and spot one of them."

Reed thought a moment and said, "It's a good idea. They could be watching from that hotel."

"Maybe we should talk with the people who work there to find out," Maddie suggested.

They left Baker to run the office and went to the hotel. They questioned every employee and the manager. They spoke with all of the hotel guests.

The two deputies were allowed to test their theory. They were led to a room on the top floor that looked out over Highway 287.

They couldn't see the door of the deserted hotel from there and tried the roof. Their view was blocked by trees.

Maddie and Reed returned to the office feeling defeated. The patrols returned without success. Baker had managed to learn that the cellphone used was purchased at the local Supercenter.

It was a prepaid phone with a limited amount of data. Recording and sending the video had used most of it. No one answered, and the voicemail hadn't been set up. He tried tracing the cell signal. It was turned off, or the battery had died.

There was nothing else the deputies could do until morning. They hoped getting away from the office would give them a fresh outlook. They went home to rest, but none of them slept.

Wade and the Fletchers stayed out of the way as promised. They paced the floor and waited for the phone to ring. Each update was the same.

Reed called to update them at ten o'clock that night, but he had nothing new to report. They prayed together before going to bed. They asked that the deputies would come up with a plan and that Lizzie would be found safe.

* * *

Lizzie was dreaming. She could hear a voice in the distance. Someone was calling her. She tried to scream, but she had no voice. She tried to pound on the walls, but she couldn't move.

She thrashed around and rolled from her burlap bed. A sharp pain woke her.

The sun was up. She'd slept too long. She had to get out.

"Miss Fletcher! Can you hear me!"

Lizzie stayed still and listened. *Am I imagining things?*

"Miss Fletcher! Are you here?"

Her captor knew where she was. The voice didn't sound like his.

"Here! I'm in here!" she shouted. "I'm in the shed."

She listened again and heard footsteps running toward her prison. Someone pulled on the door. She saw a man's right hand reach through the opening and try to push it wider. There was a mole on his wrist.

"No, stay away!" she screamed.

"I'm here to help you," he said. "I promise I won't hurt you."

"Leave me alone!"

"Stand away from the door," he ordered. "Cover your ears. This is going to be loud."

Lizzie covered her ears and heard two gunshots. She reached for the crowbar when she heard the chain being drawn through the handle.

The door opened wide, and she managed to stand up. She held the crowbar, ready to strike.

"I'm not going to hurt you," the man said. "I'm going to get you out of here."

"I don't believe you!" she said and raised the crowbar higher.

"I'm here to help you," he said, putting his gun on the ground and raising his hands. "It looks like your hurt."

"I'll use this if I have to," she said and tried to step forward. Her injured leg gave way, and she fell at his feet.

"I'm an FBI agent from Las Vegas," he said with his hands still raised. "I've been trying to protect your aunt."

"Protect her? You put a tracking device on her car!"

"Yes, I did," said the man. "We can talk about that later."

Lizzie struggled to her feet and said, "I don't…don't…feel…

The man caught her before she fell to the floor. He laid her down gently and picked up his gun.

"I'm going to get my car," he told her. "I'll take you to the hospital."

Lizzie couldn't answer. She lay still, not caring what he might do to her. She heard a car drive close to the shed and footsteps coming toward her.

The man picked her up and carried her to the car. He laid her in the back seat and carefully lifted her feet.

He closed the door and jumped into the driver's seat. They sped toward the hospital. Lizzie was unconscious by the time they arrived.

Marty Henson ran inside the emergency room and asked for help. He waited until Lizzie was being examined to call the authorities.

"Sheriff's office," this is Reed.

"I've found Lizzie Fletcher. She's in the emergency room at your local hospital," Henson said.

"Who is this?" Reed demanded.

"My name isn't important right now," he said. "Miss Fletcher is injured. She needs her family."

The call ended, and Reed screamed into his phone, "Hello! Hello!"

Maddie turned and stared at him. "What's wrong?"

"Lizzie is in the emergency room," Reed said, already dialing the number to the inn.

James answered the phone and whooped with joy when Reed

told him the news. He informed the others, and they ran to their vehicles.

Wade drove his truck with the lights flashing and sirens blaring while the Fletchers followed close behind. They made it to the emergency room in record time and rushed inside.

"We're Lizzie Fletcher's family," James said to the woman at the desk.

"Dr. Hughes is with her now," she said. "I'll let him know you're here. Please, have a seat."

Maddie and Grace were sitting in the waiting area. A man whose face Wade knew well stood beside them.

"What are you doing here?" he demanded.

"Wade," Maddie said and stood between the men. "He found Lizzie and brought her here. He called us to let us know she was safe."

"I'm sorry that I had to lie to you, Sheriff," Henson said. "I'll tell you anything you want to know once we find out Miss Fletcher's condition. She was in bad shape when I found her."

Wade nodded and extended his hand, "I already know quite a bit. Thank you for finding her."

Henson took Wade's hand and said, "I'm glad I could help. I wish I'd found her sooner."

Dr. Hughes entered the waiting area and said, "I'm going to keep Lizzie in the hospital for a few days. She's dehydrated and has lost some blood."

"Will she be all right?" Ellen asked.

"She'll be fine. However, it will take some time to recover. I've given her something for pain," he told them.

"What caused the loss of blood?" asked Wade with clenched fists.

"She has a large cut on her side," answered the doctor. "I've cleaned the wound and stitched it up. She's on her way to X-ray now. Her right ankle is injured. Did you splint it for her, Mr...?"

"Henson, Sir. It was splinted when I found her."

"You can wait here until she's in a room," Dr. Hughes told them. "I'll have a nurse come for you when she's settled."

Hughes left the room, and the family stared at Henson.

"I can explain everything now," he began. "Or I can take you to the bad guys and explain later."

"You know where they are?" Wade asked.

Henson nodded and said, "They're the reason I stayed here."

"What condition are they in?" Wade asked.

"They're in perfect health," Henson said with a grin. "I thought it best they stay that way, for now."

"Agent Henson, you and I are going to the office," Maddie told him. "We'll gather the team, and you can show us the way."

Maddie turned toward Wade and said, "You need to stay here."

He grinned at her and said, "I'm not going anywhere until I see Lizzie."

Maddie drove Henson to the sheriff's office and explained the situation to the team.

"The people responsible for kidnapping Miss Fletcher are staying in a rundown house outside of town," Henson told them. "I can take you to them."

"Do you know their names?" asked Reed. "We'll need a warrant."

"I don't know what name's their using," Henson admitted. "They have lots of aliases."

"We need to hurry," Reed said. "The noon deadline is two hours away."

"Deadline?" Henson asked.

"They believe that Grace Stewart is holding incriminating evidence," Maddie explained. "They gave us until noon today to deliver it, or Lizzie would suffer."

"We could use that to our advantage," Henson said. "I doubt that they know that Miss Fletcher has been rescued."

"What do you have in mind?" asked Reed.

Henson told them his plan. They agreed to try it and went to work.

At noon, Grace drove to the old hotel and left a manilla envelope containing a flash drive. She drove back to the sheriff's office and waited for the deputies to return.

Lodge and Baker were waiting where they could see the drop point. They watched someone approach the barrel and look around. The envelope was removed from the barrel and opened. The perpetrator took out a cell phone.

"I've got it. It's a flash drive. I'll be there in a few minutes."

Lodge and Baker made their move when the call ended. The culprit fired two shots and ran. Lodge looked like a pro football player when he made the tackle.

Baker pointed his weapon and shouted, "Don't move! You're under arrest!"

The crook rolled over and fired another round. Baker returned fire. Lodge stood and kicked the weapon away before checking for a pulse. He nodded at Baker.

"Phase one complete," Baker said. "We're going to need an ambulance.

"Let's go," Maddie said to Henson. "It won't be long before the other one figures out his partner's been arrested."

They drove to the farm where Lizzie had been held. They hid the car in a nearby shelterbelt and walked to the shed.

Maddie went inside. Henson put the chain in place and put an identical padlock on the chain. He left it unlocked and took his position behind the shed. Odom and Gonzalez waited nearby in case they were needed.

They waited half an hour before a car drove up. A man got out and ran to the shed.

Maddie drew her gun and waited. She heard the man curse when he saw the open padlock. She heard the chain being drawn through the handle.

"Stand back, Miss Fletcher," he said and chuckled. "It's time to set you free."

He opened the door and hesitated when he saw Maddie.

"Freeze," Maddie told him. "You're under arrest."

The man sneered at her and reached for his gun. He stopped before he could draw it from his belt.

"She said freeze," Henson said with the barrel of his gun in the man's ear.

The man raised his hands, and Maddie stepped forward. He whirled around, knocking Henson's gun out of his hand.

Maddie fired twice, hitting him in the arm and shoulder. She fired a third time when he drew his weapon.

The man fell with his gun in his hand. Henson kicked it away and checked for a pulse.

Maddie called the office and said, "Phase two is complete. Send an ambulance, but tell them there's no hurry."

She called Odom and Gonzalez. They drove up a moment later.

"Thank you, Agent Henson," said Maddie. "We wouldn't have found Lizzie in time."

"I wish I could have prevented it in the first place," he told her.

"I can't wait to hear your part in all of this," Odom told him.

"It's not all that interesting," Henson replied and smirked. "I spent a lot of time moving around so that you folks wouldn't arrest me."

They waited at the scene until the ambulance arrived. They drove back to town and went to the office.

"How is Lizzie?" Maddie asked Reed.

"Wade said she's in a room," he told her. "He wants to see you, Agent Henson. He'll be here soon."

"I promised him an explanation," said Henson. "Is there any chance Ms. Stewart will be with him? I'd like to explain to her as well."

"I'll call and ask him to bring her," Reed said. "What do y'all say to a working lunch?"

Reed called Wade, then ordered pizza for the entire team. The pizza was delivered a few minutes before Wade and Grace came in the office door.

"How is Lizzie?" Reed asked.

"She's coming around," Wade said. "They've been giving her IV fluids."

"It was hot in that shed," Maddie told them. "I was only there for a short time. I can't imagine being in there as long as she was."

"There were water bottles in the shed," said Odom. "It looked like she drank one and sipped the other."

"That's how they drugged her," said Lodge. "They dissolved over-the-counter sleeping pills in the water."

"It looked like they brought food and water twice," Gonzalez said. "We found two food bags and two water bottles."

"We tested both guns with the bullets we found at both scenes," Baker said. "They matched the gun we confiscated at the old hotel."

"Have you been able to get any answers from the suspect?" asked Henson.

"The surgery to remove Baker's bullet was still in progress the last time I checked," Reed replied.

"Is there any doubt that these two were responsible for Ratliff's death and Lizzie's abduction?" asked Wade.

"No, Sir," said Baker.

"I'd like to hear your story, Agent Henson," said Wade.

"I was Todd Anthony's handler," he began. "Todd was a good man and a good agent. He was also a good friend. He never failed to check-in.

The last time we met, he told me he was close to something big. All he needed was to get the evidence, and we could bust the entire gang. That's when he told me he suspected they had a man inside our department.

I knew something was wrong when he missed the last check-in. I looked for him for days, and I was getting desperate.

I happened to see Ms. Stewart on the evening news and recognized her. I'd seen her with Todd. I suspected she was more than a casual acquaintance by the way he looked at her. I took a chance and did a background check.

I watched her for days. It wasn't until she went to a salon that I thought I might catch a break. I followed her until she went into a diner. I attached the tracker hoping she'd lead me to Todd."

He turned to Grace and said, "I'm sorry that I frightened you. I didn't intend for you to know that I exist."

"I understand," Grace said and smiled.

"I went to the office the next day and discovered that someone had hacked my computer. They'd found where I'd researched Ms. Stewart's background.

I suspected that Todd was dead and that he was right about an informant. I was on leave and had a lot of free time. I decided to keep an eye on Ms. Stewart. That worked for a couple of days until she disappeared."

Grace said, "Sorry, I didn't know what was happening."

"Neither did I," Henson said. "I went into your house after you'd gone and saw the note on your mirror.

I thought Ms. Stewart might turn up in Texas with her family. I drove out here to find her. It was at the inn that I saw Jody and our two suspects. I don't know what name they used. They like to pose as brother and sister or husband and wife. I overheard them talking about a room they'd booked. I knew they were looking for Ms. Stewart."

"Are you talking about the Ketchersids?" Wade asked with wide eyes. "They're the only guests to book a room since the inn reopened."

"I have photos of them here," said Baker handing a file to Wade. "Those are the suspects we apprehended this morning."

Wade looked at the photos and said, "That's them. I can't believe we had dinner with them one night."

"The Ketchersids are members of a hit squad working for the gang Todd was investigating," Henson told them. "When I saw them, I knew that I needed to stick around to make sure Ms. Stewart and her family were safe."

"Why did they kill Jody Ratliff?" Maddie asked.

"They must have known she was an agent. They might have known she was Todd's niece," answered Henson. "It's possible they thought she had the evidence and planned to pass it to Ms. Stewart. I had the same thought, but I couldn't imagine that he'd risk the two most important women in his life.

I'm sure you already know that I met with Jody. She told me she was here for a wedding. She didn't know Todd was missing and hadn't heard from him."

"That's why she was upset when she left the restaurant," said Wade.

"She suspected he was dead, too," said Henson. "Jody was in great physical condition. She was a competitive kickboxer. She may have been killed because the Ketchersids couldn't control her."

"Why did you lie to me?" asked Wade. "Why didn't you tell me what was going on?"

"I didn't want the Ketchersids to know I was watching them," Henson said. "It was hard to keep tabs on them while looking over my shoulder. I knew you'd already had enough of the Vegas FBI. I saw Welborn and Brittain at the inn and here in your office."

"How did you find Lizzie?" Maddie asked.

"I knew they'd do something when Ms. Stewart moved to the jail," Henson told them. "I'd watched them for a while and noticed that they liked fast food.

I'd heard that Miss Fletcher was missing and suspected they'd kidnapped her. I followed them to McDonald's and saw that they'd bought extra food.

I tailed them to the house they were using and watched them go inside. He came out later with a bag and a bottle of water and drove out of town.

I couldn't follow close enough on the dirt roads without being seen. I lost him both times. I knew the general area and searched until I found her this morning."

"How did you know I was here?" asked Grace.

"The Ketchersids left town for a few days," Henson said. "I started watching the inn in case they came back. I saw you the day you arrived."

"Do you know who the mole is?" Wade asked.

"I have suspicions," said Henson. "I can't prove anything without Todd's evidence."

CHAPTER TWENTY-SIX

WADE AND GRACE left the sheriff's office and went back to the hospital. They wanted to check on Lizzie before going home for the evening.

Lizzie was awake though still weak and dazed.

"Is Aunt Grace safe?" Lizzie asked.

"I'm right here," Grace said and moved into her niece's view. "I'm so sorry."

"It's all right," Lizzie said. "I know you didn't expect anything like this to happen. Did you catch that man?"

"We got both of them," Wade told her. "It was the Ketchersids."

"The Ketchersids?" she asked and stared at Wade. "Are you sure?"

"The team caught her at the drop-off point," he told her. "They caught him when he went to the shed to get you."

Lizzie shook her head and said, "I knew there was something familiar about him, but he didn't sound like Ketchersid. He never stood where I could see his face."

"They were both putting on an act at the inn," Wade told her.

"They altered their appearances and accents for our benefit. Nothing they told us was true."

"Did they do this to you?" James asked with tears in his eyes.

"This?" she asked, confused.

"Your injuries, Honey," said Lois.

Lizzie thought for a minute before she replied, "He punched me. He apologized and said it was so I wouldn't run away."

"What about your ankle and the cut?" Ellen asked.

"I was trying to get out of that shed," Lizzie replied.

She explained what happened and told them about the rats.

"Rats!" said Lois and shivered.

"I didn't eat or drink much," she told them. "I thought it might be drugged."

"The water was drugged," Wade told her.

"How did they get you?" asked James.

"I was driving home and heard a loud pop," she said. "I thought I'd had a blowout. I got out to check and saw the flat. I was trying to get the jack out when I heard someone ask if I needed help. The next thing I remember is waking up in that shed. How long was I there?"

"Two days," Ellen said. "You disappeared Tuesday afternoon. Today is Friday."

"It's Friday!" Lizzie exclaimed. "We're supposed to get married tomorrow!"

"Don't worry about that," Wade told her. "We can get married when you're well."

"You don't understand," Lizzie said with panic in her voice.

"What's all the excitement?" asked Dr. Hughes when he entered the room.

"Lizzie and Wade were supposed to be married tomorrow," said Lois. "How long does Lizzie need to be here?"

"She's going to need surgery to repair her ankle," said the doctor. "It needs to be immobilized until then. It will be a few days before she can be released."

"We have to cancel everything," Lizzie said and began to cry. "The caterer, the cake, the guests, the honeymoon plans, all of it."

"We've already taken care of everything," Ellen said. "All you need to worry about is getting better."

"May I speak with you in private, Doctor?" asked Wade.

"Of course," the doctor replied and followed Wade into the hall.

"Can she be moved at all?" asked Wade.

"She shouldn't be," he answered. "It would be painful and might cause further damage."

"I see," Wade said. "I thought we might be able to get married here in the hospital. We picked this weekend because it fell between the reopening of the inn and the beginning of the holiday season."

"Does it have to be a big wedding," the doctor inquired.

"We've invited family and close friends," Wade told him. "I have a lot of relatives."

"I'd rather not risk moving her even a short distance," said the doctor. "You might consider going to the justice of the peace when she's recovered."

A thought passed through Wade's mind, and his face lit up.

"Would you object to our being married in her room?" he asked.

Dr. Hughes smiled and said, "No objection from me as long as her leg remains still. You'll want to okay it with the hospital, of course."

"I'll check with Lizzie first," Wade said with a bright smile. "Thanks, Doc."

"You're welcome," Dr. Hughes replied. "Now, if you'll excuse me, I need to examine my patient again before I go home for the evening."

The doctor went into Lizzie's room, and her family stepped into the hall with Wade. He told them what he had in mind.

"How do you think Lizzie will feel about being married in her hospital room?" Wade asked.

"You'll have to ask her," said Ellen. "Let us know what the two of you decide."

Dr. Hughes joined them in the hall and told them that Lizzie was doing well. The orthopedic surgeon was scheduled to see her the next morning.

Lizzie was crying when Wade went back into her room.

"I'm sorry that I've messed everything up," she said when she saw him.

"It's okay," he told her. "It's not your fault."

"You're going to lose the money you spent for our honeymoon," Lizzie sobbed. "We'll have to pick a new date and order new invitations. We'll have to start all over again."

"I bought travel insurance for our honeymoon trip," Wade told her. "All I have to do is call and postpone it."

He sat on the edge of her bed and kissed her forehead. "Your folks called everyone and explained what happened. Everything has been worked out."

"The inn is booked every weekend through New Year's Day," Lizzie said. "We may have to wait until spring to get married."

"I have an idea," Wade told her. "How do you feel about getting married right here tomorrow?"

Lizzie stared at him and blinked several times before she replied, "Are you serious? I look terrible."

"You always look beautiful to me," Wade said and smiled. "We can get married tomorrow and have the reception whenever you want. I'll call Preacher Dave and arrange everything. What do you think?"

"What about the ceremony and walking down the aisle to you?" she asked with tears in her eyes.

"We can do all of that at the reception," he told her. "The most important thing to me is that we both say I do. The rest is frosting on the cake."

"What about my face?" Lizzie asked. "I have no idea where my dress is now."

"The bruise isn't that bad," he told her. "You can cover it with makeup if it bothers you. Your dress is in the evidence locker at my office. I'll make sure you have it if you want it."

He looked into her eyes for a moment and wiped the tears from her face. He took her hand in his and kissed it gently.

"What do you think, Lizzie? Will you marry me tomorrow?"

"Are you sure you want to get married in a hospital?" she asked.

"Darlin, I'd marry you anywhere, anytime. I don't care if you're wearing your wedding dress or that hospital gown," he told her. "I understand if you'd rather wait."

"I love you, Wade Adams."

"I love you, too," he replied.

"Yes!" said Lizzie. "Let's do it!"

Wade beamed at her and said, "I'd better tell our folks and call the preacher. I'll go and let you rest. I'll see you tomorrow."

He kissed her goodbye and left the hospital happier than he'd been in days.

* * *

Maddie and Reed were entering the hospital as the Fletchers were leaving. They were on their way to interview the woman they knew as Beverly Ketchersid.

"How's Lizzie," asked Reed.

"She's going to be okay," James told him. "The doctor said she'll need surgery to repair her ankle."

"That's good news," Reed replied.

"Maddie, can we talk for a minute?" asked Grace.

The two women stepped away from the group.

"I need your honest opinion," Grace began. "Should I stay in protective custody, or is it safe to go home with my family? I don't want to jeopardize anyone else's life."

Maddie thought for a moment before answering.

"We don't know if there are more people here looking for you," she said. "It could have been just these two, or there could be more. I can't answer your question until we've interviewed the woman."

Grace nodded and said, "Would you recommend that I stay in my cell until you have an answer?"

"I think that would be best," Maddie replied. "I hope I'll have more information for you after we've talked with her."

"I'll ask James to drop me off at your office," Grace said.

"I'll see you when we've finished here," said Maddie.

Reed and Maddie made their way to Ketchersid's room. She agreed to answer their questions in exchange for protection. She knew that a member of the hit team would come for her whether or not she talked.

"We were looking for Todd Anthony when Earl broke into the Stewart woman's house," she told them. "He wrote the note on the mirror, hoping to scare Anthony enough that he'd turn over any evidence he had.

We caught up with Anthony after Stewart disappeared. Earl told him that if he didn't talk, Stewart might. Anthony went for Earl, and Earl shot him. The boss wasn't happy about that.

A day or two later, we were given an address to check out. We ended up at that inn. That's when we saw the Ratliff woman.

We had information that she was Anthony's niece. We thought he might have given her the evidence. We grabbed her so we could find out.

Everything was fine until Earl had to stop to avoid hitting a deer on the highway. Ratliff jumped out of the car and took off.

Neither of us could run fast enough to catch her. I fired a shot to slow her down. I didn't mean to kill her. We hadn't had the chance to find out what she knew."

The woman stopped and asked for water. Maddie left and returned with a pitcher of water. She poured some water into a cup and handed it to the woman. She drank it all and gave the cup back to Maddie.

"We were supposed to hang around the family in case the

Stewart woman went there," she said. "We left when we got word that she was in St. Louis. We were there looking for her when we got a text saying she was in Texas."

"Who sent the text?" asked Reed.

"I don't know," she replied. "We never know. That way, we can't rat out the bosses."

"Go on," said Maddie.

"We got back here and found out the Stewart woman was in protective custody. We decided to grab one of the Fletchers and force her to hand over the evidence. The redhead happened to be the first one to cross our path."

"Does your organization have someone inside the Vegas FBI?" Maddie asked.

"I'm sure they do," replied Ketchersid. "I don't know who it is. That's someone else's business."

"What sort of evidence were you supposed to find?" Reed queried.

"I don't know that either," she said. "We were told to get it from the woman and bring it back."

"That's it?" Maddie asked, unbelieving.

"I do what I'm told, and I'm well paid," answered the woman.

"Ms. Stewart doesn't have anything and has no idea what your bosses want," Reed said. "Is it possible that Anthony didn't have any evidence?"

"Anything's possible," the woman said, and she began to laugh. "I wouldn't want to be in the shoes of the person who told them he did."

"How did you manage to arrange flat tires for both women?" asked Reed.

"Earl drove close enough behind them that I could shoot the tire. He backed off and waited until they pulled off the road. We stopped behind them, and he knocked them senseless with one punch. We loaded them into the back seat and drove away."

Beverly Ketchersid was moved to a more secure room, and a

guard was posted outside her door. She would be moved to jail when released from the hospital.

* * *

The Fletchers dropped Grace off at the sheriff's office, and she went back to her cell. She was surprised when she heard a tap on her door.

"Ms. Stewart, there's a man here who wants to talk with you," said Gonzalez. "Would you like to meet him here or in one of the rooms upstairs?"

"I'll come upstairs," she said and followed the deputy to one of the small offices.

"Ms. Stewart," said Marty Henson. "I wanted to see you and discuss what you plan to do next."

"I haven't thought that far ahead," she replied and sat down in one of the chairs.

Henson sat down in the other chair and said, "The people behind Todd's death and the spy in my department are still a threat to you. If we work together, we might be able to bring them both down."

The pair talked for hours discussing the situation, making plans, and remembering Todd Anthony. It was decided that Grace would go back to Vegas and resume her life.

Henson would escort her home, and they would fly back to Vegas together. She had his phone number on speed dial in case of an emergency. He would warn her if he learned anything that she needed to know.

"I want to make sure my niece is okay and spend a little more time with my family before we go," she told Henson.

"I thought you would," he told her. "We can leave on Monday if you want."

"That sounds good," she said. "I should talk to my family and my boss to let them know what we've decided."

"I'll go and let you get some rest," Henson said. "We'll talk again before we leave."

Grace went back to her cell and closed the door. She flopped onto her bunk and sobbed. The stress of the past few days needed to be released.

* * *

The Fletchers were busy taking down the wedding décor when Wade returned to the inn.

"Lizzie agreed to be married in her room tomorrow," Wade told the family. "I've talked to the preacher, and that's all set."

"That's wonderful," said Lois.

"I'd like for y'all and my parents to be there," he told them. "I don't think the room is big enough to hold anyone else."

"I'm sure it isn't," said James.

"I have an idea," said Ellen. "Why don't we video the wedding and put it on social media or something? Everyone who wants to can watch it."

"That's a good idea," said Wade. "How much trouble would it be to decorate the room a little?"

"We have the stuff Lizzie made," said Lois. "We can take some of it in the morning."

"She wanted to know about her dress," Wade told them. "Can you manage that without moving her leg?"

"I don't know," said Ellen. "I'll talk to her about tomorrow."

The Fletchers finished their work, and Wade called his parents. They were happy to hear that Lizzie was safe and promised they'd be there the next day.

Wade was restless and couldn't sleep that night. He'd been surrounded by Lizzie's family while she was missing. It was the first time he'd ever been alone at the inn.

It didn't feel right without Lizzie. He found a movie to watch but still couldn't sleep when it ended. He finally drifted off to sleep, watching a documentary about Koala bears.

The Fletchers were at the hospital the next morning in time to hear what the surgeon had to say. The surgery was scheduled for Monday morning.

Lizzie's family decorated the room. It felt bright and cheerful when they'd finished. They made an arch of yellow roses, white daisies, and greenery over the head of her bed. The foot of her bed was decorated with the same theme.

They placed flower arrangements on the nightstand and the window sill. Greenery framed the doorway.

"We need to talk about your dress," said Ellen. "I'm not sure we can manage to get you dressed without hurting you."

"I've been thinking about that," Lizzie replied. "It won't have the same look lying in this bed, but I don't want to get married in a hospital gown."

"Did you get anything at your lingerie shower that would be suitable?" Lois asked.

"Nothing that I want y'all and my in-laws to see me in," Lizzie replied and blushed.

"I brought something that might work," said Ellen. "I was going to give it to you before you packed for your honeymoon."

She stood and picked up a box that she'd left on the window sill. She looked at James.

"Why don't I get something for lunch and bring it back," James said. "What do we want?"

"I want tacos," said Lizzie.

"That answers that question," said James. "I'll be back in a little while."

James left, and Ellen laid the box on Lizzie's lap. She opened it and lifted out a beautiful nightgown and matching robe.

"This is gorgeous!" Lizzie exclaimed. "It could almost be a wedding dress."

"It's short enough that you can put it on without too much

movement," Ellen pointed out. "It's a lot prettier than a hospital gown."

"I love it," Lizzie replied. "Thank you, Mama."

Lizzie admired it a little longer before she folded it and put it back in the box.

"I didn't get a chance to make my bouquet," she said. "I have some roses and silver ribbon left. I can make something small if you bring the supplies."

"I've already taken care of that," Lois said, reaching into a bag.

She handed her granddaughter three long-stemmed yellow roses adorned with baby's breath and silver ribbon.

"Thank you, Granny! I love it!"

"You're welcome," she answered. "Is there anything else we need to do?"

"Wade's wedding ring is in the nightstand by my bed," Lizzie replied. "He has our marriage license somewhere."

"We'll make sure he doesn't forget," said Ellen.

"Forget what?" James asked when he came back into the room.

"The marriage license and the rings," Lizzie said and sniffed the air. "That smells so good!"

"Me or the tacos?" James teased.

"The tacos," Lizzie said with a grin.

"I see how I rate," he joked.

James passed out the food and drinks. They talked about the wedding while they ate. After a while, James looked at Lizzie and cleared his throat.

"Tiffany came into the restaurant while I was waiting for our food," he said. "I don't want to upset you, but we need to watch out for her."

"What did she have to say?" asked Lizzie.

"She said she was sorry to hear about you and asked if I had any idea where you could be," James said. "I told her you had been found and were recovering in the hospital."

"I'll bet she was disappointed to hear that," Lizzie said and scowled.

"She said that was wonderful with a phony smile and asked if it was going to delay the wedding," James said. "I told her that you're getting married tomorrow. My number was called. I went to get the food and left. You should have seen her face when I drove away," James added, laughing.

"You don't think she'll show up here tomorrow, do you?" asked Ellen.

"I wouldn't be surprised," said James. "I didn't tell her where they're getting married. I'll stand by the door during the ceremony," James told them. "She won't get past me."

Lizzie had lots of visitors that morning. Jan and Faith were happy to see that she was safe. They were thrilled that the wedding wouldn't be postponed and thought getting married in the hospital was a good idea given the circumstances.

CHAPTER TWENTY-SEVEN

WADE WENT to the inn at lunch to shower and get his tux. He made a pot of coffee, poured himself a cup, and looked through the refrigerator for something to eat.

He looked at the back door when he heard someone knocking. He waved Lizzie's family inside.

"Happy wedding day!" Ellen said and kissed him on the cheek.

"Thank you," he said and smiled. "I was about to make lunch. Would y'all like some?"

"I'll make lunch," offered Lois. "You relax. You have a big day ahead of you."

"We want to make today special. We thought we'd have a mini reception after the ceremony," Ellen told him. "I made a small cake last night. We'll take some champagne glasses and sparkling water instead of champagne. It won't interact with Lizzie's pain medication."

"That's a good idea," Wade said. "The cafeteria will be closed. We could order takeout for dinner."

"I think that's a good plan," said James.

After lunch, the family went to visit Lizzie, and Wade went to the office. He hadn't planned to be at work, but he wasn't supposed to see Lizzie until the wedding.

He picked up the phone and called to cancel their honeymoon. He explained the situation and was given the option of a full refund or credit toward a future trip. He chose the credit and hoped they'd get to use it when Lizzie recovered.

"Are you busy, Wade?" asked Maddie.

"No, I'm waiting around until time for the wedding," he said.

"Grace wants to see you," she told him.

Wade stood and went to Grace's cell. He tapped on the door and opened it when she answered.

"Did you want to see me?" he asked.

"Yes, please, sit down," she told him and pointed at a chair.

"You look like you have something serious on your mind."

"I do," she said and took his hand. "I am so sorry about what happened to Lizzie. I never would have asked for protection if I thought doing so would cause my family harm."

"I know that, Grace," he said and squeezed her hand. "No one expected this to happen."

"I feel terrible about it," she told him. "I want to make it up to you."

"I'm sure James told you that Lizzie and I are getting married this afternoon. You can make it up to us by being there for the ceremony."

Grace smiled and said, "I wouldn't miss it for the world."

"You can go with me when I drive over," he told her.

"There's something else that I want to talk to you about. I may need your help," she said.

"Okay," he said, curious.

"I've decided to go home Monday," she began. "Marty Henson is going to escort me."

"How can I help?"

"Help me convince my family," she said. "They won't want me to go back before the informant is caught. I need to go back to work and get on with my life."

"What aren't you telling me?" he asked.

"I think if I go back and live my life, people will realize that I don't have any evidence. I could include that fact in the story I'm writing."

"That's a big gamble," Wade told her.

"I don't want to be the reason that someone else gets hurt."

"I assume you've talked about this with Henson," said Wade.

"Yes, he believes he can convince his colleagues that Todd didn't have any evidence. The word should spread to the mole and so on."

"I'll do my best," Wade told her.

"Thank you," she said. "Do you think it would be safe to spend the rest of the weekend with family?

"I think so," he told her. "Reed and Maddie talked with the Ketchersid woman. According to her, no one else was sent for you."

"I'll pack up my things," she said.

"I've got to talk to Baker about something," he told her. "We'll leave here at one."

"I'll be ready."

Wade left Grace to pack and went in search of Calvin Baker. He found him in the technology lab.

"Baker, I need your help," he said. "The family wants to record the ceremony and stream it for those who'd like to see it. None of us are that tech-savvy."

"I can set you up for live stream, or you can record it and stream it later," Baker said. "What time is the ceremony?"

"At four o'clock."

"Are you planning to stream on social media or a website?"

"Can we do both?" asked Wade.

"You can record and live stream at the same time with social media. You'll have to let people know where to find it," Baker told him. "You'll need to set up a link to a webpage for folks to view it once it's uploaded."

"We don't have a webpage or link ready," Wade told him.

"I think social media would be your best option considering that you're short of time," Baker told him. "Do you know how to do that?"

"I do. Lizzie can do it faster," Wade admitted. "I'll have her set it up, and one of the family can do the rest."

"We'd all like to see it," Baker said.

"Thanks, Baker. I'd better get ready," he said and went to his office.

Wade locked his office door and changed into his tux. He made sure he had the rings and marriage license before going to see Grace.

Grace was ready when he got there.

"You look handsome," she said with a whistle.

Wade blushed and said, "Thank you. You look nice, too."

"Oh, this old thing," she joked.

He offered her his elbow and escorted her to his truck. He helped her into the passenger seat and closed the door. He got into the driver's seat and started the engine.

"Would you be interested in recording the ceremony?" he asked. "You can use my phone."

"I'd be happy to," she said. "It'll give me something to do other than cry."

Wade looked at her with shock. "Why would you cry?"

Grace laughed and said, "That's something women do at weddings. They're tears of joy."

They arrived at the hospital, and Wade helped her out of the truck. He handed her his phone, and they made their way to Lizzie's room.

Grace went into the room, and Wade stayed in the hall with the other men. James, Dan, and Sean talked about fishing, farming, and anything else they could think of to pass the time.

An energetic young man with dark hair and a winning smile joined them. Preacher Dave was dressed in a suit rather than his usual jeans and T-shirt.

"This is going to be a unique wedding," said Dave. "I've never officiated a wedding in a hospital room. I've never stood with the bride and waited for the groom either."

Lois opened the door and said, "We're ready for everyone except Wade."

The men filed in, and Lois stepped into the hall with Wade.

"We'll let them get in position," said Lois. "I'll open the door when we're ready for you to come in. Walk slow."

"Thanks, Granny," Wade said with a grin.

Lois beamed at him and went back into the room, closing the door behind her.

Wade heard the music begin to play, and Lois opened the door. He took his time walking in and stopped near the foot of Lizzie's bed. The head of the bed was positioned so that she was sitting up.

He couldn't believe how beautiful she looked. Her hair was arranged on top of her head, with curls framing her face. Instead of a veil, she wore a sparkling headband on top of her head.

The bruise on her face was expertly hidden with makeup. Her eyes sparkled, and her smile lit up the room.

She wore an ivory gown and robe made of satin and lace. It had a sweetheart neckline that showed off the necklace he'd given her when they were dating. She held the yellow roses in her hand.

When the music stopped, Preacher Dave began the ceremony. James gave the bride away, and Wade took his place at Lizzie's side.

The couple looked into each other's eyes as Dave spoke. They said their vows and exchanged rings on cue.

"I now pronounce you husband and wife," said Dave. "You may kiss the bride."

Wade leaned toward Lizzie. She wrapped her arms around his neck. They shared a warm, joyful kiss before facing their families.

"I'd like to present to you, Mr. and Mrs. Wade Adams," said Dave.

Everyone in the room applauded. The women dabbed at tears, and the men shook hands.

The celebration immediately followed the ceremony. They all had dinner from Styrofoam take-out boxes. The couple cut the cake, and they drank sparkling water from the champagne glasses.

A nurse brought Lizzie's pain medication, and the families decided it was time to leave. A cot was brought in so that Wade could spend the night beside his new bride.

"We'll come back tomorrow and take all this down," Ellen told her. "Try to get some rest."

"Thank y'all for everything," Lizzie told them. "It was wonderful."

"Yes, thank you," Wade said. "It turned out better than I imagined."

The families left the hospital and waved goodbye promising to get together soon. Grace tapped James on the shoulder on the way to his truck.

"I'd like to stay with y'all tonight," she said. "Is that okay?"

"Of course, it is," he said. "Are your things at the jail?"

Grace nodded.

"We'll stop by and get them before we go home," he told her. "Mom and Ellen are in her car."

Brother and sister talked on their way to the inn. Grace explained what she wanted to do.

"I hate to see you go," James told her. "I kind of like having you around."

"I like being here," she assured him. "I'd like to come home, but I can't with this threat hanging over my head."

"Mom isn't going to like it," James told her.

"I know," she replied. "We won't have to communicate in secret anymore. That ought to make it easier."

"When are you planning to leave?" he asked.

"Monday afternoon," she told him. "I wanted to wait until Lizzie is out of surgery."

"Where are you going to meet Henson?"

"We arranged to meet at Wade's office."

James parked the truck at his home and unloaded Grace's bags. They went inside and told their mother about Grace's plan to leave.

"I knew you couldn't stay forever," Lois said. "I hoped it would be a longer visit, though."

"I know, Mom," said Grace. "I can visit anytime I want now. We don't have to stay apart anymore."

"That's one good thing about all of this," Lois said. "I won't stand in your way."

Grace said goodnight to her family and picked up her cell phone. She dialed Oliver Baldwin's direct line.

"Oliver, this is Grace."

"How are you?"

"I'm good," she said. "I wanted to let you know that I'll be coming home on Monday."

"Is it all over?" he asked.

"I'm not sure," she admitted and explained what she planned to do.

"Are you sure that's wise?"

"I can't run forever," she said.

"What about your story?"

"It's finished," she told him. "It doesn't have the ending we hoped for, but that could change."

"We'll be glad to have you back," Oliver said. "When do you think you'll be ready for work?"

"I'll be there Tuesday," she said.

The call ended, and Grace went to bed, hoping she was making the right move.

* * *

Lizzie's surgery on Monday morning was a success. Grace waited until she was back in her room to say goodbye.

"You can't go," Lizzie said. "You're safer here with us."

"You weren't safe," Grace replied with tears welling in her eyes. "I don't want to put any of you in more danger. I have to deal with this."

"Promise you'll come back for the reception," Lizzie begged.

Grace smiled at her niece and said, "I wouldn't miss it."

"I'm going to drive Grace to Wade's office," James told his daughter. "I'll be back in a little while."

"Grace, thank you for recording our wedding," said Wade. "I think I still saw a tear on your face."

Grace laughed and said, "I'm sure you did. I was happy to do it for you."

They left the hospital and drove to the sheriff's office. Henson was waiting for her inside.

"Are you ready?" he asked.

"I'm ready," she replied.

Her luggage was transferred from James' truck to Henson's car. They drove to the Dallas airport, talking about Todd and Las Vegas.

Henson hailed a cab when they'd collected their luggage at the Las Vegas airport. They rode to Grace's house together. He made certain that her house was secure before he left her there alone.

Grace took her luggage to her room and began to unpack. The message was still on the mirror.

She went to the kitchen and found the glass cleaner. She took it and a roll of paper towels to her room. She scrubbed the mirror until it gleamed.

She had mixed feeling about being home. She was happy to be back in her own space, but it felt lonelier than it had before she left.

She picked up the phone and called Oliver.

"Oliver, this is Grace. I wanted to let you know that I'm home, and I plan to be back at work tomorrow."

"That's good news," he told her. "Is everything at your home as you left it?"

"It's better," she said. "My front door has been repaired, and my security system is working perfectly."

"Excellent! What time will you be in?"

"I plan to get my car first thing in the morning," she replied. "I hope it hasn't been towed. I'll let you know if I'm going to be later than the usual time."

"We'll see you in the morning," Oliver said and ended the call.

Grace dialed another number and waited.

"Las Vegas Police Department," answered the operator. "How may I direct your call?"

"I'd like to speak with Officer Danny Burnett, please."

"Please, hold," the operator replied.

"This is Burnett."

"This is Grace Stewart. How are you?"

"I'm doing well," said the officer. "How are you?"

"Wonderful," she told him. "I have some information to share with you."

She told him who was responsible for putting the tracking device on her car and who had broken into her house. She explained what she'd learned about the message on her mirror.

"Thanks for letting us know," said Burnett. "How did you find out what happened?"

"I'd like to discuss that over dinner with you and Kara," she said.

"Oh, wow!" replied Burnett. "That would be great."

"I'm going back to work tomorrow," she told him. "I'll be free this weekend."

"I'll check my schedule and talk with Kara," he said. "May I call you back?"

Grace gave him her number and ended the call. She dialed a new number and waited.

"Paradise Creek Inn," answered Lois.

"Hi, Mom. I made it home."

"I'm so glad you called," Lois said. "Lizzie will be released from the hospital tomorrow. They've decided to have their reception on October first. Will you be able to make it?"

"I'll be there," Grace promised. "Do they know when they'll get to have their honeymoon?"

"They've been talking about going after the holiday season," Lois told her. "Lizzie should be completely recovered by then."

"That would be a good time to go someplace warm," Grace replied.

"It's so wonderful to be able to talk with you again," Lois said.

"Yes, it is," Grace said.

Mother and daughter chatted about her flight home. They talked about the upcoming reception and Grace's return to work. They said goodnight half an hour later.

* * *

The remainder of September was uneventful for Grace and her family. No one tried to make contact with her. No one followed her. No one broke into her home.

Grace had dinner with Officer Burnett and his wife as promised. She was pleased to learn that they were expecting their first child in March.

She took the redeye flight to Dallas after the ten o'clock newscast on September thirtieth. She rented a car and arrived at the inn the next morning.

"Aunt Grace, you made it," Lizzie said when she walked through the front door.

"I told you I would," she said and hugged her niece. "How's your leg?"

"The doctor says it's doing well," Lizzie said. "I may get a walking cast next week. I'm ready to do away with these crutches."

Grace followed Lizzie to the dining room. She was greeted by the rest of the family. They sat down at the table and talked about what they'd been through.

"Wade, have you hired your new deputies?" asked Grace.

"I was wondering about that myself," said James.

"The application window closed yesterday," Wade replied. "We didn't have any new qualified applicants. One of those we interviewed accepted another position."

"Does that mean what I think it means?" asked Ellen.

"I'm afraid so," Wade replied. "Our new deputies will be Drake Wagner and Sherri Logsdon."

"How are you going to deal with that?" asked Lois.

"I've been focusing on Lizzie and trying not to think about it," said Wade.

At six o'clock, family and friends were there to celebrate the union of Wade and Lizzie. The Inn was decorated as they'd planned for the wedding. Lizzie looked beautiful in her tea-length wedding gown in spite of her crutches.

* * *

Grace flew home Sunday evening. She drove her Silver Honda Civic home from the airport and parked in her garage.

She went inside and carried her bags to her bedroom. She was about to open her suitcase when her doorbell rang.

She went to the door and looked through the peephole. She relaxed when she saw her next-door neighbor.

"I'm sorry to bother you," the woman said. "I know you just got home."

"That's okay," Grace said. "What can I do for you, Mrs. McPeak?"

"This package came while you were away," she said. "Someone

wrote my address instead of yours. I saw on the news that you were on assignment, so I just held on to it. I thought it might be important. I'd have given it to you sooner, but I've been in Los Angeles taking care of my daughter and new grandson."

"Thank you so much," Grace said. "And congratulations. I'd like to celebrate with you, but I don't have anything in the house until I can go shopping."

"That's all right," said Mrs. McPeak. "I haven't been home long, and I'm exhausted. We'll do it another time."

"I appreciate that you've kept the package all this time. Thank you for bringing it over."

"What are neighbors for?" the woman asked with a smile and walked toward her house.

Grace closed the door and locked it. She made sure the security system was on. She didn't know what was in the package, and she didn't want to take any chances.

She looked at the label. It looked like Todd's handwriting. She didn't know what to expect.

She removed the wrapper and opened the box. Inside was a cell phone and a note. Tears ran down her cheeks as she read.

My dearest Grace,

I'm sorry that I couldn't meet you for our date. My cover was blown, and I've been trying to stay out of sight.

I know it's a matter of time before they catch up with me. Give this cell phone to my friend Marty Henson. Don't give it to anyone else. He'll know what to do.

I love you, Grace. I wish things could have been different. It would have been nice to have a normal life with you.

Love,

Todd

Marty Henson's phone number was written with his name and address at the bottom of the letter. It was the same number that Henson had given her.

She wiped her eyes and took out her cell phone. She dialed Henson's number and told him what she'd found.

He rushed to her house and read the note. He opened the cell phone and searched through it. He found a video with a date and time. He smiled as he watched it.

"May I download this to your computer?" he asked Grace.

"Yes, of course. I don't know if I have the right cables."

"We'll figure it out. I'll make multiple copies of this," he told her. "I don't want to risk our only copy being mysteriously lost."

"Is that what everyone is looking for?" she asked.

"It is," he told her. "It's more incriminating than I expected. No wonder they were willing to kill to get hold of it."

Henson downloaded the video to Grace's computer. He saved the file on the cloud and sent it to his computer.

"I have to take this to my boss," he told her. "He'll want to make an arrest right away, but I don't want to leave you here alone."

"I'd love to come with you," she said.

"Come on," he said. "I'll call him on the way and have him meet us at the office."

She grabbed her purse and cell phone and followed him to his car. He put on his emergency light and raced to the FBI office.

He parked the car, and they ran inside. He flashed his badge at the door.

"She's with me," he said, and they ran down the hall before anyone had a chance to stop them.

They stopped in front of a door that read *Grant Beckenholt, Deputy Director, Las Vegas*. Marty knocked once before going in.

"Henson? What's so important?" asked the man sitting behind a huge oak desk.

"We've got it, Sir," Henson said.

"Anthony's evidence?"

"It's right here," he said. "It's been in Vegas all along."

"Let's see it," said Beckenholt.

Henson found the video and handed it to his boss. He watched the video twice before he said anything.

"Has anyone else seen this?" asked Beckenholt.

"I've seen it," said Henson. "I haven't shown it to Ms. Stewart."

Beckenholt seemed to see Grace for the first time.

So, you're Ms. Stewart," he said. "I understand you've had quite an ordeal."

"Yes, Sir," she said.

"Would you like to be in on the arrest?" he asked.

"I'd love it," she said. "I'd also like the exclusive story."

Beckenholt laughed and said, "It's yours. You should watch this video while I see about getting a warrant."

Henson showed her the video while Beckenholt called a judge. Grace couldn't believe her eyes. Charles Brittain was the informant. She'd have wagered everything she owned that it was Welborn.

Brittain was arrested without incident. The leader of the gang and several of his men were injured in a gun battle with the FBI.

Grace witnessed it all. She interviewed Beckenholt and added his commentary to her story, along with a description of the arrest.

On Monday evening, she settled herself at the anchor desk and smiled at the camera.

"Welcome to the news at five," she began. "I'm Grace Stewart. In today's headline, corruption in the Las Vegas FBI."

She went to her office at the end of the newscast and called home.

"Hi, Mom," she said when Lois answered. "I have great news. It's all over. Everything's going to be okay."

The End

Sign up for Dianne's newsletter at diannesmithwick-braden.com for the latest news and announcements about upcoming books. (use the QR code below for a direct link)

If you've enjoyed *Gambling with Murder*, follow Wade Adams and Lizzie Fletcher in Book Five of the Wilbarger County Series, *Murderous Opportunities* (use the QR code below for a direct link)

PREVIEW OF MURDEROUS OPPORTUNITIES

Chapter One

Andrew Clifton could hear the hum of a large fan turned on high. He thought he heard strange music as well. *What is Maddie doing?*

He opened his eyes and quickly closed them again. He didn't know where that bright light was coming from, but he wanted it to disappear.

"Maddie, will you turn that thing off?"

There was no response.

"Maddie! Turn that damn thing off! It's the middle of the night!"

Still no answer.

He covered his eyes with his hand and peered through the space between his fingers. He looked around the room.

This isn't my bedroom!

Drew tried to sit up but fell back onto the bed with his eyes closed. It felt like his brain was trying to pound its way out of his skull. The room spiraled and twisted like he was looking through a kaleidoscope.

He waited until the room stopped spinning to look around again. He was lying on a twin bed covered with a navy-blue quilt. An identical bed was across the room. Matching curtains hung on the windows. Dallas Cowboy and Denver Bronco posters adorned the walls.

He slowly sat up. The hammering in his head intensified with every movement. He rested his elbows on his knees and held his head in his hands, waiting for the waves of nausea to subside.

Where am I? When did I get here? How did I get here?

He searched his pants pockets. His cell phone, wallet, and keys were missing.

Oh, this isn't good! Think, Drew, think! Where did you go? What did you do?

He held his head in his hands again and tried to focus. He remembered arguing with Maddie. He remembered leaving the house. He remembered driving.

I went to a bar. I ordered a couple of drinks. I talked with a woman. We had a few drinks together...

Drew lifted his head, and his eyes opened wide.

No! No, I couldn't have! Maddie will never forgive me if I...

He got to his feet and staggered toward the bedroom door. He stumbled into a hallway and shouted.

"Hello! Is anybody here?"

No one answered.

A door was ajar a few feet from where he stood. The bright light, music, and fan noise came from inside the room.

He teetered toward the door and shouted over the noise, "Hello! I'm sorry to bother you, but I need to get home."

When there was no response, he pushed the door open. His eyes, unaccustomed to the bright light, began to water. He shielded them with his hands and shouted again. The music and fan were too loud for anyone to hear.

When his eyes began to adjust, he peered inside. There was someone in the tanning bed. Stepping into the room, he saw clothing lying on a nearby chair. Realizing the tanner was nude, he covered his eyes with one hand and knocked on the top of the tanning bed with the other.

"Hello! Can you help me!"

There was still no answer.

He raised the top of the tanning bed enough to get the tanner's attention and kept his eyes directed toward the face.

"I'm so sorry to bother you, but…."

Drew screamed in horror. Bile rose in his throat. He tore from the room and ran through the house. In his flight, he toppled over an ottoman and knocked a lamp off an end table.

At last, he reached an exit. He jerked the door open and stumbled off the porch, falling to his knees. The contents of his stomach spewed onto the lawn.

He heard heavy footsteps coming toward him. Looking up, he saw a dark form framed in the glow of the porchlight.

"Looks like you've had one hell of a night," said a gruff male voice.

Large hands picked Drew up and roughly dusted him off.

Drew tried to tell the man what he'd seen, but the words stuck in his throat. He pointed toward the house and tried to break free.

"Had a few too many," said the voice. "I'll get you home."

Again, Drew tried to explain. He struggled to show the stranger what had happened when the words wouldn't come. He gestured wildly and stammered. "In the there…somebody…in there."

The man led Drew to his car and pushed him into the passenger seat. Drew struggled to get out. The man punched him in the face and closed the door.

The stranger got into the driver's seat and fastened his seatbelt.

"Tryin' to tell me somethin'?" the man chuckled. "Guess it can wait."

He started the engine and drove away with Drew unconscious in the passenger seat.

* * *

The morning sun streamed through the bedroom window and woke Sheriff Wade Adams from a sound sleep. He rolled over and looked at the clock.

"Lizzie! We've overslept!" he shouted and bolted out of bed. "I should be on my way to work by now!"

Lizzie jumped up and hurried toward the kitchen. "I'll find something for your breakfast while you get dressed."

"I don't have time," Wade called after her. "I'll get coffee at the office."

"Aren't you hungry?" Lizzie asked with concern and turned toward him.

"I'll send somebody for donuts," he answered while he dressed. " Or I'll have a big lunch."

Wade put on his cowboy boots and stood. He took his bride of thirteen months in his arms and kissed her.

Lizzie snuggled into his arms. "I wish you didn't have to go in today."

"Me too. Do you have a full schedule?"

"Not too bad," Lizzie answered. "I have four client meetings.

The couple walked arm in arm to Wade's truck.

"I'd rather stay here with you, but I'd better get going," Wade said.

"We'll be all alone this weekend," Lizzie reminded him. "We should take advantage of every minute."

"I like the sound of that," Wade said with a mischievous grin and kissed her goodbye. "I'll see you tonight."

"Have a good day," Lizzie said and watched him drive away.

The newlyweds lived at the Paradise Creek Inn. It was located on the Fletcher farm in western Wilbarger County, Texas. The Fletchers owned and operated the family business.

Lizzie was the managing partner. She had lived at the inn since she returned from Chicago six years earlier. It was her education and experience that made the venture a success.

Arson forced the business to close for more than a year. It had been a struggle to recover the family's primary source of income.

Business at the inn had been steady since the newlyweds returned from their March honeymoon. Lizzie had been booking events and guests every day. The upcoming holiday season looked promising.

The couple decided it was best to begin their life together at the inn. Lizzie needed to be on-site for overnight guests. She often worked late during scheduled events. Wade didn't work late unless it was crucial.

Wade drove into town thinking about how his life had changed since marrying Lizzie. They'd taken a short weekend trip to celebrate their first anniversary. Since then, there had been little time to call their own. He and Lizzie were both looking forward to the weekend.

Running the inn was more demanding than he realized. Before they married, he stayed at his place when the Fletchers were busy with guests or events.

Now, there was nowhere else to go. The house he once leased had a new occupant. Deputy Brandon Lodge allowed him to use the guest room when needed. But it wasn't the same.

Wade parked in his space at the Wilbarger County Sheriff's department and went inside. Lost in his thoughts, he was startled when a deputy greeted him.

"Morning, Sheriff."

Wade tried to mask his surprise and said, "Good morning, Wagner. You're here late. Was it a busy shift?"

"No, it was another slow one," answered Drake Wagner. "I was waiting for someone else to come in before leaving. Maddie called and said she'd be late. Something about her son."

"I'll hold down the fort," Wade said. "Go home and relax."

"Thanks, I'll see you tomorrow," said Drake and left Wade alone.

Wade strode into his office, put his hat on the shelf, and sat down. He drummed his fingers on the desk. Wade didn't like Drake Wagner. His feelings made attempts at casual conversation awkward. He would have stayed to chat if his other deputies had been there.

When the Wilbarger County Commission approved the funds to hire two new deputies last year, he'd been excited at the prospect of being fully staffed. His excitement waned when Maddie presented him with Drake Wagner's application.

He'd thought it best to leave the decision to the rest of the team. In the end, they chose Wagner and Sherri Logsdon.

Both were a good fit for the department. The only things against Wager were his lack of experience and the fact that he was Lizzie's ex.

Wade would have preferred to remain shorthanded, but that wouldn't have been fair. The team had worked overtime and extra shifts far too long. He promised his team that he'd put his personal feelings aside and make the best of the situation.

He could ignore his animosity for Drake when they were busy. Unfortunately, it appeared that the criminals of Wilbarger County had collectively decided to take a break.

The low criminal activity was good for the county. But it made for long, dull days at the Sheriff's department. Wade knew from experience that the lull wouldn't last long.

A light tap on his door interrupted his thoughts.

"Hi, Maddie. How are the party plans going?"

Maddie gave him a weak smile and wiped a tear from her cheek. "Do you have a minute?"

Wade looked at his deputy and realized something was seriously wrong. Maddie seldom cried, especially at work. He stood up and walked toward her.

"Of course, sit down. Do you want some coffee?"

"No, thanks. I'll get some later," Maddie replied.

Wade closed his office door and sat down in a chair beside her.

"Are you all right?"

"Not really. I'm sorry I was late this morning. I had to take Brody to daycare and check on something."

"I thought Drew took him to daycare every morning."

"He does, but…he couldn't today."

"Maddie, what's wrong?" Wade coaxed and took her hand.

"I…I…can't find Drew," she said and broke down.

Wade got up, took a box of tissues from a shelf, and handed it to Maddie. He returned to his seat and waited until she was ready to talk.

Maddie sniffed and said, "I haven't heard from him since last night."

"Tell me what happened."

"We had a big fight, and he stormed…out…out of the house. I don't know…if he even realizes that…that today is Brody's birthday," Maddie said between sobs.

"I see," Wade replied. He didn't know what else to say.

"I've called his cell at least every thirty minutes," Maddie continued after she'd regained control. "It rang at first, but now it goes to voicemail. I started texting him, but he hasn't answered."

"You've had arguments in the past and managed to work it out, haven't you? I'm sure you'll be able to work this out too. He might have gone to his folks' or a friend's house."

Maddie blew her nose and shook her head. "His family and friends haven't heard from him. I went by the bank after I dropped Brody off. He didn't show up for work this morning."

"Drew probably needed some time to clear his head," Wade said, trying to reassure her. "I'm sure you'll hear from him soon."

"Wade, you don't understand," Maddie said and swallowed hard, trying to find the right words. "Drew hasn't been himself lately. It's…it's hard…to talk about."

"Maddie, you know I'm here for you," Wade began. "And what

you tell me won't go any further. But wouldn't you be more comfortable talking with someone else, a minister or professional counselor?"

Maddie shook her head and wiped a tear from her cheek. "I know I can trust you, and you're the one person who might understand."

"All right, I'm listening."

"First, I have a personal question to ask, if you don't mind."

"You can ask me anything. I'll tell you if it's too personal."

Maddie looked down at the tissue in her hands for a moment, summoning her courage.

"Do you ever have nightmares about the day Craig was killed?"

Stunned, Wade took a moment to answer. He'd been expecting a relationship question.

"Yes...I...had them all the time...at first," he admitted reluctantly. "I don't have them as often now. Are you having nightmares?"

"No, not me," she said and looked at Wade. "It's Drew."

Wade could see the tears brimming in Maddie's eyes again. "What's been happening?"

"He's been having nightmares on and off for the past four years," she began. "They were terrible right after the murders in Rayland. I used to find him standing in the barn in the middle of the night, running his fingers over the bullet holes."

"That was a horrible experience," Wade said with compassion as he recalled the details of the case.

Maddie nodded. "The nightmares eventually stopped, but the anniversary of Paul Randolph's death triggers them again. The dreams have started in October for the past two years and lasted a month or two."

She paused and took a deep breath. "This year has been different. For the past six weeks, Drew's been waking up screaming almost every night. There have been times that I woke up in the middle of the night, and he'd be gone. He always answered when I called or texted. Nothing that I've done for him has helped. I don't know what else to do."

Wade gently squeezed her hand. "People handle terrible experiences in different ways. I struggle with Craig's loss every day. I had to have help to deal with it."

"What kind of help?"

"A counselor from the hospital helped me through the initial part. I came out of the coma to learn that Craig was dead, and I survived. His funeral was over, and his body was already buried. The rest of you were further along in the grieving process. I had no one else to talk to about it."

"I didn't realize that," Maddie said. "I don't think any of us did. I'm sorry we weren't there for you."

"You did the best you could. I was the only one there that day. No one else could understand how I felt…how I still feel about it."

Maddie could see the anguish in Wade's eyes. "I'm sorry to dredge up painful memories. I didn't know where else to turn."

"What was the fight about?" Wade began, "If you don't mind telling me."

Maddie's eyes filled with tears again when she said, "It was my fault. Drew came home and plopped in his chair. Brody wanted to talk to him about his birthday party. Drew acted like he couldn't see or hear him. Brody climbed on his lap and put his hands on either side of his dad's face. He said, 'Daddy, can you hear me?'"

She cried at the memory for a few minutes before she could continue. "Drew pushed Brody to the floor and started yelling at him. You should have seen Brody's little face. He was crushed."

"I can imagine," Wade replied and shook his head at the thought.

"That's when I lost it," Maddie continued. "I told Drew that he needed to get help before he destroyed our lives. We argued for over an hour. Then he just walked out."

Wade reached across his desk and picked up a notepad and a pen. He wrote a few lines, tore off the page, and handed it to

Maddie. "This is my counselor's name and number. He's been a tremendous help to me."

"Thank you," Maddie said and wiped her eyes. "I don't know if Drew will talk to me about it. He sits in his chair, staring into space. It's like we aren't there. When he does interact, he's impatient with Brody and short with me. The argument last night was the worst we've ever had."

"Why don't you go home and see if Drew's there.," Wade suggested. "Maybe the two of you can talk it out."

"And if he isn't?"

"We can file a missing persons report. It will be easier to find Drew with all of us on the case."

"Thanks for listening, Wade. I'll go home at lunch and see if he's there. I'll let you know if I'll be late getting back."

Maddie left the office at noon and drove home. Her mind was so full of thoughts about Drew that the fifteen-minute drive to Rayland was over before she realized it.

Drew's SUV wasn't in the garage. She went inside and searched the house. There was no indication that he'd been there since she left that morning.

She took out her cell phone and called the Sheriff's department. She asked to speak to Wade when Lodge answered the phone.

"Drew isn't here," she said when Wade answered. "I think it's time to file that report."

"I'll get it started," Wade replied. "You can fill in the missing details when you get back."

The call ended, and Maddie went to the refrigerator. Opening the door, she stared inside. Her mind wasn't on food. She was thinking of Drew.

Why hasn't he called? Where did he spend the night? Why didn't he go to work? Is he hurt? Could he be in the hospital somewhere?

She closed the refrigerator and wandered around the house, wiping tears from her face.

I can't let my imagination run wild. Drew's probably safe. He's taking some time to get himself together.

She went to the bathroom and splashed cold water on her face. She stared at the bottle of Polo Black cologne on the counter.

"Drew, where are you?"

To read more of *Murderous Opportunities,* use the QR code below to purchase a paperback book.

ABOUT THE AUTHOR

Dianne Smithwick-Braden is an avid reader of fiction but mysteries are by far her favorite genre. It seemed only natural that her own novels would be mysteries.

The Wilbarger County Series is set near Dianne's home town of Vernon, Texas. She was raised on the family farm in the western part of Wilbarger County. She graduated from Vernon High School in 1979.

Dianne currently lives in Amarillo, Texas with her husband, Richard.

Please take a few moments to rate and/or review this book. Dianne would love to know what you think.

Subscribe to Dianne's monthly newsletter at www.diannesmith-wick-braden.com.

ALSO BY DIANNE SMITHWICK-BRADEN

Coded for Murder

The Wilbarger County Series

Death on Paradise Creek (Book One)

Death under a Full Moon (Book Two)

Flames of Wilbarger County (Book Three)

Gambling with Murder (Book Four)

Murderous Opportunities (Book Five)

Subscribe to Dianne's newsletter at:

www.diannesmithwick-braden.com

Follow Dianne at:

www.facebook.com/smithwickbraden

www.instagram.com/smithwickbraden

twitter.com/smithwickbraden

www.pinterest.com/smithwickbraden

www.goodreads.com

bookbub.com